Praise for the novels of

ROBIN D. OWENS

"Strong characterization combined with deadly danger make this story vibrate with emotional resonance. Stay tuned as events accelerate toward the final battle."
—*Romantic Times BOOKreviews* on *Keepers of the Flame*
(Book Four of The Summoning)

"Fans of Anne McCaffrey and Mercedes Lackey will appreciate the novel's honorable protagonists and their lively animal companions."
—*Publishers Weekly* on *Protector of the Flight*
(Book Three of The Summoning)

"[A] multi-faceted, fast-paced gem of a book."
—*The Best Reviews* on *Guardian of Honor*
(Book One of The Summoning)

"The story line is action-packed but also contains terrific characters...Robin D. Owens enchants her readers."
—*Affaire de Coeur* on *Guardian of Honor*

"Owens takes...elements that make Marion Zimmer Bradley's *Darkover* stories popular...and turns out a romance that draws you in."
—*Locus* magazine

W9-BUJ-924

"Owens excels at evocative, sensual writing."
—*Romantic Times BOOKreviews*

ECHOES IN THE DARK

ROBIN D. OWENS

LUNA™
www.LUNA-Books.com

LUNA™

ECHOES IN THE DARK

ISBN-13: 978-0-373-80293-7
ISBN-10:   0-373-80293-5

Copyright © 2009 by Robin D. Owens

First printing: January 2009

Author Photo by: Rose Beetem

Recycling programs
for this product may
not exist in your area.

Printed in U.S.A.

To the Song that moves within us all.

"Poets are the hierophants of an unapprehended inspiration; the mirrors of the gigantic shadows which futurity casts upon the present."
—Percy Bysshe Shelley

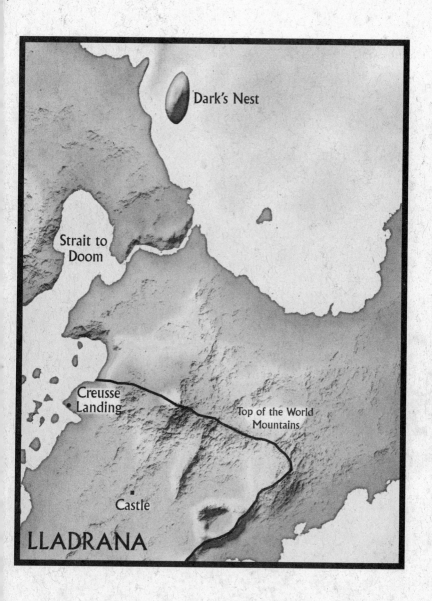

Dark's Nest

Strait to
Doom

Creusse
Landing

Top of the World
Mountains

Castle

LLADRANA

I

Ghost Hill Theater, Denver, Colorado
Late August, Night

Jikata was taking her last bow on stage and soaking in applause when her great-grandmother died. The odd thing was that Jikata actually felt Ishi Yamuri pass away in one of those increasing moments of hyperawareness. As if the old woman touched Jikata with her stubborn disapproval even as others yelled and clapped.

The bond with her great-grandmother vanished. Ishi hadn't waited to see Jikata tomorrow, the date Ishi herself had insisted upon.

Jikata had added her old hometown of Denver to her touring schedule because she'd sensed her great-grandmother's time was near, though she hadn't heard from the woman in years.

Suddenly the applause, the only thing that had satisfied

Jikata for a long time, rang hollow and empty. Like the rest of her life.

Jikata lowered her head, closed her eyes against the lights made brighter by tears. Then she stepped back on the polished wooden stage and let the heavy maroon velvet curtains descend.

The crowd whistled and clapped louder, but she had no more to give. This final event—the reopening of a newly renovated small Victorian theater—was the last in her tour. Fitting.

Her career was skyrocketing. She neared the pinnacle of success for a pop singer, a female half-Japanese no less, and found herself alone and panting after the climb.

Her life was tanking. Fans adored her. No one loved her. No man, no good friend female or male, no child. As her great-grandmother would have said, her soul was withering from lack of nourishment.

Applause came from stage right and the philanthropist behind the renovation strode forward, beaming, accompanied by his wife. Jikata pasted a smile on her face, hoping that it might turn into the real thing since she usually enjoyed the company of Trenton Philbert III. He stopped clapping and held out a hand and she put hers in it. "Great job. Definitely the next star. I'm looking forward to that last zoom to the top." He squeezed her hand and let it go.

The praise warmed her a little. "Thank you."

"You did the inaugural event of the Ghost Hill Theater proud. Thanks again for agreeing to perform. We sold out." He glanced around, the backstage was still shiny with cleanliness and held the faint scent of wood stain. "This place should be good for another hundred years."

"It's a lovely theater," Jikata said. Now. She could remember when it had been a ruin.

He radiated satisfaction. Turning to his wife behind him, he said, "We have a gift for you. Darling?"

Juliet Philbert stepped forward with a large fancy birdcage fashioned like the Taj Mahal. Jikata gritted her teeth...no, please, not a bird. Her great-grandmother had kept finches when Jikata had been younger. "I'm sorry," she said, "but I—"

Then the bird opened its beak and pure liquid notes warbled out, like nothing Jikata had ever heard. As if it were more than song, a communication. The bird didn't look like any she'd seen before, either. All scarlet red, but with a fancy cockatoo comb of red, yellow and white. About the size of a cockatoo, also. It fixed a yellow eye on her and let loose another stream of notes. This time sounding a lot like the underlying melody of the last ballad she'd sung. Jikata blinked.

"Her name is Chasonette," Juliet said. "She's a Lladranan cockatoo and has the most beautiful birdsong in the world. She's quite rare, but I knew such a lady would be perfect for you. And Trent indulged me." She thrust the cage at Jikata, so she took it. It was lighter than she'd thought.

Juliet tucked her hand into Trenton's elbow and he covered her fingers with his own, shaking his head as he looked down at his wife. "I always indulge you. The bane of my existence." He kissed her temple. "People say I'm going soft."

Fast footsteps came from backstage and Juliet's assistant, Linda, who appeared distressed, hurried to them. Jikata remembered, and the small moment of normality shattered.

"I'm sorry." Linda stopped, inhaled a breath that raised her thin chest. Looked at the Philberts, hesitated and said, "I'm sorry. I have bad news. We should...ah...let's go to your dressing room." Linda pulled Jikata backstage, past the greenroom and into the star's dressing room. The Philberts followed.

The small room was elegant in cream and white, but four people made it crowded. Jikata placed the birdcage on the dressing room table. Chasonette stepped nervously back and forth on her perch, then apparently caught sight of herself in the mirror and preened.

Linda led Jikata to the cream brocade Victorian fainting couch that took up most of one end wall. She figured she had to sit. The moment she did, Linda released her hand—a blessing since both their palms were sweaty.

Linda grabbed a box of tissues from the dressing table and dropped it in her lap. "I got a call. Your great-grandmother has died, Jikata."

"I was supposed to visit her tomorrow," Jikata said, still shocked.

"Sorry," repeated Linda. She was a young intern with the University of Southern California who'd traveled with Jikata during the two-month tour. Though they'd managed well enough, neither of them expected the job to transform into anything more.

"She was an old woman and had a good life." Isn't that what Jikata was supposed to say? "I want to be alone," she choked out.

"Of course. We'll take care of your crew and fans." Juliet, patting Jikata on the shoulder, trilled her tongue. Chasonette perked up and warbled a low, soothing melody. "I'm sure you don't want to attend the opening gala."

"No, I don't." It had completely gone from her mind.

"We'll make sure your room in the hotel next door is booked for you through the next week. It's been a gruelling tour for you, I know. You need rest."

"Yes, I'd planned a long break." Rote answers seemed to

work. Jikata didn't know what she felt except…empty. Nothing new about that.

"You just go next door when you're ready," Juliet insisted.

"Fine."

The bird continued to croon, soft background scales that tugged at Jikata, reminding her of the chants and chimes that had haunted her. She rubbed her temples.

Trenton squatted down, as if setting himself in her vision. "Jikata, if there's anything we can do…."

She nodded. "You go on to the gala. You're the star of that show."

"All right, but if you need us here in Denver, let us know."

She watched blindly as the Philberts left. They *were* the only people she felt she could call on in Denver, and they were acquaintances. All her old ties had withered.

"Um, Jikata?" Linda said.

Oh. The girl had looked forward to the end of the tour and the big party to celebrate the renovation of the theater. With another nod, another blank gaze, Jikata said, "You go ahead. You don't have to stay with me the next couple of days. Let's call this the end of the internship."

"I don't know, if you need me…." But Linda sounded relieved.

Jikata was prepared. She went to her designer backpack and got the card—with bonus—from an inner pocket. Held it out. "Thanks for all your help. I've already turned in my last report. You're free to go."

"Thanks!" With a smile showing the job was already history, Linda hurried from the room.

Jikata sat and listened as the theater emptied, then dragged herself into the shower. Let the heat and steam flow over her as she prodded her feelings about her Japanese great-grandmother. Regret, as always, they hadn't ever seen eye-to-eye. Her great-grandmother had refused to speak to her after she'd legally changed her name to Jikata, had hated that she'd become a pop singer. At eighteen, Jikata had left the dust of Denver for L.A. and prospered.

Well enough that she could buy whatever she wanted, keep her great-grandmother in style. Which, of course, Ishi had refused, liking the little house in east Denver she'd bought a few years after leaving the internment camp in southeastern Colorado. Both of Jikata's grandmothers had died before she was born. Both her grandfathers had been unknown, a bond between her parents who were killed in a car accident when she was fourteen.

Sad. Jikata felt it, mostly for the lost opportunity to reconcile, though she'd known in her bones that was wishful thinking.

Now she was truly alone. No more family.

She wondered what to do. Knowing Ishi, all her affairs would have been arranged. Jikata was ambivalent about seeing the old house. At the end of a tour, she usually found the nearest bed and fell into it. But lately her sleep had been troubled by dreams that had her sweating and tangled in sheets when she woke. Or, worse, visions that were pure beauty she strove to put into words and sing.

Those songs always bombed. She did much better when she sang others' melodies and lyrics, and that was a raw spot in her soul.

The pipes creaked and water cooled and she turned the shower off. At least the makeup and sweat of the last show, of the tour, was finally gone.

Wrapping herself in a large towel, she stepped into the dressing room. The mirror was foggy with steam so she opened the door, dressed quickly in jeans and a blue silk blouse and packed a small suitcase, put her backpack in order and swung one strap over her shoulder.

She turned to do a sweep of the room and froze.

The birdcage door was wide open. Jikata blinked—could the bird have unlatched it herself? Apparently so. A very valuable, rare bird.

Her gaze trailed to the open door of the dressing room. Shit! She looked wildly around the room, but it was small and a foot-long scarlet bird was not evident against the cream-and-gold background.

Dammit!

She hadn't seen or heard the wretched bird leave. No trilling of a goodbye song. No soft *whoof* of feathers.

Sliding her feet into ballet slippers, she opened the door wider, then heard a tinny chime. She glanced at the table where the chiming-ball necklace Juliet Philbert had given her when they'd met had been. Pretty and shiny on a gold satin ribbon, it was gone, too.

Jikata grimaced. She was ambivalent about chimes. She'd included them in her own compositions that hadn't been successful, then the last one that had made it big. It was hitting the top of the charts now. The strange concoction of bells and chimes and an occasional gong tone. She'd sung—chanted—a mishmash of words in English and Japanese and French and had layered her voice in the track again and again over four octaves. She barely had a full four-octave range and had worked hard on that track until each note was strong and perfect.

"Come to Me" was going platinum.

The tune wasn't really her composition and that's what bothered her. She'd heard odd patterns of notes, of chimes, of chants, the occasional gong beat in her head over the past two years. It had started here in Denver, her hometown, two years ago February. A February as dreary as her life. Ishi hadn't wanted to see her then, either.

She shook the thought away. Stop dithering! Go hunt the bird. She stepped to the door, called, "Chasonette!" Would a bird come to her name? Cockatoos were supposed to be intelligent for birds, weren't they?

Another chime. Faint. But her hearing was good and she was sure it came from the stage area. She hurried past the greenroom, angling toward stage left, which had more space than stage right. A bird would want more space to fly in, wouldn't it?

Only a few dim bulbs were on and she moved through light and shadow. She pushed through the curtains to look into the house—even dimmer—and saw a flash of a red wing through the door to the lobby someone had propped open with a broom.

Damn!

So she hopped from the stage and ran up the plush maroon aisle, through the door to the equally elaborate lobby.

Then she heard the wonderful song of a woman's voice, with the slightest of quavers that made Jikata think the singer was old. An elder and perfect master of her craft. The wordless Song compelled Jikata to *listen*. Not to hear, but listen, and the mistress of that voice had the range of Jikata's own, a full four octaves, richer for years of use.

Other music lilted. Crystal singing bowls, chimes, and the jangle of Chasonette's ball melded perfectly into the whole.

"Chasonette?" she called.

Chasonette chirped. Jikata ran after her, misjudged the distance of the sound and went *through* the mirrored wall.

No!

That couldn't have happened. Could it?

She stood in a gray mist. Wind whipped at her hair. There were no walls around her, just an echoing distance. Where *was* she? Her toes curled in her shoes, felt solid ground through the thin soles of her slippers. Shouldn't it be new, plush carpet?

She hesitated, but more chimes and the voice and the bowls and the sheer magnificence of the sound drew her. How often did a person hear this sort of concert? *Never.*

There were cadences and tones to this Song that outclassed all her composition attempts. As if she'd…heard through a mirror darkly…. She chuckled, but she yearned. This, *this* was what she'd been trying to achieve for the past year. If only…

Another questioning chirp and Jikata realized she was humming her "Come to Me" hit. Light was ahead and walls looked cut from rock. That reassured her a little. Everyone knew there were tunnels under Denver. She'd somehow made it into one of them.

Then the woman's voice twisted the melody and the notes seemed to hit physical points inside Jikata. She literally *felt* her heart squeeze. So wonderful, and there was more, she heard the reverberation of the chant she'd included in her own work. *Come to me.*

The woman's voice caressed her with a soothing cadence. Jikata blinked, she saw the woman, a tiny, aged, Asian woman standing in light that reflected off mist around her, giving her a glow. Chasonette perched on her shoulder, the ribbon of the chiming ball in her beak. She shook it. The sound shivered over Jikata's skin. She glimpsed people behind the woman, playing singing bowls.

Stranger and stranger, but not threatening.

Jikata hurried forward, met a thickness in the air like a membrane, surged through it. More wind. In a tunnel or dreaming. She could have fallen asleep on the Victorian fainting lounge in her dressing room after her shower. But she plunged ahead. Then she was with the woman, and Chasonette hopped from the woman's shoulder to Jikata's, dug in her claws. Ouch, she felt that!

"Welcome to Lladrana," the older woman said in English. She gestured and cymbals clashed and chimes sounded and a shudder went through Jikata.

Brightness flared before her eyes, blinding her. She flung out her arms, trying to keep her balance. Another clang as if from a gong, but the percussion was slightly off and she knew it came from many cymbals. *What the hell was going on?*

A dream. Just a dream.

Hair had risen over her skin, and she'd gone clammy. The air she sucked in smelled like incense and was heavy and humid. She shook her head, trying to think beyond the sound.

She couldn't.

The music strummed her as if she were a taut string, vibrating through her.

Another clang of cymbals and she fell, panting, to the floor. Starburst. Darkness. Then Chasonette was beside her on the ground, rubbing her head against Jikata's cheek. So soft.

Jikata could see the bird's yellow eye and thought she was finally back to reality. She leaned on an elbow, but her support didn't feel like a padded lounge, or carpet. It felt like rock.

She looked around and saw a large cave, people wearing long robes standing in a circle. Some had small tables holding crystal bowls before them and held the thick glass wands to set them humming. Others held cymbals of brass, silver, gold…?

Her mouth was open so she sucked in deep breaths. The small woman gazed down at her with triumph, crinkling deep wrinkles around her eyes even as her throat moved with renewed song, music that lowered down the scale as if ending a long piece.

We are here! I am back! A warbling voice came in her head and Jikata slowly turned to see Chasonette. She could have sworn the bird winked at her. *There's magic here,* the bird said.

Jikata sat up, craned to look around. Just beyond some people she saw the pale pink and deep maroon lobby of the Ghost Hill Theater amidst a blue fog in the distance. Strangled noises came from her throat as she jumped to her feet.

Then that glimpse of *known* vanished and she was in a cavern, large enough to hold the musicians surrounding her, all taller and sturdier than the old woman, than Jikata herself.

Chasonette fluttered to her shoulder. The bird's fragrance was the same, as if her feathers held a faint lavender oil.

Once more the bird took wing, and the chiming necklace was dropped over Jikata's head, rattling to shine silver against her dark blue blouse. Then Chasonette was on her shoulder again, yellow gaze serious. *You are where you belong.*

"I am the Singer," the old woman said.

She certainly was.

"Now to test your tuning," she continued. That didn't make sense. But she opened her mouth and hit high C with ease. At the same time the cymbals clashed, someone rang chimes and the singing bowls sounded. Every note reverberated in Jikata until she felt like only pure vibration.

She crumpled. She didn't understand anything.

2

Lladrana, Singer's Abbey, a few minutes later

Luthan Vauxveau, the Singer's representative to the warrior Marshalls, stood in the green landing field just downhill from the Singer's Abbey. He'd been about to return to the Marshalls' Castle, when he'd *felt* it, the Summoning of another Exotique from their land to Lladrana.

The soles of his feet had tingled with a joyous outpouring of Amee, the planet, that her last savior had arrived. His winged horse and the rest of the herd had trumpeted.

A shout tore from him, joining other exclamations.

Even as he felt the planet's joy, his own anger welled and the back of his neck burned with humiliation. He hadn't felt this stupid since before his father had died. The Singer had manipulated him, used him, played him for a fool. Again.

Soon the vibrations of the act would notify every person

with a modicum of Power that a new Exotique had crossed the Dimensional Corridor and entered Lladrana. That would include the five other Exotiques who would demand immediate answers from him. All he had was questions himself.

People from Exotique Terre were supposed to be Summoned by the Marshalls, the strongest team in the land. But the Singer had Summoned her own. Luthan ground his teeth.

He was the representative of the Singer to the Marshalls and all the other segments of Lladranan society. *He* was supposed to know what she had planned, be informed. *He* was the one people would come to, ask questions of.

Especially the other five Exotiques.

He'd known nothing. The Singer had kept this Summoning, and other matters, secret from him. This was the last straw, and time to tell her so.

Simmering with anger, he turned back toward the central Abbey. He'd find her in the caverns, a place off-limits to him, but that wouldn't stop him. Not now, not ever again.

He'd tried his best over the past two years to liaise with the Singer and the Marshalls, the Chevaliers, even the Sorcerers. And over the past two years the old Singer herself, the oracle of Lladrana, had become more secretive and capricious.

Striding to the high wall enclosing the Abbey's jumbled buildings, he swung open the gate with Power, shaping a bubble around himself so he could not be detained. His force field gently shifted robed figures of the Singer's Friends from his path as he wound through the buildings toward the towers of the main Abbey.

The Singer's Friends reached out to pluck at his white leathers, stood in front of him, yet all were moved aside. He was a Chevalier, a fighter, had fought battles against the Dark and its monsters for most of his life. With respect, he'd bent his will under the Singer's. No more. He could *feel* the location of the Singer and the new Exotique, could *hear* it.

A fifth-level Friend, the highest in the hierarchy, stepped in front of him just where the mazelike path narrowed to allow only one person. The man stood his ground, but Luthan's Power pushed him and he had to back quickly. "Don't get in my way, Jongler. I must speak to the Singer about her Summoning the last Exotique without telling anyone."

The man stared at him from under lowered brows. He sighed. "It is done. The final Exotique is for the Singer. It is appropriate that our lady Summoned her instead of the Marshalls."

Luthan continued walking. "Fine. You tell that to the other Exotiques when they swoop down on this place in a couple of hours." He smiled. "I estimate that the Distance Magic of the volarans will bring them that quickly." He hesitated a step. "Of course Bri has the roc, and roc Distance Magic is even faster."

The man paled, the giant bird liked flesh. "Not the roc."

Luthan let his sarcastic smile widen. "If you're lucky, it will be Bri, the healer, riding the roc instead of Lady Knight Swordmarshall Alexa."

"Not...not...Alyeka."

That first Exotique was considered to be the most unpredictably dangerous. Alexa, pronounced correctly, had no fondness for the Singer and her Friends.

"Wait, you must stay and explain to them!" Jongler said.

"I know nothing *to* explain." That nettled him so much he wanted to hit the man. His fingers itched. But he was not his father. After a couple of years of rebellion, Luthan had built his reputation as the most honest man in Lladrana. He would not betray that for an angry impulse, not for the Singer herself.

Shrugging, Luthan said, "You'll be the one explaining."

Jongler backed rapidly, by his own feet, bowing repeatedly. "Ah, Hauteur Vauxveau." That was Luthan's title and surname.

"I've been beyond courtesies for months." He didn't slow down, but bared his teeth. "I'll speak to the Singer in person."

A quick darting of eyes by Jongler. They'd reached a wider space that curved around a circular building with paths to the left and right between it and others. Luthan swung left.

Jongler coughed. *The closest door to the caverns is to your right.* Luthan heard mentally, privately. Now when had he become sufficiently connected to Jongler that they could speak mind to mind? Didn't matter.

Luthan pivoted and stared to his right. A small octagonal tower stood with dark arches below, leading to what he'd thought was the Friends' meeting room. The arch was matched by the second-story windows, the whole was capped with a conical roof and weather vane. Though the blackness beyond the arches was deep, he didn't hesitate, moved swiftly and found two doors. One would probably lead to the meeting room.

He glanced back at Jongler, who now smiled with an edge, hands folded at his waist.

"Which?" Luthan asked.

Jongler lifted his nose. "If you have the bond with the Singer that you think you do, you will know how to find her in the maze of the tunnels, won't you?"

Nodding shortly, Luthan settled into his balance, grounded himself, banished anger and *probed*. Behind the left door he sensed the dampness of rock walls, the slope downward into the heaviness of earth, the secrecy of the Caverns of Prophecy. The atmosphere behind the right door Sang of laughter and petty quarrels and the range of human concerns.

He set his hand on the left doorknob. Shock! Gritting his teeth he absorbed it, knew the knob was brass that now had left a fancy pattern on his skin…and told the Singer he was coming. Wrenching open the door he stepped inside. The door slammed behind him as if on tight springs. Another security measure. The dark in here pressed on him, whispering, whispering…

He found himself swaying…falling into a trance that would trigger his own gift of prophecy, and by the great, evil Dark, he didn't want more visions!

"*Light!*" He snapped the word and the resulting brightness shocked him, coming from a great chandelier dripping with crystals, each one emitting sparkling light.

This anteroom was pretty with a stone mosaic floor and smooth walls of gold-patterned white silk. Three doors were set in it. He knew exactly which one led to the Caverns of Prophecy; dread filled him when he looked at it. Another led to the chapter house, the third resonated strongly of the Singer, probably went to one of her personal suites. The beauty of the room masked the threat of the caverns.

For a moment he considered his options. Going down into the bowels of the planet, subjecting himself to whispers and vapors and misty visions of the future…many futures. He didn't have to endure this. But he didn't like giving in to fear. And he didn't like being used as he had been used for the past year.

He could avoid confronting the Singer in her place of Power, abandon trying to rescue the new Exotique, who *was* meant for the Singer and her Friends. Might even be the *next* Singer. He could wait for the other Exotiques to arrive and they could all speak to the Singer herself. He shook his head.

The Singer would be a stone wall to the others, and the more they pushed, the more adamant she'd be.

So he squared his shoulders, opened the door and Sang himself a light spell for illuminating underground chambers—usually hot springs or bathing pools rather than caverns or dungeons. Light flickered along the top of the smoothly worked dark brown stone tunnel twisting downward.

Luthan headed into the depths of the caves, ignoring the susurration of the whispers around him, the vague mists that floated near, sparkling with images if he cared to *see*.

Hair prickled along his body, and he quashed apprehension.

As he descended and breathed the vapors of the cavern that triggered prophecy, it became impossible to block visions of the future. The first bad one was his brother's nearly unrecognizable burnt body, skin black and bone white. Luthan fell to his knees, gasped. A broken-fingered dead hand was clasped in Bastien's, Alexa's. Luthan's pain rose as he saw his brother holding what was left of his mate. Beyond them were a pile of dead; he saw the staring blue eyes of Jaquar, and Marian's red hair. He forced nausea away, his gorge down.

Since they were all planning to invade the Dark's Nest, ready to die to stop the evil alien being, this wasn't an unexpected vision, but it hurt his mind, his body, his heart to contemplate such a future.

After a few breaths, the image faded. The cave was dark and echoing with a faint swirl of mist near the top. Shuddering, he rose to his feet, felt clamminess on his face and didn't know if it was vapor or tears or sweat.

When he came to a three-way fork in the tunnel he closed his eyes and listened. He could hear the Singer, the echo of her words or Song, and the sound told him how to go. More, it seemed like the bond they'd established between them was true, because he could *see* a link also, a deep blue and occasionally glittering silver thread. She was in the direction of the middle path before him, but it was not the way to her. It was the left-hand path, again, that reverberated with Song, and showed the cord winding between them. So he took the left.

Descending deeper, the scent of weeping rock and incense came to his nostrils, the mists of prophecies became full, iridescent wraiths, tempting him to look and study. The Songs of them increased from whispers to a steady hum. His skin itched. How did the Singer stand it? How had she stood it for over a hundred years? Did it diminish or grow stronger or was it her own strength and control that grew? If so, he was a fool to set himself against such a being.

Concentrating on her, he held off most of the visions.

But not all.

Dark encroached. His mouth dried. The light dimmed, his field of vision narrowed. He set his jaw. The Dark had encroached into Lladrana for centuries, particularly in his lifetime, especially in the past decade.

He drew his gauntlets from where they were folded over his belt and put them on so he could trail his hand against the cavern wall.

Four steps down the corridor his solid steps wavered, the mist pushed around him as if it knew he had the Power of Sight. Wisps curled in his nostrils and he couldn't help breathing them.

Six steps and the heat was vicious—like that of an active volcano. The Dark's Nest.

Seven steps and a horrendous explosion occurred, the heat searing his eyes, but not before he saw a mountain island explode flinging bodies into the sky—volaran and human.

One of the bodies wore white leathers like his.

Again his legs gave way and he gasped, fell to the floor, knees bruising.

Endured the horrendous noise of a dying Dark, the screams of volarans and the Exotiques echoing in his brain as they died, too.

Then nothingness.

For a long moment he lay and ached…body, mind, soul.

He rose once more and wiped his arm across his forehead, glad these were his regular white leathers and not dreeth skin that wouldn't absorb his perspiration. Panting, he staggered through the dank mists and discovered he was humming. The realization jerked him to a stop. Bracing himself on the wall, he converted the hum to a Song and immediately felt better, his vision cleared. The tendrils of mist still lurked, but he'd developed a shield against them. He thought of the words he chanted—"I am fine. I can handle this. Not all visions are true." Rough words, not harmonious to the ear. But he'd Sing them until he could craft a potent poem.

He was still working on the wording when he saw an ancient door and beyond the door he felt a great cavern where the Singer and some of her Friends waited—Friends who didn't have any prophetic Power, as she did. As he did.

He heard the murmur of real human voices and the last fading note of crystal bowls. He realized that though it had seemed like a trip of hours, it had been less than five minutes. Nevertheless, his skin was bathed in sweat. He hoped his undergarments were releasing a pleasant scent as they were supposed to. The Singer had a nose as sensitive as her hearing.

When he opened the door the ghosts of prophecy faded. He let out a breath of relief and stepped into the large, rough cavern. The circle of Friends, some behind small tables holding bowls, some with cymbals, the best Singers with no instrument at all, circled a flaming blue-energy-lined pentacle. The Singer, a tiny woman especially for a Lladranan, looked down at a figure.

Then the Singer looked at him, her pointed brows rising high, and pitched her voice so it sounded next to his ear. "You made it all the way to the Summoning Cavern."

He couldn't tell whether she was impressed or dismayed or both. Then a slight, secret smile lifted the corners of her mouth. He didn't ask what she knew. *He* didn't want to know. "I was not mistaken in you," she said loudly.

Luthan looked her straight in the eyes. "I was in you."

Striding to the outside rim of the circle, he stared down. As expected by all, the Summoned Exotique was a woman. A lovely woman, beautiful more in the manner of his own people than that of Exotique Terre: long, dark hair flowing around her torso, old ivory and gold complexion, lush lips. He swallowed hard and waited for his innate revulsion for Exotiques to hit.

Marshalls' Castle, the same time

Raine Lindley found her feet carrying her to the great round temple in the Marshalls' Castle. Again.

There'd been something in the air of her small purple home office that wouldn't let her settle. Time and again she'd erased the line of the ship's prow she was designing. When she looked out the window, rainbows seemed to dance on the air and somehow she caught a scent of incense and the reverberation of a gong.

So she'd mounted her flying horse, her volaran, for the short two-mile trip to the Castle and the temple, accompanied by her companion, a young magical shape-shifting being called a feycoocu. This compulsion was more than was natural or healthy.

Because look what happened when she last followed a compulsion. At home in Connecticut she'd been so obsessed with her grandmother's mirror that she'd stare at it for hours, think about stepping *through* it, and how strange was that?

Then she'd thought that giving the mirror away to one of her brothers—newly engaged—was the right thing to do. To top off all this foolishness, instead of driving around the inlet, she'd packed the mirror and taken it onto the open sea in a new boat she'd built. In the winter. It was a mild day and the water was calm, but the action had been unwise beyond belief.

Thunder, lightning…storm from nowhere. The quilts and ropes around the mirror falling away magically. The glass blazing white like nothing she'd seen. The boat breaking up under her, the wind whipping her *into* the mirror, then landing her in the cold sea of here—an alternate dimension or universe or whatever. Lladrana.

She'd been Summoned by the Seamasters, who'd done it on the cheap. They hadn't even known they'd succeeded. Just called a person from Earth and when she didn't seem to show, they wandered back to a market gathering.

That forced Raine to fend for herself in a strange land where she knew *nothing*, and, in fact, got sick if she were more than a couple of miles from the sea.

Of course the worse had happened. One of those Lladranans who had an instinctive, irrational repulsion for people from Earth—Exotiques—had found her, been in a position of power over her. Tormented her. She'd lived like that six months before she could escape.

A winged horse had found her, brought a nobleman—Faucon Creusse—to her, and then she'd been *tuned* to this world and the sickness had gone away. Maybe that was why she was here, in the temple. The ritual to tune her had been here, in this large round building separated into sections by fancy screens.

Now the feycoocu was playing in the pool as a baby seal. Raine glanced at her, then stared at the crystal chimes that had run through her body last month, plucking inner chords she didn't know she had, and shivered.

There were seven chimes, and her friend Bri Masif, another Exotique, a healer, said they corresponded in sound and color to the chakras. The chimes sat on a large marble altar carved with symbols of the four elements, one on each side. Raine's, like Bri's, was water, which was the only thing that really made sense. Because she was a shipbuilder and would create a vessel that would carry an invasion force to fight the Dark.

One fast ship that might escape notice, loaded with the best fighters in Lladrana, and the Exotiques to Sing and trigger a weapon knot that would probably explode the whole damn island.

Raine peeked inside the chimes. She was sure that during her ordeal these had been lit somehow, but there was no candle wax inside. They were probably storage crystals like the ones embedded in the beams above her. She cleared her throat. She was learning all about Power—magic—and how it manifested in music. She hummed, true C. The red chime sounded the same note and lit, staying bright. Raine ran the chakra scale and grinned when all the chimes lit.

Then she stared at the silver gong, nine feet in diameter. Naturally it was suspended in the frame with Power, didn't have holes in it. She narrowed her eyes. Did it have an aura? Probably from all the magic in the temple, all the times it had been used in ritual, still… She circled the altar to look at it from the back. As she watched she thought she saw it vibrate faintly, heard a soft, trembling note. But when she shook her head it went away. She examined the gong again, there was something about it.…

"What are you doing here? Do you have a final model for the Ship yet?"

Raine jumped. She hadn't heard the doors open. The Castle staff was keeping them too well-oiled. Slowly she turned to face the man who was also a great draw for her to come to the Castle. The sexy guy she'd longed would notice her, Faucon Creusse.

3

Since Faucon had been dumped by another Exotique—okay, the whole lot of them—he didn't give Raine the time of day.

For some damn reason she swallowed sudden tears, hoped they didn't show in her eyes. How humiliating. She dragged a silk handkerchief from her pants pocket and stumbled over to the low stone built-in benches that circled much of the temple. Sank down onto one of the fat jewel-toned cushions and sniffled.

I am here. We are fine. Her feycoocu levitated over to her, leaving a dripping wake, then glared at Faucon. The little creature didn't give Raine any advice, a blessing since she wasn't very wise.

"Pardon," Faucon said stiffly. "I shouldn't have been so rude." He was cold, which was worse. His face was expressionless, masking the irritation she'd seen the first time they'd met and every time since.

"Is something wrong with the Ship?"

"The ship." She bit her own irritated words off, tried for the chilled courtesy that he'd mastered. "Nothing is wrong with the ship. I should have a final model this week." She bent her lips in a smile. "As for my welfare, I am a little touchy since all anyone cares about is my crafting of the ship, but I will get over my mood in a bit, thank you for asking."

She thought his golden skin tinged red. He inclined his head. "I am sorry to intrude." He hesitated. "Did you touch the gong? I thought I felt…thought I heard…"

She blew her nose and tucked the handkerchief away in a pocket. "No, I did not. But Summoning a new Exotique seems to be on all our minds. I wasn't *asked* to be Summoned."

"By the Song," he muttered. "Only Alyeka was asked and came of her own free will."

"Didn't know what she was getting into," Raine said.

"But the others have stayed with us to fight the Dark. I don't remember them being so fussy during the time they were making that decision."

He misremembered, she was sure, she'd read their accounts. But what came out of her mouth was, "My family! They still think I'm dead. And I don't know what's going on with them!"

He flung up his hands. "Is that all?" Now he strode to her, locked elegant fingers around her wrist in a strong grip, pulled her to her feet.

The feycoocu hissed, had turned into a little snake when they weren't looking.

Faucon ignored the small being, and said, "Why haven't you talked to mirror magician Koz about getting a mirror to your family so you can see what's going on?"

Raine shook her head. "He hasn't been around, has been in the east studying advanced mirror magic or something."

"Well, he's here now. We'll go see him."

Turn her over to Koz, Faucon meant.

She shrugged out of his grasp, turned again to the gong. She was sure she'd seen it tremble. A strange *push* of air popped her ears. She put a hand to her head. Faucon frowned, lines digging into his face, and steadied her with a hand to her elbow.

We must stay until it's done, said the feycoocu.

Singer's Abbey

Luthan stared at the new Exotique and waited for the screeching of all his senses into a cacophony. An awful Song that *hurt* until he learned to know the person behind the pummeling sounds that shrieked "mutant."

Those who didn't experience the horrible Song called the effect "an instinctive repulsion" and it was that, but it was more. An assault on his inner ear, his inner sight, his inner self. He'd learned to control it, of course. There was no honor in attacking an innocent person who had no knowledge that their Song was hurting him.

He waited and it didn't come. Instead he saw the long legs of the woman dressed in that sturdy blue material the Exotiques liked so much. Soft cloth draped her breasts and a harmony ball gleamed against their round fullness. She had equally full lips. Her eyes were as tilted as his own, as his people's, her skin not as golden as most Lladranans, but not that strange paleness of the other Exotiques, or Marian's hint of olive.

Studying the length of lovely legs and slender torso, he knew she wouldn't have the height of Lladranans. Marian would still be the tallest, this one was near to the size of Calli, the Volaran

Exotique with the yellow hair. But this woman's hair wasn't yellow, or the red of Marian's, or the browns of Bri and Raine. Nor the black with varying deep colors of his people. It seemed to be a very dark brown with black mixed in, not the other way around.

No repulsion. Had he finally mastered it? Squeezed the hideous moment from full minutes to less than a second? He didn't know. He didn't care. He only blessed the Song that this lady brought no instinctive repulsion and following shame.

In fact, her Song was vaguely muffled, heard dimly and not with the clarity of everyone else's in the world. Odd, but relieving.

A red cockatoo watched over her.

His anger at the Singer had dissipated. It would return, but now he felt only extreme wariness. He inclined his torso to the Singer, not the full bow he had given her when he'd first become her representative two years ago.

"Sweet Song salutations, Singer." Difficult not to hiss the greeting, to keep the proper rhythm and lilt, but that's how she judged her Friends, judged him. Irritation would have made his tones hard and he was glad he'd lost it. He'd be courteous until the new Exotique was settled.

When his gaze met the Singer's, he knew she *saw* that he doubted her deeply. There was a flash of arrogance there, her own annoyance.

A long glint caught his eye and he peered into the shadows of the cavern wall opposite them and saw a huge mirror, the glass covered with a faint sheen of blue that he thought could be sapphire dust.

He'd taken part in tuning Raine to the vibrations of Amee. Grimly, he said, "I see that you have chimes, and the crystal bowls for additional Song, cymbals to approximate the gong. But not the gong itself. You brought the Exotique by mirror magic."

The Singer's eyes flashed Power. She lifted her chin. "Do you presume to think that *my* Summoning could be inferior than the Marshalls' puny chanting Song? Especially now that Partis has died and cannot lead them?"

A shaft of pain speared him—Partis had been his loved godfather. Luthan held his ground, narrowed his own eyes. "Your Song is incredibly more Powerful than the Marshalls—"

Her expression relaxed.

"Your voice magnificently trained, your Friends almost as good a team as the Marshalls."

"Almost!"

"I have fought with the Marshalls, been mentally linked with them as a team in battle, in healing circles after battles. They are the premier team on Lladrana." He gestured to the people in colored robes around them. "Neither you nor these Friends have experienced life-and-death circumstances that form such a bond. Further, the Marshalls participate within their bond as equals. Your Friends will never be allowed to be equal to you. Could never be equal to the Singer."

Her expression showed pride mixed with irritation. Not many told her the truth. "But my team must have done well enough. We drew her here."

Luthan nodded. "She is here, but how tuned are her personal Exotique Terre vibrations to our planet of Amee? You have the chimes, the crystals, cymbals. But you do not have the gong."

"And the gong is so necessary?"

"I have been at four Summonings and a tuning, have seen and felt and heard what occurred. You have not attended. Yes,

I believe the gong is necessary. Unless you want to limit and cripple this Exotique to stay near the Abbey, as the Seamasters crippled their Summoned one."

Again the Singer's eyes flashed with Power. Her lips thinned. "If the gong is needed, the gong will sound and be heard!" She raised her hand and fisted her fingers in a snatching, twisting gesture.

The low note of a gong—could it really be the silver gong in the Marshalls' Castle so many leagues away?—resonated throughout the chamber.

The woman, who'd sat up, flung back her head. A cry came from her throat, but the sound held music.

The Singer's gaze snagged his again. "How many times?"

She knew, he'd reported the damn ritual five times, hadn't he? "Three."

Another clench of her hand, pull of her elbow. This time the gong note held longer, echoed loud against the cavern walls.

Another long wail from the woman, a thrashing of her limbs. By the time her body finished shuddering, she'd changed her position, sat cross-legged and hunched. She raised uncomprehending eyes and stared at him. He was watching her, but the Singer's gaze had not left him.

"She felt the tuning with my cymbals thrice already," the Singer said in her musical voice. "Now you insist that she experience the gong. Do you think she will be pleased with you?"

He forced his stare from the beautiful woman to the Singer. "Doing what is pleasant isn't as important as doing what is right."

The Singer lifted both of her hands, fingers straight. She nodded. "As you will, then. And *three!*" She closed her hands.

The sound was massive, clanging against his ears. He staggered a step, saw Friends fall from the corner of his eyes. A long, ululating cry came from the woman, matched by the warble of the bird.

There was a tinkle of chimes, and the mirror in the cavern faded—was it real or illusion? How much was truly needed for a portal between the worlds?

Marshalls' Castle

Raine staggered away after the third sounding of the gong, her ears still ringing despite her hands over them. Faucon had kept her upright with a grip on her upper arms.

The huge wooden doors from the courtyard burst open and Alexa, the first Exotique, and Bri, the healer, shot into the room, along with their men.

Raine stared at them in surprise.

Alexa, hands on hips, with the aura of the most Powerful warrior in the country, small and silver-headed, examined the large room in one whirling turn. "Where is she? Why did you do it?"

"What are you talking about?" Raine asked.

Bri, medium-brown hair gleaming, creamy complexion pale, rubbed her hands up and down her upper arms. "I felt it, a great change in Lladrana, in Amee. I heard the gong!" She glanced at Alexa, who was nodding.

"A Summoning," Alexa said. "Just a little while ago, and now the gong has sounded."

"No Summoning here." Raine and Faucon spoke together. He released his grip on her and she missed it. But Raine knew about sounding gongs, at least. "Tuning an Exotique to the world," she said between dry lips.

"Ayes," Alexa agreed. "But you didn't sound the gong."

"No." Then in Lladranan, "Ttho." Raine swallowed. "What's going on?"

"I can guess," Bastien, Alexa's husband, said grimly, towering over his mate. "The last Exotique is for—"

"The Singer!" Alexa shouted. "And that sneaky old woman has Summoned her!" She broke from Bastien's grasp and ran into the courtyard, yelling for her flying horse. Bastien followed.

Bri sent Raine a look and said, "Sevair and I rode the roc up from Castleton, we'll get there quicker. Are you coming?"

Everyone had been overprotective of her, and the Marshalls' Castle nearly a cage. Now, to leave it in the dark and fly south to the Singer's Abbey that she'd only heard spoken of in awed tones, seemed scary. Still, Exotiques stuck together. "I'll come," she croaked. *Blossom!* she called her own winged steed mentally. *Prepare for a flight to Singer's Abbey.*

Bri drilled a look at Faucon. "You?"

He shrugged. "Ayes."

Bri nodded and ran out, hand in hand with her serious husband.

But Faucon wasn't as casual as he seemed. Just standing near him, Raine could feel his tension. He strolled to the door, threw her a look from over his shoulder. "Come along, though I'd wager that this will be a futile quest. Despite everything, we won't wrest the new Exotique from the Singer's clutches."

Raine was cold and her throat too tight to reply.

As they flew away, the Castle alarm sounded, calling warriors to battle. Raine saw Alexa and her volaran flinch, but she didn't look back.

Knowing that Chevaliers and Marshalls were running through the Castle to their volarans, rising in a cloud to the North to fight monsters, Raine didn't look back, either.

She'd learned that looking forward was always best. That way you sometimes saw doom coming.

Singer's Abbey

Jikata was barely aware of what was going on around her. She thought there was a big, gorgeous Asian man looking down at her, wearing white…leather? Then he stepped out of her line of sight and she was surrounded by the people in rainbow robes. Most of them were smirking and she didn't like it.

A couple of them had looked at her in horror and disgust, had trembled and shrunk away from her gaze, pressing themselves against the cave walls.

Cave walls?

She had an uneasy feeling that she wasn't in Denver anymore. But she was more than confused, she'd just begun to figure out her surroundings when wave after wave of *sound* ran through her, electrifying her nerves. It felt as if she'd been struck by lightning. By the time it was done she could only lie quivering.

The older woman who'd said she was the Singer gestured to two women and they lifted Jikata gently, set her on her feet, steadied her as if she were a precious child learning to walk. She wasn't sure she liked this extreme care any better than the revulsion. Looking around for the one being who was slightly familiar, she saw Chasonette on the man in white's broad shoulder, staring at him. He was staring back at her in surprise, then he turned and met Jikata's gaze with a dark chocolate one of his own that made her tremble in more ways than she understood.

Then the elder was in front of her, demanding attention. "This cavern and the tunnels leading to and from it are filled with the tunes of prophecy. I am the Singer and have Summoned you!" She spoke English.

Jikata saw White Leather Man's grimace and an odd expression flicker on his face. She'd seen him come from that door to the tunnels, right? Now that she scrutinized him, he looked a little worse for wear, lines around his eyes and bracketing his mouth that she didn't think were usually noticeable. There were also smears of grime on his forehead, his face, his white leathers and gloves.

Chasonette warbled and again words sifted through Jikata's mind. *Let Luthan escort you. Best for you both.* The bird tugged a strand of the man's hair from a tie in the back and Jikata realized it was longer than shoulder-length. A good look for him.

She took a steadying breath. "Luthan?"

The Singer frowned, the man strode forward, lifted his arm and Chasonette walked down it to his wrist. Keeping that arm raised, he bowed, brown eyes never leaving Jikata.

"Luthan Vauxveau," he said. As he straightened he rolled a gesture from himself to her and spoke more words. French-like. She knew some French from songs and thought he said something like, "I am at your service." He held out his opposite arm in a formal offer of support and the women's hands on her tightened. The Singer's eyes narrowed and her lips pursed.

Jikata didn't know what was going on, but the emotional currents around her spoke of power plays. From the sheer force of the Singer, Jikata thought she was *the* major player in this situation, the turf was hers, the...minions. And the Singer had such life force, such *ki*, that Jikata could literally feel it.

Best even things out a bit, though the man, too, was a presence to be reckoned with. Jikata had been dealing with movers and shakers in the music world the last few months and knew authority when she saw it. This Luthan Vauxveau must represent another faction. Of what or whom, she didn't know, but it couldn't hurt to follow Chasonette's continued murmurings in her mind to go with Luthan. So Jikata put her hand on his arm and the cockatoo warbled approval even as a small shock went through Jikata. The hard muscles under her fingers tensed and she became all too aware of him, most particularly the melody *coming from him.* As if he had a personal theme in the soundtrack of her life.

Her fingers curled hard around his arm, but he didn't falter. The women who had been steadying her let their hands fall away. Everything—*everyone*—around her was…giving off… sound, from a ripple of notes to Luthan's harmonic melodies, to the Singer's full orchestral symphony. Jikata thought the cave itself issued long, deep tones.

She *did* have a soundtrack in her life now, and the thought was daunting.

Luthan took a small step toward the door and Jikata followed. Her stomach clutched. She stopped and looked around, peered back where she'd seen the theater, hesitant to leave this place. A slight mist hovered in that direction, beyond which was dark, no sheen of a mirror or electric lights.

Nothing but rock walls arching to roundness above her. Excellent acoustic chamber, but…not Denver? Couldn't be, if she listened to both her mind and her heart. Did she dare leave?

How could she stay? There was nothing here. She had to go with them to get answers.

The Singer had glided beyond them to the door, along with a woman in a royal blue robe who opened the door. Luthan hissed through his teeth and began singing. He had a strong tenor. Beautiful. Great breath control. His chant was simple and strong. The Singer had begun her Song, too. Intricate and forceful but with a delicacy, and, again, a slight quaver.

A sense of impending change flared in Jikata. Her life would never be the same again, and the moment of decision had passed by so quickly she hadn't been aware of it. She wanted to slow events down, felt the edge of a tide of exhaustion lapping inexorably to her. Maybe she *had* fallen asleep on the chaise lounge in her dressing room and this was all a dream.

Chasonette fluttered from Luthan to Jikata's shoulder, and she felt the small prick of claws. Then the bird Sang, too. So much music from everyone overwhelmed her as she tried to sort it out. The others were lining up behind her and Luthan, the Singer was no more than a small pace ahead.

The tunnel was larger than Jikata expected, with a smoother floor though the walls remained rough. When they stepped into it a mist coalesced around them, wisping into faces she knew—the major record producer, her agent, other singing stars—and with all of them came more tunes that seemed to suit their personalities. And they seemed to be leaching the heat from her.

She blinked and saw herself singing with a huge Grammy behind her. Fabulous!

When they turned a corner the mist formed into five women in front of them, Caucasian women—a small white-haired one, a redhead, a blond, two brunettes. They all scowled at her, gazes hot. The sound they made was incredible, going beyond Jikata's hearing range in each direction. Waves of heat rippled around them, reached out to lick her with flames, and she was almost glad, she was so cold.

"We trusted you!" they snapped in chorus. "You betrayed us."

The heat of the anger and the cold of the tunnel and the tide of exhaustion was too much. Jikata slid into blackness and blessed quiet.

Luthan swung the new Exotique up into his arms, the bird fluttered around them, making soothing sounds, a lilt of encouraging notes. The Singer took the lead.

Oddly enough, his muscles eased. The muffled quality of her Song held most of his visions at bay. But he'd seen the future again: a wondrous ship, rough seas, the looming volcano of the Dark's Nest in the distance. The battle. Monsters against Chevaliers and Marshalls. The Exotiques and their mates Singing the Weapon Knot loose, the City Destroyer spell.

Death and destruction. Again and again. Only one thing remained the same. Calli, the Volaran Exotique, and her bondmate, Marrec, lived. For that Luthan gave thanks. If even one Exotique lived the outcome was good. Usually the Dark expired, too; when it didn't, it was too wounded to rise for generations. Good.

He plodded after the Singer, trying to keep his mind shielded from the prophetic wraiths.

Luthan, what the hell is going on! Bri, the healer, demanded, and he sensed her within the Abbey proper, arriving by the roc sooner than the others. She and her husband, the formidable Citymaster, Sevair Masif, were spiraling down on the roc to the main courtyard. They would sense Luthan, come to him, might even sense the new Exotique.

For years Lladranans had fought invading monsters sent by a great Dark until the magical northern boundary began to fall and the Marshalls had dared to Summon the first Exotique,

Alexa. She'd found the way to mend the fence posts, but had set them on a course to defeat the Dark itself.

Marian had come then, for the Circlets—the Sorcerers, Tower community—had discovered that the horrors invaded to regain some specific item. Marian agreed that the battle should be taken to the Dark. And she'd found the knot that would be their greatest weapon.

Then Calli was Summoned for Luthan's own portion of society, the Chevaliers, and the volarans. She'd scouted the Dark's Nest.

When a sickness sent by the Dark had swept the country, the Cities and Towns had paid the Marshalls to bring a medica from Exotique Terre. Twins had arrived, Bri and Elizabeth, and had fulfilled their tasks...and Elizabeth had returned with the Snap, when her home planet called her, opening a portal in the Dimensional Corridor, giving an Exotique the choice to stay or return.

Unknown to the rest of Lladrana, the Seamasters had tried a Summoning—Raine—and had thought they'd failed, and left. Now she was to build a great Ship to carry an invasion force to the Dark's Nest itself and kill it.

The fractured communities of Lladrana were combining for that one purpose. To kill the Dark.

To send one swift and stealthy Ship to the Dark's Nest, manned with the best warriors of Lladrana to fight the horrors and the Master defending it. There the Exotiques would untie the mysterious Weapon Knot Marian had found—the City Destroyer—with Song and...and leading the Song would be this last woman.

The sixth and final person to be Summoned to battle the Dark.

4

A cold wind whipped around Luthan, whistled through the tunnel, some of the Friends' voices broke and were silent. Luthan drew on his Power to keep going, to protect the woman in his arms, as the bird shrilled a distress call.

The Singer remained untouched and serene, her pace regular, her Song soaring.

But she knew, like everyone else, that all their lives hung in the balance.

When they reached the white-and-gold anteroom, her Song faded. She turned toward Luthan with a flinty gaze. "I will not let you take this one away. She is mine to train! Her voice is not sufficient, yet, to master the spell Circlet Exotique Marian discovered to destroy the Dark. This one must develop her full range, as I have. She is the key. She will lead the others."

The Singer gestured and a hefty man hurried from the rest

of the Friends' to stand before him, arms outstretched to take the burden of the new Exotique. Luthan held onto her.

The door to the caverns was still open, the room was small and not everyone could crowd into it. Friends in the tunnel whimpered. Then their ranks broke and a line of them hurried by the Singer and Luthan and the large Friend, through the door to the chapter house. The Singer ignored them. Luthan couldn't, he sent what Power he could to soothe their fears. They didn't acknowledge him.

He'd made the right decision. He would no longer represent the Singer.

"Look at her," the Singer said, pointing at the woman in his arms. "The shadows beneath her eyes, the gray tone to her skin, she is exhausted."

Luthan? Bri called. She, Sevair and the roc were just outside the octagonal tower door that led to the caverns. He was connected to her through his bond with his brother, who was pair-bonded with Alexa. All the Exotiques except Raine were strongly linked to Lladrana men—and to each other.

"Summoning is hard on a person, she'll recover, better she be with her own kind," he said.

The Singer's smile was knife-edged. "*My* Song has reverberated in her life. She was fated for me, will probably be my successor. That means she has prophetic Power, untapped and untrained. Can't you sense it?"

Focusing now on the inner woman and her Power—her great Power—instead of her outer beauty, Luthan studied her. He'd never heard such a complex Song, and as the Singer had pointed out, there was a well of Power within her that appeared to be trapped behind a door just cracked open—recently. She'd seen visions in the caverns, he realized. His gut tightened.

"You can take her from me—" the Singer's voice held a mocking note "—but her Power for prophecy has already been unlocked. Will you take the task of training her? Do you forget, then, how it was when you had your own first visions?"

He suppressed a shudder. He would never forget the visions that had come to him as he'd gone from boy to man. Terrible to experience that alone, to fear for your sanity.

Luthan, I know you're nearby! Bri kicked the outside door.

"So, what will you do, Luthan Vauxveau?" the Singer asked.

His lips firmed as he considered. If he broke ties with the Singer now, he'd be leaving an Exotique solely in her Power, with no connection to the others from Exotique Terre.

Or he could let the Singer think he was yet her dupe, come and go freely in the Abbey. So he bowed his head. "Very well."

"You'll explain to the others?" She smiled again.

He wanted to refuse. "I'll do my best." But his loyalty had changed, from the Singer to the... Not the Marshalls, even though Exotique Alexa and his own brother Bastien led them. Not the Chevaliers, he'd outgrown them and their specific concerns.

He'd serve Lladrana itself, the planet Amee, and the Exotiques. They were the spearhead against the Dark.

He would double-check all the Singer's statements. Reluctantly, he transferred the lovely new Exotique to the burly Friend. Chasonette settled on the man's head and he winced.

Bri, Luthan said mentally, keeping his tone calm and unhurried. *The Singer has convinced me that the new Exotique should remain here.*

But—

There are good reasons. The last Friend sidled through the chapter house door. The Singer went to her own door and flung it open for the man holding the Exotique. There was a tinier room that Luthan understood was a box that moved between floors. The Singer stepped in, watching him.

"She will be taken to a luxurious suite that has been prepared specifically for her," the Singer said, her smile turning satisfied.

Luthan didn't like any of her previous smiles, nor the smug one she sent him now. She lifted a hand. "You have been an excellent representative. Take care of the problem of the other Exotiques. We will talk later."

Anger welled again. She'd held great Power—the Power of the Oracle of Lladrana—for too long. And her secrecy had helped separate the factions over the past decades.

He had much to discuss with the Exotiques and they didn't totally trust him because he'd been the Singer's man. He'd have to talk fast.

If he were clever and lucky enough, he could speak with them one at a time and convince them to let the new one stay with the Singer. Save himself grief. Not a good position for a man who'd once been called the most honorable in Lladrana to be in.

Luthan opened the door to Bri and Sevair. The healer's husband had a grip around her biceps and she shifted from foot to foot. She'd cut her brown hair again and it was shorter than most men's, some standing out in spikes at the top. In style, she was the most outrageous of all the Exotiques, but at least the purple streaks were gone. She wore a medica's red travel tunic with a white cross.

The roc had moved to a spacious courtyard within earshot, eyes gleaming and wicked beak slightly open as if ready to pounce.

Bowing, Luthan addressed them, "Salutations."

Bri frowned. Sevair had taken to carrying his stonemason's hammer as a weapon in a sling on his hip. His fingers touched the handle, but he inclined his head. "Salutations, Luthan."

Luthan raised his voice. "Lady roc, if you are hungry, the Singer's cattle herd is to the northwest."

Thank you, Chevalier, the roc said, projecting her thoughts into all their minds. Her tone, too, was mocking and Luthan was getting damned tired of that, but he'd brought this situation upon himself by trusting the Singer and following her orders.

Using the common link between the Exotiques and their men, Luthan spoke mind to mind. *Perhaps we can adjourn to my home estate? It's not too far from here.*

Sevair frowned. *Castle Vauxveau is far northwest.*

Not my father's home, but my own, Luthan said. It was the house he'd inherited from his mother's aunt that he'd claimed as soon as he could leave his father. Not that he'd made it a home then. He'd run wild for a couple of years until he realized his younger brother was following in his footsteps.

Past mistakes, he'd made a couple of bad ones. Then he'd done fine for years, but recently…

He waved toward the entry station of the Abbey and the volaran landing field beyond. "While the roc is feeding, we can fly to my home. I'm sure the Singer won't care if you use a couple of her volarans." Not if it meant getting disruptive people away from her domain.

Bri's face went stubborn. She crossed her arms under her breasts and adopted a militant stance that looked more than a little like Alexa's. Habits were rubbing off. "I'm the Exotique Medica, I want to examine our new addition." Bri shook her head. "Summoning is tough under any circumstances, but by the Singer—"

"The most Powerful person in Lladrana," Luthan ended smoothly. "I saw the lady myself."

"Female?" asked Sevair.

"Ayes, one who looks more like our people than the others."

As expected, curiosity lit Bri's eyes, but she stuck to the topic. "She appeared well, and tuned to Amee?"

"Ayes. The Singer Summoned her through mirror magic without my knowledge. There were the chimes, and cymbals to approximate the gong." He raised his hand when Bri opened her mouth to speak. "When I refused to accept that the cymbals would be effective, the Singer drew the sound of the gong to us." He shook his head. "Amazing."

Bri huffed a breath, her stance softened. "We heard it."

"I'm sure everyone did."

Fingers drumming on her opposite arm, Bri searched his face. "She was well?"

"I give you my word. She appeared as if she was weary before she arrived, and the Singer immediately sent her to bed to rest. If we petition the Singer now to see her, she may deny us simply because the new Exotique is sleeping." He paused. "She *is* meant for the Singer, you know."

Bri seemed unconvinced. Luthan saw a man in the shadows. "Jongler!" he called. The man hesitated, shuffled forward. He bowed briefly, looked at Bri's hair, glanced away. "Ayes?"

"The Singer has Friends who are medicas?" Luthan asked.

"Of course." Jongler's forehead lined. "She has been ill and is of a great age. We have the best medicas in the land here, two came from the Marshalls' Castle last year." He bowed, deeper, to Bri. "I should say the best medicas other than yourself, Exotique Medica." A gleam came to his eyes. "If you would stay with us, I guarantee that you would be well paid." He turned to Sevair. "And there is always work for a skilled stonemason and architect on the Abbey buildings. The Singer is delicate, and the person of the greatest importance in Lladrana. Her visions are so necessary for the future, please stay—"

But Bri was backing away, hauling Sevair, who was studying the conglomeration of buildings within the compound. "Thank you." She glanced at Sevair, then planted her feet, raised her chin and stared at Jongler. "I insist you have a medica examine the Exotique...Singer tomorrow morning and send me a report at my tower in Castleton. You do have a crystal orb?"

Jongler was bowing again. "Of course, of course, the very best crystal, bespelled by the great Circlet Sorcerer himself, Bossgond. We also have mirrors, though none of the new, advanced ones. Yet. Still, they will do."

"Crystal," Bri said firmly. "You know my address?"

"The ancient Ronteran's Tower in Castleton." Jongler breathed the name reverently. "Ronteran was not only a Circlet Sorcerer, he was a Singer's consort." Jongler waved. "He designed a few of the buildings."

"Thought I recognized his ornate style," Sevair said. Luthan followed his gaze to a row of gargoyles.

There was a belch overhead and the scent of sweet grass— from the roc. A magical creature indeed. The great bird fluttered down. Jongler sent its bloody beak a glance of abject terror, scrambled back, still bowing to Bri. "If you ever want to change venues..." He vanished around a corner.

I flew around the compound, the roc said, eyes glittering a rainbow of dark colors. *The new Singer is Powerful, healthy, resting. She is where she must be.*

Bri and Sevair matched Luthan's sigh. Magical creatures were usually cryptic.

Bri stared at Luthan. "Have you had any visions of her?"

He could feel a prophecy coalesce, didn't want it. "No." The vision came in a flash anyway. Despite his wishes he'd become expert in deciphering flashes of prophecy. "Only that she and I will meet you on a road, still summer."

After searching his face, Bri nodded. "Then we'll leave." Again she shifted. "This place makes me nervous. *I* don't want to be kidnapped."

Luthan's jaw flexed before he said, "I did what I had to do."

Wincing, Bri said, "I didn't mean— Before my time. Anyway, let's go home. I'll contact Calli at her estate and give her the info." Bri took Sevair's hand and led him to the roc.

Sevair still scanned the buildings. "Perhaps some time in the future we can visit…."

"Maybe." Bri mounted the roc, then Sevair settled behind her. With a short, "Bye!" they flew away.

Luthan's home

Luthan flew, intercepted Alexa and Bastien, Raine and Faucon in the air and led them to his home. A few minutes later they all landed in the yellow cobblestone courtyard between the small manor and the moat.

Alexa and Bastien went inside, but Luthan lingered to talk with Raine and Faucon, neither of whom had dismounted.

He convinced these two that all was well, he'd explain everything to Bastien and Alexa. Raine and Faucon could return to Castleton. He sensed they were glad to go, and didn't want to spend any more time together. Faucon would grimly escort her to the Castle, flying with Distance Magic, and they wouldn't need to converse or interact. Their relationship was interesting, and he made a note to tell the Singer— No, he would not be reporting anything of importance to the Singer.

Faucon had the opposite reaction to Exotiques than Luthan. Luthan had never spoken to the man about his innate attraction to Exotiques, could only imagine that Faucon heard a siren's song of love where Luthan experienced a painful clash of sounds screaming "wrong." But of the two of them, so far Faucon had been the one most emotionally hurt.

Raine looked back over her shoulder, frowning, as her volaran rose into the sky. Wanting again to be reassured that she wasn't abandoning her friend, Alexa, or the new Exotique. Luthan sent her mental soothing—*All is well, I promise. This is not like your own experience, the Singer will cherish the lady.*

And you are an honorable man, Raine replied, her expression easing. She waved.

He waved back, then entered his home, passing his housekeeper, who'd brought brandy and tea to the shabbily masculine sitting room where Bastien and Alexa waited.

Now to convince Alexa not to storm the Singer's Abbey.

5

Luthan strode in. Bastien lounged in his chair, sipping brandy. It was good to see him there. During the two years they'd lived together, after Luthan had put aside his wild ways, the seat had conformed to Bastien's butt. That was years ago and Bastien was a hardened warrior now. He was even a Marshall like their father, not a troubled young man with strange and spiking Power that went with his striped black-and-white hair.

He was grinning, watching his bondmate pace the room. Since Alexa was an Exotique and smaller than Lladranans, and the shortest one, too, it took her more paces than it would have anyone else. Luthan noted that Bastien watched *her* butt. "So what's so wrong about the Singer Summoning the next Exotique?" Bastien prodded his wife.

She scowled and stopped in front of him, fingering her jade baton, her best magical weapon. That would have made

Luthan nervous except Bastien was a good judge of his wife's moods. Bastien continued, "You just wanted her to bond with you and the rest of the Exotiques first, before you handed her over to the Singer. Raging curiosity, lover."

Alexa pouted then plopped herself on Bastien's lap. He wrapped an arm around her, and Luthan felt a stinging surge of envy.

Bastien met Luthan's eyes, his expression unusually sober. "Fact is, we Marshalls have been working as a group on the complex Summoning spell. We had the chorus harmonies right, but…" He shrugged. "We lost Partis, and his was the voice with the strength and timbre and heart that brought the Exotiques through the Dimensional Corridor."

Luthan froze as he noticed tears dribbling down Alexa's cheeks. He didn't think he'd ever seen the strong woman cry.

Bastien cradled her against his chest, gave her a cloth.

"It was Partis's voice that drew me," Alexa said between quiet sobs. "He comforted me for the loss of my friend. He was so strong and so gentle. Such a serene man."

"An amazing quality in a Marshall. They tend to be fierce and passionate," Luthan said, pouring her a cup of the tea she favored and that he kept on hand, dumping in a couple of lumps of sugar and stirring it.

She sniffed, took the cup with watery eyes, steady hands and a crooked smile. "A compliment, thanks." She drank, then sighed. "We Marshalls *are* determined." She patted Bastien's cheek. "Even him."

Bastien's arm tightened on her. "Determined that you aren't going to face the Dark alone. I am your Shield."

The Shield was the defensive person of the Marshall Sword-Shield pair, though Bastien had many years of outright battle as a Chevalier himself. He tucked her head under his chin. "We were training Marwey for the main solo, but she didn't have the range. There's a young Chevalier we were encouraging to test for Marshall." He rubbed Alexa's back. "Just as well the Singer brought her over. Mirror magic, you said?" He raised his brows.

"From what I saw." Luthan squinted to bring details back. "The Singer called the cave the 'Summoning Cavern' so—"

Alexa continued, "—Other Singers have brought people through. She had some sort of crystal that showed Calli this world when she was growing up on Earth." Alexa shot Luthan a dark look. "I'm still mad at you for hurting Calli and Marrec."

Luthan closed his eyes.

Bastien said, "It was more than a year ago, give it a rest. And he made a mistake, didn't you?" he asked Luthan.

Luthan opened his eyes and stoically met Alexa's frowning gaze. "No. It wasn't a mistake. I followed the Singer's orders." He walked to a table and poured himself a short brandy, downed it. His jaw flexed. "I am sorry for any upset I caused—"

"To Marian and Jaquar and Bossgond and me and Bastien—" Alexa obviously still kept a list and a grudge.

"I didn't upset Bastien," Luthan protested.

"You upset me. My upset disturbed Bastien," Alexa ended frostily.

No way to escape this. Again. "I am sorry for the upset I caused, but looking back, I believe that Amee, and destiny, was well served by my actions." He sank into a large, comfortable chair. "The Singer was right in that instance."

"I don't think so," Alexa said. "I think that if she, or you, had considered the matter, you'd've found a better option."

Luthan shrugged. "I don't know. Perhaps."

"It's past," Bastien said.

"*But*, I am done with being her representative," Luthan said.

Both Alexa and Bastien straightened. Bastien nodded. "Good."

"Good!" Alexa echoed.

"When she first requested I become her liaison to the Marshalls and other segments of Lladranan society, I thought it was good the Singer and Friends would be less isolated in the Abbey. At first she kept me well informed and I knew why she gave the orders she did and followed them, even if I did not agree totally with her. The past year or so, though..." He shrugged. "After that last illness...she's become secretive, autocratic. I'm done with her, and will tell her so...soon."

"Hmm." Alexa finished her tea and set the cup on a side table. "Now the new Exotique will be the one to integrate the Singer and her Friends into the rest of Lladranan society. What did you say her name was, again?"

They hadn't been introduced, but Luthan thought back, recalled the trilling of the bird's mental voice. "Jikata."

Alexa gasped. Her mouth dropped open. She put a hand on her heart. "*The* Jikata?"

Luthan frowned. "It's a title?"

Alexa was shaking her head. "No. She's a singer."

"Of course," Luthan said.

Alexa hopped off of Bastien's knees and strode over to Luthan. "I mean she's a popular singer in our world." Her hands waved. "A local star going national—international."

That was gibberish to Luthan.

Alexa began pacing again. "A...a well-known troubadour?"

Luthan shared a glance with Bastien, for Alexa to be impressed meant the lady was *someone*.

"Wait, wait," Alexa muttered. "Didn't I hear...yes!" Her eyes went bright. "I read that she had a four-octave voice."

This time they all shared a glance.

"The requirement for the City Destroyer spell while unloosing Marian's weapon knot," Bastien murmured.

"Wait 'til I tell the others! Especially Marian." Alexa settled onto Luthan's lap, looked up at him with a winning smile. "She's from Colorado, too. How did she look? Tell me all about her."

He met Bastien's gaze over Alexa's head. His brother smiled and raised his mug to him.

So Luthan told Alexa all he knew of the Summoning.

Luthan waited up after Alexa and Bastien went to bed, prepared to convince Circlet Marian and her husband Jaquar that Jikata should remain with the Singer.

He sat in his firelit study. Like all the other rooms in the small manor, it was comfortable but worn. The walls had faded to an even duller color than the original beige. The sturdy wood and leather chairs showed nicks and scratches. Occasionally there was a settee or couch with a dim pattern reflecting his great aunt's taste.

He still liked this place. Couldn't imagine living in the great, cold castle where he and Bastien had been raised by a whining, disinterested mother and a dictatorial father.

Since Bastien had formed an unexpected bond with their father before his death and told Luthan about their father's foreknowledge of his own death, Luthan understood the man better. Luthan didn't despise his father anymore, but he would never be able to respect his sire.

Tonight the Sorcerers—Circlets—would come, Exotique

Marian and her bondmate Jaquar. Since the weather was clear with only a few drifts of mist, they wouldn't ride lightning, but fly on volarans. He didn't know what experimentation they might have been conducting when they felt the Summoning, but they'd been on their island in Brisay Sea. His stable master had been alerted.

Luthan would wait for them, get the confrontation out of the way when there were only two of them, no matter how formidable. Taking the Exotiques one at a time was the best strategy.

Besides, he didn't want to go up to bed. Bastien and Alexa tended to be noisy in their lovemaking. He didn't begrudge them that, but it did remind him of his loneliness, his single state. The invasion of the Dark's Nest was preliminarily scheduled for less than three months from now, perhaps as little as a month, determined by the building of the Ship and the trip. Though they hoped they'd survive, they were all prepared to die.

He'd never thought he'd die single, always had believed he'd find a bondmate—was that fantasy or wishing or a vision that had gone awry?

It was near midnight when the doorharp sounded. He rose from the chair where he'd been dozing and went to the door. Beyond the thick wood he sensed great Power. Marian and Jaquar were here.

With a low whistle, he set the spell torches lighting around him in the entryway, then opened the door and bowed. "Salutations."

Marian, the Exotique Circlet, was tall and voluptuous with long, dark red hair, blue eyes and a slightly olive tone to her complexion.

"Salutations," Jaquar said. He was tall with silver streaks of Power at both temples and eyes a little darker blue than

Marian's. Some old strain of Exotique blood was in his background.

Neither of them appeared angry, but both looked as if they had prickly questions.

"Come into the sitting room," Luthan said. "I have brandy and mead."

"Prepared as usual," Marian murmured. "I don't sense the new Exotique here."

The skirmishing had begun.

Luthan continued to the sitting room, poured brandies for Jaquar and himself—he was drinking more tonight than he did in an entire month—and Marian the mead she favored. As the couple sat together on a loveseat, Luthan caught a half smile on Jaquar's face. The Exotiques' men were enjoying him trying to handle their women, and Marian could literally be a force of nature. She was a weather mage like her husband.

Thankfully, she began sipping her mead. She leaned against Jaquar and closed her eyes for an instant. Like the new Exotique, Marian had shadows under her eyes. Ayes, she was interesting with her blue eyes and red hair, but not lovely like the new Exotique. Jikata's delicate features, long dark brown hair with black, tilted brown eyes and complexion close to the golden of the Lladranans appealed to Luthan more.

Best to begin. "There are many reasons why the Singer Summoning the last Exotique was best. Time is of the essence and the Marshalls were not prepared to do the Summoning, since they'd lost Partis." Luthan lifted his hands as Marian sizzled a glance at him. "No, I did not know the Singer was going to do so. She did not inform me, nor did she ask me to participate. My taking her orders is at an end, but I haven't cut the association yet."

Frowning, Marian said, "I've been concentrating on the City Destroyer Weapon Knot and the Songspell to untie it, training my voice with others. I knew Partis was the lead singer of the Marshalls, and of course knew of his death, but I didn't…" She shook her head, and a distant expression came to her eyes, recollection of when she was Summoned, Luthan supposed.

"He was a strong, quiet man, a Shield to his Lady's Sword, more important than we all knew," Jaquar said.

With a watery sniff, Marian nodded. "I should have paid more attention to Alexa, or she should have told me. The Tower community has several good teams now, including good Singers…between all of us, the Castle and the Tower and the Chevaliers and the Cities, we could have forged an excellent team." She shrugged. "Well, the Singer took advantage of our distraction and inaction."

Jaquar put an arm around her waist and squeezed. "It is our duty to figure out the Weapon Knot."

"And you have?" Luthan asked.

"Pretty much," Marian said. "It's for an ensemble of at least three and no more than fifty, and the lead solo must have a four-octave range."

"The Singer would Summon no one with less," Luthan said. "And she's the best to train such a range since she has it herself, and since the spellsong will be complex and difficult—" he raised his brows in question and Marian nodded, "—the Singer is the best to train anyone in Power made by the voice alone."

Jaquar shifted. "Her voice isn't the only Power of the new Exotique, is it? All the signs indicate that the lady will be strong in prophecy, too, like the Singer herself. And you."

Luthan didn't want to recall the visions he'd had in the caves. "The new Exotique is Powerful, and like all the other

Lladranan communities, the Singer would have requirements for the one she Summoned."

"Which would include prophecy," Jaquar pointed out.

"Which would include prophecy, though I wasn't with the lady long enough to gauge her Power," Luthan said, then told them every detail of the Summoning, his talks with Bri and Raine and Alexa.

"Hmm," Marian said at last. "This Lladranan cockatoo, I've never heard of one."

Another squeeze from her husband. Jaquar said, "You all have animal companions, why shouldn't she?"

"If you consider the feycoocus animals," Marian said. "They are more beings of pure magic."

"Who take various animal forms," Jaquar added. He looked at Luthan. "Was this cockatoo a real bird or a feycoocu?"

Luthan hadn't considered the matter. He went with his gut. "A real bird."

Marian sighed. "Looks like my feycoocu will be mostly bird in the future, along with his mate and the baby, since Bri has the roc. I must admit I prefer mammals."

"Birds may be more useful during the trip," Luthan said. "A Lladranan cockatoo comes from the forests of the southeast, a beautiful, intelligent bird."

"Ah." Marian yawned, stretched and rose.

"One last thing," Luthan said. "Alexa recognized the name of the new Exotique."

Marian tilted her head.

"The new Exotique's name is Jikata."

Marian stared at him for a long moment. "I can't believe it," Marian said. "What is *she* doing *here*? And why would she possibly want to stay?" She seemed shocked.

Jaquar stood and put an arm around his bondmate's shoulders. "With that attitude, perhaps it's wise that the Singer has charge of her." He glanced at Luthan. "For now."

"For now," Luthan agreed.

But tears shone in Marian's eyes, and she clutched Jaquar's biceps with both hands. "But we all know that the Snap to return an Exotique home doesn't come until after she finishes her task. If she's a four-octave Singer who'll lead us in the City Destroyer spell, that means her task—"

"Is to go with us when we invade the Dark's Nest and kill it," Jaquar finished.

"The most dangerous task of any of us. Does she have any free will at all?" Marian asked.

Singer's Abbey

Jikata awoke, stretched luxuriously, smiled at the velvet canopy above her head. The Ghost Hill Hotel was lovely and she had the Presidential Suite.

But what was truly excellent was the music. She didn't know what radio station the hotel carried, but it was primo, something she thought she'd never find in Denver, though that public station in Greeley came close.

The piece was new-age ambient, full orchestral with rich, intricate melodies, and the acoustics of the room were wonderful since the sound surrounded her. Better than her home system. She'd get her sound engineer here to talk to the management.

She frowned, rubbed her face. She *had* ended a tour yesterday, that meant the crew was officially on vacation and—

She was due at her great-grandmother's at ten! She scrambled up, shoving the binding covers down, bad dreams again.

Weird dreams—

Ishi would never forgive her for being late.

Ishi was dead.

That came flooding back, along with all the regrets and emptiness of her life. She fell back against fat pillows.

A flash of scarlet and there was a beautiful red bird sitting on a perch near the bed. It trilled a liquid melody. *We are in Lladrana, where we belong.*

Jikata blinked and blinked again. Cleared her throat. "I beg your pardon?" Her voice was raspy. Everything seemed slightly off.

The bird fluttered to the bed next to her. Jikata wrinkled her nose but didn't smell musty feathers or bird manure. She smelled lavender.

I am Chasonette. We are here, we are home, we will triumph!

A mind-singing bird. Not slightly off…way off.

Music all around. Jikata concentrated and thought she could hear music coming from the very walls of this place and that sent a little shiver down her spine.

Harp notes rose and fell, then came the creak of a door, followed by the wonderful smells of eggs and bacon, freshly baked bread. Saliva pooled in Jikata's mouth. A plump young woman walked in bearing a tray, obviously breakfast. Jikata shouldn't eat so heavily…but she *was* coming off a long, stressful tour.

She noticed the food first then her gaze went from the red lacquered tray to the woman and she stared in disbelief. *Music* streamed from the maid in simple, repetitive notes. Jikata shook her head hard enough to dizzy herself. But when she stopped, the woman's music was still there.

Chasonette fluffed her feathers. The bird, too, emanated

music without one warble from her throat, a high lovely tune that seemed to pierce Jikata's heart.

Jikata recalled the notion that she had a soundtrack for her life. True again this morning. More disturbing now. Surely it had to be in her mind, but she could live with it.

The woman dipped a curtsy and flushed a little. Jikata scooted back, wary, but ready to be served. She didn't keep servants herself, but had stayed at homes of both old wealth and nouveau riche where maids were common.

After a tour she treated herself to resorts where she could be pampered. Perhaps this was just one and she'd forgotten the travel, or the Philberts had arranged for her transport. She wondered what sort of spa facilities this place had.

Speaking in a Frenchlike patter—or perhaps patois—Jikata didn't understand, the serving woman set the tray on Jikata's lap. Chasonette nipped half a slice of bacon and after crunching a chunk, dropped the rest in a small china dish on the corner of the tray that held a mixture of seeds.

The bird was going to *eat* from Jikata's tray? That couldn't be sanitary. Chasonette buried her beak in the bowl.

A word from the woman caught Jikata's ear with the rising inflection of a question. "Po-tat-oes?"

Jikata stared and the servant repeated it. "Potatoes?"

Potatoes for breakfast! Glancing at her plate, Jikata saw scrambled eggs with cheese decorated with pepper and dill, and two strips of bacon. She shouldn't even be having this. An egg-white omelet with fresh vegetables and a touch of cheese, an in-season fruit cup. Nothing like this. The thought of the cheesy eggs on her tongue made her mouth water all over again.

"No," she said. "No potatoes."

The woman's eyes sharpened. "*Ttho*. Ttho potatoes."

Jikata shifted in her bed, she'd been hoping that despite everything, this really was Denver. Pushing down panic, she decided to go with the flow a bit until she could discover more.

With a steady movement, the servant pulled all the bed curtains open and tied each section to the carved bedpost. Jikata gasped. In front of her was a wide rectangular window. The near distance was a field of white stone towers and spires, some embellished. Beyond that was land of a green that Colorado rarely saw except for a couple of weeks in a very rainy spring. Nothing like California, either. Or the tropical island she'd planned to recuperate on.

In the far distance were hills of various shades of green, highlighted by golden streaks of sunlight, a blue, blue sky and puffy, white castle-clouds. It all had an exoticness that spoke nothing of the rocky hills and rockier mountains around Denver.

Jikata's mouth dried and she swallowed. She needed something to drink.

As if on cue, another woman and a man entered, both older than the first plump maid, who was dressed in yellow. The woman wore blazing red and held a beautiful folding table. The man wore rich blue and carried a tray loaded with fabulous china in a wildly colored chintz pattern on the tall coffeepot and fluted cups rimmed with gold.

The fragrance of jasmine tea rose from the spout of the pot and Jikata's nose twitched.

None of the three had a bone structure that Jikata could quite place, not northern Chinese, or Mongolian, Korean, Thai. Definitely not Caucasian. Gorgeous all the same. And they all had streaks at their temples, the younger one silver, the older ones the color of spun gold. Jikata recalled that the old woman last night—the Singer had pure gold hair. Those streaks and that hair must mean something. Another frisson slid through her.

The older woman in red set the table beside Jikata's bed, stepped back and folded her hands, but her sharp gaze scanned the room as if checking to ensure everything was correct. Jikata had seen that professional housekeeper's glance before. The man poured the tea, lifted the lid of a sugar bowl as if in question.

Jikata shook her head, then remembered the word, *ttho*.

With exaggerated movements the younger maid shook her head and said, "Ttho." Then nodded vigorously, smiled and added "Ayes."

"Ayes," Jikata said faintly.

Everyone echoed her, and the sound of the word was sometimes *eyes*, or *ice* or even *ah-yes*.

Deciding that her language lesson had progressed well enough and not wanting to think or talk about it further, Jikata fed her rumbling stomach. The first mouthful of eggs nearly melted on her tongue, with a nice garnish of spice, and a small bite of what might be something like paprika or even chili.

She was famished, as if she hadn't eaten in days—or after a major performance, which was the truth.

"Velcome," said the older woman and bowed.

"Velcome Lladrana, Exotique Singere," said the man with a self-important incline of his head.

Since her mouth was full of soft buttered bread giving joy to her taste buds, Jikata merely nodded in return. He reminded her of a thin-nosed agent who'd rejected her and now was probably regretting it. That gave her a warm feeling, too. Always did.

He gestured and the younger woman came forward, took the tea and handed the thin china cup to Jikata. She sipped it. Great tea, but she could have done with some strong coffee. She wondered if they had coffee...not thinking about that!

The man spoke in halting English. "Ven yu dun, she weel take yu Singer." He pointed rudely at the maid, whose eyes flashed, but she bowed her head.

Jikata nodded again and continued eating, said nothing to his raised brows. He swept from the room, followed by the housekeeper, who sent a last look around the chamber and lowered her own brows in a stern gaze to the younger maid.

With a sideways glance at Jikata the maid stood tall and sang a perfect round C. The door swung shut.

Jikata choked.

6

Marshalls' Castle

Luthan didn't sleep well. So he rose early and mounted his volaran, flew to the Abbey. There he told Jongler of the evening with the Exotiques—an abbreviated report for the Singer. As a courtesy, he would have to keep her informed, but he wouldn't be blindly following any orders.

Jikata wasn't awake, but he flew close to her window, startling a maid, to see her sleeping peacefully in luxury.

Luthan flew back to the Castle surrounded by the Songs of his good friends Alexa, Marian and Jaquar, his brother and Powerful volarans. He rolled his shoulders, it felt like a great weight had fallen from them. He was no longer the Singer's Representative to the Marshalls and the other segments of Lladranan society.

He was free.

He hadn't felt so carefree since he'd left home at seventeen and run wild.

Of course he'd been honored to be the Singer's first Representative in ages, but that had tarnished over the two years he'd served her. Smudging his honor, too, he thought. *That* was why he'd been so angry with her, with himself. After he'd set his wild ways behind him, he'd been spoken of as the most honorable man in Lladrana. He'd earned the title, and he'd liked it. Been prideful of it. A trait to be proud of.

Now, once again, he'd have to mend some relationships with people who'd grown distant, specifically Marrec Gardpont and his wife, the Volaran Exotique, Calli. He'd missed the chance to become closer to his godmother and godfather, they'd died in battle a couple of months before. The ache of the loss of them still swept through him now and again.

They all descended to the Landing Field at the Marshalls' Castle. For a moment Luthan wondered if he should move his rooms from the Noble Apartments back into Horseshoe Hall, where most of the Chevaliers lived. But though the baths of the Hall were the best in the Castle, the building was busy and noisy. Luthan much preferred quiet. When had he grown staid? The thought stung.

But Alexa was hugging him and murmuring in his ear, "I've never actually known you when you weren't the Representative of the Singer. Now you can kick up your heels like Bastien told me you used to do." She was gone with a wink before he could do anything but stare after her.

Bastien snorted laughter and elbowed Luthan in the ribs. "Those days are long gone, eh? I'm the rebel and rogue now." He swaggered after his wife.

It was a bright, sunny day like they hadn't seen most of the summer. Luthan's vision blurred and he *knew* now that the last Exotique had arrived, the weather would be sunnier and warmer. *She* had brought something to the planet of Amee that it had lacked.

Hope, perhaps.

A belief that the alien Dark battening on Amee and leeching life from her *would* be destroyed.

Frail humans would kill the Dark, and many of them would die doing so. Luthan had little hope that he'd survive, thought Alexa and Bastien felt the same way, so they were doing their best to enjoy every moment. Song grant them joy.

A throat clearing attracted his attention, and he glanced over to see Marian's considering gaze on him. As usual, her bondmate had his arm around her waist.

"Ayes?" Luthan asked.

"Just wondering if you noticed that your streak of Power over your right temple has widened?"

He hadn't looked in a mirror that morning—he rarely did.

"And," Jaquar continued smoothly, "your left temple has a definite streak now."

"Hell," Luthan said.

"Must be the effects of the Caverns of Prophecy," they said together. Both blinked then beamed at each other as if cherishing the way their minds meshed.

Luthan's shoulders tensed. He handed the reins of his volaran to his squire with thanks, then turned back to the Circlet couple. "I suppose you think that means my prophetic Power will be stronger, come more often?" His voice was rougher than he wanted. He shrugged to unwork a kink.

Both Circlets nodded. Marian stepped forward and brushed

a kiss on his cheek. "Take care, and tell us whatever you want us to know." She made sure squires tended their volarans, then took Jaquar's hand and they strolled toward the lower courtyard of the Castle.

Dread uncurled in Luthan's gut. His Power was increasing in potency and intensity, wouldn't be going away no matter how he neglected it. He'd have to accept the talent and use it— a lesson he hadn't wanted to learn.

He strode toward the Assayer's Office and Upper Ward beyond. The Exotiques tended to avoid the Assayer's Office with the mounted monster body parts on the walls, and usually a horror or two laid out on the counter ready to be "processed," like for the stupid hat that Bastien had designed and was now all the rage.

Faucon Creusse intercepted Luthan. He suppressed a sigh. The man was frowning, radiating irritation. Faucon was one of Luthan's friends with whom he hadn't been completely honest while he'd worked with the Singer. Luthan stopped and bowed elegantly, dropping his eyes, a bow requesting forgiveness that Faucon would understand. "I am no longer the Singer's Representative, I am sorry for any slights when I was under her hand."

"Forgotten," Faucon said on an exhalation.

Luthan straightened, met his friend's gaze. "She didn't inform me of what she knew or guessed about the Seamasters secret Summoning of Raine. Had she done so, I would have acted."

"We all would have acted." Faucon shifted his feet.

"How is Raine? She seemed tense last night. The farthest volaran flight for her yet, right? Not much to see of Lladrana in the dark."

Faucon hunched a shoulder. "She's always tense around me."

The man didn't want to acknowledge the attraction between them. Luthan didn't blame him. Loving an Exotique was dangerous to the heart. Yet Luthan didn't need a vision to tell Faucon and Raine belonged together. That was obvious to anyone with a little Power. Luthan had once prophesied that Faucon would have a love worthy of a bondmate—that blood ritual that tied people together for life and death—and Raine was Faucon's woman.

Perhaps Faucon was ignoring the growing link between them because once Raine finished her task of building the Ship, her Snap would likely come and she would probably decide to return to Earth. Luthan hesitated, then decided not to meddle. Restraint from "fixing" others' lives was all too rare, especially by and for the Exotiques. Everyone wanted them here, wanted those who had not committed to Lladrana to stay.

Luthan, himself, would feel much better if Raine captained the Ship on the trip to the Dark's Nest, and didn't vanish back to Exotique Terre.

"Aren't you going to ask how the Ship progresses?" Faucon said.

"The Ship will progress as it needs to, in the amount of time it takes," Luthan replied and frowned. He could understand how long it took for others to accept their gifts and their tasks, but had been impatient with himself. But he wasn't the only one. Those Exotiques were trying to push and fix again. He wondered what sort of culture they came from that they hurried so. Or perhaps it was the hard circumstances looming over them all. That could agitate anyone.

Faucon grunted. "You're a better man than I am, thinking about Raine instead of the Ship. Or thinking about her first."

"I'm not as involved with her as much as you."

"I'm not involved with her at all!"

"But you need to be," Luthan said, his turn to prod. "You are the closest thing to a Seamaster that she can trust. If she needs advice, you must provide it."

"Suppose so," Faucon said grumpily. "I came to ask of the new Exotique. Will she stay for the battle with the Dark?"

"I don't think she has any choice," Luthan said.

"Damned shame, but our need is too great."

"Ayes," Luthan agreed. He saw a larger number of Chevaliers loitering around the Landing Field. The Assayer's Office was unusually crowded, too, with people eavesdropping. No one interrupted the pair of them until they were crossing Temple Ward to their suites in the Noble Apartments. A tall, broad-shouldered man rose from a sunny stone bench. Koz, Marian's brother, once a Chevalier, now a mirror magician. He'd moved from Horseshoe Hall to the Noble Apartments. He could easily afford them.

"The new Exotique?" Koz asked.

"With the Singer," Luthan said.

At that moment the Castle klaxon rang in a short pattern that meant "Meeting in Temple Ward for all Chevaliers and Marshalls." The siren could be heard all the way to Castleton, so Chevaliers in the town—and any Exotiques there—would arrive soon for the discussion.

Koz turned to Faucon, rubbing his hands. "I've got some ideas about putting transdimensional mirrors in Raine's father's and brothers' houses so she doesn't fret as much."

"She always frets. Doesn't like to be asked about the Ship design," Faucon muttered.

"We don't want an unhappy Exotique who must still per-form her task. She'll be distracted." Koz sounded cheerful at the challenge.

The klaxon stopped and the quiet was wonderful, then people began filling the courtyard.

"I wonder if the Singer will be keeping her Exotique happy," Koz said.

Singer's Abbey

Jikata stood before a carved and gleaming wooden door that rose in a pointed arch several feet above her head. Everything she'd seen in her walk from her rooms to this soaring round tower was on a scale larger than Earth human. And a feeling was rising through her that she really wasn't on Earth. But everyone was treating her very well. For her mental health, she'd consider this a resort.

There were buildings as small as a ten-foot airy pavilion of embellished gothic arches, and as large as a huge square stone tower, and something like the chapel at King's College in Cambridge, England.

At least she hadn't gaped open-mouthed. Stared, yes. Everything was surrounded by a high stone wall, equally white, as for a castle or a college, a city in itself. The whole place spoke of immense effort over ages. Like for a king, or queen.

Or the prophetess of a country.

The maid had told her that much, despite Jikata's wariness. The Singer was *the* oracle of the country. She had the magical skill—Power—of prophecy. *Everyone* listened to her, came for personal Song Quests and more, the woman did quarterly Songs on the future of Lladrana. Then the maid had shut up. She'd left Jikata here. Everyone in the castle-keep-like building wore jewel-toned colors at the dark end of the spectrum, and the maid wore yellow. Jikata had deduced the clothing indicated rank.

This door led to the Singer's "most formal" personal apartments, the most impressive. The Singer had been impressive enough last night with her four-octave voice, commanding people right and left, including one very impressive man in white leathers—a Chevalier, a knight, the maid had said. Not a Singer's Friend who lived in the Abbey compound.

Jikata herself wore her own underwear and a long, midnight blue robe that slid over her skin like the silk it was, embroidered in what appeared to be real gold metallic thread around the long bell sleeves and the hem. The dress fit perfectly, which made her nervous.

She was alone. Chasonette, the mind-talking bird—that was the only strange thing Jikata would accept—had flown away as soon as they'd stepped out of the building into the bright summer day. Jikata wished the cockatoo back.

"Entre!" demanded the melodious voice of the Singer from beyond the door, apparently deciding Jikata had paused too long.

The door opened and a golden room dazzled her. A woman took her arm and drew her forward. Jikata blinked. The focus of the room was the Singer, who sat on a throne so encrusted with shining gems that the gold could hardly be seen. The throne was much larger than her small form. But she commanded the room by her manner, the depth of her dark brown eyes and the Song that filled the room even when she herself was silent.

Sound overwhelmed Jikata—the woman holding her arm had a strong one, there was another servant hovering by a silver tea cart in one of the octagonal corners of the room, her blue robe nearly matching the deep blue silk of the walls. Jikata could hear a melody coming from her, too.

"Entre," the Singer said again, this time with less demand and more like pity or smugness in her tone. One word and Jikata heard layers of meaning, of emotion.

With a flick of her fingers, the servant with the tea tray

finished placing a table before the Singer's throne, setting two places and pouring two cups of floral-scented tea. The china was so thin that light filtered through the cups. The woman holding Jikata's arm curtsied and left, and so did the other one, closing the door behind them.

Jikata walked to the table, drew up an ornate chair with deeply padded velvet cushions in a gold-leaf wooden frame and sat. Eyes as sharp as her hostess, Jikata waited. She wasn't sure whether it was a battle of courtesy or patience, but felt she'd take a misstep if she drank first. The tea could freeze to ice in the winter before she lifted the china to her lips.

After several minutes, the Singer chuckled, picked up what looked like a shortbread finger and nibbled it. Jikata sat with folded hands until the woman drank, then sipped herself. The tea tasted like spring blossoms and Jikata yearned for strong black coffee. She replaced the cup in the saucer without the slightest clink and said nothing.

"I am the nine hundred and ninety ninth Singer," the woman said, "and I am old. No one in Lladrana has my vocal range or Power to match mine." She swallowed tea, and Jikata could barely see her throat move behind crepey wrinkles, but the sun highlighted the thick gold of her hair.

The Singer continued, "Or perhaps I should say that there were none who could match my range and Power yesterday. That has changed since last night."

Muscles tightened under Jikata's skin, she kept her expression impassive. She'd better get up to speed, and fast, which meant accepting this whole thing at face value.

"Look around you and see my wealth, my lifestyle, my authority and power."

This time Jikata didn't think the woman meant Power like

magic with a capital P, but power like a queen, or high priest-
ess, or oracle.

"I have contact with the Song that infuses us all, everything.
From the stars around us to this planet, Amee, to the smallest
feather of that bird, Chasonette—" the Singer lifted her little
finger "—to the tiniest cell on the tiniest baby's finger in this
land."

Hmm.

The Singer leaned back, another graceful gesture. *"Listen!"*
The word rang in Jikata's head, flaring with colorful layers,
resonating with equally rich nuances of sound. "Hear the
Songs of Lladrana." She settled back into her throne.

Though her nerves quivered, Jikata leaned back in her chair,
breathed steadily, relaxed her muscles one by one, all the while
listening. Hearing notes…dense clanks as if they came from
the very blocks of stone surrounding her.

Once again the sound of music that she'd been holding
back as she spoke with the Singer overwhelmed her. Music
came from *everywhere*—the stones must have absorbed magic
or Power or Song, whatever, as well as contributing their own
low, slow bass note. Every person had notes or a tune or a
melody. She might even be hearing sound from trees, bushes,
flowers. Birdsong, the Abbey attracted a great many birds. She
might be sensing rhythms of the land, of the sky, of the sun
rays filtering down on the planet and the sun itself. Maybe the
stars that could not be seen during the day.

She let everything wash over her, holding herself still. The
only silence was in her own body, her own mind.

Finally she began to untangle the mixtures…simple notes
and small tunes, melodies quick and short, or long and lilting
and extravagantly complex. She *knew* this simple chime was

a rosebush with a single flower, this little tune—along with whistling—was a Friend walking down an incline to...what? Beyond him was a luscious sounding combination of melodies so sweet and rich they seemed to stimulate all her senses, as if the music had magic. Or the magic was music.

Dizzy! With a deep breath she drew back, to the room. She'd closed her eyes, but could still *hear*. There was a small chamber on one side of the room and Friends waited in there, ready to be called for any wish of the Singer. They had stronger, more developed personal Songs. Because they associated more often with the Singer, or she'd chosen them for that? Probably both. Jikata realized all the higher Friends who wore the deepest shades of jewel tones had streaks of silver at their temples...or... Jikata frowned as she puzzled it out—the older ones had streaks of gold blond. The Singer had golden braids.

The older and more magical—Powerful—the more gold hair you had?

"Listen..." The Singer Sang the word, more a command than an request. "Listen to the room. Can you hear what surrounds us?"

The Singer's Song was ever varied, but Jikata followed the long pattern, the harmonies and variations.

Since Jikata could get lost in the woman's voice, she set it to the background. There was something more in the room. And she *felt* the sound. There were gems, crystals embedded in the throne and the furnishings and even the wall and the chandeliers and in the molding around the ceiling and floor. Crystals that held energy. Power. Magic.

She was beginning to believe in this place more, to like it.

"Cast your hearing beyond the room, now, to the Abbey."

Following the Singer's instructions seemed natural, something she wanted to do. She heard a theme, comprised of many sounds, of many personal Songs, the theme of the Abbey. "Care for the Singer." Hundreds of notes, all flowing to one Song, one purpose. "Care for the Singer."

What might that be like? To wake up and hear everyone around you working toward your care? No wonder the woman was arrogant.

It would be humbling at first, wouldn't it?

"Farther," the Singer said.

Jikata sensed the sounds of the land beyond the walls, sniffed and smelled something like crumbling amber. More Songs that could snag her so she'd listen to them forever.

"Send your mind, your Power, your hearing beyond the Abbey." The Singer's voice lilted, persuaded. "What do you hear at the farthest edges of the west?"

The west was cooler, the sun had not passed its midpoint for the day. Jikata inhaled deeply, sent her "hearing"—more of the mind than her ears—toward the hills, then longer…surely that was surf? "Ocean," she said, then noise impinged on that, tugged at her a little to the south. "A port city, busy, mixtures." Sounds that were not what she already knew as the rhythm of Lladrana and its people.

"You cannot!" The Singer's voice was so harsh, it snapped Jikata from her daze. She blinked at the old woman.

"Only I, and after years—" The Singer snapped her mouth shut, glaring.

How irritated was she? What next?

7

The Singer clicked her tongue and one of her attendants hurried in and curtsied. "Singer?"

"The map of Lladrana," the Singer said.

The Friend in dark blue hurried across the room, grabbed a stand that held a cloth tapestry stretched on a square frame, rolled it back toward the Singer and Jikata. It had four wooden balls as rollers, but they moved so easily they could have been the best steel, each machined to exactly match the other. Could something be carved so precisely?

With magic it could. More and more Jikata was believing in it.

The Friend set aside the tea table, put the map in front of them. It was about two and a half feet square. Then Jikata's gaze was caught by the map of the green country in front of her. This was not any place on Earth.

"Lladrana," the Singer said impatiently. She lifted a hand and the servant left quickly and quietly. Jikata shifted slightly at the power of this woman.

"Look!" the Singer demanded.

Jikata did.

"The map is shown here as straight up and down, but in truth the 'northern' border is angled northeast on the planet Amee, you understand me?"

"Yes."

The Singer scowled.

"Ayes," Jikata amended.

Stabbing a well-kept finger with age lines at the map, the Singer said, "My valley is here."

There was a tiny three-dimensional conglomeration of buildings on a mound ringed by hills. The old woman drew her finger to the left, the west. "Here is Brisay Sea." She tapped a spot below it. "This is the city of Krache, a city belonging to both Lladrana and our southern neighbor, Shud." Brows low, her inflection went up. "This is what you sensed?"

She sounded as if she didn't believe Jikata. Jikata straightened. This was like when producers or voice trainers asked her range. Four octaves, and she could prove it. "Ayes."

With a sniff, the Singer gestured and the map rolled back to its spot. The tea table moved—*lifted*—back into place. Why hadn't she done that earlier?

She'd just proven to Jikata that she held two types of power—the power over people as the ruler of the Abbey, and magic. Neither of which Jikata had.

Her stomach clenched at the realization that she was entirely in this old woman's hands. Jikata could barely swallow. She could disappear, totally and completely, and no one…wait, there was that attractive man in white leather. She hadn't heard his personal Song this past hour, had she? She sent her thought questing, shooting around the Abbey, weighing each person. Her throat closed with nausea at the effort. She thought she sweated but her dress absorbed it.

She didn't feel the man. So he wasn't at the Abbey, but he knew she was here, had arrived last night. The Singer might have to explain to *someone* if Jikata vanished. Relief trickled through her and she found that she'd shut her eyes again. When she opened them she saw the Singer watching her, as if the old woman knew she used Power but not *how*.

The Singer shuttered her gaze, curved her lips and relaxed back in her throne. "Your talent is raw, but I can train it and shape it and free your Power. Power like you've never experienced." Again she raised her little finger, touched her shaped fingernail. "The Power you used today is like this to what I can give you."

What Jikata already had, she knew. Like her voice, the Power was *hers*. But like her voice, it could be trained. *That* the Singer could do, she could train, but what was inside Jikata was her own. She'd had plenty try to suck it from her.

She studied the old woman. Yes, power and Power cloaked her like a queen's huge and enveloping state robe. Innate and developed, as well as given to her by the people of this land.

Jikata sensed the Singer had sent her own mind to the city with the merest effort. Everything Jikata had done this morning had left her exhausted, using unaccustomed mental skills. The Singer looked as if she'd had no exercise at all. She placed her hand on her cup of tea and hummed a note. Steam rose and Jikata was sure it was the exact temperature the Singer preferred.

Jikata's own tea was cold, and the woman had not warmed

the teapot that they both used, only her own cup. The lesson smacked Jikata in her gut. She, herself, had begun to get used to stardom, to flatterers, to people around her wanting to please her. That was heady and lovely. But to be so very Powerful that her own wishes were preeminent—that notion caused Jikata deep unease.

She didn't want to be like that. She'd have to beware of becoming so selfish, so arrogant. This woman might remind her in some ways of her great-grandmother, but Ishi would have been shocked at the Singer's hubris.

So not only was Jikata at the Singer's mercy, but all the lovely things the Singer tempted Jikata with were also part of a sharp, double-edged sword. Talent was like that. To follow her heart, her destiny, she'd had to be more public than her great-grandmother had wanted, had to forsake tradition. Had broken with her great-grandmother. Her child-self still hurt from that, from disappointing her great-grandmother, and perhaps always would.

"You might have questions," the Singer said, and Jikata wondered how long she'd been musing. She thought she caught a flash of satisfaction in those long, dark eyes, that Jikata was not and never could be the Singer's match.

Thin eyebrows raised, the Singer repeated, "Questions?"

Jikata did, but with the Singer's complacent half smile, Jikata decided she should surprise the woman. Since that lady hadn't hesitated to make rude comments, a personal question wasn't out of order. "Why are you so small?" Everyone else she'd seen was larger than Jikata herself.

The Singer looked startled, then her face became expressionless. Her brown eyes darkened and burned coal-black. When she audibly inhaled, the quaver was back. "There is a price for everything. You understand?" Her accent was so strong that Jikata was finally able to place it—Bostonian.

"Ayes." Jikata didn't like being treated like a rude pupil.

"My Power was understood from when I was a child. I was brought here to the Abbey." She lifted a hand and her fingers showed a fine trembling, then she put them back on her lap. "The old Singer had had prophecies, of course. I would be one to Summon an Exotique." She breathed through her nose. "Not once, but twice. I would be an extraordinary Singer, at the cusp of a great age. Whether I did my duty would ensure whether many people would live or die, would—" She stopped, shrugged. "I was told, and given to experience Songs and visions of my own. I could grow large, as large as my people and have less Power. Or stay small and have greater Power. I chose to say small." Her lips curved in a travesty of a smile. "The decision was made when I was passing from child to woman. Not many Singers have a consort. Few men or women can match the Power of a Singer, and most of us want a partner, bondmate. More visions came and I knew if I stayed small, I would have a chance for a consort, a man from Exotique Terre. He would find me more attractive if I were small. At the threshold of womanhood, I longed for the love of a man, dreamed fantasy dreams of a mate." She shrugged again. "I Summoned him, my Thomas. He came, taught me English. Left with the Snap. He did not love me enough to stay." Her gaze shifted from the distance to bore into Jikata with a penetrating spear of disapproval that she actually felt.

Jikata's mind whirled at the strange words: Exotique, bondmate, Snap. "What are—"

"We will discuss other concepts later." The Singer leaned

back and closed her eyes. "I am tired." She snapped her fingers and an attendant sidled into the room. Obviously snapping the fingers was an indication of a bad mood. "Send the medica to me. I promised that the Exotique would be examined."

Oh. Fun.

A tall, strong woman wearing a red tunic with a white cross over a long red robe entered and went to the Singer, gently took her hands. The old woman didn't open her eyes. The medica began to hum in an excellent voice, head cocked as if listening to responses only she could hear. Then she placed the Singer's hands back on the arms of the chair. "You are doing well, Lady Singer. As we anticipated, the new Exotique has help—"

"Examine her for Bri," the Singer said.

Jikata wondered what *bri* was.

The medica dipped a deep curtsy, turned to Jikata. She'd stretched out her legs and crossed her ankles in a casual pose. She would not act like a scolded puppy. She'd asked a simple question. But she was sure, now, that all of her simple questions would have complex answers, and her blood thrummed in her veins at the thought of duty and prices to be paid.

But the medica made a curtsy almost as deep to Jikata as she did to the Singer, and her eyes were curious and kind, not condemnatory. "You will please sit up straight, feet on the floor." Her language was simple and accompanied by gestures. Jikata sat, realized that with her feet flat on the floor, the chair was too deep to support her back, and stood.

The medica nodded and moved in front of Jikata, smiling. "I at Marshalls' Castle last year. Know Exotiques." Was what Jikata heard.

The Singer sniffed.

The medica let out a little breath and held out her palms, obviously for Jikata to take them.

Reluctantly, recalling the nastiness of the ordeal the night before when chords were painfully plucked inside her, Jikata put her fingers in the other woman's larger hands. They were unusually warm. The woman Sang and it was as if pulses within Jikata warmed and glowed and vibrated almost pleasurably. "You healthy, more rest and good food," the woman said. "Potatoes—"

"Potatoes?"

The medica beamed. "New wonder food."

Jikata narrowed her eyes.

A chiming filled the room and she followed the sound to a round lump in the medica's pocket. The sturdy woman took out a crystal, and Jikata stared at moving wisps of mist within the orb. "Apologies, Lady Singer, third time Bri—"

"You may report to Bri somewhere else," the Singer said.

The medica left hurriedly. So Bri was a person.

"'Jikata' is how you are called," the old woman said.

"Ayes," Jikata said. The Singer still had her eyes closed. Not vulnerable, showing that nothing and no one could assail her defenses. Ishi had been like that, had refused to let anything bother her.

"We will have lessons. Stretching for the body, our instrument. Then voice lessons both in range and in Power. Then, training in prophecy. We are done for the day. You may go."

Jikata's mouth dropped open. *Training in prophecy!*

She had a hunch that all the previous hunches in her life had been true.

And her life had taken another unexpected twist.

Castleton/Marshalls' Castle

Raine had tinkered with the latest design of the ship at her pretty house in Castleton, then left her drawing board. Before she made a model, she liked it to simmer in her head.

Restlessness claimed her and she found herself walking the two miles up to the Marshalls' Castle. It was good exercise and she never did it alone. There was always a guard or two, or some Chevaliers who'd been in town for one reason or another, or even Bri and Sevair, who'd accompany her if she didn't fly on Blossom. Today she walked with some Chevaliers who let her brood.

She hadn't gotten much sleep, she'd been so churned up about the Summoning and Faucon that she couldn't settle.

Then one of the recurring nightmares had come. She'd awakened in a cold sweat, thinking for long, confused moments that she was back to being a despised potgirl at the rough tavern, The Open Mouthed Fish.

She'd dragged herself out of bed late when the daily housekeeper had come in to leave food and tidy up. Not that there was ever much out of order. Having slept in a corner for six months and not had any place to call her own, Raine now prized the exquisite furnishings of the lovely house. She certainly took nothing for granted anymore.

Enerin, her companion, the baby feycoocu, was with her parents, being schooled in magical shape-shifter business.

Raine was at the front gate of the Castle when the alarm sounded and everyone tensed. The monster invasions of the north had diminished in frequency if not in ferocity. But the siren blared a pattern requesting folk gather in Temple Ward.

An announcement about the Summoning last night. Of course Alexa would do something publicly and to anyone who wanted to hear—merchant folk at the Castle, guards, Chevaliers, not just the Marshalls. Raine didn't know a lot about how the Castle had run before Alexa became Lady Knight Swordmarshall, but knew things had changed.

Since the great round white stone Temple continued to tug at her, Raine shuffled along with a crowd through Lower Ward to Temple Ward to listen.

Alexa beamed at Raine, giving her mixed emotions. The other Exotiques were good with their support and not putting pressure on her, but their unspoken expectations were weighty. Raine spotted Calli, the Volaran Exotique, first, the sun glinting off her blond hair. Raine blinked. Most of the summer days had been cloudy and cool. Sunshine today would please the Coloradan Exotiques since they were all used to more sun than she. Then Marian and Jaquar, the Circlets, joined Calli. They'd just flown in from Luthan's southern estate, Raine realized. Calli held the hand of her adopted son. Marrec had their toddler, also adopted, sitting on his shoulders. Raine felt a wave of dread as she walked toward them with a false smile that wouldn't fool anyone.

No wonder she was dragging her feet about the ship. Once she was done, everyone, including Calli and Marrec, would be committed to destroying the Dark that had sent monsters from the north for ages. Raine had little hope that they'd kill it, or any of them would survive.

Calli, the nurturer, wrapped her free arm around Raine, and they listened to Alexa, who fully believed that leaving the new Exotique with the Singer was important and right, and that relieved Raine. No one should go through what she had.

When Alexa was done, the crowd stayed, discussing the news. They all approved of Alexa's actions, of course. Reluctantly, Raine went with the other Exotiques to hash over everything again. The guys had made themselves scarce. Before they entered the keep, she scanned the crowd one more time.

Faucon was there, ignoring her. Though her gaze lingered because he was so darn handsome, she looked for someone else.

"Where's Koz?" she asked Marian, his sister.

"Around, he'll see us shortly," Marian said.

Raine sucked in a deep breath, "Really?"

Marian linked her arm with hers. "Ayes, we'll talk of the mirrors for your family."

Swallowing hard, Raine said, "Thank you."

"Welcome," Marian replied absently. Then they were climbing the stairs to Alexa and Bastien's suite.

To keep anticipation from eating her alive, Raine, too, thought of the newly Summoned one. She'd heard of Jikata, though she hadn't listened much to her music or bought her albums. Raine had liked industrial. Past tense here in Lladrana. They did have some of Marian's and Bri's music. But Marian preferred longhair and Bri had strange things like atonal chants by Tibetan monks or African women clapping and singing. Not a jammin' track in the bunch.

"Jikata." Alexa rubbed her hands with glee as she paced the sitting-dining room. Raine hoped the munchies would arrive soon, eating usually kept Alexa still for a few minutes.

"It was obvious that we all knew of her," Marian said. "That made it easier for everyone to accept her being in the hands of the Singer."

"How on Earth did she get here?" Raine asked.

Alexa stopped and put her hands on her hips. "One name, or maybe two. The common thread among us, I think." She

studied Raine. "I don't know that we asked you about them."
She cleared her throat. "Trenton Philbert the third, U.S.
District Court Judge in Denver." Alexa waggled a thumb at
herself. "I was acquainted with him during my very brief legal
career. Brief, ha!"

Marian winced. "Really, Alexa." The Circlet rose when the
doorharp sounded and took a loaded tray from Alexa's maid.
The scent of French fries—"twin fries" as they were called here
for the two women who introduced potatoes—filled the air,
making Raine's mouth water.

"Marian had a significant encounter with them," Alexa said.

Marian put the tray down on a large round dining room
table and they all took chairs. "Yes, I did. Juliet Philbert is the
owner of a Denver new age shop called Queen of Cups. She
gave me the Lladranan weapon knot book."

Calli added, "The Philberts have had a ranch next to our
spread for generations." She took a ham and cheese sandwich
on a croissant. "And you, Bri?"

"Dad's roomie in college," Bri said around a fry. "Elizabeth's
and my godfather. Only met his wife once, though."

They all looked at Raine. She nodded. "Yes, they commissioned a seagoing yacht from my family last year after buying
some oceanfront property. Big gossip in Best Haven."

"So anyone know how they got Jikata?" Alexa asked.

"Think so." Bri wolfed down another fry. "When I last
talked to my folks in the magic mirror they said something
about planning to attend the grand opening of a rehab project
Uncle Trent funded." She raised a fry dramatically. "The Ghost
Hill Theater. The jewel of the opening gala was a performance
by one Jikata, local girl made good."

"Little did we know that Jikata would be our new Exotique,"

Marian said, cutting her sandwich into smaller rectangles. "The opening would have been last night, I presume."

"Probably. By the way, the Singer's medica has reported that she's in good health," Bri said.

Calli frowned. "Bert, I mean Trent, is sure throwing a lot of money around." She shrugged. "But he has it."

This whole talk of Summoning was too much. Raine pushed her plate away. It had smelled good and she'd eaten some fries and a bit of sandwich, but the conversation had dried her taste buds. "When do you think Koz—"

Her impatience was stopped by the strum of the doorharp.

"Bet he hasn't had lunch." Alexa drew her plate close. "He'll want our fries."

"He can have mine," Raine said.

"I'll cut half your sandwich for him," Calli said, "but you should try to eat the rest."

Alexa swallowed a fry then called, *"Entre."*

Koz strode in, a big man with big bones. He was roughly handsome but nothing to compare with Luthan or Faucon. His face was animated, showing a lively mind behind the dark brown eyes. An Earth mind. The Lladranan body carried an Earth soul.

He greeted them, pulled up a chair and looked at Raine.

"Salutations, Koz," she said belatedly.

Nodding, he said, "Hey."

She found her fingers had twined together tightly. "Mirrors for my family?" was all she could force out.

He hadn't brought anything with him.

8

Koz said, "Yes, I can establish connections with Earth through my mirrors. Links I think will even survive when the Dimensional Corridor shifts and Earth is no longer accessible from here."

A mirror set in her father's house! Or one of her brothers', or even all of her brothers'! She hadn't really hoped for so much. She gasped. Calli came and rubbed her shoulders.

Reality cleared her mind. "There is no way my father or brothers will believe in mirrors that suddenly appear in their houses, in talking mirrors, in any of this."

"Doesn't mean we can't get something there, and you can't check up on them once and a while," Koz said. He lifted his forefinger. "However…"

Raine tensed.

"I can't place the mirror or mirrors myself. Bossgond must do that."

Raine's spirits sank.

She'd had a few sessions with the most brilliant Sorcerer in Lladrana—the cranky old man. She didn't think the CIA could debrief better.

"Sorry." Koz gave her a half smile.

Marian coughed. "Maybe he'll be reasonable...."

Everyone stared at her.

She shrugged. "All right, he won't, but we should try, and right now." Pulling out a small crystal sphere from her pocket she called Bossgond.

The ball hummed for about a minute, then came a voice but no image. "What! I'm working!"

"Koz and Raine have a project for you."

A heaved sigh, then wisps in the ball solidified into the image of the skinny, wrinkled Sorcerer. He sat with arms crossed and listened as Koz explained what he needed.

Bossgond sniffed. "It will cost you."

Raine had anticipated this, but anger spurted through her anyway. She jumped to her feet. "Cost *me!*" Glaring at him, she said, "Am I or am I not the one who spoke to you for *hours* about every little detail of my Summoning here and my life? Haven't I given you *masses* of information about...stuff. My grandmother's mirror that originally came from Lladrana. The Summoning. Living here on my own. Travys who had the innate repulsion." She waved her hands. "Whatever. You should owe me!"

"She's got a point." Koz rocked on his heels, grinning.

"Excellent strategy," Alexa said.

Another big sigh from Bossgond, though Raine thought she saw the eternal curiosity that marked a Sorcerer in his eyes. "You can locate your father's home?"

"My father and four brothers." Raine stuck out her chin. It

didn't matter that none of them would believe in talking mirrors or interdimensional communication. She wanted a connection to them all.

Bossgond let out an undignified squeak. "Five!"

"Yeah, tough," Raine muttered. "I love them all, and they love me." Even if there hadn't been much understanding among them. She'd wanted to take the family shipbuilding company into the second millennium with double hulls and metallic alloys. The guys had insisted on staying with wooden sailing ships. She probably would have left the company by now, but that was all in the past. Her future, for the moment, was on Lladrana.

"I want to get a message to them that I'm okay, too."

Koz gave a little cough, gazed at Raine, then switched to Bossgond. "I have an idea."

"Ayes?" asked Bossgond.

Koz looked Raine in the eyes. "Are your father and brothers honorable men?"

Raine had rarely given that phrase much thought on Earth. Here in Lladrana it was important. "They're known for always keeping their word."

"Right." Koz nodded. Again he swept a look from Raine to Bossgond. "What say we send the mirrors to their attorney. You know their attorney?"

"Yeah, I know him well."

"You could locate his office," Koz said. A gleam came into Bossgond's eyes. He loved discovering new places of "Exotique Terre."

Raine shrugged. "No problem. They're a family firm, too. A family firm run by men doesn't often change drastically. They've been in that building for twelve generations. The Lindleys were upstarts in Best Haven at four generations."

She looked around and Marian anticipated her, whisking a piece of paper and pencil in front of Raine. With a few quick strokes Raine laid out the plan of the office.

Koz took the layout with a low whistle. "You are one good draftsman. Draftsperson." He studied the map for a couple of seconds. "What if we deliver five mirrors to this attorney, along with money, saying it's an inheritance from your great-grandfather's lover's estate…"

"That would be the Singer here on Lladrana," Raine said. She still marveled that her great-grandfather had been an Exotique, the last one Summoned before Alexa.

"Yes. A mirror for each of your brothers and your father. To be hung in their living rooms for…say…three generations. With the mirrors will be some sort of payment. We'll think of that later." He waved a hand like a man who's never known poverty. "Like helping convince my sister that I should be on the invasion force."

"I can't—" Raine started.

"How soon do you wish this project to be done?" asked Bossgond from the crystal ball.

"I have a stock of mirrors ready," Koz said.

The older man raised golden brows. "Ayes? You don't want to consult the Singer on *her* mirror, one that can be tuned to the Dimensional Corridor, too?"

Marian said, "You old fox. You just want Koz to do some research for you."

Bossgond pursed his lips, said, "The Singer does not answer my calls to her crystal."

"What of her Friends?" Koz asked.

Silence from the old man.

Koz rubbed his chin. "Okay, I'm hooked. I'd like to visit the

Singer, in case she'll give me more and better info." He glanced at Raine. "That all right?"

"Whatever's best," she said.

Nodding, Koz said. "I'll fly to the Singer's Abbey first, shouldn't take more than a day or so if she's cooperative."

Marian snorted, and Alexa said, "Not likely," then stared into the crystal ball. "These old, Powerful folks don't do anything they don't want to. Pity they're so stuck in their ruts."

Bossgond huffed, said, "I will be on the invasion force."

Koz turned to Raine. "After that, you and I can go to Bossgond's island and the dimensional telescope. You can leave a note with the mirrors, say you ended up in France with your great-grandfather's lover's family or something."

Raine tottered. She'd never considered what she could say to her family to reassure them, explain without explaining, and not sound like a selfish, insensitive bitch or raving lunatic.

But she did know something. She swept her gaze around the room, meeting everyone's eyes. "I don't want to go. It would be faster if you went alone." She met Bossgond's gaze in the sphere. "You have my notes and a good enough map of Best Haven. Pearson and Pearson is located in their own three-story building on the southwest corner of Main Street and Seadrive Boulevard. Koz can find it."

Koz raised his brows, then grinned, rubbing his hands. "Fun." Then he winked at Bossgond. "More time to look around the town, than if Raine came with us. You know Marian likes us to limit our time, but without Raine…"

Marian frowned, turned to Raine and asked, "Are you sure you don't want to go yourself, see your home?"

Raine didn't think she could bear it since there was no way

she was going home before the ship was built…but if she had strong moral support… "Would you be coming with me?" Raine trusted Marian.

"I can't, I have—"

"I have responsibilities, too—the ship," Raine said. "My task for Lladrana, Amee. My turn, now."

Koz said to the crystal, "I'll be there no later than tomorrow unless the Singer cooperates. I'll let everyone know if that happens. See ya," he said to Bossgond, then waved the crystal ball dark, leaving a grumpy sound coming from it.

He paused with his hand on the doorknob, looked at Raine and again sympathy was in his eyes. "I'll give you time to think of a story, write a note."

Raine raised helpless hands. "What can I tell them that they might believe?"

Shrugging, Koz said, "I dunno." His grin was fast and charming as he scanned them all. "Bunch of very creative women, you'll think of something." He sketched a bow and left, whistling "(I Can't Get No) Satisfaction."

Babble erupted as the women began to brainstorm. Alexa and Bri concocted the most outrageous stories. Marian frowned and tapped her lips with her finger, Calli just shook her head.

A few seconds later Koz popped his head back in. "Oh, hey, down payment could be a hat like Bastien's. Thought it was ugly at first, but every Chevalier who *is* a Chevalier has one."

"Guys wear those hats," muttered Alexa. She sniffed. "*We* have cowboy hats. The Exotique Gang."

Koz winked again, this time at Raine. "'Kay, I'll take one of those, too." He shut the door.

It was going to happen! She would be able to see her father and brothers after nearly a year. The emotions swamping her were too huge. "I have to go." Raine bolted to the door. "Arrange stuff with the master tailor in Castleton." That lady would have Koz's measurements.

The talk stopped, the other Exotiques shared a glance.

Calli said, "Honey…"

Raine didn't listen but heard Marian's voice in her head as she hurried down the flights of stairs. *We'll figure out some story.* A soft sigh. *But I think Alexa and Bri are right. It may have to be a sailing accident, amnesia, a wealthy foreigner with pressing business and a private jet. A love affair in Europe. We're thinking Sweden. Your memory has just returned.*

Raine gritted her teeth—sounded like some novels she'd enjoyed but didn't believe. Obviously the others had the same taste in fiction.

Her body remained tense until she knew nobody was coming after her, though from the buzzing in her mind she understood that the others were discussing her. Fine.

She'd meant to turn back to town, but her feet took her to the Temple. As usual, the hum of Power in the building enveloped her, merged with her own, and she felt less anxious, more able to handle anything that happened.

She wasn't the only one in the Temple. Knots of Chevaliers were discussing the new situation and she sensed they were all relieved not to have been in a Summoning circle.

Some individuals were Singing—praying. Raine heard one soprano requesting she do well on the trials for the invasion force and be chosen to go on the great adventure.

Raine shuddered.

Though people nodded at her, no one bothered her and she went to the altar again. The chime candles were lit.

She stared at the gong. There was something about it. She

walked around it, brushed it with fingertips. There was an energy she couldn't quite understand but thought she should….

Raine! Puppy Enerin bulleted to her, jumped into her arms.

Looking up at her with huge brown eyes and tongue lolling, Enerin said, *I can now do many, many shifts and forms. As many as I like!* The puppy rolled from Raine's grasp to under the altar cloth and emerged as a kitten.

You like this form best. She smiled a little cat smile showing baby teeth.

Raine smiled back.

Now I can go with you on the Ship.

Raine stopped smiling.

Singer's Abbey

The next morning, Jikata awoke late and only thought she was in Denver for a few seconds. The new soundtrack of her life reminded her she was in Lladrana. For better or worse. She was managing to deal with the day-to-day stresses. Still, she'd need some answers soon.

Chasonette chirped, "Salutations, Jikata."

"Hello, Chasonette."

Apparently the bird took that as an invitation to fly through the open side bed curtains and perch on her knee. Chasonette tilted her head and revved up her personal Song. Jikata eyed her. "So, Chasonette, what do you want?"

The cockatoo shifted from one of Jikata's knees to the other, her tail lifted and dipped and Jikata had misgivings but the cover stayed clean. A tiny sound almost like the clearing of a throat came from the bird.

I am your companion.

"I suppose so."

So I should be with you all the time.

Jikata chose careful words. "I don't believe that's true."

The bird seemed to perk up. *No?*

"No."

The feycoocus and volarans said so. One yellow eye turned to consider Jikata.

"What are faycouscous and volarans?"

Chasonette preened. *I am with you to help you learn our ways.*

"Thank you."

Feycoocus are magical beings. A trill of Song, full of wonder. *They can shape-shift into many bird forms. Animals, too.* Chasonette clicked her beak in disapproval. *They are about my size, whatever shape.*

"Ah."

Volarans are winged horses.

"Oh, right." The maid had used that word last night when Jikata had opened the curtains at the foot of the bed. Jikata had been nude and that hadn't seemed to bother the young woman, but leaving the curtains open had. They'd had a mimed discussion that got vigorous, particularly after Jikata had asked who'd see her from the third-story window, with no close buildings around. The maid had flapped her arms like a bird, then galloped like a horse. Jikata hadn't believed her, they'd both thrown up their hands, then the maid had made a pleading face. Jikata had given up and gotten into bed fully intending to open the curtains but had immediately fallen asleep.

The afternoon before had consisted of a quick tour, then

lunch, then bathing in a wonderful spa-like pool under one of the buildings, a massage, then dinner.

Learning to live with a soundtrack had taken a lot out of her and she'd retired early.

Now she said, "Flying horses?"

Of course.

They stared at each other. Chasonette clicked her beak. *Come to the window, then.* She flew there.

Jikata slid off the high bed, grabbed a robe hanging on a garment rack, slipped it on, tied the belt, then sauntered over to the window.

Chasonette gave a piercing whistle that had Jikata stumbling back, then the bird turned her head and ruffled her comb. *Wait. They are not as fast as birds.*

Jikata shrugged, looked for her backpack. Obsessive or not, she always checked it every morning and every evening. The bag, and smaller pouches within, were all she had of her own…world. Everything was there, but a little jumbled, not in the order she liked. She arranged the smaller bags.

Chasonette whistled again, and Jikata looked up, irritated.

And froze.

Hovering outside her window was a gorgeous animal.

It looked like a horse with wings.

The song coming from it was ravishing.

It is one of the Abbey volarans. It is glad to see you so it can gain status with gossip. But it is not good at staying in place. Chasonette tapped the window glass with her beak. The horse flung up its head, then fell away, wings beating.

"Wait!" Jikata dropped her pack, but by the time she reached the windows it was out of sight.

I am your companion, Chasonette said. She slid a glittering gaze toward Jikata. *But I don't think I need to be with you when you have your lessons from the Singer this morning or visit the Caverns of Prophecy this afternoon.* She fluffed up her feathers as if cold.

Jikata felt a chill, too. Of change, of premonition.

9

Marshalls' Castle

Raine watched her beautiful model boat cruise around the sacred pool in the Temple. She was pretty sure this design would work to take an invasion force to the Dark's volcanic island. It had room enough for crew, provisions, twenty-five pairs of Marshalls, twenty of the top Chevaliers, six Circlets of the sorcerous persuasion, six Friends from the Singer's Abbey, flying horses for all of them, the four Exotiques and their mates and the remaining two Exotiques, which included her.

She didn't want to go invade a hideous evil so huge and ancient it could suck the life out of a planet.

It was the biggest ship she'd ever designed by herself or with her family in Connecticut. It was all wrong that she should be working on a galleon, a battleship, instead of a yacht. It was beautiful.

She'd gotten used to building models by magic here in Lladrana, designing them on heavy handmade paper, cutting and folding them until they looked like the ship she'd seen in her mind, setting them in water, then concentrating hard with her Power, and making the pulp in the paper into wood that was a model ship. She didn't think the process would work for a real, full-sized ship.

Not to mention it lacked a power source.

The model floated and cut through the water of the pool fine, pushed around by her Power. She couldn't imagine even the most Powerful of the mages on Lladrana mentally propelling the ship. Wouldn't it drain them quickly and leave them stranded?

Of course it had two big masts, two small ones and sails. They could take advantage of the wind.

Except no one had consulted any sailors. The anger of most of Lladranan society toward the Seamasters who had messed up Raine's own Summoning was still in force.

Raine's early days on Lladrana were fading into a bad dream.

But right now she was all too aware that she couldn't build the ship, power it, sail it, alone.

That meant she had to release the last bit of grudge against the Seamasters and make the first overture, bring them into the fold to help plan the defeat of the Dark.

She'd spent a month understanding the needs of the Lladranans, designing and revising the ship. It was a fine vessel and a work of art and would carry exactly what everyone told her it needed to carry. She had different versions for different power systems, steam and diesel.

Here in the Marshalls' Castle and her tidy house in Castleton, she'd hidden and healed. Now she was nervous about the time it would take to build the ship. All the prophecies of this land stated that the battle would take place this year.

Since time flowed the same here as at home, that meant they were in the beginning of August. Casually, she'd dropped questions about shipbuilding to Marian, who spent most of her time working on the final "City Destroyer" spell. Marian thought it could take out the Dark's island.

Probably with all of them on it.

But most were primed for the suicide mission, to sacrifice their lives to destroy the Dark.

Raine had never planned to "go" that way.

So she'd concentrated on the ship instead, as all of them wished, and had asked Marian how long it took to build a ship. Marian had gone all distant, as if recalling something she'd read. She'd absently replied, "Three days with Power," turned her mind back to her studies and didn't see Raine stagger away.

Looking again at her model, which had floated to the center of the pool and sat in dead calm, Raine shook her head. She could do another test of seaworthiness on it—making the pool ripple with huge waves to batter it. Raine had lived with tides and oceans all her life and knew to the salt of her blood how they moved. But the ship was excellent, one of her best efforts.

It had no Power source.

Time to look at a real ship.

Everyone had been very protective of her. Except for the strange flight a couple of nights before, Raine had stayed in the Castle and the city for the past month—she'd never lived inland and away from the sea for so long. She yearned for the scent of the beach, the sound of the surf.

Just as the month before that she'd yearned to be able to go inland more than a couple of miles.

She really wanted to come and go as she pleased.

She left her ship in the pool and exited the Temple to a cloudy summer day, cool for Connecticut and cool for Lladrana. The planet was dying under the onslaught of the Dark, the weather chilling. She'd welcomed the two previous days of sun.

The courtyard of the Castle bustled, as usual. That morning there'd been an alarm that monsters were invading from the north. Marshalls and Chevaliers had flown to battle. Raine had clutched her newest model in her hands and run to the Map Room, had seen that the incursion was minor, and forced herself to finish her last experiments in the Temple. She had really wanted to stay and watch the animated map, particularly the orange-red shields that were Faucon and his team. But she had her own task.

Now she heard the clang of the siren pulse in notes that told everyone the Castle teams had been triumphant, and waited, heart squeezing, for the pause then the indication of casualties. The quiet went on and on and she heard a couple of soldiers next to her sigh as she did. No deaths.

They bowed to her, a man and a woman, and she smiled back, cleared her throat. "How long will it take for the Marshalls and Chevaliers to return?"

The man's forehead wrinkled in thought. "They were north and far to the east. Quite a distance. A few hours."

"Thank you."

"You're welcome, Seamistress Exotique."

She jolted inwardly at the title but didn't let it show. They walked away, the woman whistling.

Seamistress Exotique. The title was wrong. She could design pretty ships, make sure they were seaworthy, but knew little enough about the seas and oceans of Lladrana—the Brisay Sea dotted with islands off the western shore, the colder waters north on the way to the Dark's island, the narrow channel between continents that was the only way to approach the island.

Time to remedy that, to finish her job. When her particular task was done, the Snap would come. The Snap was the call of Mother Earth to her wandering child to return. Earth was a lot stronger than the planet Amee. If Raine wanted to return, and she did, all she had to do was let herself be taken home by the Snap.

She only hoped that part of her job was *not* invading the island, prayed it was only finishing and building the ship.

But she had to take the next steps and the sooner, the better. She knew of one ship only that she could study in complete safety, Faucon Creusse's yacht. Surely it would have an additional power source other than sails.

He didn't like her and she was wildly attracted to him. But she wasn't going to get involved with a Lladranan. Four out of five women from Earth had already fallen for sexy Lladranan men and forsaken their birth homes.

Raine was ready to return to designing fast, double-hulled vessels of cutting-edge metal alloys. She'd been unhappy with her place in her business, but hadn't been willing to cut the bonds.

With the Seamasters' faulty Summoning, the bonds had been cut for her. She loved her father and brothers, suffered at the thought of their grief in thinking she'd been lost to the sea, but when she returned she wouldn't stay with the business. She was tired of wooden ships.

She snorted. One last, huge, wooden ship to build, then freedom.

Now was a good time to go to the coast and look at Faucon's yacht while he was flying back from battle.

Raine called her very own winged horse mentally, *Blossom!*

I am here, Raine, Blossom replied, sending along a wash of love that had Raine sniffing back tears. She was so blessed now. She had a being who loved her, who would put *her* first before any other person. That was a gratitude she clutched close to her heart, so much different than six months ago, when she'd been a despised potgirl in a fishing village inn. Raine *sensed* Blossom at the Landing Field. Raine had magic now, a great deal of it, called Power. And *that* was so different than a year ago when she'd been much younger and rebelling against family tradition.

Lladrana was so different, so scary in those first isolated winter weeks that, looking back, she wasn't quite sure how she survived.

But she had, and now she was an Exotique, a person valued above all others—except by those who had an instinctive repulsion to the alien women.

Time to see how free she really was. *Please request one of the Castle squires prepare you for a flight.*

Blossom squealed in joy. *We are flying? More than just exercise?*

Ayes, we go to Faucon's castle, Creusse Crest, and back. She should have made up her mind earlier. Even with Distance Magic, the trip to the coast and back would be a long haul…if she'd accepted the land the Lladranan's had offered her, she'd have had a seaside estate and could have stayed there tonight. But she was minimizing strings, already had bonded with too many to be comfortable.

Raine started walking through the flagstoned courtyard called Temple Ward to the keep where she wended her way through the building and the maze outside to the Landing Field. Blossom was waiting, a beautiful white volaran with big brown eyes and wings of subtle white shades. Gorgeous creature. As soon as she saw Raine, she trotted across the field, fully caparisoned in colorful tooled sky blue leather and gold thread. She wore a saddle for Raine's benefit, but only had a hackamore around her nose for reins. Raine had been instructed in "volaran partnering" and gave Blossom most of her cues mentally or by shifting her body.

We go to Faucon's? Blossom repeated as Raine mounted and they took to the sky, flying west.

Ayes.

Blossom lapsed into silence. Raine was glad that she was quiet because she wanted to enjoy the flight. As always her spirit soared riding on the winged horse. She inhaled deeply, the clean air of a land that knew no machines. Beneath her the landscape was one of green and rolling plains, a low ridge of hills that tugged at her heart. When she caught the distant scent of the ocean, her pulse picked up.

Since she'd been unconscious when she'd been brought from the coast to the Castle, all she'd seen were maps. The land was far more beautiful.

Blossom caught an updraft and rose higher, the sound of the wind swishing through her feathers a soft accompaniment to the rush of the air against them.

Distance Magic now?

Raine sighed. *I wanted to see Alexa's and Bastien's estates.*

We do Distance Magic for a little bit, then come out, look at their estates, Blossom said. *Then do more to Creusse Crest.*

Won't that take more Power?

We have plenty of Power.

All right. Then Blossom drew on their combined Power, fumbled to merge it for the spell. A tweak, some disorientation and a clear bubble formed around them. Each beat of Blossom's wings took them much farther, as if the magical bubble had no inertia and it zoomed through the atmosphere. Propelled by magic? Could a ship travel like that, too? Raine didn't think so. Power would be a part of the energy source but it wouldn't be Distance Magic that made a ship go. Sails couldn't be used by people who couldn't see or feel or scent the air. Fishing folk couldn't have a bubble around them to haul in a catch.

Pop!

Alexa's and Bastien's estates.

They were side by side and looked comfortable and well-established. A volaran herd running free on Bastien's land lifted their wings in salute.

They are old or tired or lost their riders, Blossom said, her voice laced with pity. She lifted her head, rose higher.

Blossom had lost her rider, too, but not from battle. One of the Summoned Exotiques had returned home, Blossom had been her volaran. Raine's stomach sank. *You know I don't want to stay here in Lladrana.*

You were treated bad. When you are treated good you will stay.

Raine winced. There was another pop as Blossom formed the Distance Magic bubble around them.

We will fly due west, then south, she said with a cheer that sounded a little false. Raine realized she'd poked a sore spot and shook her head. She was just getting her balance here, why did she have to make decisions right away? But what decision was there to make? Could she really see herself facing the Dark and fighting and staying here forever? No.

Blossom was flying due west to the coast because that was where the estate the Lladranans had offered Raine was. She'd seen drawings, and pictures from Bri's camera, but not the place itself. She shouldn't be curious.

And the island where the Exotique Circlet Marian lives is due west, too, Blossom reminded.

Raine gritted her teeth and called up a map in her mind. *I think we need to angle south.*

Faucon's main estate is almost due south of your land.

It's not my land.

A big beautiful seaside estate. Lots of room to fly and run, a nice stream, good stables for volarans and horses.

Raine had never been on the back of any sort of horselike creature until she'd met Blossom.

Big house for you, too. Bigger than where you live now. Blossom didn't care for Raine's house in the "city" of Castleton, there was no room for a volaran stable. From what Raine had seen in the pics, the place on the tiny peninsula was a small castle.

The world blurred outside the bubble, but Raine thought she smelled the ocean. Mixed emotions welled inside her. She loved the ocean, couldn't imagine not living close to one, but her first months in Lladrana had been hideous.

Now she only had a few more, one way or another.

10

Singer's Abbey

Jikata's voice lesson with the Singer went well, they treated each other with exaggerated courtesy. Before actually doing the exercises, they did some body stretching. After the scales and range practice, the Singer spoke of Power, and spells initiated by sounds, notes, tunes, "songspells." Jikata opened and shut windows and doors, locked them, released the locks. She learned various humming bits to Summon Friends.

The Singer watched with a careful eye as Jikata stirred water, lit a fire in a fireplace, made wind chimes tinkle and moved dirt in a planter. By the time she was done with the "simple" spells, Jikata was exhausted and would have smelled of sweat except her gown absorbed perspiration. Since the dress released an herbal scent, it was obvious how hard she worked.

The old woman, of course, demonstrated all the tasks serenely and with little effort.

Jikata ate lunch by herself, a light one of fruit and cheese and crackers with a hardboiled egg. Then came the baths, massage and rest. She could almost believe this was a resort—Club Lladrana, a retreat specifically for singers. She'd reluctantly decided differently, let the knowledge that she was in another place incrementally filter through her, and focused on the incredible instruction she'd been getting.

In the afternoon she went with the Singer to a suite of personal rooms above an octagonal tower. The old woman had several suites throughout the compound for various activities—or various levels of visitors. Certainly the Friends in different buildings were of different status.

"These are the rooms where I receive Marshalls who come for a Song Quest," the Singer said. "I do not use them otherwise because they are very close to the Caverns of Prophecy. Listen and *feel*."

Jikata recalled her Summoning, the caves, the sounds, the visions, and didn't open herself up fully. She'd already learned how to tone down the soundtrack around her, hear selectively. It was a matter of control, like breath control. If she opened herself fully, she'd be overwhelmed by Song, especially in the Singer's presence. She thought of her Power like the flame of a gas oven, opening a valve and giving the burner more energy.

So now she set her Power on low, *listened*.

Hollowness under her feet. She knew the sound of stone—worked and raw around her, beneath her. The different, deep chord of the planet itself. Only now, when she heard that strange Song, did she realize that she'd always heard a rhythmic beat quite different, that of Earth.

Whispers. Perhaps even hissing like gas. Dangerous if she were open and defenseless to it.

Jikata! Pay attention! It was the Singer's voice, in her head. Jikata sucked in a breath. All right, she should have expected that people could speak telepathically, too.

"One moment!" She wouldn't let the woman rattle her. She wasn't a tyro in the music business.

But the Singer had that smug smile Jikata was beginning to intensely dislike. Eyes widening, Jikata realized the Singer had spoken to Jikata with her mind, while she'd answered aloud.

The Singer had spoken *Lladranan*.

Jikata had understood.

She was learning the language through Song and telepathy and hearing it spoken around her. She'd been a fairly quick study before, but nothing like this.

Letting her knees soften, becoming aware of her *ki*, she let Songs sift into her, or into her awareness and Power.

Her senses slipped down from this chamber to below to the Caverns.

Whispers coalesced into sound, into language—English. A vision formed.

She saw the man in white leather. They were walking along a sandy beach, surf foaming near their feet.

They were talking. No, they were *flirting*. Warmth tingled through her, then and now. A half smile curved his lips, lightening his serious expression and making him dangerously attractive. There was an easiness between them, as if they had a lot in common. His eyelids lowered over a very male glint, and he took her hand, raised it to his lips.

His mouth on the back of her hand sent frissons through her and she knew that this night they'd make love.

Then he froze, dropped her fingers, reared back, shock on his face.

Followed by utter revulsion. Pain. He shook his head, slapped his hands against his ears.

She stared at him in horror. Worse, she could feel tears backing up in her throat, rising, rising. She had to get away.... She stumbled, blinking frantically to keep tears back. Why hadn't she learned a spellsong for *that*?

Jikata! The Singer's voice.

Suddenly she wasn't there and then, but here and now. That was Zen, this is Tao, she thought with ironic humor. Her throat still burned.

The Singer was frowning, her face wrinkled into a thousand lines that spoke of age and experience...and some of them of lost love. "What did you see?"

Jikata cleared her throat. "The man from the other night."

"The night you were Summoned."

"Yes."

"Ayes."

Did the Singer mean her to parrot "Ayes?" Jikata didn't want to play games. She nodded.

"That is Luthan Vauxveau, a wealthy, Powerful noble of the Chevalier class. He wore Chevalier leathers and is my representative to the rest of Lladrana," the Singer stated.

Chevalier meant what? Horseman? Knight? One of those who flew on the winged horses?

A knight in white leather. Was that as good as in shining armor? He looked more like a Western knight than a shogun. No, he *acted* more like her idea of a Western knight, though her ideas of both knights and samurai were formed by the media.

As the Singer crossed to a dark red door, Jikata understood that though the woman had spoken telepathically, she hadn't seen into Jikata's mind and that was a blessing. She didn't want anyone to do that.

The Singer opened the door and gestured Jikata into what looked like a closet. She wasn't claustrophobic, but it was hardly big enough for three people. Everyone on Lladrana seemed to think personal space was a lot smaller than Jikata believed.

The Singer waved her hand up and down. *A moving box.*

An elevator.

We descend to the Caverns of Prophecy now.

Jikata hesitated. The Singer lifted her brows. *I promise neither will hurt you.* Jikata wasn't accustomed to being patronized in her own mind. She shrugged and got in.

The Singer Sang a scale, starting at the top of her range and descending. The elevator moved gently and silently down. *This is the only moving box in Lladrana, and I am the only one who can Sing the songspell.*

Then the door opened and they were in the caves. As Jikata watched, mist gathered into wraithlike shapes and solidified….

A piercing high C and the mist dispersed. Middle C and Jikata's vision blurred and she understood the Singer had curved some sort of force field around them. Handy. From her last time in these caves, Jikata figured that the man in white, Luthan Vauxveau, didn't know that particular spell. But Jikata had also sensed that the man didn't know the Caverns. Thinking back, the majority of the Friends didn't know the caves, either.

The Singer walked with a sure step through dark brown rock tunnels, following a spell light brighter than Jikata had learned to make…yet, in the two days she'd been here. "Time passes the same?" She wanted reassurance.

"Ayes." The old woman didn't pause, but as they turned left, Jikata saw a tiny marking on the rock wall at about her eye level. High for the Singer, lower for the rest of the Lladranans. The Lladranans, like most Earth peoples, had grown bigger and taller over generations? The sense of the caverns was ancient. Long smoke smears—from torches?—were even with Jikata's head.

They jogged right and went through an old door. Jikata didn't recall going through the door before, but now the Power was stronger. It slid smoothly across her skin with a touch that sent warning throughout her body. Danger, visions ahead!

Seven Mile Peninsula

Blossom dispersed the Distance Magic bubble without a sound and she and Raine spiraled slowly downward to a tall gray keep on the bluff overlooking an equally gray sand beach. This was the estate the Lladranans had offered Raine. The place itself was well-kept and looked old and weathered, but still seemed a good stronghold. It was on the southwest side of a small piece of land thrusting into the ocean called Seven Mile Peninsula.

Around it were green fields. The village that supported the castle was farther south, where the land smoothed toward the ocean and provided a good port. Part of the income for the village would come from fishing. Raine wondered if any of the folk could help her if she accepted the estate or whether they'd be as suspicious as the Seamasters themselves. As she and Blossom flew south, still within the boundaries of "her" land, Raine saw a huge building and docks with several boats, one being built the old-fashioned way.

They would owe fealty to you. Want to descend?

No! She could imagine what her father and brothers would say if some clueless guy from the government showed up. But she spotted a couple of men dressed in bright green who shaded their eyes as they watched Blossom and her fly over the open sea. The men raised their arms and waved. Raine thought she even saw a flash of teeth through bearded smiles.

She would rather figure out things on her own. A matter of pride, particularly since she'd been considered useless when she'd first arrived. Her ego and pride had been battered out of her, then, and were just reviving. A thought struck—*Blossom?*

Ayes?

The land where you found me…the hamlet where I worked, is it owned by anyone? At the time she'd thought the place was owned communally by the Seamasters since it was near Seamasters' Market, where the great fisherfolk held seasonal fairs.

Blossom snorted. *Owned by a great Chevalier. She now knows to keep a better eye on it, and on the Townmaster.* The volaran snapped the Distance Magic around them once more. Raine relaxed into the ride, checked Blossom's and her own energy levels, which were good, and let the flight soothe Blossom's irritation—that Raine hadn't committed to staying on Lladrana, hadn't adored the castle or the estate, and at the memory of Raine's mistreatment.

Raine went quiet, was sorry she couldn't see their route to Faucon's castle, but could tell when they flew over ocean or island on their trip. The *feel* of the water, more than the sound of surf against land, filled her.

Singer's Abbey

Caverns of Prophecy, Caverns of Prophecy, the syllables pattered a rhythm. Jikata had a wonderful voice, an instrument, she knew that. Since arriving on Lladrana she'd felt Power.

Magic outside her that ruffled, pulled at magic *within* her. She'd enjoyed learning magical spells.

Did she really think she had a "gift" of prophecy?

Uneasily she recalled the hunches she'd felt all her life, even before the chimes and gong the last couple of years, though her intuition had flashed more often since then. She'd *known* that to further her career she would have to leave Denver, disappoint Ishi, who wanted her to be a teacher. Jikata could never see herself in a classroom, only and always on stage, singing. Was she supposed to ignore the gift of a beautiful four-octave voice?

Arguments with Ishi buzzed around her head and she grew irritated with the past and herself for dwelling on it. She'd accepted being disinherited.

Ishi's death, and now the air around her, brought it all back.

Flashes of intuition, vivid dreams that sometimes came true. She hadn't believed she was psychic. It was easier, even here, to believe in magic outside herself.

They moved into smoothed rock hallways. These floors had thick carpets and their footsteps were lost in fine wool. Jikata still sensed the layers of sediment of the ages above her. Below her was the throbbing heartbeat of the planet. The dim sound seemed to ignite a glow of light in her chest and expand it.

A few minutes later they came to a door of black wood with a rounded top and strap work and hinges that seemed like iron, but were tarnished silver. Beyond the door was a hum of great Power.

The Singer looked at her and for the first time dissatisfaction was gone from the back of her eyes, leaving them serene. Whatever Jikata dimly sensed beyond the door, the Singer felt a hundredfold more strongly.

"You have trained enough to open the door. Listen closely." She inhaled from her diaphragm, Sang crystalline notes from four octaves in a pattern that stirred Jikata's blood.

The doorknob glowed, an intricate design of gleaming silver. The Singer touched the knob, said "Lock," and the knob turned black-on-black again. Then she waited, gaze fixed on Jikata.

Jikata ran a couple of scales to warm her vocal cords. Had she known the Singer would make another of her impatient demands, Jikata would have limbered up her voice as she walked. Then she replicated the Song and the doorknob glowed once more.

"Good." The Singer nodded shortly. She touched the knob and they both stepped back as the door swung outward.

The Singer went in first. "This is the true Chamber of Prophecy, where Power gathers. This is the room where every Singer for time out of mind has listened to the Song—of Amee, of the universe, of the great creative being we name the Song. It can be many tunes or one or even pure silence." Her voice had sunk to a whisper.

Jikata stepped into the room and onto layers of thick, colorful rugs and gaped. In the middle the rugs became a pyramid, smaller and smaller until one just long enough to cradle the Singer was on top. There was a down mattress atop it.

The glitter of the walls took her breath. She was in a massive geode, a domed chamber with walls of protruding crystals all colors of the rainbow. Every color of quartz. Or were they tourmaline, precious gems, colored diamonds? She didn't know. She couldn't imagine the number or the color variations, the sizes of all the crystals, all of which would resonate with a different note.

They seemed to emit sound beyond her hearing. She quivered like a tuning fork.

"It's the Power," the Singer said with relish. "Some of the crystals store it, some project it, some even dampen it. The Song is endless and various."

Jikata couldn't speak. She blinked and blinked again, then narrowed her eyes to slits and shaded them with her hand. Even the filters she'd been building didn't stop the unheard melodies affecting her so she rocked on heels and toes.

The Singer breathed deeply and Jikata understood the Power here supported and refreshed the Singer, probably led to her great age. But one thing Jikata *had* agreed with Ishi on was that living to a great age was not a goal to be sought at all costs, not even if the quality of life was acceptable.

For everything there is a season. She'd recorded that song because she'd agreed with it.

The Singer went to the pile of rugs and sat on an edge. She gestured. "I do not need the tools in the four directions of the room, but you may. We must explore which divination tool is best for you. Look around."

The room wasn't big, perhaps twenty feet in circumference, enough space for the rugs in the middle and the largest rug— surely commissioned for this chamber. As Jikata turned in place, she saw four different…thrones, and noticed that where they sat there was a shading streak of the same color. Deep blues spearing down to the palest shade of blue that seemed almost clear; the same with reds through orange to citrine with only a hint of yellow; dark purple amethyst to the lightest of lavender; great milky crystals that became more and more translucent until only the reflections on their facets showed they were there.

Each streak of color was equidistant from the others. The chairs were of silver, of gold, of polished wood, of slick obsidian. All had fat pillows near them in bright contrasting colors for seat and back. All had a pedestal she could barely see between the back of the chair and the wall.

She walked to the clear stones. On the pedestal was a harp that appeared to be fashioned from thick glass, shaped like an ancient lyre.

"Ah, my own element, air," the Singer said approvingly.

Jikata yearned to touch the instrument. "I don't know how to play it."

The Singer's laugh was sincerely amused, her face crinkled with humor, and Jikata saw the vibrant woman she'd been before age and sickness and something else—worry…the burdens of being a great oracle?—had taken their toll.

"It is meant to be strummed, a tool to vibrate the air around you so the visions come. Sit, try it."

Jikata hesitated.

"We will not be leaving this room until we have found your best tool," the Singer said calmly. "I was first here when I was nine. Two days after I arrived at the Abbey."

But she was a Lladranan. The small woman's hand was on Jikata's shoulder, urging her down. Jikata sat on the silver chair and took the glass harp in her hands. It wasn't large— about a foot and a half and fit easily in her lap. She didn't know how to hold it, so she put her arm behind the glass top and set the bottom at an angle on her opposite thigh.

"If you have a question, ask. If not, just let your mind relax and see what comes." The Singer's voice lilted, hypnotic.

Creusse Crest

Blossom dropped the Distance Magic for the final time and Raine saw it was late afternoon. In the near distance was a crescent between two jutting promontories that was Faucon's land. His castle was built of a golden-toned stone and both sprawled and rose like a small city in itself.

Raine said, *We—I—don't need to go to the castle. I want to look at Faucon's yacht down on the dock, it shouldn't take very long.*

But Blossom was licking her lips. *I have flown far and deserve good food.*

Raine shifted uneasily, enough to have given Blossom wrong cues, if they hadn't been ignored. Raine hadn't asked Faucon's permission to inspect his ship, to come here and demand food for a hungry volaran. She'd hoped to pop in, look at his yacht and pop back out, no harm done. She should have asked, even if he did avoid her.

Blossom said, *You should go up to the castle to greet the people. You did not thank them for your care last month.*

Because I was knocked out and taken away! But Blossom had said enough to prick an underlying guilt in Raine. The housekeeper of Faucon's castle and a couple of maids had been the first people to treat her decently since her arrival on Lladrana. Raine would have written thank-you notes but she still didn't know how to write.

Blossom alit on the dock near the yacht and Raine dismounted. She'd no sooner began to stretch her muscles before the flying horse took off to the castle above. Raine ground her teeth, then turned to the yacht. Beautiful lines, wood painted white, it was about two hundred feet long and one glance told her no money had been spared in her making. She walked to the stern and probed with her Power, her magic, for a rope ladder, then found and lowered a gangplank that had fancy carving on the sides. Raine just shook her head and gently settled the plank on the dock, then hurried up it.

The rocking of the ship under her feet made her catch her

breath, and swallow hard. She hadn't been on a boat in eight and a half months. She closed her eyes and a small moan of pleasure escaped her as her soles tingled and she got her sea balance. Somehow the water beneath her wasn't like Earth oceans. Were the tides and the ocean swells that different? Lladrana had a moon that looked only a little larger than Earth's. Maybe it was the difference of the planet Amee under the ocean, or with the ocean, or whatever. Raine sniffed and again shook her head at the fanciful notion.

Singer's Abbey

Letting her mind wander, Jikata strummed, closed her eyes against dazzling brightness. How odd that such a conglomeration of crystals should form a hemisphere focusing Power and prophecy. Surely it couldn't be natural.

I made it. Crafted it like you craft your melodies. A rippling laugh and Jikata angled her head to see a Lady dressed in a white toga, a Lladranan woman with long silver hair, dark eyes that showed a brilliant white starlike pupil. She held her hand against her lower abdomen. *I wanted my peoples to listen to me.* She smiled and it was the sweetest, most heartbreaking smile Jikata had ever seen. *There are places like this in many lands, but only my Lladranans listened.*

"Who are you?" Jikata breathed.

II

I am the planet Amee thanking you for coming. But air is not your element and you know that. Try others before you settle on the one you love.

Jikata started from her daze, opened her eyes. Placed the lyre carefully in the stand. Then she went to the blue crystals and the dark wooden chair inlaid with a lighter wood in a complex pattern. On a wooden pedestal was a delicate stone bowl. In the bowl was swirling water.

"Go ahead," the Singer said. "Look into the water. Feel the Power around us. See what the bowl shows you."

Jikata had no sooner glanced into the bowl than Amee was back, her face troubled. *I have called you and the others here for a purpose. You give me hope after ages of despair.* Her star-pupil eyes flashed like a supernova, tears ran down her face, then she vanished.

With a shaky breath Jikata levered herself from the chair, moving within a dream. The air around her was thick with sound, tinkling crystalline whispers and vibrations she couldn't hear, could only feel.

She went to the obsidian throne. The Singer had placed a fat red pillow on the seat. Jikata sank into it, looked at the top of the obsidian pillar for a few seconds before she saw the mirror. Reaching out, she found its edges and tensed, not wanting to cut herself. She raised it until she saw her own face, ghostlike, brown-black hair, brown eyes, more amber than chocolate. Behind her the opposite wall with the red streak glowed. Then it wasn't her face but Amee's. Her gaze reflected wariness, too. *I am fighting and will fight. I ask you to do the same.*

The mirror fell from Jikata's fingers, thumping onto a soft black pad she hadn't seen. Once again she rose and with measured steps went to the red-orange fiery wall that had drawn her from the first. As she came near, flames ignited and danced in a brass brazier.

She sat and was enveloped in warmth. Amee stepped from the fire, wearing a red gown, hand again at her side. She nodded to Jikata. *Jikata, you are here, at last.* The sweet, terrible smile. *You must know that should you wish, you can become the thousandth Singer. All you have seen here could be yours. The comforts and the Power and the joys of living a life full of music, of listening to your gift of prophecy and thereby helping others. Composing. That can be yours.*

One corner of her beautiful lips twisted. *Along with the temptation of Power, the burden of foreseen knowledge, the duties and responsibilities of the Singer.*

"I'm just becoming accustomed to here," Jikata said.

Amee's smile saddened, her star-spark pupils shone behind

tears. *I brought you to help me, to fight with me and for me. But you are not alone in this endeavor.* Finally she removed her hand from her side. A black, hideous swollen sluglike leech gnawed on the woman, and the red of her dress was nothing compared to the red of her blood. *Help save me.*

Jikata stared in horror at the evil thing, then skin on its head rolled back and she saw shiny, depthless, black eyes that sucked the light from the room as it sucked the energy from Amee. It smiled. *First her, then you.* It cackled in her mind.

Everything went dark.

Creusse Crest

Faucon's yacht was two-masted with red and orange sails furled and tied down. A gorgeous Tall Ship. Soon Raine would make her own ship. Joy blossomed in her. Who knew after all those bitter wars with her family that she'd wanted to build a Tall Ship…? There must be more of her family in her than she expected.

The future of ships on Lladrana was what she, Raine Lindley, would make it. That sent a shiver down her spine. It would be more like a galleon than a schooner or pleasure yacht. Good thing she'd designed hundreds of hulls and sails, and now if she remembered her doodlings in middle school, a Tall Ship or two….

Her ship would be as beautiful as this yacht, grander than anything her family had made. As for yachts…she could build something for Faucon, or other rich Lladranans, faster, sleeker than this pretty lady.

But her Tall Ship was one thing only—a troop transport. She set her mouth. No reason it couldn't be lovely, and they'd want fast.

She just didn't know how fast the thing would go without real power or Power—magic. She walked along the upper deck, all tidy. No doubt Faucon had a top-notch crew. No indication here of any other propellant source than the sails ready for the kiss of the wind. There was a polished stick where a wheel would be on Earth and she was sure it connected to a rudder, but nothing more.

She went down a level, found the crew's quarters, hammocks hanging, and grimaced. That was the most efficient way for people to sleep on a ship. She wondered about the fighters. She thought of their tired and grim faces and realized that they wouldn't care much as long as they had a chance to destroy the Dark and its Nest and the monsters it kept sending to Lladrana.

Raine only hoped that her last task was building the ship, not fighting the Dark itself.

The galley, sitting area and cabins were all gleaming wood. The crew quarters had been in the stern of the ship, and Raine's eye had told her that there was no "engine" compartment between that room and the ocean.

Now she stood in Faucon's large and luxurious cabin and studied the wall behind the big bed. There was something beyond that wall, snugged in the forecastle, the front of the bow.

"Your reason for being here is?" Faucon asked.

Singer's Abbey

Jikata awoke on a fainting couch and jolted upward, but as her mind spun she realized she wasn't in Ghost Hill Theater but in Lladrana.

"The first true vision can be intense," the Singer said. "Especially if you touch the Song, or if you see your future."

Without saying a word, Jikata took a few deep breaths, looked around. "How did I get here?"

The Singer smiled. "I used Power."

Which could have meant she dragged Jikata through the caverns or teleported her or something altogether different. Jikata decided she didn't need to know. "We're in your suite above the crystal room?"

"Ayes. Only Singers are allowed in that room. It is where the *Singer* experiences the Song. Others—Chevaliers testing to become Marshalls, those who wish a Song Quest—are given drugs to open their minds to our innate Power and we link with them here. Now go to your own rooms and rest and eat, perhaps meditate." The autocrat was back in full force. "I have had a blank journal placed on the desk in your suite. You should record today's vision." The Singer grimaced. "In English since you have not begun to learn written Lladranan."

Jikata thought she was doing well to learn spoken Lladranan so quickly.

There was a pecking on the door.

Another moue from the Singer. "Your bird companion awaits. Go listen to its silly chatter."

Jikata was glad to escape.

Creusse Crest

Raine should have known someone would tattle on her. Blossom had told some person or some volaran and here was the man himself. "I needed to see a Lladranan ship," Raine answered. "Figure out the Power source." She would *not* let his Power or his wealth or his sheer attractiveness intimidate her.

"Why didn't you ask Marian?" He didn't move, lounged with a shoulder propped on the doorjamb.

She threw up her hands. "I have, time and again! But she only shoves a book at me and I can't read Lladranan. Then she goes off to craft a Songspell that will destroy the Dark and am I supposed to follow her and interrupt *that?*" Her voice rose with irritation, but she didn't modulate it. The man didn't like her anyway, no need to put polite manners on. Though she did wish he didn't cause her insides to quiver with incipient lust. He'd always been sexually appealing to her, and had never shown that he even liked her with the flicker of an eyelash. Had refused to let her on this yacht.

She stood her ground, rolled with the slight swell of the ocean beneath her feet, jutted her chin. "Or should I have gone down to the nearest fishing village to look at a boat, hoping I'd find someone I could trust who wouldn't kill me?"

His expression, which had softened at the mention of Marian, went hard again. "I assure you, your attacker has been punished. He was banished from Lladrana. I made sure that he shipped out on a merchanter from one of the City States. He's half an ocean away by now."

Raine inclined her head. "Thank you. Now I know this has interrupted your day—" she'd seen enough Chevaliers to understand the fresh stains of monster gore on his leathers "—so if you will point me to the power source, I'll be glad to get out of your way and let you go about your business." He probably *did* have business, he was a merchant prince.

Then he smiled and had her heart flopping in her chest with the contrast of white teeth against his golden skin and the sensual curve of his blush-colored full lips. Uh-oh. Thinking about him too romantically.

He'd turned on his heel and that saved her from looking like a fool since her mouth had dropped open and she was sure her eyes had glazed. It hadn't been one of the sarcastic smiles he usually aimed her way, this one had had real humor in it.

"Here," he said.

At his voice she pulled her feet from the deck and hurried after him outside the door and to her right. He'd drawn back a curtain and opened a narrow door that led to an equally narrow passageway. "Light," he said and the tiny corridor lit, still paneled in pretty wood. He took three steps and was out of sight, behind his cabin's wall. When she joined him, he gestured. "The Power source." He tucked his thumbs in his belt, grinning fully now, liking her slack-jawed shock as she stared at four huge slickly smooth stones, each nearly five feet in circumference and arranged in a diamond pattern.

She squeaked a sound, didn't even know what she'd intended to say so couldn't cover it up with rational words.

"Brighter," Faucon said and the light in the room intensified.

He tapped the top of the stone nearest them and Raine saw a beautifully faceted emerald inset into the sphere.

"Directional stone, west," Faucon said, touched a forefinger to the shiny great stone beneath—surely it couldn't be hematite? "Power stone."

Raine shook her head, trying to make sense of this. "I don't understand."

He indicated the jewel in the sphere nestled in the prow, a shining golden topaz. "Directional stone, north." He pointed to the one to their far right, a sapphire, "Directional stone, east." The last was a richly red ruby.

"Huh," she said, brilliantly.

He laughed and some of the lines in his face eased. He would have fought hard in the battle. And he didn't have to. He could have stayed here in the south of Lladrana where no monsters had ever reached and tended to his estates and wealth and business. But he'd answered the call to arms a few years ago and fielded two teams on the battlefield.

Hell, she really was falling for him and he'd done nothing to encourage her.

She marched back into the sitting room. Her gaze fell on her model that she'd left floating in the Castle Temple.

He was still chuckling as he closed the door and pulled the red drape over it with the sound of brass rings running over a curtain rod.

He picked up the model and one of his long elegant fingers stroked it. "Come up to the castle and have dinner." His smile hadn't faded as he'd made the offer and she thought that was a good sign he was beginning to tolerate her. "We'll talk about ships." He studied the model, turning it in his hands to observe the detail. "I've never seen anything like these designs of yours, but I do understand how they would make a ship go faster, or, in this case—" he held up the small wooden ship "—carry a number of us to the Dark's Nest."

He'd included himself in the invasion force. Raine's stomach knotted. "Have they chosen the Chevaliers who will go?"

Raising his brows he said, "Do you really think that the Exotiques will make me test like the others? I field two teams and will help finance this expedition. There will be a couple of us that will go without testing. Luthan, for another."

Raine crossed her arms, would have liked to hitch her hip on a table to add to her attitude, but he was between her and it. She met his eyes with a cool stare of her own. "Ayes, I think the Exotiques will expect you to test like the rest of the Marshalls and Chevaliers who intend to destroy the Dark." She didn't really know, but it sounded good.

Faucon shook his head and laughed. "I suppose I shouldn't be surprised." He shrugged. "Very well, I'll test. I'll 'make the cut'—that's the Exotique phrase, ayes?"

"Ayes."

Bells chimed. Faucon said, "That's the dinner signal, come along, Raine." He turned and went up the stairs. "You can spend the night. I think that Blossom has already settled in my stable to have a good chat with my volarans."

Raine followed, her pulse beating hard. She'd wanted to grill someone on ships and building. Some part of her had also wanted to get closer to Faucon, learn to know him better, but that part was more like a sailor drawn to the siren's call.

She was sure she was already in over her head.

Faucon seated Raine at the small table for two that his housekeeper had set up in the outside dining nook on the main terrace of the castle. The surf at the bottom of the cliff was a low, rumbling accompaniment to their dinner, a sound he hadn't known he'd missed until Raine had tilted her head to listen to it and sighed in enjoyment.

He was making more than one mistake, getting close to this woman. Of all the Exotiques who had been Summoned to Lladrana, including his lost Elizabeth, she stirred him the most. Her skin was pale and translucent, her hair a dark, rich color of brown that proclaimed her no native Lladranan, though not quite as startling as Marian's red or Calli's blond. Raine's eyes were the green of the deepest ocean.

And she suited him better. Underneath all her outer

defenses, he sensed she'd been more tender than the others when she'd come, younger in spirit, not quite as tough.

She'd developed whatever toughness she had here on Lladrana. That angered and shamed him. One of those who found Exotiques instinctively repulsive had abused her, nearly killed her.

As for him, he was, as always, instinctively attracted to her as an Exotique. But he'd learned his lesson. For once in his life Faucon Creusse would not get what he wanted—an Exotique for a wife—as he'd hoped for since the moment he'd met Alexa. His reaction was only physical. He'd get over it. He wasn't sniffing around the other Exotiques now, was he?

Because their Songs had changed when they'd pairbonded, their music didn't seem as potent and beautiful to him. Raine's Song was delicious, the tastiest he'd heard.

But that was what he'd thought of Elizabeth and he'd been wrong about her loving him enough to stay in Lladrana. Now he felt like an object of pity among the Marshalls and the Chevaliers, noble Creusse who couldn't convince his Exotique to stay. He fought all the harder in every battle.

At least Raine wasn't aware of his physical reaction around her—dreeth leather helped conceal that—and he kept his manner brusque. He'd changed into another set of fighting leathers instead of trousers when he'd washed up.

He caught a fragile expression on Raine's face as she looked at the fine china and the scented candles that his housekeeper had lit now that evening was deepening into the blue-purple of night. No one had treated Raine to an elegant meal, had they? He cursed inwardly for doing exactly as he'd done with Alexa and Elizabeth—but no, his housekeeper had arranged this, and he wished she hadn't. Still, the softening of Raine's face made him want to rub away that rough shell Lladrana had layered on her and see the true pearl beneath, the woman she'd been before.

The serving maid set mixed greens before them with dressing and they ate in silence. He was enjoying the moment too much, the gentle pulsing of her fabulous Song, twining with the wonderful Songs of home. He treasured his home now.

At this point in the past he would have led the conversation to the fascinating topic of life on Exotique Terre, but he didn't want to know any more than he'd learned and seen in his lover's—Elizabeth's—mind.

He wasn't going to court or care for this Exotique. More than any of them, she'd seen the harsh side of Lladrana and would *not* stay. "So, you don't come from the same place the other Exotiques do?" he said and was appalled. He stuffed a bite of crisp greens in his mouth before something else came from it he didn't want.

Raine gave him a cautious look. Because he was being civil? Because he'd asked a question he already knew the answer to? Faucon chewed longer than necessary.

"Ayes, I come from the east coast of the continent." A small, charming smile flashed across her face. "The others' home is landlocked, they know very little about boats." She speared a curl of onion and ate it. "I've never been to their area, either. I don't know much about mountains." She stopped abruptly.

The mountains of Lladrana were in the north, where the horrors invaded, sent by the Dark. Hardly anyone lived there now. Since Faucon didn't believe in ignoring a topic once it was brought up, he said, "We won today, no casualties." Another sharp pang, he'd lost the man he'd considered his father a couple of months before. His chest tightened. What would Broullard have said about this situation? But he knew. Broullard would have told him to grab all the pleasure life had to offer, even if it hurt later.

"We are winning more often, replacing the old magical fence posts that fall." He hesitated. "Of course we must repel the invading horrors, but the main effort of the Marshalls and the Chevaliers is on planning the invasion."

Raine put her fork down, a third of her greens remained. "When will they have trials for the invasion force?"

"Soon. Now that the last Exotique has come, everyone thinks the time of the Singer's prophecies has also arrived and this cycle has passed." Determination strengthened every muscle. "We must rid ourselves and our planet of the Dark or watch Amee die."

12

Raine shivered, but Faucon knew it wasn't from cold. The summer evening was nice, the sea breeze only freshening. He raised a hand and the maid came and took away the plates, bustled back into the castle. She should have done that without his request. Broullard would have been disappointed in her.

The fading of the day was working on Faucon, bringing depression. He should have stayed with his Chevalier team, gone carousing with them to a tavern, not come to check on what this strange, lovely woman was doing at his castle when his volaran had told him she was here. No one would treat her poorly, nor would any be less than discreet about his affairs. He'd guessed she'd gone to examine his yacht.

She looked away and Faucon followed her gaze to see the incoming tide break whitely against the rocks curving into the northern headland of his estate. She rubbed her arms. Maybe she *was* cold. Faucon lifted a finger and a footman came.

"A shawl for Raine," he said.

Her look was surprised and again he was irritated by the thought he'd been less than courteous. He was walking too fine a tightrope—fighting his awareness and attraction on one side, and on the other thinking of his grief at losing Elizabeth, and trying to treat Raine as a gentleman and nobleman should. He was juggling, too, wasn't he? Like some damned player come to the fair—his business affairs, his Chevalier teams, his sessions with the Marshalls and other Exotiques. Plenty to juggle. He wanted to shove back his chair and pace. Instead he smiled charmingly and Raine's expression became even more wary.

The footman came back with a shawl and handed it to Faucon, who stood and went to Raine. He draped it over her shoulders without actually touching her. Since she tensed, she must have noticed.

"About ships…" she said as he took his seat again.

"Ayes?"

"How *are* they built here?" Her brows dipped. "Marian seems to think that my ship will be built in a few days, maybe a week." She shook her head. "Magic, Power," she muttered.

"Most are built by hand, with Power imbued in them as they are constructed."

The serving maid was back with the fish entrée—lightly breaded and spiced, caught that day. Faucon's mouth watered before he cut into a flaky slice. On the side were green beans and thin rounds of potatoes in an herbed cream sauce.

Raine's eyes widened. "I haven't had creamed potatoes since…" Remembrance and hurt flashed in her eyes and Faucon knew it was before she'd come to Lladrana.

"From what I understand, all noble cooks are experimenting with this new vegetable," Faucon said easily, staring at the stuff on his plate. He hadn't eaten anything like it, either. Even with Power helping them grow, potatoes were rare.

But Raine had dug in, savored a mouthful, closed her eyes. "Mmmmm. Could do with a little pepper, though."

"Pepper?" Their meal was interrupted by the chef herself. She bowed to Faucon but didn't leave. Her hands clenched in her apron. "On behalf of the noble households I am asking the Lady Seamistress Exotique if we could have recipes other than twin fries and Mickey potatoes that the Exotiques might remember. No one has been forthcoming. Concentrating on other things than food, they say." She gestured to the plates. "This is my own concoction."

Raine licked her lips and desire stirred in Faucon. Raine said, "Have you tried them baked and loaded?"

"Baked?"

"Um...wash, bake in a hot oven for about an hour, incredible," Raine said. "Good with just butter, but some people can make a meal with them by adding bacon bits, sliced peppers, cheese, sour cream—" Raine waved "—other stuff. Very good."

"Hot oven, bacon bits, butter." The chef nodded.

"Also cheddar potatoes, sort of like these," Raine said.

"Cheddar?"

"Potatoes in a cheese sauce," Raine said, taking another bite, eating with more gusto than she had her greens. All the Exotiques loved potatoes, enough to have the twins bring some from the Exotique land three months before.

"Cheese sauce!" The cook turned.

"And mashed and whipped," Raine said.

The chef whirled back.

"Mashed potatoes and gravy. You peel them, boil them, mash them when they're warm to...uh...different consistencies, maybe add a little milk if you want them fine, then make gravy from meat drippings and thickened with flour and more milk and put it to the side." She frowned as if searching her memory. "I come from a house with men so I didn't make them with my mom, she died when I was little, or with my grandmothers—"

But the cook was already racing back into the castle, on a mission to pummel potatoes, Faucon didn't doubt. He found himself again smiling genuinely. Just being with Raine lightened his spirits. He should shut that door hard, but couldn't, heard Broullard admonishing him to choose joy.

He watched as Raine ate with fierce delicacy, the worry about whether she'd have a next meal was ingrained in her now, and he suppressed a sigh. "Have you been assured of your future?"

She glanced up, the frown between her brows again, a line that didn't belong there. "I'll be building the ship. I'm hoping that's my task and the Snap will come after that." Her gaze slid away from his, she put her silverware down. "I'm not a fighter, I don't want to go to the Dark's Nest and Sing that Song Marian's crafting to destroy it." She pulled the shawl more tightly around her. Then she lifted her chin defiantly as if in expectation of his condemnation.

"I think you *are* an excellent fighter when you must be," Faucon said quietly. "You survived what many would not."

She sniffed, still didn't meet his eyes. "All of the other Exotiques would have survived, too."

"Probably..." He kept his voice matter-of-fact. "Those who are Summoned are always exceptional."

With a flicker in her eyes, she said, "Even those Summoned in a half-assed way?"

"Especially those," he said.

The moment spun between them, a gentle moment, his absolute belief in her and her acceptance of that. He continued eating and she picked up her cutlery again and ate, slower this time, savoring every bite.

When his maid came to clear, he said, "Thank you. Since the meal was light, we'll have dessert."

"Crème brûlée, Hauteur, your favorite."

Raine made a little noise, her hands crushing a thick linen napkin. "Crème brûlée?" she asked in a sexy, breathless voice with a tiny whimper of anticipation that stirred his body. She looked at him, licked her lips and his blood heated so he could barely hear the last of her words. "My favorite, too."

Finger bowls had been placed with soapy water on the table and she used hers. "Thank you. *Merci.*" She shut her eyes and her whole body seemed to go lax. "I'll have my crème brûlée for breakfast, please," she mumbled and fell asleep.

Faucon shook his head. She was doing too much, had no one noticed that? She felt too good in his arms when he carried her to a guest room.

Singer's Abbey

Jikata had dozed the rest of the day and through the night, starting awake from nightmares of the leech or disturbing dreams of the crying woman, lifting a sword that was too heavy.

Her own heart hurt, simply ached, with a depth of compassion she hadn't been aware she'd held. She *did* want to help the world—Amee—fight. The idea of becoming the Singer—a different sort of Singer than the old woman before her—tantalized.

Magic was in every sound all around her and she loved the music of her new life.

She knew there would be a price to pay.

Killing that evil leech, whatever it was.

She didn't think that destroying it would be easy.

Creusse Crest

Raine woke in sheer luxury. For a moment she was disoriented as her blurry vision focused on the gold-toned canopy over her bed. She wasn't in her little house in Castleton, not even that bed was as soft and decadent as this one.

A rap came at the door and Raine realized that's what had awakened her. Clearing her throat, she called, *"Entre."*

The housekeeper strode in with a maid, and Raine gripped her covers in a dizzying moment of déjà vu. This had happened the morning after Blossom and Faucon had rescued her. Memories of that day—more horrible than pleasant—washed through her and had her shaking.

"The room is too cool," the housekeeper snapped and immediately rectified it with a little Song that heated the air. She shook her head at Raine. "You should have pulled the bed curtains."

"In the summertime?" The room was fine, now overwarm.

"It's been cooler than usual," the housekeeper said, and gestured to the maid with a tray holding a steaming pot of tea and a plate of eggs and bacon. "You eat this and you can have crème brûlée with Faucon in a half hour in the breakfast nook."

Raine did and didn't want to eat with Faucon. She liked him, and he'd been so kind! As she scooted up on the pillows, she touched the yoke of a fine nightgown accented with little green ribbons.

"We undressed you and put you in the nightgown," the house-keeper said, but Raine had had no doubt about that. Faucon never touched her.

"Hauteur—" that was Faucon's title "—said you were working too hard." She sniffed. "We should never have let you go to the Castle, they aren't caring for you properly."

"Thank you."

"Quite welcome. Your flying leathers are being cleaned, but will be done after breakfast." The housekeeper gestured and Raine saw underwear and several lovely dresses of crushed velvet being placed on the chest at the end of the bed. "These were made for you and we kept them here. Hauteur requests that you stay since he has called his cousin the Seamaster from his northern estate to consult with you and Corbeau won't arrive until this afternoon. Those Marshalls," the housekeeper tsked. "Expecting you to build a ship and not giving you any information. Besides, the Ship will depart from Faucon's northern estate, Creusse Landing, of course."

"Of course." Had that been decided? Raine knew some of the Circlets had wanted to depart from a northern island. All her problems swooped down on her like crows. Like they did every morning. Her surroundings might have been upgraded a thousandfold, but so had her responsibilities.

The maid and housekeeper curtsied and left.

The pot of tea smelled wonderful. She was a coffee girl, but like many, associated tea with comfort in stressful times. The eggs and bacon were perfect and she wasn't sure whether to be glad or not that the Lladranans hadn't learned about home fries.

But her mouth watered for crème brûlée, and her mind demanded answers about how huge round stones could make a ship go and how a troop ship could be built in less than a week.

She had a busy day in front of her.

13

Raine stroked her hand down a pretty sapphire gown, visualized how Faucon might look at her if she wore it.

Foolish.

Why couldn't she banish these foolish feelings for the man?

So she took a quick shower. When she came out her leathers were on the bed. She cast one last glance at the dresses, then put on the thin silk long underwear, leather pants, lawn shirt, leather vest and coat. They were supple against her skin and she realized she was finally breaking them in. Good.

When she entered the breakfast room, Faucon set aside a stack of papers and rose to seat her, smiling.

"Thanks for your hospitality," she said.

"You're welcome," he said, and she didn't think he realized he'd said it in accented English, which just reminded her that he'd loved a previous Exotique who'd dumped him. Keeping her wince inward, she sat opposite him at the damask-covered table that held a plate with a small bowl of crème brûlée.

She glanced at Faucon, who'd continued to smile, and said, "I suppose your cook disapproves of this breakfast."

He nodded and dipped a shining silver teaspoon into his own treat. "And the housekeeper, and the maids. I don't think the footmen care, though."

Raine savored the custard and crunchy sugar and spice crust melting on her tongue. Perfection. She glanced around the place from under her lashes as they ate in silence. She hadn't actually been in the castle. This was the ground floor of an octagonal tower room, with long windows in every section of the wall. She couldn't see to the beach, but could watch distant waves rolling in from the ocean. Wonderful.

Faucon cleared his throat. "The propulsion of ships is usually based upon sail and Power."

The crème brûlée became a little less tasty. A working breakfast, nothing personal. "Figured that," she said. "You have those huge stones…."

He nodded. "Ayes, Power stones, they store Power and are magnets set for the four main directions."

"The jewels."

"Ayes. The jewels are tuned to each cardinal point."

Raine had an idea. "Magnetic north and south poles?"

"Ayes."

"But what about east and west?"

Faucon shrugged, then bent down and retrieved a book, opened it to a bookmarked map.

For a minute Raine expected to see little animated notes on the paper, then realized it was static and two-dimensional. With one long, well-shaped index finger, he indicated two gray rectangles on the coast of other continents, one to the east of Lladrana, one to the west. "Amee made these ages ago for us to tune our spell stones to." He smiled briefly. "Legends say the locals worship the great plinths, but they're only navigational tools, though huge and resonating in the proper frequency."

An idea flashed through Raine's mind, some strange connection, then was gone.

"So your jewels are tuned to the north and south magnetic poles and these, uh, plinths."

Faucon nodded.

It sounded weird to Raine, but if she tried to think about Power logically most of the things on Lladrana were weird. "Your ships *do* have a rudder."

Again Faucon nodded. "There are corresponding stones on the rudder and it controls the ship's course. But it is also, ah, *pulled* by the magnetism of the great Power stones toward the cardinal directions. That makes sense?" His smile was crooked.

Not really. "Uh, how are the stones, um…how does one indicate the direction to the stones, steer the rudder?"

"Oh, a steering stick, of course."

Huh.

She stared at him. "Wouldn't a force that strong—" She waved her hands. "The magnetic poles and the monoliths, if they can *pull* a ship—" she was still having difficulty with this one "—pull the stones right out of a ship?"

He smiled indulgently. "The Power is not only in the monoliths. Those are like…beacons. The Power is in the stones, they hold huge stores of Power and are drawn to the poles and the beacons at a particular rate."

"Particular rate," Raine repeated.

"The direction and rate are controlled by the helmsman." Faucon touched his right temple where a wide streak of Power showed. The streak was larger than it had been. In preparing for this battle, everyone was taking on duties that increased their Power. "One *wills* the stones to go a certain course and applies the—ah—spark to Power them." His forehead wrinkled and his tone became stiff. "I don't entirely understand the matter, myself. I understand wind and sail better. If you want a complete technical explanation, speak to Marian."

Raine lifted her brows and made her eyes big. "Oh, I *couldn't* bother her. Her explanations…" She winked.

Faucon looked startled, then laughed. "Yes, hardly anyone talks to Marian these days. She's apt to go off on a lecture and usually loses me three sentences in." After swallowing his last bite, Faucon said, "My yacht needs a crew of ten, but I had my sailboat brought around to my private dock. It's small, two sails, a beautiful, responsive boat. We can handle it easily." Another smile but his eyes were intense. "Would you like to go out on her?"

Raine's heart jolted with a hard, fast thump. She hadn't been sailing in more than half a year when she'd been used to being on the water at least one day a week. Tears stung behind her eyes. She couldn't show them to him.

"I'll be the crew. You can captain," Faucon said softly.

She couldn't speak at all for a moment, then unthinking words came. "Why are you being so nice to me?"

He straightened in his chair and his face became impassive, but color showed under his golden skin on his cheeks. Meeting her eyes, he said, "I did not treat you well when you arrived. I apologize."

Raine had already said too much, too rudely. She flushed

and it was much more evident. "And I apologize for my rudeness." She glanced away, then back at him to see him watching her with wariness. "If the offer to sail is still open, I would love to." Now tears clogged her voice. Dammit!

He put the book on his stack of papers and Raine knew that no one would touch them until he returned. Definitely the master of the castle. "Excellent," he said, standing. "Shall we go?"

The walk down to the dock seemed all too long once the offer of a sail had been made. But her deck shoes had to be sent for. Like the dresses, some shoes had actually been cobbled for her when she'd first arrived a couple of months ago. If she'd known...

She was deluding herself. She wouldn't ever have returned here unless she had to, to learn of ships. A castle wasn't her idea of "home." More like her idea of something that had to be toured with her father and brothers on a family trip to England and France.

Though her own great-grandfather had been an Exotique, had come to Lladrana in his youth for the purpose of teaching the current Singer the English language. Which was all too woo-woo for her, especially since that woman was still living. From what the other Exotiques had said, and what she'd read in their journals, Raine had no wish to meet the woman.

She wondered briefly how the one Summoned for the Singer was getting along, but both Bri and Luthan had said she would not suffer at the oracle's hands and Raine believed them.

Then they were down the winding path to the docks and a small sailboat bobbed gently.

It was the most beautiful boat she'd ever seen, because *she* was going to sail it, after all this time. Every muscle fiber in her body quivered with anticipation, the feeling more intense than looking forward to some of the sex she'd had in her life.

She tasted the salt air and other sea smells on her tongue, drew the air deeply into her lungs, gaze fixed on the little boat. Even if it had been an awkwardly shaped tub, she'd have yearned for it like a lover, but it was a pretty thing, carefully made, and it would go fast. She grinned. Oh, she'd show that Faucon—who had yet to call her "Seamistress"—how fast she could make this boat go, wring more speed out of her than he had, she'd bet.

Rubbing her hands, she considered actually betting him and turned to him, mouth ready with the wager. But he was looking down on her with understanding and amusement in his eyes and the words stopped. She was reminded how well they'd gotten along the last day, how much he'd done for her. No, she wouldn't take the man's money—zhiv—on an easy bet.

"She's lovely," Raine said instead.

Faucon beamed. "I had a hand in designing her."

Raine kept her mouth shut. Obviously ship design on Earth was ages ahead of Lladrana, or, for all she knew, the entire planet of Amee.

Despite that her feet itched to feel deck rolled by wave under her feet again, she stopped to glance at it, then at the elegant Faucon. "It's red."

"It is indeed, and the sails are bright orange. The Creusse colors, you know."

Garish...not at all fitting with his image. She could see blue-gray and silver, or black and silver...

His smile lingered. "My ancestress, the founder of our house, liked bright colors."

Raine said, "She got them." Tilting her head, she said, "At least it's not purple." The color assigned to Exotiques.

Faucon laughed, eyes crinkling. Raine liked seeing him lighten up.

He waved to the sloop and she stepped aboard.

The moment she was on the boat she could feel the difference in the sea from Earth. She wasn't sure what it was, the size of the moon or the distance of it from Amee, or what, but no ocean of Earth ever felt like this one. Being smaller, the boat rocked more than the yacht and her heart caught at the feeling. She sniffed. This was home. A boat was home. Not the pretty house in Castleton, the Marshalls' Castle, the small castle on the estate they wanted to give her. A ship. Nothing else.

Odd that she'd come all the way to Lladrana to learn that.

The boat had a tiny cabin for bad weather. "Where're the stones?" But she was walking to the bow, saw a small trapdoor with a rope handle. Faucon passed her, lifted it, and she saw four small round stones, gleaming silver, each with a tiny gem embedded on the top, again in a diamond pattern. Well, no need to worry about getting an engine wet.

Faucon put the hatch lid back down, then headed for what was obviously the steering stick. There was no wheel, but a short stick at ninety degrees that looked like the curved and polished wooden hilt of an old dueling pistol, not in the stern where a tiller was most likely to be.

With a lopsided smile, he said, "Let me get her out of the dock."

It was only sensible, but she wanted to sail *now*. Still, she stepped back from the control and let him take her place. She gauged the wind and the water with narrowed eyes, and hoisted a sail.

He grinned at her, and she sensed the barest tickle of Power, a slight lift in his personal Song and the boat moved without wind, but magic. No roar of the diesel catching, not the faintest hint of fumes. She could get used to this.

They communicated with hand gestures that seemed easy to both of them. Raine anticipated the boat's needs. She thought that after a few minutes he actually forgot she was there.

Then she saw the true man. The man who was nothing but a guy enjoying a wonderful pleasure. He wasn't the nobleman running his castle, the merchant planning his next trade, leader of men into battle. The man facing a suicide mission. He was simply Faucon, head raised to feel the breeze against his face, eyes narrowed at the horizon, his body easing into the natural rhythm of a sailor.

Feeling for him caught her in the gut, tightened her throat. She could love such a man. She backed away from that thought, stumbled, and he glanced at her and a mask dropped down over his expression. He still seemed more open, and smiled charmingly, but his eyes held a hint of surprise. That he'd forgotten about her in the enjoyment of the sail? That she wasn't the woman he had pigeon-holed?

Though she itched to get her hands on the wheel—the steering stick—Raine saw he was caught up in the sailing and put aside her desires. She didn't know how long it had been since he'd sailed, but not as long as she'd known him.

Finally, a long hour later, he seemed to wake from his personal sail-induced trance and gestured to her.

Singer's Abbey

For Jikata, the next morning was a repeat of the first two, with breakfast and pampering, being amused by Chasonette, though the bird didn't tell her anything new. The cockatoo *did* insist that Jikata write down her experiences from the moment they'd met in the Ghost Hill Theater. Chasonette told her to title her musings "The Lorebook of the Exotique Singer," which had an archaic and pleasing ring.

Then came physical and vocal limbering up and voice training. Jikata had rarely worked so hard at her craft, and it had rarely come so easily. It seemed as if her very pores were soaking up Power…or it was being released from them. Glorious Song continued to surround her, and she was getting used to a soundtrack to her life, would stop and smile when a lovely combination of Friends, the buildings and trees occurred.

She found the Singer's primary personal chambers oppressive, the music too strong and structured and with a restrictive beat. Chasonette was banned from them. Jikata also sensed that the Singer knew training in her rooms was uncomfortable since the woman stated that it was good for Jikata to learn to Sing under adverse circumstances.

She was also becoming aware of odd silences, of hesitations and gaps in what she was being told, but she didn't press. The training schedule was rigorous enough that it kept her mind and body fully occupied learning new things—songspells and how to work Power with the voice—and older lessons like extending the strength of her vocal range.

Club Lladrana pleased her, giving her challenge for her current skills, showing her new ones, all in a beautiful setting where she received the utmost respect, as if she were a superstar. Of course she couldn't have imagined this, but it was just what she'd needed after the last tour and Ishi's death.

Jikata had come to terms with her great-grandmother's passing, accepted that they'd never have reconciled, accepted there'd always be a spot inside her heart that would ache and grieve for her relationship with her great-grandmother, that it couldn't have been different, couldn't have been more supportive and pleasurable for both of them. Being on Lladrana had been good for this.

Though she'd accepted her past and all the decisions that she'd made, she shied away from the future that might include who knew what. She lived in the moment and enjoyed every second.

The setting itself was pastoral and everyone except the Singer treated her with a deference that buoyed her ego. Furthermore, compositions were beginning to simmer in the back of her brain and she knew in a few days she'd be putting notes to paper, creating again.

She didn't know if the Singer composed or simply Sang extemporaneously, but creating music was vitally important to Jikata. If she'd been a dry wisp of a wrung-out rag spiritually when she'd ended her tour and arrived on Lladrana, now she felt like a fat sponge bursting with Power and music that would pour from her. She'd *create* tunes that others would like to sing, play, dance to.

That was the best. *That* fulfilled her.

Creusse Crest

Faucon said, "We're out of the shelter of the headlands. I'll let you have the helm."

They'd been out of the bay for a while, but Raine nodded, letting the wind separate the strands of her hair and whip them around her face. She should have braided it.

Frowning, he reached into a pocket and pulled out a knit cap, handed it to her. She could have used it earlier, thought her ears might be red. "What about you?" she shouted.

In answer he set her hand on the steering stick, went over to a compartment and got a cap for himself. It was a tightly knit orange with his coat of arms on a red shield, a falcon with wings lifted as if ready to soar or having just landed, atop a black circle around an even-armed cross. Obviously a "captain's" cap.

His eyebrows dipped, then he took the utilitarian red hat from her head and handed her the one with the insignia. Giving her the captaincy of the boat? Her eyes stung from the wind as she put it on and tucked in her hair.

Perhaps better to speak mind-to-mind for instruction, he said, his mental tone brisk.

Definitely not something she was used to doing while sailing, but if she could learn to fly volaranback and hear telepathic instruction while doing that skill, it should be a snap while sailing, so she nodded.

This is the steering stick.

She'd figured that out.

With his index finger he touched the four tiny cabochon gems separated by two bits of hematite inset along the slightly curved top. *Send a little Power to these points as you move the stick when you want to increase the speed.*

She glanced around. There were some fishing boats hovering in the distance, and she got the impression that people on them were watching her as they worked. The most open sea was west by northwest. So she looked at the stud, recalled the amount of Power Faucon had used and thought of a thin thread between her mind and the hematite and *sent* Power along the thread to the gem.

The boat zoomed forward and the rounded polished handle slipped from her grip. She fell back against Faucon and they both fell to the deck in a tangle of arms and legs. The man's body had no give at all and she elbowed him in the chest as she rose to grab the tiller grip.

She didn't know how to stop.

14

Frowning, Raine *dampened* the boat's Power.

They slammed to a stop. Faucon, who'd risen to his feet, fell again, then just held his ribs as he gasped, laughing.

She'd never seen him belly laugh like that and it was worth the embarrassment of echoing laughs from the fishing boats. Keeping her own face as straight as she could, she said mildly, "Do you need a hand up?"

Faucon hooted. "And have you throw me overboard with your Power, lady? I don't think so."

"Ah." Heat crept up her neck and cheeks, she turned to the wind so he'd think that was what was causing it. "Guess I don't know my own Power." She'd thought she had, but not here, not on the sea, her element.

Rising, Faucon shook his head. "Guess you don't."

"'Least I didn't run into anything."

"Ttho." His lips twitched. "Good job."

Yeah, right. She sniffed. "Perhaps you should teach me a little more."

"Just send the tiniest amount of Power to it. Feel." He took the handle of the stick from her and clasped her own hand in his own, swept a glance around at the positions of the other craft and the southern headland. Then he zipped a tiny amount of Power to the northwest. The boat moved smoothly through the water several hundred yards.

"You felt the increment that I sent?" he asked.

"Ayes." But it was her turn to frown. She'd done pretty close to that. Could her Power be greater than Faucon's? She studied him from the corners of her eyes. He had thick streaks of silver in his hair, the indication of magic. On the other hand, most of the Exotiques from Earth had more Power than the natives. The reason they were Summoned.

"Your turn." Faucon moved her hand to the tiller.

Maybe it would be better if there were finger indentations, she might consider that for her ship... He moved to clasp her left hand and the scent of him came on the sea breeze and scrambled her wits, dissolved the thread she'd spun from her mind to the north. She'd wanted to make sure they'd go nowhere near Faucon's southern headland jutting rockily into the sea.

As she inhaled, she dribbled Power down her reformed thread and the boat shot forward. Raine kept her hand on the rudder stick as they skimmed the waves. This was *not* good for the sails and she heard canvas snapping like wet clothes in the wind.

Faucon jerked back, but kept ahold of her. His stance was wide and he didn't fall. When the boat slowed to a stop as the energy diminished, the sails flapping, he went to tie them down. Obviously they would be exploring driving and Powering a boat with magic and not sailing.

Pity.

Faucon studied her, being more natural again. She raised her eyebrows.

"You have more Power on the sea than anyone I've ever known," he said.

That sent a jolt through her.

He was shaking his head. "Not surprising. We need Powerful people to destroy the Dark."

Just that easily the shadow of death moved over the boat. Raine shivered.

"Amee would ensure the Seamasters Summoning you would find the right person. I noticed you formed a thread to send the Power," he said. "Why don't you try just *thinking* of the gem-direction you want to use." He smiled and it was sincere.

Raine shifted, tested the breeze, noted the fishing boats in the distance, outside the clasp of the headlands, but in the middle of them. She and Faucon were almost directly west of the point of land.

Raine wiped her hand on her pants to rid her palm of sweat and stray droplets of spray, and took the helm again. Once more she stared out at the rolling vista, and decided to go due west. She looked at the line of semi-precious stones. Would the colored jewels be more Powerful than the hematite? She let their individual sounds come to her ears, separated the notes from physical sounds, the strong Song of the man beside her, and the psychic Songs of the boat and the land and the sea.

No, each stud lined up in the handle of the steering rod was equal in Power, logical.

She smiled at Faucon, took his hand and liked the connection between them. She wanted to close her eyes to listen closer to the gems and envision them, but didn't dare. So she drew in a cleansing breath of sea air and *brushed* the deep green emerald that meant "west."

The boat moved smoothly through the sea and came to an easy stop.

Faucon laughed again.

And when she looked up at his golden face, his deep brown eyes, his smile, she tottered on the edge of love. She stepped back from that cliff and, experimenting, sent the sailboat into a wide sweeping turn, reversed easily, then did a circle, a figure eight.

These weren't three-dimensional figures like she'd learned with Blossom in the air, but they came much quicker and easier to her than partnering a volaran.

Finally she stopped and rubbed her hands, glanced at Faucon, who was sitting easily on a side bench, arm along the boat rail. Again his smile was pure enjoyment and a little spurt of pleasure went through Raine. She had given him this simple contentment at being on the sea.

She grinned at him. Now was the time to truly show her skill. "Set the sails, crew."

He stood and saluted smartly with a hand flat to his shoulder. "Ayes, Captain."

Raine had gotten the measure of the wind and the sea, sensed currents running shallow and deep below the surface.

The water, the sea, was innately different. She'd traveled a fair amount to Earth ports, and though each place had its unique qualities, the innate feel was the same.

It was as if the *substance* of water was different. Maybe there was a little something extra in Amee's oceans. A tiny bit of magic, Power, in each droplet. She didn't know how that could be, but the previous minutes had convinced her. The sail had gone more smoothly than it should have—would have done on Earth—with the chop of the waves, the currents they'd navigated.

But now Faucon was staring at her with narrowed eyes and she lifted her nose and sniffed the sea. Studied the expanse before her, empty of other vessels. With gesture and learning words, concepts through voice and mind, she ordered Faucon to angle the sails and they *went*.

They skimmed through the water, and Raine wrung every bit of speed from the wind and the boat and the water.

They *sailed*. The breeze tore a delighted laugh from her throat as she saw Faucon's wide eyes and admiring glance. She knew she would have won that bet.

He put his hands on her shoulders and his touch, the downright beauty of his personal Song, sent every other thought out of her head. If she paid attention and listened to her own Song, she could tell that they complemented each other well, would fit together in a complex pattern. Was that why she was so attracted? Because their Songs fit? Or did their Songs fit because she was attracted? Or was it because he had helped rescue her? She'd escaped the Open Mouthed Fish and the stalker on her own, might have made some sort of life, then had met Blossom. That meeting would have changed her circumstances, but when Faucon flew back on Blossom to find Raine, he'd taken matters into his capable and elegant hands and the change in her lifestyle had been quick and dramatic.

Faucon said nothing of returning to shore, and one of the seat lockers held a lunch that was all the more tasty from the activity and setting and company.

Seagulls fought for the few scraps of sandwich crust and cheese crumbs that Faucon threw into the air.

Then they took turns at the helm and sailed more.

Contentment flowed between them. He didn't hide long looks at her, as if reevaluating. They shared laughter, and admiration came to his eyes. More than her spirit felt refreshed. She became aware of her body, how she moved with the boat, bent in the wind, how that wind kissed color into her cheeks, tangled her hair. And somehow the sailing of the vessel became a silent dance between them, the lift of her hand, shift of stance indicating to him how he should set the sail. Being on the water transformed from a wonderful physical activity to an emotional bonding. Something she didn't think was wise, but couldn't deny.

Singer's Abbey

Early in the afternoon, the Singer and Jikata went to the Caverns of Prophecy. Soon she realized there was less than a meeting of minds with the Singer about the prophecy business. The old woman spoke of "that land swell of notes," "the volaran flying melody," "the home pattern," and when she said the phrases, Jikata heard distant Song, but it was evident that the Singer didn't actually see visions, but *heard* the future, and interpreted it that way. It was too strange for Jikata and for the first time she truly felt she was in an *alien* land.

She'd had hunches, flickering bits of visions all of her life, and many had come true. This woman had been trained from a child to recognize what melodies meant and portended for the future. There must be thousands of patterns the Singer recognized.

Jikata could never learn that. She *had* been playing with the idea of staying, not having to worry about her career on

Earth—remaining fresh and innovative, and young. Americans put a premium on young entertainers. She had no one whose heart would break if they missed her.

Being the most important person in a country, revered, set for life.

But she couldn't learn the notes that meant different things in this alien culture, not enough to nail it every time. Oddly enough that thought was depressing and she wandered the compound accompanied by Chasonette, who chittered bird style and added a layer of music to the surroundings. Jikata admired the buildings once more, the juxtaposition of styles, as if each new wave of architecture was adopted by a past Singer and a new building had to be erected in that style. It was whimsical and endearing, and she might miss it, too.

There was a commotion by the gatehouse and Jikata walked that way, curious.

Chasonette said, *It is a Chevalier from the Marshalls' Castle.*

Again that phrase. "Explain."

The Marshalls are the greatest warrior team in the land and they have a Castle.

Jikata envisioned a shogun's holding, eaves sweeping outward, tiled roofs. But looking around her she knew it would be more like some gloomy medieval European place. She sniffed. Obviously these people borrowed from the wrong culture.

"Chevaliers?"

They are lower than the Marshalls… Chasonette hesitated then added, *Though they can be wealthy noble lords. This one must be like that because his volaran has so much pretty trim.*

Jikata hadn't even noticed a volaran flying overhead.

Let's go see!

"We're on the way."

Faster, they are not letting him in! Chasonette rose and zoomed to the stone arch and the wrought-iron gate that was the main entrance.

A man. One who wasn't sworn to the Singer. An outsider. Maybe like the man she'd seen the night she'd arrived? The one in white leather? Leather would be good for riding—flying—and fighting, and he had held himself well, a noble...Luthan.

So Jikata sped from a stroll to a brisk walk and saw a man arguing with the gatekeeper Friend.

"I'm a mirror magician now, and I know she was brought here by mirror magic. Knowledge should be shared, dammit!"

The last word was said in *English,* though the man had the Asian features of a Lladranan and the skin tone. Jikata stopped about twenty yards from him and met his eyes.

He looked startled, then swept a bow. "Lady Exotique," he called in Lladranan, then in accented English. "I'd like to speak to you."

"Ttho. Go away, orders from the Singer that you will not be allowed in," the Friend said, then stepped away from the grill and unlatched a heavy door, slammed it shut, while Jikata still stared. Running footsteps sounded, a shout, wings.

Some of the feathers in the wind came from Chasonette, who landed on an eave close to Jikata. *It is Koz!* She snapped her beak. *I have never seen him. But I have heard of him. He is a special man, part Lladranan and part Exotique Terre.* She craned her neck. *Look!*

Jikata followed the bird's gaze to see a pretty roan volaran outfitted in red-and-white trappings. A shield was on the side showing a triton symbol. She blinked, stared—that was definitely a Maserati symbol. The winged horse looked nothing like a car. She choked on a chuckle.

The man circled the compound waving a helmet at Jikata. He wore leathers of a deep reddish cognac color.

She lifted a hand and saw his teeth flash.

"How come he doesn't come down inside the walls?" she asked Chasonette.

Because there is a magic shield.

Of course. When Jikata narrowed her eyes she thought she *did* see a wavering in the air.

"You'll see me again, I'll be back!" he yelled, again in English, then grinned. "And I'm not a terminator!" His expression sobered. *"Ask questions! Learn the truth."*

Then more volarans surrounded him, with Friends on their backs, and herded him and his volaran away.

Jikata dropped her gaze from the sky, looked around. Some high-level Friends were streaming her way.

All right, she knew this wasn't really Club Lladrana. That things were being hidden from her, but she'd been on the point of physical, mental, emotional exhaustion when she'd come here. Perhaps spiritually bankrupt, too. Had pretended this place was a retreat, gone along with the idea that nothing was wrong, even when she heard more than a few references to Chevaliers and Marshalls, who were definitely warrior classes. Warriors usually meant a war going on.

She had no doubt that a person who could partially predict the future would be an excellent weapon.

But that wasn't her. She couldn't *hear* like the Singer did.

She couldn't master the patterns. Didn't know that she even wanted to.

Guiltily she thought of the lady of the planet, Amee, and

her wound and the leech. Jikata shuddered. She definitely wasn't ready for this, so when Friends surrounded her and gently suggested a nap, she continued to be silent.

Chasonette sat on her perch just beyond the end of the bed and warbled Jikata asleep.

The Lady walked in her dreams, dressed in a silver kimono tied with a golden sash.

Amee held out her hand and Jikata took it. They walked in a misty garden beautiful beyond belief, green and full of birdsong.

"Goddess," Jikata said.

Amee's smile was amused. "No. I am *not* a goddess, merely a sentient being like yourself."

Jikata didn't think so.

Amee spread her arms and flowers bloomed, white and pink and blue and red...a rainbow of colors. The grass was studded with tiny blooms, too, and seemed to become an iridescent green as if each blade were coated in dew.

"Not at all like me," Jikata said, her voice like a croak to Amee's liquid tones.

"Ayes," Amee said. "Sentient." She paused, her eyes saddened. "Finite." She bent to a red lily-like flower, inhaled, then said, "Fallible." She stepped away from the bush and continued down a path of crushed stones, making no noise.

Jikata crunched behind.

Amee shrugged her shoulders. "An alien came, a small foul-smelling slug, and I did not squash it. I was not the kind of being who killed such things. A great mistake."

Jikata didn't want to hear this.

Amee's star-pupils flashed. "But it was a being that killed, that went from place to place and drained a planet's force. It battened on me and I was too surprised and too weakened by its bite to fight. Then," She turned a face of terrible purpose upon Jikata. "But I have become a great fighter, have watched fighters and mages and Singers born and die in my service—native and Exotique. Have had my people Summon others who vow to fight for me, for my life and their own."

Day faded with quick suddenness. The garden dimmed to full night, Amee flung up a hand and Jikata thought she saw swathes of galaxies *move*. "The Song is with me, with us. For all is in a balance, good and evil, and this evil has tipped the balance with me, until it will feast on me as it has planets before. It has left death and sterility in its wake, dead cultures and races and worlds. It must be stopped, and it is my fate—and yours—to stand against it here."

Jikata wanted to put her hands over her ears, but couldn't move. A great Song blew around her, through her, showing how much she was a part of the whole.

"Our Dimensional Corridor is out of balance, and now we must try to right it. We will not be the first to attempt it, and if we fail, it will move onto its next feast, stronger." Amee tilted her head toward Jikata. "You know where the closest portal leads."

The enveloping Song diminished and Jikata felt chilled. Earth. It spoke of her home.

Such a huge battle! She couldn't.

"You can," Amee said, holding out her hands palm up. "I have learned that the Song does not give us burdens or tests that we cannot bear." Again the terrible, sweet smile that tugged so deep into Jikata that it hurt.

"Your gifts of voice and prophecy and music were given to you by the Song, encouraged by Mother Earth and by me.

You *can* do this." There was a slight sigh and Amee's face became implacable. "Indeed, you will not be called home until you *have* done it." Tears overflowed her eyes and ran down her cheeks. "I am sorry for that, but it is our fate. All of our fates."

"The Singer…" Jikata gasped.

"Is old and has lived longer than your kind to fulfill her own destiny. But you have doubts and so I come. Your gift is not for interpreting the Song, but you *can* be the Singer."

"Lladrana needs those who *hear* the patterns."

Another shrug from Amee. "Not now, for the others are more visual, too. And Luthan was given that gift." Amee smiled. "The Song bestows blessings as well as challenges. When you become the Singer, you will share your visions. Your successors will be blessed with the gift of *hearing* prophecies."

But a certainty welled up in Jikata. "Not *when* I become the Singer. *If.*"

Amee bowed her head. "If. If we survive. For if you fail, I fail, others fail, we die."

They wept together and Jikata awoke with tears on her cheeks and the knowledge that though she still didn't want to know more about what was going on, it was time to start asking questions. Club Lladrana had always been a pretense.

15

Marshalls' Castle

Luthan jolted awake from the trance with Jikata and Amee.

"This is only watching practice. Sleeping during trials will not win you a top spot on the invasion force," his brother Bastien said, elbowing him in the same sore spot in his ribs that he'd hit before. "If you were meaning to apply for this suicide mission, that is."

Drawing his hand down his face, Luthan wasn't surprised to find beads of sweat.

Bastien glanced at him with a smile that snapped into a frown. Then he looked away. "Sorry, thought you were sleeping, not in one of your trances." He held up a hand, face still averted. "I don't want to know." He sucked in a big breath. "It's best if I think we will die. Thank the Song, I will not live without Alexa." His crooked smile came. "I cherish her every moment of every day, just in case we don't come back."

His expression sobered as he watched young Marshalls and Chevaliers training in the practice ring, grunting and kicking up a lot of dust. "Who would have thought it would be my fate to destroy the evil that has been plaguing Lladrana for centuries."

Gesturing to the men and women before them, he said, "Father wouldn't have expected it." Bastien shook his head. "Like them, Father would have wanted to be in on the fight, for the glory. Me, I'd prefer life stayed exactly the same as it is now…a few minor horror incursions as we renew the fence and fence posts, a good life."

"Father was a bastard and a fool. Everyone should want a good life over a glorious death," Luthan said.

"So you don't think living forever in a saga—'cause you know every name of every person who goes will be celebrated in Song and story for as long as there is a Lladrana—you don't think being famous forever is worth the price?"

"Ttho."

Bastien turned to face him. "I didn't ask you, just presumed. Are you going to test for the expedition force? Will you go with us?"

"Ayes."

"It would please me, brother," Bastien said softly, "if you stayed behind. If you survived."

"Can't stay. May survive." He met Bastien's eyes. "All three of us might."

Bastien's shoulders relaxed in a sigh. "Not one hundred percent death then?"

"Ttho."

Throwing back his head, Bastien laughed and the sparkle was back in his eyes. "I've always liked long odds." He waved to the ring. "Now let's go show these youngsters what *real* fighting is. I bet I can take seven of the twelve."

Luthan looked down his nose. "I'll be the one who takes eight of the twelve."

"You're on!" Bastien vaulted over the fence.

"Those are good odds," Luthan murmured under his breath. "You have your very long odds in surviving the Dark." He saw Alexa running toward the ring, love in her eyes. She hopped over the fence using Power, not bothering to whip out her jade baton before she joined the fray. "We three have the long odds." Then Luthan jumped over the fence himself, but felt no joy.

Creusse Crest

Raine let Faucon take the helm for the trip back to his dock and manned the sails. The duty didn't keep her fully occupied and she could truly appreciate the shoreline, the headlands around the crescent beach, the sand, and the castle sitting atop in just the right place to look great. The views from the castle windows were great, too. She'd had glimpses of several land masses that had to be Circlet Islands. She'd come close during her own sailing, but hadn't wanted to exchange the pleasure of being at sea and only with Faucon, who was becoming a friend, to being on land with Powerful strangers.

Her soul was quiet, full of serenity.

Enerin, as a small red bird with a multicolored comb, was hopping up and down on a piling when Faucon handed Raine off the boat to the dock.

This is where you are! Enerin scolded. *You were supposed to be back last night!*

Raine just smiled and shook her head. "I decided to stay."

Enerin ruffled her chest feathers. *You were not at your land—*

"I don't have land."

And I tracked you here by your Song all by myself.

"Really good." Raine set her cupped palms together so the young feycoocu could jump into them. Her feathers were as soft as kitten fur.

So I came.

"Thank you."

And so did my mother and father, Sinafinal and Tuckerinal, and so did all the Exotiques and Luthan and Koz—

Raine winced, she wasn't ready for another long briefing on the ship and the invasion, her spiritual peace was eroding. "A full house, then."

Faucon glanced up at his castle and slanted her a smile. "Not very full."

Sighing, Raine put Enerin on her shoulder, welcomed the little scratch of claws as the birdling dug in. Her companion. She was glad of the loyal friend. A being of pure Magic; even as a youngster, Enerin's Song was awesomely beautiful.

Enerin swivelled her head to look at Faucon. *Your cousin came, too. They are all at the large pool where you have made a miniature model of Amee. Raine's Ship is there, too.*

Raine tried to imagine a model of the northern continents of Amee in proportion to her own ship and couldn't.

With a tiny peck-kiss, Enerin said, *Even though it's too big, it's ready to sail to the Dark's Nest.*

All Raine's peace vanished.

The "large pool" made Raine's eyes widen. It *was* a map of the northern part of the world, land carved and set into the pool from the north pole to the southern border of Lladrana.

But Raine's gaze arrowed to the island of a single volcano that was the Dark's Nest. She stared, then realized it didn't match the maps she'd seen. That had been Calli's task, to map the island. There weren't any good harbors, especially not for a ship the size she'd designed. So the invasion would take place on volaranback, God help them all—beautiful winged horses and the crazy, determined people who flew on them.

Then Raine noticed that the pool and the growth looked *old*. She glanced at Faucon, who was using a long stick as a pointer to indicate his northern estate. "How is it that you have this?" A tingle went down her back. It was so very much what she needed.

He shrugged. "I had a couple of Circlets in my ancestry. One of them made this. He said never to fill in the pool and was respected enough that we didn't."

The group of the Exotiques were standing around the north end of the pool, staring at the ovoid shape of the island. A man who looked a lot like Faucon, except thicker around the waist and shorter, stood tugging at his lower lip. From his roughened face and hands, Raine recognized him as someone who'd spent time on the sea, a fisherman once if not now. A Seamaster now. One of the loose guild-masters of that calling.

"You really think we'll raise the Ship at our northern place," Faucon's cousin asked, obviously uneasy.

"I do," Faucon said. "It's the best place."

Raine looked at the tiny U-shaped building sitting on the northern edge of the easternmost peninsula of Lladrana, Creusse Landing—the manor house where this man and his family lived. He had a new baby, didn't he? No wonder he was concerned.

"Not one of the Circlets' islands?" the man persisted.

"We'll discuss this later," Faucon replied with an underlying tone of command.

Alexa swaggered around the west of the pool, hand tilting her baton sheath. "Don't worry, Seamaster, we've replaced all the northwestern fence posts. No horrors will come through."

"The monsters can manifest the farthest south any one of them has come with Power," he said doggedly.

Alexa's brows lifted. "We have not experienced that phenomenon of *retrousse* since the old master of the horrors died and a new master took his place. We believe it was a skill of the old master's and either the new one doesn't know it, hasn't learned it yet, or doesn't have the Power to do it." Her words were clipped and carefully enunciated. Though Alexa was the first, she was still the one who had the most difficulty with Lladranan.

The man reluctantly nodded.

"Where's my ship model?" Raine asked.

Faucon's cousin jerked straight from his slouch and aimed a penetrating look at her. He bowed. "Seamistress." Raine nearly smiled at the respect in his voice, something he hadn't shown Alexa, who was so much more dangerous than Raine. "Your Ship is brilliant, absolutely brilliant."

Warmth washed through Raine. "Thank you."

"Raine, Exotique Seamistress," Faucon said formally, "please let me introduce you to my cousin Corbeau."

Raine dipped her head, "Pleased to meet you."

"And I, you," he said fervently.

Alexa rolled her eyes at Raine, stepped back into the group of Exotiques.

"Your Ship's over here, on the estate pond." Faucon moved to the left of the continental pond, to the north.

Raine followed. "Estate pond?"

"Ayes." His smile curved, reaching his eyes, and once more she was distracted by his charisma. Then she saw a long rectangular pond that showed a portion of the western coast of Lladrana. She caught her breath. The southernmost edge was Seamaster's Market, where she'd been Summoned. She swallowed. She saw the tiny village where she'd lived and nearly died.

Then Faucon was by her side, hand under her elbow. "Easy," he said, and Raine realized she was hyperventilating. She steadied her breathing with a long inhale.

Her ship was there, rocking in the pond, massively out of proportion.

"It belongs in the Creusse Landing pool," Faucon said.

"Hmm, a series of ponds showing Lladrana and your estates," Jaquar, the Circlet Sorcerer and Marian's husband, said. "Wonderful." The rest of them had followed Faucon, and Jaquar glanced back at the other pool. "All the islands are correct, and the largest, Bossgond's, has good detail."

"Should have, one of our female forebears lived there," Faucon said.

His cousin stood tall. "Our family has contributed members to every segment of society." His voice took on a note of awe. "We even had a Singer, once, ages ago."

"The second of the Creusse name," Faucon said. "He was Powerful in Song." Faucon slid his gaze to Alexa. "Which is another reason I should be allowed to go on the expedition. We know our responsibilities to Lladrana, have contributed much to the country. We love her."

"You test and are in the top twenty and you go," Alexa said absently as she studied the new pond. Then she shrugged. "We should be studying the other pond, the one that shows the Dark's Nest. It helps a lot to see it like this, in land and water to understand the dimensions."

"We will return to that pool," Faucon said. "As soon as we show Raine how the Ship will be built," he said softly.

"She doesn't know?" Jaquar stared at Raine.

"Ttho." She lifted her chin. "I've asked Marian a few times but never got a short, straight answer."

Everyone looked at Marian, who flushed. "Pardon," she muttered. "I get caught up…didn't realize." She drew in a deep breath as if readying herself for a lecture. You could take the prof out of the school, but not the school out of the prof.

Faucon smiled charmingly. "I think it would be better to demonstrate." He gestured to his cousin. "Corbeau?"

Corbeau was staring at Raine, his mouth slightly open. He glanced at her model. "You did all that without knowing exactly how a ship is built?"

"Ayes," Faucon responded with a pride that surprised Raine. "She *is* the Exotique Seamistress. You should see her on the water." Now everyone was staring at Faucon. "Pure magic and Power." He winked at Raine, nearly made *her* jaw drop. The sexual sizzle between them was back, greater than before.

Alexa made an approving noise. She wasn't the only one. Raine glanced at the clump of Exotiques and their men.

"Must we—you—always travel in a pack?" Raine asked

"Well, I haven't ever seen a ship raised, either," Alexa said cheerfully. "Not even built the regular way. Anyone else?"

"I saw one raised here," Marian said. "During research—"

"Of course you did," Alexa said, grabbing her bondmate's hand and pulling Bastien faster than his usual saunter. Bastien, too, winked at Raine. It wasn't the same.

Alexa continued. "We'll get out of your way tomorrow and you can be all alone with the man." *She* winked.

Raine felt her cheeks warm.

"Coming, Raine?" Faucon said.

"I will not pick up that straight line," Marian murmured.

"Thank you," Raine said weakly and hurried to Faucon. Obviously all the others sensed the sexual tension between herself and the noble Chevalier. Also evident was that they approved. She should return with them in the morning.

She caught the scent of the sea, a wisp of Power sent in the air from it, and knew she wouldn't. Didn't want to be very far away from an ocean ever again.

No physical constraint this time, but emotional. Seaside was her place.

The next series of pools showed three places—Faucon's northern estate, the one here, and, of course, the one she'd been offered. She stared at it—she'd been told it was empty.

"We divested ourselves of that piece of land a while back. The owner to the north wanted it." Faucon shrugged. "Eventually her family had financial troubles and it came back on the market just a few months ago. We hadn't quite decided to buy it back—"

His cousin grunted.

"—when Marian suggested it would be a good place for you."

Raine looked at Marian and she said, "It has a shipyard."

"Does now," Corbeau said. "The village is smaller on this reckoning. Features haven't been kept up here." Another frown as he strode to the northern estate where he lived. "This isn't quite right, either."

"I've been fighting," Faucon said, "you haven't been down."

"No quarreling," Marian said. She held out her hand to her husband, Jaquar, then took Faucon's gesturing hand, then sent a grin to Raine. "This will be like my training. Form a very detailed image in your mind of the land, Corbeau."

He took Faucon's hand and Jaquar's, forming a small circle of Power, the lines of his face deepening in concentration.

"Gonna be fun," Alexa said to Bastien, who was at her back, his arms around her. She wiggled in excitement.

"Later," Bastien said.

Raine's mouth *did* fall open as she watched. She could tell through her link with the other Exotiques that Corbeau was providing the image, backed by Faucon. Jaquar was keeping the link between them all clear and steady…and Marian was shaping the land with wind and the wave of the pond. It was like watching the forces of nature carve the estate over years. Raine had seen the Exotique Circlet do mundane spells, and some esoteric ones Raine couldn't grasp, but this was the first time she saw Marian work her true craft.

Awesome.

Corbeau grunted. "We have more sandbars."

The land was raised in certain places, pulverized to sand.

"Wow," Alexa said.

"That's it, I think," Faucon said. "Blessings of the Song." He dropped his hands, shook them as if ridding himself of energy. Sparks flew from his fingers. Corbeau yelped, stepped back and then sank into his balance, studying the result. His mouth curved. "Ayes. Perfect. Good job." He looked at Marian and Jaquar and shook his head. "Consorting with Circlets."

"We don't bite," Marian said.

"Later," Jaquar said.

Raine snorted.

But Corbeau was walking out on the peninsula, jutting into the pool's waters. He pointed to a particular spot. "I think this would be the best place to raise a ship."

The continued use of *raise* finally clicked in Raine's brain. They couldn't possibly mean…

But Enerin, as a seabird, cawed as she dropped a stick that looked suspiciously like a rudder on the place Corbeau had indicated, then fiddled with it a bit until her parents came with more twigs. It looked as if they were setting up a ketch.

Raine bit her lip. "You actually *raise* the ship like a—"

"Barn," Marian confirmed. "A person in the local community sends word out that he or she needs help for building a boat, the materials are laid out, others come and a circle is formed around the boat and it is 'raised.'"

"By magic," Raine said, shaking her head in disbelief.

"Let's show her," Faucon said, and the birds lifted to Alexa's, Marian's and Raine's shoulders. Once again she welcomed the light weight of her companion.

You will see! warbled Enerin.

Faucon splashed into the shallow water and held out both hands to his cousin. They positioned their linked arms around the planks and bit of cloth that was the outline of a ketch.

Sinafinal, the original female feycoocu who came for Alexa and was her companion, dropped a tiny hematite sphere in the bow. She sprinkled gem chips on the outline—one in the bow, one where the rudder stick would be and one for the rudder itself.

Corbeau began a rolling chant that matched the rise and fall of a boat on deep waves, then the Song quickened as if it were coming to shore, the waves more shallow, with a hiss of surf.

Raine stared as the "planks" rose, formed, snapped together

with…Power? Small bits of twine unfurled and set themselves in minuscule blocks and tackles, the sails straightened. The ketch tottered on the piece of land, then lifted from it and moved to the "sea," bobbed there, complete and functional. Raine couldn't believe it. She stared.

Alexa sloshed into the pool and dunked it, the little boat righted itself and bobbed back up. "Incredible."

Sinafinal chirped in satisfaction on Alexa's shoulder.

She scooped the boat up, held it at eye level, examined it from every angle, including upside down. "No teenie-weenie nails. No glue. Huh." She jumped through the pond to Raine and handed it to her. "You look."

"Smooth lap construction. Very smooth," Raine's voice squeaked with surprise. "But no glue."

Faucon raised his brows. "Power."

Corbeau came over, took the little boat from Raine, studied it himself. "A good job." He glanced at Faucon. "We do good work together."

"Always," Faucon said.

Setting the boat back into the pond, Corbeau gave it a small push. The little round Power stone took it to magnetic north.

"I want one," Alexa said. "I want my own boat. A prettier one." She fixed her gaze on Raine.

Faucon met Raine's eyes with a challenge. "Let's try it again, with Raine."

16

"Ayes!" shrilled Enerin, an actual word instead of mind-talk. She shot off to nearby bushes and began scruffing about in the underbrush, muttering to herself. "Too thin, too long. Look, look, a cord for rigging!"

They all stared at the little bird.

She is a feycoocu, Sinafinal said. *If she wishes to speak aloud, she can do so.*

Raine shared glances with the other Exotiques. Just what were the limits of feycoocu Power? They all knew the magical beings could move a lot faster than volarans or even Bri's roc. They looked at Marian, who said, *I ask questions but am mostly ignored. I will not experiment on them.*

Of course not! Raine's shock was echoed by the others.

Tuckerinal, Marian's ex-hamster, flew to her shoulder as Sinafinal went to help Enerin gather appropriate shipbuilding materials. Raine shook her head at that thought.

I do not know all that I can do, Tuckerinal sent to them. *I surprise myself.* His head cocked and beak clicked. *I cannot heal as well as Bri, I cannot revive dead things.* He gazed northward. *There are very few of us feycoocus and we cannot defeat the Dark by ourselves. It falls to humans for that.*

"Raine!" Enerin's cry was piercing. She was standing next to the outline of a boat.

With a little shock, Raine realized that some of the "planks" had been colored, and if she visualized the boat in 3D, it would correspond to the last boat she'd built for herself—the one that had splintered when she was sucked to Lladrana.

A great wave of homesickness rolled over her.

Then Faucon was next to her, hand on her shoulder. He murmured, "I asked Koz about your mirrors. He's finished them and has been to Bossgond's island. He'll soon arrive here." Faucon made a sweeping gesture to the arrangement of sticks, cord, tattered triangles of cloth and a tiny hematite sphere.

Alexa lifted her chin. "*My* boat!"

"Snot," teased Marian.

Alexa just smiled. "I never had a toy boat."

She'd been the most financially deprived of them all.

"Neither did I," Calli said, sauntering over to watch the raising.

"Neither did Elizabeth or I," Bri said.

These women, like sisters she'd never had, understood Raine more than her brothers ever had, lifted her spirits. Along with Faucon's touch. Their connection was steadier, stronger, since they'd shared the sail.

She smiled up at him. He looked startled, took his hand away and walked toward the "boat."

Raine shrugged and followed, took Corbeau's hand, then held her free one out to Faucon.

"Maybe we—" Alexa started.

"Not now, Alexa. We don't know the Song," Marian said.

Raine glanced at them. "I don't, either."

"Of course you do," Corbeau rumbled. "Better'n Faucon or me. You've been building ships all your life."

She met his eyes, so like Faucon's chocolate-brown.

"It's in your blood and bone and Song," Corbeau said.

Faucon took her hand and she felt a zip of energy go around their closed circle. There was the attraction between her and Faucon, which they both ignored. She heard Corbeau's personal Song better, sounding much like her brothers' would. A solid, practical man who loved the sea.

Dragging in a breath, she put away her feelings and stared at the sticks arranged slooplike on the ground. The three of them surrounded it.

"Focus," Corbeau said.

He meant magic, Power, of course, but she heard the echo of her brothers', "Concentrate, Raine, don't let your mind wander."

Then Corbeau began the ship-raising Song again, and she *did* know it. The notes she should Sing came bubbling to her lips and fell from her mouth droplet by droplet without thought. From her link with the men, she learned the words. Words that referenced the ocean and waves and wind and sail and the Power of working on and with the sea. Words she recalled hearing when she was a potgirl…but not often. Those who frequented that tavern were more interested in drink and sex and games, the occasional story.

The men's strong tones pulled her from that depressing memory, brought her to the here and now.

She heard the distant bustle of people in Faucon's castle,

preparing food and chambers for guests. She heard the first trio of stars blink brightly into the deepening blue sky.

She heard the Songs of people who cared for her enveloping her.

Raine ended on a high note, a little sad that their melody was done.

Both Corbeau and Faucon squeezed her hands. "Look," they said at the same moment.

She glanced down and was only a little surprised to see a small, perfect sloop. She'd missed the raising!

"Don't worry." Faucon's smile was almost sad. "You'll get plenty of practice. Your warship isn't as simple as this sloop."

Alexa squealed and Raine and the men dropped their hands. The Swordmarshall swooped in and got her ship. She grinned. "It's mine."

Bastien, her husband, who was leaning against a tree, smiled brilliantly at Faucon. "We'll be wanting a room with a large tub so my lady can play with her *new* toy."

Much snickering at Alexa's surprised expression.

Faucon bowed with a flourish. "I'll make sure of it."

There was a flurry of wings and a volaran landed delicately among them. Atop the winged horse was Koz. He lifted a large padded velvet bag. "I'm here and I have Raine's mirrors."

Faucon stepped farther away from Raine as Koz dismounted. "Dinner, first," he said.

Too late for Raine to prefer Koz. During the night before and the time with him today, she was falling for Faucon.

After dinner they all gathered in one of Faucon's sitting rooms on the castle's main floor. Or all the humans did. The feycoocus were off on their own mysterious business.

Along one wall of the room were French doors, looking out into a night spangled with brilliant stars and moon. Just beyond those doors swished the everlasting tide.

The room was comfortable with faded orange-and-red patterned rugs and well-worn leather chairs in a butterscotch color.

As always when working with his mirrors, Koz had settled on the rug and placed the velvet bag beside him. Raine sat on the floor, too, but gave him plenty of elbow room.

Koz drew out the mirror, then unfolded it to gasps of amazement. First it was a triptych, opening like a triple wallet, one side to the left and one to the right, all backed with what Raine recognized as soulsucker skin. Then Koz flipped up a mirror to the top and down the bottom until the whole array looked like a cross.

"I'm pleased to say these are the best magic mirrors ever made." He gave a deprecating cough. "Probably couldn't have been done without my advances in the field."

"Better the mirror magic field than the battlefield," Marian said, patting her brother on his shoulder.

Koz switched his gaze from the others to meet Raine's eyes. "I've calibrated them to the mirrors now in your brothers' and father's homes."

Huge feeling rose in her, so big she couldn't speak. To be able to see her family! Even if she couldn't communicate with them like Bri did, she'd know they were safe and happy. A horrible noise came from her, a groan, then she was heaving with sobs so deep she could barely breathe.

Bri came to her left and wrapped her arm around her, and with Calli to her right they held her as she wept. She cried as she hadn't since she'd arrived on Lladrana.

"You're safe, you're valued, you're safe now," Calli murmured. Raine let her body shake, all her emotions out.

To their credit, the men hadn't stampeded to the door, but all except Koz had withdrawn to the far corner of the room—backs against the wall, protecting each other? Raine snorted a chuckle and realized she'd been wrong when Faucon handed her a large white linen handkerchief to blow her nose.

She did and wiggled a bit to let the other women know that the crying was over. From their supportive mind-tones, she knew that each one of them had suffered through bouts of tears.

Separation anxiety, Marian sent, matter-of-factly.

Separation from our own world, Bri said, *and my parents and twin.* Her bondmate, Sevair, strode over to pick her up in his strong stonemason's arms and cradle her.

So half of Raine's vision was unblocked. Faucon, the handsome hunk, was crouched before her. When she met his eyes, he said, "I have double-checked with the ship's captain who has your stalker in his crew. Being unused to hard work and of a nature to boast, the man is not faring well."

"Too bad," Alexa said. She'd risen from a couch and stood, chin out, hand on her baton. She glanced at Raine. "Better than if he was here. No future for him in Lladrana."

"No," Koz said. He'd moved away down the rug and was fiddling with his mirrors, which reminded Raine.

"Koz, I ordered and paid for your hats—"

He looked up at her with a grin. "Thanks, the feycoocus have already delivered them."

They must have gotten the hats from the tailor. No one would deny the magical beings.

She coughed. As if that was a signal the rest of the men sauntered back to drape themselves over or lean on various pieces of furniture near their ladies. Looking at Koz, she said, "The mirrors were going to be delivered with something that would make my guys keep them in their houses for three generations?"

Koz smiled and it was charming and her pulse might have fluttered once upon a time. "Ayes." He reached into a little belt pouch, withdrew his hand and opened his fingers. She goggled at huge diamonds. They must have been four carats each.

Raine blew her nose again, better than gaping at the jewels. "I can never repay you!"

"Raine," Koz said, "I have more riches here than I or any children I might have will ever spend. Even in four generations, or maybe even in ten."

Faucon glanced at the diamonds, then at Raine. "These gems are costly in your world?"

"Ayes," Raine said, still staring at the beautiful facets shooting rainbows.

Faucon shook his head. "They are common here, not worth much."

"Huh?" Raine stared at him.

Chuckling, Koz said, "I can barely buy a bit of land with these. A mistake bringing them from Earth. Your father and each brother got two. So what was a huge payoff to your father and brothers is actually covered by the hats." He lifted up a finger. "One like Bastien designed, low crown, extra-wide brim, of soulsucker—" he lifted another finger "—and a cowboy hat. Hand-made to fit."

"Thanks," Raine said, gulping back more threatening tears. "About your time and effort—"

Koz waved a negligent hand, eyed Faucon and scooted back over to give her a firm kiss that left her lips throbbing.

She stared at him, then leaned back, smiled.

He winked. "A good kiss from a pretty girl is enough, 'specially since the project itself was damn fascinating." Leaning over, he snagged the mirror array and velvet bag.

"Bossgond and I had a good time exploring Best Haven. Nice town. Your map of the main streets and the Pearsons' building was perfect, of course. We addressed the package to the senior Pearson and moved it to his office. Good idea signing Judge Philbert's name to that note, Alexa."

Bri chuckled. "He's a U.S. District Court judge and has clout."

Raine nodded. "The Pearsons had been courting him, invitations to the country club, the yacht club." She shrugged. "You know."

"Sure," Koz said. "Now, the mirrors." He straightened the array. "The center is your father's mirror. The left is your oldest brother John's." Again the self-deprecating smile. "I couldn't figure out the birth order of the rest, but the right is Simon's, the top is Terry's, and the bottom is Nathan's."

He hesitated, then said diffidently, "This is the original set, but I made a duplicate and left it at Bossgond's Tower, where it should be safe enough." Koz grimaced. "In payment for that and helping you I did have to give him the access word to your father's mirror. I hope that's all right."

Raine swallowed and bobbed her head. When she spoke her voice was crusty. "If that was his price, that's fine, and I'm glad there's another set." She touched a corner of the mirror.

Koz said, "When the mirrors are live we have video and audio. The procedure for these mirrors is the same as Bri's.

There's an access word to initiate the spell to see through the mirror. One for each person—" he cleared his throat "—or household. Your brothers John and Terry are married."

"I was at John's wedding," Raine said, making an effort to keep her voice steady. "I was taking Granny Fran's mirror to Terry as an engagement gift."

She must have sounded shaky. Faucon came and sat near her.

"Right," Koz said. "Anyway, I gave the mirrors access words that you'd remember, based on what I saw when the mirrors were mounted. Here's the list." He tossed her a small piece of paper. The phrases were written roughly, as if his Lladranan hand formed English awkwardly.

The first, for her father, was "Follow your heart," and Raine sniffled. That was a sampler her mother had cross-stitched when she was a bride. The piece of embroidery had hung in the family living room for as long as Raine could remember.

The rest of the words made her smile. "Yo, ho, ho" for Simon's pirate ship in a bottle. "Bottle of rum" must mean Nathan had put in that bar in his living room as planned. She swallowed. "Quiambog" and "Cos Cob" meant John and Terry still had maps on their walls. Their wives sailed, too. "Thank you," Raine whispered thickly. Faucon reached over and took her hand. His fingers were warm and the Song that spun between them was nearly painful in its intensity.

"Right," Koz said again. "If you want to try to communicate with someone, you tap the mirror and say, 'Testing, testing, testing.'" His grin came crooked. "If they actually don't jump outta their skin and reply or whatever, to end the session you say, 'Signing off.'"

"That won't happen." She glanced at Bri. "Any way your

folks could visit and convince—" Raine held up a hand and answered her own question. "No. My guys wouldn't listen."

She looked at the mirrors, drew in a big breath, exhaled. Then she squeezed Faucon's hand and let it go to hunch over the array. Who to check first? Not her father. She looked at Marian. "Time's the same there, right?"

"Ayes," Marian said. She sat in a loveseat with Jaquar.

"Perhaps we should leave." Jaquar stood.

"No, I don't mind," Raine said.

"It's not only you," Alexa said, "it's your father's and your brothers' privacy." She frowned. "Bad enough Bossgond is a Peeping Tom."

The image of a boney old man peering into a mirror, eyes wide with apersonal curiosity, seemed to strike them all at once and there were a series of snorts and chuckles.

"Please stay," Raine said.

"Okay." Jaquar used the English word. He drifted, casually, over to the mirrors so he could see what was going on during this experiment. Fooling no one since they could all hear his personal Song pick up beat. Marian drifted, too.

Alexa strode over.

"Good thing we're not testing the two-way video. Having loads of people loom over you could freak a guy out," Koz said.

Touching Nathan's mirror—his mind was the most flexible—Raine muttered, "Bottle of rum" under her breath.

The mirror flicked on, showing a masculine room of cream-colored walls, a huge TV screen on one wall, a green leather recliner and, straight ahead, a multitude of bottles on the bar.

"Is that liquor?" Faucon asked.

"It certainly is," Koz said genially.

Nathan's apartment wasn't large and Raine knew he wasn't

home. She tapped it again with another whispered "Bottle of rum" to close the video, then tried her other brothers in turn. It hurt to see things from home, the map of Connecticut, the silver vase she'd given John and his wife for a wedding gift. So she spent little time at her brothers'.

Finally she tapped her father's mirror and whispered, "Follow your heart."

The mirror came on. Her entire family was sitting on the curving sofa facing the fireplace. Holding drinks and diamonds.

17

Raine's father swirled his rum and Coke and stared at two diamonds twinkling in his hands. "Damndest thing," he said in a way that meant he'd said it more than once. His hair was all gray now and Raine grieved for the vanished brown that had been the same color as hers, for the lines engraved deeper in his face. A tiredness showed in his eyes that was carried throughout his body.

John was holding his wife's hand—they were solid, both of them individually and as a unit. He glanced at a folded sheet of paper that looked stiffer than most and Raine realized with a little shock that it was Lladranan-made. Her mouth dried. Something here *had* made it there. Oh, the mirrors, too, but she couldn't actually *see* this mirror, only out of it. She knew it was rectangular, width longer than the height, and hung over the mantel where an old mirror had always been.

John said doubtfully, "They say truth is stranger than fiction."

"They say," Nathan agreed. "But this whole damn thing sounds fishier than the cove at low tide."

A small moan escaped Raine. All of this looked, sounded, so familiar. She put the handkerchief to her mouth to muffle any noise so she could hear better. Faucon slipped his arm around her shoulders and she leaned into his muscular body.

"You think she really is all right?" Terry's wife asked.

"Yeah, I do," Terry said firmly. He'd always been the most optimistic. "She looked okay in the photos."

"She looked like she was recovering from a sickness in the photos," Raine's father said.

"I don't know about all this," Simon, the pessimist, said.

Nathan stretched his legs. "Old Preston was too cheerful."

"That Trenton Philbert had him snowed," Simon agreed. "I always thought there was something off about that man."

"He was a good client," Raine's father said.

Nathan said, "Maybe we should have a sit-down with him."

The doorbell rang. The Lladranan men looked puzzled at the sound. "Our doorharp," explained Marian.

Terry's wife went up and got it. "Judge Philbert," she said, surprised, stepping back and letting him in.

Raine's father got heavily to his feet. "Speak of the devil." He still offered his hand.

The hair on the back of Raine's neck rose and everyone on her side of the mirror stilled. The men and Alexa stared at the judge with a predatory light in their eyes.

Here was a man with answers. Raine's family seemed to think that, too. Nathan made him a martini.

Though Philbert was dressed casually, his clothes were

tailored. Raine had always thought he was much more hand-some and sophisticated than his silly-sounding name.

Then he glanced at the mirror, his gaze fixed, and he stared. He lifted a hand as if acknowledging the Lladranans and turned to the Lindley men.

"He knows!" Koz said. "He fucking knows about the mirrors."

"More," Jaquar said, tapping Koz's shoulder. "He knows we're watching now."

"By. The. Song," Faucon breathed.

Philbert propped himself against the mantel near the mirror and they saw his profile.

"I thought that you didn't totally buy the 'sailing accident, amnesia, wealthy Swedish lover' story," Philbert said smoothly.

"The sailing accident bit, yeah," Nathan said, running his hand through his dark hair. It was almost odd to see strong people without streaks of Power in their hair. "We found pieces of her boat last year after that freak winter storm."

"But you must admit the rest is difficult," Simon said. "You know anything more?"

Philbert shifted as if he put his hands in his pockets. He replied mildly, "Would you believe that she has been, ah, co-opted by an agency that will remain nameless to design a state-of-the-art stealth ship?"

Bri said, "Ohmygod, Uncle Trent sounds so sincere." Bri moved to watch the man who'd been a big part of her life.

"That's because he's telling the truth," Marian said. "He knows the truth. I wonder how?"

"The Singer has a mole on Earth," Koz said.

Raine's brother Nathan was pounding his fist in his hand. "I knew it! Raine's definitely second-millennium cutting edge.

Her work with alloys..." Nathan shook his head. "Her notes were far ahead of anything I'd seen before."

"They'll believe *that* easier than our amnesiac love story?" Alexa sounded offended.

"They like spy fiction," Raine said drily.

Raine's father came within a couple of inches of the judge, getting into his face. The men were about the same size, but her dad was larger and more muscular. "You telling the truth this time?"

"I didn't lie the last time." Philbert waved to the letter. "If you run a graphology analysis, you'll find that isn't my signature. One of Raine's friends, I think, trying to reassure you. What I told you was the truth."

"You've seen Raine?" her dad barked.

"No. But I've been assured that she is fine."

"Now," John said. "She was sick. I know my sister when she looks sick and she *was* sick."

"That is what my source tells me," Philbert said.

Questions peppered him and the judge raised his hands. "My unofficial, under-the-table source who should not be talking."

"Is there a man?" asked Terry, totally surprising Raine. She wouldn't have thought he'd care.

Raine felt the weight of Faucon's arm on her shoulders.

"There usually is under such circumstances," Philbert said.

"What circumstances?" Raine's father asked.

"Intense working situations."

Raine's dad kept his stare on the judge. "Is it dangerous?"

The judge hesitated an instant too long. Raine's father grabbed a fistful of shirt. The judge answered, "Building the ship isn't dangerous. Piloting it in the action would be."

"Will Raine be the pilot?" Raine could barely hear her father.

"I don't think anyone knows, even Raine," the judge said steadily. "But she has the best-of-the-best special teams guarding her."

"That would be me." Alexa preened and laughter broke a little of the tension.

"Dad…" John put his hand on Raine's father's arm and the older man dropped his grip, not that Philbert had appeared the least intimidated. Raine's father turned away.

"Raine won't pilot," Terry said. "She's a big weenie."

"Thanks, bro," Raine muttered.

"What's a weenie?" asked one of the Lladranan guys.

"What's the timeline?" asked Raine's father.

Another hesitation by the judge. Raine's father whirled back to face him, the mirror, his face stark, his eyes grieving. His expression was a blow to Raine, and she moaned.

"We're not sure of the timeline. That depends on Raine and the Ship. It will go down before the end of the year. Maybe even next month."

"Next month," Raine's father repeated.

"We prefer not to hear 'go down' with regards to a ship, particularly one we've built," Terry said.

Raine's father tossed back the last of his drink and when he turned his gaze back to the judge he asked, "Why Raine?"

"Because she's the best."

"Yes, she is." Her father threw his glass in the fireplace. It shattered with an ugly noise. "She'll pilot. It's her ship."

Singer's Abbey

That evening Jikata and the Singer held the dreamquest of a female Chevalier who wished to become a Marshall.

The Chevalier's Song, dreams and images were dark. She wept during the process and Jikata felt an odd tug as she watched the woman—girl, really—cry. She was lying on her back, fingers twined tightly in the Singer's and Jikata's grip.

"Why do you wish to test?" the Singer said in a soft voice that the hypnotized woman answered.

"Because my lover tested and became a Marshall, and will be going through the trials." The girl flailed her arms.

"But you do not want to go through the trials."

"No, it's suicide. Talk is, it's a grand adventure, but it's suicide." More tears a Friend wiped away with a soft cloth as the woman's head thrashed back and forth.

"You could stay," the Singer insinuated, rather evil-snake-like, Jikata thought.

"No." The woman calmed. "No. She's my Shield. I'm her Sword. We're a Pair."

"But not pairbonded," the Singer said.

Jikata tried to keep up with the strange words, concepts.

"Not yet," the woman said, "but if we bond, I think it will be better. Ayes, it will." Now a note of determination.

"My apprentice will awaken you now," the Singer said, and withdrew her fingers from the girl's.

Jikata set her teeth at the title, but did so. The young woman sat up from the mat of rugs on the floor with a watery smile. Jikata and a Friend helped her to her feet, the Singer had already gone to her throne. Taking the warm, wet cloth from the Friend, the Chevalier wiped her face, kept the smile on, though her personal Song screamed she was nervous. She ran one hand down her scaled armor. There were odd-colored stains on it, along with old blood. "Did I pass?" she asked brightly.

"It is not a matter of passing or failing," the Singer said. "It is a matter of sensing the future and deciding how to act."

The young woman lifted her chin, her mouth was mulish. "I've decided how to act."

"Then I will tell you what I told your partner," the Singer said. "You are a Marshall now. Pairbond."

The girl broke into a smile. *"Merci!"*

"Do not undertake the trials. Your partner has a rare gift and could contribute more if she remained behind."

A low breath whooshed from the Chevalier. "The fence posts, she's canny in drawing horrors to make fence posts."

"The fence is not yet whole. Some must guard the northern border while others are gone," the Singer said. "Do you not think Alyeka knows your Shield's worth?"

"Ttho…ayes…ttho." The ex-Chevalier threw her hands up. "I don't know."

"Speak to Alyeka."

Now the girl was glancing at Jikata from the corners of her eyes, but she bowed to the Singer, deeply, and only a little less deeply to Jikata. "I'll speak to Alyeka," she said, jaw set. "She's a little scary." The new Marshall looked at Jikata more fully as she walked to the door. "Exotiques are so Powerful. They are all scary."

All the Friends accompanied her when she left.

Slowly Jikata turned to look at the Singer, definitely time for answers. The woman had her eyes closed and looked unexpectedly tired, her lined face reminded Jikata of the texture of crepe, as if it might be tissue thin. She appeared older than Ishi had been and for the first time Jikata wondered just how many years the Singer had. She'd always been so intense.

Then the Singer opened her eyes and pierced Jikata with a hot, bright gaze that stopped her breath like a force of nature.

"My Thomas taught me to count in your language. I am one hundred and thirty years old."

A tiny gasp caught in Jikata's throat.

The Singer's smile was as sharp as her eyes. "You have never met someone as old as I?"

"No. Ttho."

With an incline of her head, the Singer said, "It is a great age, even here where we are bigger, stronger, older and more Powerful and beautiful than you." Her gaze traveled down and up Jikata. "Though you have possibilities. I am weary. Your questions can wait until another day."

Jikata had opened her mouth, but respect for age had been instilled in her and she could not deny the Singer since Ishi had returned to her thoughts. It suddenly struck Jikata that she was missing Ishi's wake, would miss the funeral, and whatever daily memorials there would be…she'd been so busy here…

So busy pretending on so many levels—denying Ishi's death?—that she hadn't thought. But the funeral would be long past, and any of Ishi's old friends who were still living would think Jikata a totally ungrateful person not to show up. That hurt arrowed to her heart and she breathed through it.

Not her fault. She hadn't been present because this old woman had Summoned her.

For some purpose Jikata had yet to learn. But as she raised her gaze to meet the Singer's forceful one, Jikata knew the Singer, this live old woman, needed her. Ishi, if she'd ever needed Jikata of late, had not indicated it by the lift of a finger, let alone calling her. The needs of the living must always precede the needs of the dead.

Jikata gave a little curtsy. She was wearing a damask robe, richly embroidered and it was heavier than most fabrics. She'd loved it, but now felt stiff. Stiff from hurt, from anger, from confusion. "Until tomorrow," she said.

The Singer closed her eyes again and clicked her tongue and several Friends hurried in. Jikata walked out. Her escort of a bodyguard-type man and the housekeeper of her building were there. Both would ignore her if she asked questions.

Chasonette swooped down and lit on Jikata's shoulder, gave her a bird-peck kiss, then flew up to perch on a gargoyle a few yards ahead of them, and tilted her head. *You are weary and sad. I will Sing for you.*

The bird did and that Song and the soundtrack of Jikata's life rose to fill her, gave her peace. She let out a soundless sigh, concentrated on keeping her carriage proud.

I will Sing you home and Sing you asleep. Music is the cure for all.

Jikata smiled, let the music of the growing things, the buildings, the people, surround her. Music was wonderful.

Ishi had never been able to appreciate that. She'd been tone deaf.

Tears trickled down Jikata's face.

Creusse Crest

Faucon walked Raine to her room and she was glad of his undemanding company. Servants were moving around, preparing the castle for night, helping the retiring Exotiques and their men, or getting it ready for morning. She didn't know what all. But it was a lot quieter than being with a bunch of people, or watching a bunch of guys.

Just having Faucon hold her hand and match her steps was soothing. She still got a little sparkle inside from him and his Song, and even his nearness, but it wasn't overwhelming. Somehow the events of the day and night had given her more inner balance. Maybe it was the time on the water, maybe it was just that so many experiences had crowded in this day that she was numb, perfectly happy to sort them all out later.

Then they were at her door and she glanced up at him. God, he was handsome. Steady brown eyes, sculpted mouth, strong jaw. Looking just like a nobleman should.

"I'm not captaining that ship for the invasion," she said.

A line formed between his brows. "We all know that. You've made that clear, including tonight. You are free to choose."

"Ayes."

"But you are designing and building the Ship."

"Ayes."

Keeping his gaze on hers, he lifted her fingers and brushed a kiss over them and suddenly the sexual attraction was there, rushing through her, heating her skin from the inside. She put her hands on his shoulders and somehow the floor beneath her feet began to rock like the deck of a boat and she hung on tight.

18

Faucon bent his head, closer, closer, until she scented the liquor and dessert on his breath. She yearned for his taste, had for longer than she'd admit. Her neck tilted back and her lips parted. A whisper away, he said, "It's not just the innate attraction, Raine. It's just you."

"I know."

Then he pressed his lips on hers and she swept her tongue across his mouth and was lost. He gathered her close and it was just where she'd wanted to be, caught safe in someone's arms, in *his* arms. The lovely sparkle went hot. She opened her lips, tasted his tongue in her mouth and knew that finally, something she'd needed all along was within her grasp.

He was strong, and hard, and his Song thundered through her like the surf. Her arms curved under his, around his shoulders as she let him taste her. He angled the kiss deeper and she clung. He was a shelter, a harbor. She could almost believe he was hers, her man.

He trembled and it was sweet and heady. His hands stroking her back was the touch she'd missed all this time.

Then his mouth tore from hers and she moaned. He kissed the sweep of her cheeks, her brows, her temples. Lips hovering above her own, he made a rough sound and stepped back.

She let him go. It seemed he was always pulling back and she was always letting him go.

But, like all the other times, this time it was the right thing to do.

Standing on tiptoe, she kissed his chin.

"Raine…"

"Ssshhh." She stepped back and came up against the door, beyond it she could hear the ocean, or perhaps that was her own tide of blood. She found the doorknob with her fingers, kept her eyes on his. "Thank you, Faucon. *Merci.*"

He jerked a small nod, his fingers came up and touched her face. "Sweet dreams."

"You, too." She opened the door and backed in and fell on the bed. She didn't sleep.

Fool, fool, fool! Faucon ran lightly through his castle, knowing how to avoid everyone. Suppressing his Song, his turbulent emotions that threatened to burst out of him in a cacophony alerting all that he'd been a fool.

Raine would be going home after the Ship was raised, he wasn't deaf to that fact, had agreed with those who'd bet in the Nom de Nom against her staying. Despite what her father said. That man didn't know this Raine, she'd changed from the pretty young woman he'd seen in an image hanging on her father's wall.

Faucon was a fool to want her in his bed, and especially in his heart, which was in bloody shreds from the loss of Elizabeth and Broullard. He flung himself through a door to the outside, couldn't prevent a rough curse, shed his vest, shirt, undershirt as he ran until he reached the smooth spot on the cliff and dove into the sea.

The impact was hard on his fists, the water sliced cold along his body. He let his breath out in a cleansing scream as he plunged. When he ran out of air, he shot to the surface, gasped for breath between wave ripples, shook his head so his hair was out of his face. And saw two pure white ducks with yellow beaks and one fuzzy duckling paddling serenely near them.

He stared at the three feycoocus: Sinafinal, Tuckerinal and Enerin.

A little cheep came from the duckling, Enerin, Raine's companion, a lilting Song. *Why do you fight your destiny so?*

Sinafinal gave her child an admonitory peck. *Because he is human.*

Tuckerinal, the male, swam close. *Raine will stay if she loves you.*

"She has family at home. I saw those pictures of ships on the walls, the metal ones with two hulls, near her image. We can't give her that challenge here."

Snorting, Tuckerinal said mentally, *She has plenty of challenge here.*

Faucon couldn't argue with that.

She will stay if she loves you, Tuckerinal insisted.

Faucon didn't believe that.

Sinafinal came and rubbed her feathery body against his face. *You have lost your faith. I am sorry.*

Peeping, Enerin said, *You must find it again. Know that she can stay, that you can love her, that you can destroy the Dark together.*

His eyes stung. From the ocean.

Tuckerinal gave him a look Faucon couldn't decipher.

"A lot of that going on, tonight," the male feycoocu said. "Here and on Earth."

Faucon rubbed his face and swam to the pier.

He'd ruined his boots.

He was falling in love with Raine, might already love her. One more lost love would shatter his heart forever.

She was waiting for him on the dock, wearing a long robe that shimmered in the moonlight. He climbed from the water and shivered. Her gaze was as deep and fathomless as the sea. Her tongue touched her lips nervously.

Their Songs had mingled and the links between them were stronger than ever, but her Song had a little hitch that betrayed those nerves, no matter how serene she appeared.

He wanted her, again and forever.

"I couldn't sleep." Her hands pleated the sides of her gown.

She was beautiful beyond compare in the moonlight. When he said nothing, she lifted her chin. "You were all churned up, and so was I." She swallowed. "I want you, have wanted you from the moment we met. Is it wrong to wish for pleasure and comfort and companionship with a man you want in times like these?"

He couldn't think. He should definitely say "ayes" in the answer to her question, "ttho," to her…or was it the other way around? He wished he was anywhere else.

A lilt of a woman's teasing laughter came from one of the castle's open windows and he was swamped with loneliness. Not just for friends, but for a lover who understood him, an intimate companion. In the past months he'd lost his lover and his father-friend. He needed…he needed. And he needed Raine. For herself, the person whose Song he'd finally heard yesterday and today. The friend-woman-companion he'd found on the sea, sailed with and meshed with.

Raine's eyes widened, her face fell into those soft, sad lines that hurt him. "It's not time," she whispered, as she made an awkward gesture. "Still too early or too late." She turned.

And the sea breeze flattened her nightgown against her and his body reacted as usual, even encased in cold trousers. His blood wasn't cold.

"Wait," he croaked. He couldn't step away this time, couldn't protect his heart, had to trust the Song. His breath whooshed out and when he inhaled the air was delicious, freeing. All the masks he'd used with her fell away. Denial was over. "I want you, too."

Overhead three seabirds called out and he thought a cheerful blessing settled over him—and Raine. "I want you, too." He slicked water from his hair. He glanced up and down the pier. There was his yacht and the boathouse. Both would have towels.

The boathouse had a better bed.

"I'm having a hard time knowing what I feel, knowing what I truly want." And those words that came from him emphasized his foolishness. Was denial back? What was foolishness, giving in to his and her need, or running away from her?

But she smiled. "Thank you."

"What?" He was incredulous.

"Why should I be the only one floundering around in a net of tangled emotions? Thank you." She took a gliding step toward him. "You are the most beautiful man."

The breeze of the sea was offset by a flush of embarrassment. "No—"

Her delicately arched brows raised. She touched outside her eyes. "To me you are the most handsome of all." She held out her hand. "And the kindest."

He felt even warmer, hunched a shoulder, didn't move a step.

"That responsibility bred into you," she said, and walked up to him, took his cold, wet hand in her own. She glanced at the castle, sighed, her mouth turned down before she said, "I'd love to go there, but we are always aware of the future, aren't we, Faucon? That's why there's been so much friction between us, we both know there will come a time when I'll leave."

Her hand was hot, as hot as the licks of desire heating him, his blood pooling below his belt, as fast and strident as his Song. He could barely hear her words as his body angled to hers, wooing her with brushes of skin against skin.

"And when I leave—" Her voice broke and he sensed it was from that confusion of emotions in her…sorrow for what might come, grief at what was past. Once again he lifted her fingers to his mouth, kissed her hand gently, tasted Raine and the sea.

She quivered, shook her head as if to clear it. "You will see me in places I was, after I am gone. So I will leave you your private castle rooms. You'll not see me there."

He didn't know what to say. She, too, was kind.

And terrible with her knowledge.

"Come to bed with me in the boathouse, Faucon. Where you sheltered me that first night we met. We will find a harbor together."

And desirable.

Then she hesitated. "Perhaps it will be worse for the both of us if we do this—"

"No." The time for questions was over. His fingers trembled as he tilted her pale face up so he could study it, wished he could see the green of her eyes. She didn't want heartache, neither did he—who did? "This time between us is meant to be. Don't deny us this."

She smiled with her lips but her eyes held sorrow. "No."

He stiffened at the hurt, then her hands covered his that were cupping her face. "No, I won't deny this."

Raine felt his hand warm in hers, but the rest of his body quivered and she thought it was more from the chill of the breeze than desire. Concentrating, she thought of hot Mediterranean winds, and a low rasp of tuneful notes came to mind. She sent *that* heat through her hand to warm him. He stilled and she looked up into his eyes—serious eyes though she'd heard he'd been lighthearted once.

She stood on tiptoe and kissed him on the lips as lightly as the last droplets of sea spray. His mouth opened, his tongue swept out and her brain went fuzzy. She didn't want that, wanted to keep this easy and gentle and tender as he had their kiss before. If she glanced down, she'd see his body wanted hers and just the thought of that had her body readying, too. But now was not the time for fierce and mindless sex.

What was between them should never be simply fierce and mindless sex.

So she led him the few yards to the door, hummed the small spell to unlock and open it. The scent of the place—seaside and fresh cleaning—took her back to the night she had saved herself and he and Blossom had come and flown her away from her old life on a moonlit ride.

"No," he said thickly. "No. You don't need to remember."

But she did. The attack and fight the next morning.

"No." Faucon swung her up in his arms, held her close to his warm body. One of her arms went naturally around his neck, the other slid along his lightly furred chest to his heart that beat with a rhythm of passion she couldn't deny.

She let him carry her up the steep path, but as he went to the gardens, she wiggled and said, "I want to be an equal partner, Faucon."

So he slid her down his body and her own thrilled to the strength and muscularity of him, his need.

Again she linked her fingers in his, glanced around to see they were near the ponds. One little boat showed white sails as it moved on the water.

She kept her eyes slightly unfocused so she could pretend the pools were just pools, water and land, and not maps. Beyond the land was green and beautiful, the plants lush from all the cool rain of the spring and summer, the tangy wind off the ocean mixed with other fragrances that added piquancy to the soft night. Leaves rustled from trees, rising in verdant levels from small fruit-bearers to tall and thick-boled ancients. On the opposite side of the garden was Faucon's castle, appearing like a fantasy of bold lines and turrets and warm yellow squares of windows, with the slight murmuring of distant voices.

All her senses increased. Most of all, she was aware of the man walking beside her and her own throbbing pulse. "You have a lovely home." Her words sounded breathless.

Faucon stopped, looked down at her, smiling. "I do." He bent and pressed a small kiss on her lips. "Thank you."

His arm tightened for an instant, then he relaxed it, though his heart had picked up a beat. His gaze lingered on her and she felt her breasts swell, her limbs go heavy.

Again he leaned down, this time kissing her temple, then he shook his head. "I've tried to avoid my fate for too long."

Her spine stiffened. "I don't care to be thought of as part of your fate."

He slid his arm from her waist to link fingers, just held her hand, and her throat tightened. The connection they'd established during their time on the water, that link of joy of wind and water and sail, the laughter, the learning—her of Lladrana, and both of them of each other—unfurled between them. It was a shining bond like she had with no other. Small sexual tugs came from him to her, or was she the one doing the tugging?

He met her eyes, then his gaze dropped to her lips, his thumb caressed the back of her hand. "You would be the best of my fate."

She shook her head, but didn't pull away from his calloused grasp, kept in pace with him. "I'm not."

His smile curved deeper. "You felt the connection between us, the attraction flowing one to the other and back immediately, as I did."

She didn't want to think, analyze—couldn't they just pleasure each other? Not a phrase she would have used on Earth, but somehow it fit the night. And the man.

Breath unsteady, she said, "You feel that way for all Exotiques."

His smile faded. "Perhaps so, but the intensity between us has always been...more." His grip tightened a little. "Believe that, Raine. I deluded myself with Elizabeth." Now his expression turned grim, worse and worse. "I won't lie and say that I didn't love her—I did. And if she'd stayed, we'd have made a good marriage." He let his breath out on a soft sigh. "But what we had at our best was weak compared to what you and I had from our very first meeting."

Then, he opened himself and his Song flooded her, strong and male and fabulous, making her tremble. Her mind swam and she instinctively leaned toward him, her Song *reached* for his, found his, meshed.

When his soft lips touched hers, all her senses focused on their mouths, their mingling breath. Her body heated, needy, wanting more of him touching her than just his mouth, his linked fingers. She opened her lips and took him in, felt the slight roughness of his tongue, like the slight roughness of his hands still holding hers. There was only sensation. She surrendered to the desire for this man that she'd fought, that she'd thought she was alone in feeling, and finally *knew* he'd wanted her all along. Had fought her...resisted *fate*...until this moment.

Her senses throbbed with stimulus. His taste was of man and crème brûlée and some sort of liqueur, a taste she didn't know that she'd craved but was exactly right. He dropped her hands and she could press herself against his hard body, slide her arms around his neck, let herself arch so she could feel more of him, the solid breadth of his chest, his strong thighs, his thick sex.

She moaned and his hands went to her butt and lifted her to fit her against him and it felt so good she strained against him, rubbed. He made a rough sound, moved his tongue against hers, then broke the kiss and set her aside. Her knees wobbled and he supported her with a hand to her elbow. She was panting, her vision blurred, her body pulsing with need. "Faucon." It was a gasp.

"Not here, there's a place…over there," he said between ragged breaths. He lifted her into his arms and she was against his chest and she could slip her hand around his nape and feel the tickle of his hair against her hand. That set off sparks again. "Hurry," she said.

He groaned, ran lightly across the ground to an odd-looking domed structure that appeared to be made entirely of vines. The bower was covered with pretty white five-petaled flowers, as if indicating a special place only for lovers.

"Flowers," she breathed, and he understood her.

"No, they were not there before, they're night blooming."

Then the scent of them came to her, sweet temptation, a light, sensual fragrance.

When she spoke the words, she wanted to cry, but they had to be said. "I'm going back."

19

"I know," Faucon whispered. "My fate, but we'll have a wonderful time until you do."

Her mind swam away again and she felt his hands on her, untying the gathered ribbon of her nightgown above her breasts, sliding it down until she was naked. The soft summer air against her legs, now the scent of the ocean. Perfect.

She fumbled with his pants. Damn dreethskin, why did he wear it?

He laughed shortly, answered her question. "It kept you from noticing I was aroused when I was with you."

"Fighting fate," she breathed. For one clear instant she wondered what this act would do to *her* fate, her resolve to return home. But then his hands were over her breasts and nothing was as important as his touch. She arched and moaned.

He muttered something and pulled away.

No! She jumped toward him before she saw him unbuckling the waistband of his pants, stripping trousers and loincloth down until he stood nude before her.

Definitely the most beautiful man she'd ever seen.

Her hands curved over his shoulders to bring him down. She felt scars, round raised bumps, a slice, and something she'd been guarding inside herself burst through a locked box and swept through her like a fresh rain of her name.

He grasped her hands, set her on her back on the thick, soft grass. His intense gaze met hers, he was biting his lip.

"Can't," he gasped. "Can't control myself."

She set her hands on his face, felt beard, a little rough like all of him except his manner. "Please don't," she said.

A wild noise came from him, sent their Songs into a drumming beat, and he surged inside her.

She screamed at the pleasure and let the tide of passion take her to break like wild surf against the shores of ecstasy.

Sometime later Faucon rolled until she was atop him and she lay, satisfied, listening to the rapid beat of his heart slowly diminishing to an even thud. She fit on him.

"I'm taking you back to my rooms," he said. "I want to spend as much time together as possible...."

"Not just now. The night is so beautiful, this place is so lovely." The fragrance of the flowers was all around them, the breeze brought a hint of the ocean. She could see the huge scarves of galaxies in the sky, and the white moon. "So many stars. Lladranan night is brighter than home."

"I didn't know that."

"No?" She realized she'd said the word in English, but was speaking Lladranan better. The other women had told her this would happen if she took a Lladranan lover, but she hadn't realized she'd get other images and feelings and experiences from his mind. Some of his lost father-figure, Broullard, many of sailing. None, thankfully, of Elizabeth.

She didn't think he'd gotten any hint of her few past lovers, either.

He pillowed his arm under her head, but lay on his side, looking at her. She gazed back at him.

Tracing her lips with his forefinger, he said, "Preparation for the trials begin tomorrow, and the trials themselves the day after. I need to go back with the others in the morning."

She didn't want to talk about this. Didn't want to think about that or any ramifications of the trials. She put her fingers over his lips, and he kissed them, but continued on. "I think you should stay here, near the ocean, where you belong, Sea-mistress. Practice building your Ship."

A slightly better topic. She stroked his brow, his cheeks. "Ayes, I'd rather be here." Didn't want to be in a Castle where people were excited about preparing for war.

He licked her fingers, and his eyes were serious. "You will always be welcome here. Always."

"*Merci.*"

There was the whir of wings, a little squeak cut short. Raine stood, reached both hands down to him. He took her fingers, rose on his own, then flashed a wicked grin and scooped her up in his arms once more. "Now I can carry you, my prize, my lover." He kissed her hard. "My wonderful fate."

"Our…fate."

They loved several times in the night and in the morning had breakfast in his suite.

She helped Faucon dress in his battle leathers—in case an alarm was sounded on the way to the Marshalls' Castle. Then she accompanied him arm-in-arm out of his castle and toward the landing field, where the others waited.

Passing the ponds, Faucon stopped. Raine didn't want to, but she halted, too. A series of pools that some long-ago ancestor of his had ordered built—for just this time? She didn't know and it was too scary to think of.

Despite herself, she looked at the large pool of the northern continent and her model. She studied the course it—they, not *she*—would take. There was the sweep northwest around the last big peninsula of the continent, then back east to the narrow S-curving channel between two continents, then nearly straight east to the volcanic island that was the Dark's Nest.

There they'd find monsters, the horrors she'd seen mounted as trophies. The worst for the invasion force and her ship were dreeths—looking like the flying dinosaurs of old Earth, but with spines and claws and sharp rows of teeth. The large ones were big as a house, the smaller ones breathed fire.

Staring at her ship, she wondered if there was any way to protect it from dreeth fire. They would need it to get back, wouldn't they? The survivors.

"It's a beautiful Ship," Faucon said.

She gave him a resigned smile. "It could be better with more Lladranan input."

He inclined his head. "Ayes. Corbeau will be here for the days I'm at the trials, then I'll return and we'll consult more on ship design and model building." His smile widened. "Corbeau has five children, I'm sure all of them would like a ship from the hands of the Exotique Seamistress."

"Thank you," she whispered.

He held her for a moment, then they walked to the landing field. None of the Exotiques said a word about Raine's new intimacy with Faucon, and she thought she heard caution-ary humming between the women and their spouses and the men kept quiet, too. The acceptance was a blessing, since she was feeling tender this morning, like she'd stepped onto a dangerous path.

Or maybe it was because she looked like she might cut and run.

She endured the grins of the women, said farewell to the others with an embrace. She hugged Luthan, who'd seemed preoccupied and hadn't said a word throughout the evening before. He held her, too, and felt solid and good, completely brotherly.

Koz winked at her and she winked back. He'd fallen into a sudden sleep after working with the mirrors and the last she'd seen him, he was snoring on the rugs. "Good hunting," she said, giving him the standard Chevalier goodbye.

"Not hunting," he said cheerily. "Testing." He flexed. "I'm gonna win."

There were several snorts.

Raine turned to Faucon and gave him a passionate kiss. As she watched them fly away, she knew she'd made the right decision to stay. This was where her own work should be done, by the sea.

And she knew that this leaving showed faith in her. That she'd be fine on her own, was a mature adult who could handle her own problems, be it a stalker to raising the ship. And she understood that if she sent a mental call to any of them, woman or man, they'd hurry to her side. Even now their link was open.

Friendship.

Independence.

The mixture was heady.

She walked back to the ponds.

The Song between her and Faucon was strengthening, from attraction to affection to tenderness. More than desire and passion. That, too, made her smile. She didn't think she'd ever had such an impact on a man. It made her feel all woman.

She was alone. Corbeau was out with the fishing boats. She knew his Song now and sensed it coming from the sea.

She sensed a lot about the sea since yesterday.

There was a small mew and she looked down to see an orange tabby kitten staring up at her with big blue eyes and cream on her whiskers. Enerin.

"Hi, Enerin."

Enerin's eyes widened more. "Hello, Raine."

Raine sighed. "What do you want?"

A wide kitten smile. "Last night we made many ships like your design."

So that was the feycoocu business! "So?"

Enerin waved a paw and a little flotilla came sailing from behind a grassy knoll. There must have been ten ships. Enerin said, "Sinafinal and Tuckerinal also modified the ponds to look like the best maps." She lifted her chin and beamed. "Especially this big one that shows all of Lladrana and the way to the Dark's Nest." The kitten bounded over to it. "It is perfect. So you can see how the course must be."

Raine sent a hard stare at Enerin. "Do you want to make me afraid and sad?"

Enerin looked surprised. "Ttho."

"Then why do you say things that you know will make me afraid and sad? You're my companion."

Enerin crouched down, lowered her head. *Sinafinal would say such to Alexa.*

"You're not Sinafinal and I'm not Alexa. I don't need to be reminded of my task, or what awaits the invasion force in the north. I don't need to be motivated by fear and depression. I've had enough of that here on Lladrana." She turned her back on that pond, looked toward the east where the volarans had already flown out of sight. "I don't think Alexa or anyone else needs to be motivated that way."

Since the kitten looked miserable, Raine picked her up, held her so their eyes met. "Maybe in the beginning, when we all didn't know what needed to be done, Sinafinal or Tuckerinal might have been good at spurring the Exotiques on. But now we need all the moral support we can get. You can tell Sinafinal and Tuckerinal that, too."

Enerin squeezed her eyes shut. *They hear. All Exotiques hear.*

"Good. Now I know that feycoocus are special." Raine cradled Enerin in one arm and petted her. "We all know that you hear the Song of Amee, of the universe itself, better than any human, that you might have other agendas that we don't know about and you don't want to tell us. But if there's a direction you want us to go, I think we'd all appreciate it if you simply asked us to do something, not manipulated us."

Go, Raine! came Alexa's mental voice.

You're absolutely right! Marian said.

Thank you, echoed Calli and Bri.

Raine sighed and Enerin looked up at her, whiskers rising from their droop. "I want you to stay here, with me and with Faucon and with the others when the Snap comes."

"I know that, but I'm not ready to make that decision."

Enerin continued, "And I know it will be better for everybody if you Captained the Ship. It is like that man on Exotique Terre said, the Ship is a stealth ship and will *be* a stealth ship if *you* pilot it."

That jolted Raine. She hadn't thought of that. "Ayes?" she whispered, but she knew all the others—the Exotiques and the feycoocus—were listening in.

There had been less shock from the others, as if they'd anticipated this. Raine wasn't sure whether she was glad or not that they'd kept the idea from her.

"Ayes." The kitten nodded. "The sea and the oceans of Amee love you and will mask you and the Ship. The Master of the Dark, he who sends the monsters, doesn't know you or sense your Song. You, too, are a weapon."

Another shock. Never in a million years would she have considered herself a weapon.

Soothing came from the other Exotiques along their bond.

"And the last Song, the Untying of the City Destroyer Knot Song, will be better if you are there, adding the lilt of the oceans," Enerin said.

"I see." Raine swallowed.

Enerin tumbled off her arm and Raine reluctantly turned back to the continental map. Blood hummed in her temples, merging with the sound of the ocean and the surf endlessly rolling in and out. Then she heard a soft clicking and saw a duckling near her feet…Enerin.

"Now you know all," Enerin said. "And we should practice raising little ships, then Powering the Ships my parents and I raised through the waters." She quacked, wriggled her bottom. "We've simulated the ocean currents. They are correct, too."

"Oh," Raine said, staring at the various-sized models.

No one else commented.

Singer's Abbey

The lessons with the Singer began in earnest the next morning. They worked on scales over four octaves, then higher level spellsongs—Songs that provided energy for the Abbey compound that entailed moving from building to building, finding the pentacle that indicated the perfect place to Sing, and Singing to crystals storing Power. This kept Jikata so busy that she had no breath to ask the questions she'd lined up.

The most important was *who or what were Exotiques?* She thought she had the answer—a person like her who'd come from another world, probably Earth. As she'd noted in her journal, her first vision had been of Caucasian women the night she'd arrived. Since then she'd heard echoes of voices in her dreams, seen more blurred images.

Her lunch break was taken on the balcony in her rooms with the Singer. The old woman had scanned the place and nodded. "A fine small suite, well kept."

Jikata's housekeeper and maid curtsied and looked relieved.

Their meal—skinless chicken breast and a soothing drink—was bland, as if the Singer had lost her taste, or her elderly stomach preferred that. Jikata didn't ask. More important questions buzzed in her brain. She knew she'd only get one.

"Who are the Exotiques?"

The Singer looked down her nose. Put down her fork, dabbed her lips with her fine linen napkin and rose. "I don't have the time to answer all your questions. Matters are pressing. *Amee* is pressing. It's time for you to learn a very specific technique. We must also visit the Caverns of Prophecy. You and they must become accustomed to each other."

Jikata *didn't* rise. "Ayes, I've seen and spoken with Amee."

The Singer hesitated.

This was *not* Club Lladrana, the image of the man on the flying horse nagged at Jikata and she realized he'd worn a sword. There had been another weapon, a long dagger strapped on his saddle. "I know I've been brought here to do—" What?

"Fulfill your task," the Singer ended smoothly. She raised her hand and a Friend hurried in, holding a stack of five books.

"*Merci,*" the Singer said, and inclined her head.

The Friend flushed and smiled, dipped a curtsy. "Anything, Singer."

The Singer smiled. "I know."

The Friend left, glowing.

Jikata eyed the books. They were all thick, and only one of them, the last, looked as if the binding was of a leather she recognized. She got a jolt as she realized she could read the gold lettering on the spines, another shock when she saw the titles: *The Lorebook of Exotique Swordmarshall Alexa Fitzwalter; Lorebook of Exotique Circlet Marian Harasta; Lorebook of Calli Torcher, Chevalier and Volaran Exotique; Lorebook of Exotique Medica Brigid Elizabeth Drystan; Lorebook of Exotique Medica Elizabeth Brigid Drystan.*

Five. She'd seen five women in her vision.

"Come along," the Singer said. "You can read those this evening after your training."

She swept from the room. After one yearning glance at the books, Jikata followed, mind on the books and not appreciating the sunshine and soft breeze of the afternoon until she was back in the Singer's incense-laden suite.

That night Jikata propped pillows high on her headboard, snuggled under a sheet and, with one note, flashed a lightball into existence to hover near. Again she eyed the books. The first was fat, the second thicker still, the third looked thinnest. She set aside the top two. Chasonette swooped down and pecked her hand. *Read me Alyeka's first.*

Scowling, Jikata rubbed the back of her hand, "What?"

Read Alyeka's first. I was not here for that. I remember Bri and Elizabeth. I was in Castleton then, but I want Alyeka's and Marian's and Calli's first.

With a grumble, Jikata took the first book, read the title, glanced at the bird. "It says 'The Lorebook of *Alexa* Fitzwalter.'"

Chasonette swivelled her head to groom a wing feather and didn't answer.

Jikata opened the book and yelped as a three-dimensional image sprang up of the face of a small Caucasian woman with a head of silver hair. The book tumbled off her lap and the holograph disappeared. Chasonette gave a bird chuckle.

After puffing out a breath, Jikata picked up the book again, opened it again, looked at the image, and began: "'My name is Alexa Fitzwalter, late of Denver, Colorado, where I practiced law. One cold March night I trudged through crusty snow on a hiking trail near Berthoud Pass....'"

Colorado! Jikata smiled.

As she read aloud, she couldn't stop the heaviness of sleep. What with Chasonette's asides and Jikata's own thinking— Alexa had heard chimes and gong and chants just as Jikata had—she didn't get far. A silver arch was coalescing before Alexa when the book was too heavy and Jikata let it fall from her fingers. Chasonette whistled the light out and began warbling her usual lullaby and Jikata slept.

Nightmares haunted her sleep.

20

Marshalls' Castle

Finally the first day of trials had come, and Luthan was in the first group to be tested. He looked out his apartment window at Temple Ward and smiled at the shimmering waves of early afternoon heat rising from the flagstones. The first *hot* day of the year. Amee was rallying. The last Exotique had arrived and the Lladranan Chevaliers and Marshalls would finally carry the war on the Dark to its very Nest.

Every day he'd had the feycoocus discreetly check on Jikata to confirm she was as well as he sensed. He and she must have formed a bond during that short, intense time in the Caverns of Prophecy. Enough of a connection that he could sense her emotions. She'd been cheerful during the day, blossoming with Power. And having nightmares. Like everyone else.

He tightened the last buckle of his tunic at his waist,

smoothed down the reinforced flap of white dreeth leather that covered the fastenings, then ran his hand down his chest, initiating a protective spell. No need for a cleaning spell on dreeth leather, nothing stuck to it, but he Sang a whitening spell. He was known for white leathers, and there were no white flying lizard-birds. He'd kept an eye out for the palest dreeths on the battlefield and had helped kill them, claiming a portion of their skins. The light buff skin was easier to brighten into white than the pale gray.

And he was delaying.

For once he wanted to make a dramatic entrance—onto the volaran Landing Field where the trials for being included in the invasion force would soon start.

Those who were favored by the Chevaliers and Marshalls and who had proven their worth were up first. He, as Bastien's brother, the brother-in-law of the Exotique Lady Knight Swordmarshall Alexa, was one of those. Luthan was the former representative of the Chevaliers to the Marshalls, the putative representative of the Singer to the Marshalls, the "most honorable man in Lladrana."

He thought he'd reclaimed that title. Last night he had dined with Calli and Marrec, talked until he was hoarse about the events last year, explained himself to them as he had no other in his lifetime. As he'd talked, he'd seen Calli relax against Marrec, and eventually Marrec himself relaxed.

Luthan apologized to them for following the Singer's orders without asking for more explanation himself.

When they'd brought in their children, he asked forgiveness from them, too. The little girl had come straight to his arms, charming him. The older boy had said he'd forgiven Luthan, had reluctantly shook his hand, but had hung back until

Luthan brought out his reparation gifts. A small golden bracelet with a tiny flying volaran for the girl, a miniature hat like the one Bastien had designed for the boy.

The gift had had the boy yelling with joy. He was the only youngster to have one. His eyes had gleamed and he'd hugged Luthan enthusiastically and had said against Luthan's neck that he *had* forgiven him. Since the pattern of his Song had changed, Luthan believed him.

Seeing their children's acceptance of him had eased Calli and Marrec even more.

They had been the last people he'd had to apologize to, his actions against them the worst. In the flush of the feel-good moment Luthan had left their suite in Horseshoe Hall and gone down to soak in the Chevalier baths, the best in the Castle.

At first there was wariness at his presence, but after he'd engaged in a couple of water fights and taken some dunkings, the men and women had relaxed. Furthermore, they'd treated him as if he were still their representative and confided some concerns that they evidently hadn't told his successor, Lady Hallard.

The Chevaliers were worried primarily about the scoring of the trials, which weren't based on play dueling but on a point system: for flying, teamwork, speed, teamwork, fighting technique, teamwork, and strength of Power and Singing.

Luthan had moved to the largest pool and laid out the scoring structure—developed by Alexa, Calli and Bastien, with input from Marian—and word had spread until people sat thigh-to-thigh and bumping knees to listen. Someone asked about the Exotique Singer, the events of that Summoning. Others wanted information about what happened on the coast with the Exotique Seamaster. Wanted his reports.

The long talking had been worth it. By the time Luthan had taken his shriveled toes to bed in his room in the Noble Apartments, the Song between him and his fellow Chevaliers, which had broken or gone flat, had been completely mended.

Many greeted him with a personal word as he strode from his rooms across the courtyard to the Assayer's Office, through it to the Landing Field. He even heard a mild cheer as he arrived that lightened his heart.

He was the last of the first nine.

As he donned his helmet, he nodded to Faucon, also a favorite. Faucon was a noble Chevalier who fielded two teams to fight the invading horrors, and fought with them. He was rich, Powerful, provided a large measure of the funds for the expedition, and had been a lover of *two* Exotiques.

Luthan snorted. The fact that Faucon had finally succumbed to Raine's charms the night before last had been all around the Castle yesterday morning, despite it taking place on the coast. Everyone was eyeing the man, betting on whether the sex had tired or energized him, whether any bond with her strengthened him. Warriors were an earthy lot.

Also in the first set was Koz, once a tough and skilled Lladranan Chevalier flying under Luthan's father's banner, then Alexa's. His soul had flown his body, and that of the dying Andrew, Marian's brother, had taken its place. Andrew had remained a Chevalier—less skilled in technique but a better strategist—until he'd been badly wounded. Then he'd become *the* mirror magician. No one was surprised to see him in his Chevalier leathers, ready to test. Extreme determination showed in the lines of his face, rose from his Song. Plenty of Chevaliers had bet against Koz in the Nom de Nom tavern, but Luthan hadn't been one of them. The man had unplumbed depths…and he'd never been missing in Luthan's visions of the final battle. Dead ninety-five percent of the time, but there. A fact Luthan kept quiet about. If he'd learned anything in his life—and after his father's blows—it was not to speak of his visions. Which had been occasional and now were constant.

Lady Hallard, the current Chevalier representative, was there, along with her new Shield. She nodded coolly to Luthan.

Two Marshall pairs were there—the newest, named the day before, a male Pair, who'd been Bastien's and Alexa's squires. And one of the oldest Marshall pairs, Swordmarshall Mace and his wife and Shield Clua, were there. Mace had a mean and resolved glint in his eye, his Shield had a serene gleam in hers.

Alexa had already announced the other Marshall pairs who were going with them. Out of respect, she'd left out some of the older Marshalls as well as her own seconds-in-command, Swordmarshall Pascal and his Shield, Marwey. Alexa had convinced Pascal and Marwey that they must stay and hold the Castle. Mace and his wife had *not* gone along with Alexa's decision.

"First group up!" shouted the new Loremaster. The previous Shieldmarshall Loremistress and her partner had died in battle, defending one of the Exotique Medicas.

Luthan finished his stretching-fighting-meditation pattern.

The trials weren't against each other but against time, and a test of skill and technique that were awarded a certain amount of points. But the competition would be fierce.

Mace and his Shield, Lady Hallard and hers, and the new Marshalls would have the advantage since they were paired.

As for him, the trials—the fighting—would be better with a partner, a Shield to his Sword. For one ludicrous moment he had a vision of the new lady, Jikata, in battle armor, long legs around a volaran, long hair flying back in the wind. He shook his head. Ludicrous, indeed. The lady was not a warrior.

He understood from the others that she must have fought to become what she was—a famous troubadour in the Exotique Land—but she'd never been in bloody physical battle.

His smile at her image on volaranback vanished and his face hardened. It might have been better if she had.

But she was the Exotique Singer. If all went better than he dared hope, *the* next oracle of Lladrana.

The rules were read—as if they hadn't been posted on boards of the Castle and many cities and towns, and Sung in taverns and along roads. Luthan could only hope that traitor-ous mouths wouldn't whisper and traitorous ears wouldn't hear or believe that an expedition against the Dark was being mounted.

For every rumor they heard, Alexa and the others had fostered four to cycle around.

The alarm sounded and he went to his volaran and mounted. His steed quivered with anticipation, said mentally, *We will do well. We will show the best. We will retain our high status.*

"Ayes." Luthan stroked his volaran's neck, focused on winning.

By the end of the two-hour trial he was soaked with sweat. His smile at Faucon and Mace and his lady had more than a hint of teeth. Faucon and the pair had tied with Luthan. Faucon was the best with speed and flying, Mace in teamwork. Luthan had edged the others out in sheer fighting ability and with one point better than the others in strategy. They all had the same score and from the cheering of the crowd, it was the score to beat.

Luthan laughed when he saw money changing hands.

Koz stumbled over to him, flung an arm around his shoulders and did the same with Faucon. Gasping, he said, "Let's go eat and get something strong to drink."

"We can barely stagger," Luthan said.

"True," Koz said, "but I want drink and food. The Marshalls' Dining Room." He winked. "I deserve it for managing to come in just a point behind the top."

"Along with Lady Hallard," Faucon said easily as they walked slowly back to the keep. He glanced at the drooping shoulders of Alexa's former squires as they walked hand in hand, then shook his head. "Several points down. Pity."

The siren blasted a short note again, and the crowd fell silent as the Loremaster shouted, "Go!" to a second set.

"I think your score will stand." Koz shrugged. "Mine, too." He glanced back. "But I'd bet all the scores will be high. Only the crème de la crème will go."

"Defeating the Dark will need the best," Luthan said.

Singer's Abbey

Every day Jikata and the Singer practiced scales, making sure each note was pure and sustainable. That meant breath control and timing was, as always, critical.

It was the hardest Jikata had ever worked. She realized then that previously she'd been depending upon her great natural talent, taking classes as she pleased.

This was the discipline of learning, of real training.

More than just Singing, there was the *magic,* the *Power* of it. How much Power to use, at what place—which phrase, syllable, note. The drawing of it into her from the elements around her, the use of it to enhance her voice and her range, the richness of the sound that came from her vocal cords.

The lessons weren't only for her. Each day the Singer rotated Friends in and out of sessions. When Jikata thought about it, she became uneasy, because it seemed as if the Singer were building a chorus around her...though if the personalities weren't right, a person was dismissed. As if the old Singer were building a community of Friends for Jikata.

But the training didn't only help Jikata, as they Sang together, the Singer's voice lost some of its quaver and Jikata could almost *see* the Power she gathered to her, to strengthen her voice and her very self.

As an exercise in magical Power, it was awesome to witness.

So the days fell into a pattern—breakfast, morning lessons, lunch, afternoon lessons...or private practice while the Singer did consultations. Late afternoon meditation and any dreamquests in the evening. Most of the dreamquests consisted of Chevaliers or young Marshalls with regards to trials taking place.

Jikata was so tired that she progressed slowly through Alexa's Lorebook. The books were the only sources of information regarding the Exotiques that she had since no one would talk with her about the other women.

Now she knew who the Marshalls were and wasn't too fond of them and how they'd treated Alexa. The magical being, Sinafinal the feycoocu, intrigued her, and there was this mysterious man mentioned....

Also mentioned was Luthan, the Chevalier who wore white and was the Singer's representative. The most honorable man in Lladrana. That eased the concern that she was isolated and subject to the Singer. Occasionally she thought she heard his Song, in her mind or at the Abbey.

The other man, Koz, hadn't appeared yet. Perhaps he came later in the story.

Jikata's brain and Power were buzzing so much by the end of the day that the stack of books seemed like a daunting tower she'd have to climb. Reading the stories was all well and good, but she wished there was an index in the back so she could easily find the information she wanted.

She'd also been tantalized with the concept of "the Snap" when Mother Earth called her home. She *had* asked others—the household staff, the gatekeeper—about feycoocus and the Snap and had received strange and contradictory answers. The general idea was that after her task was done, Mother Earth opened a door home, and she could decide whether to stay or go.

One evening after dinner with the Singer and her closest Friends—all subordinates to the Singer, none equal, none *true* friends—they adjourned to a small sitting room. A few minutes later five people entered, a couple of boys and three women who were smaller than most Lladranans. The boys wore the pale colors of new acolytes, the highest ranked one wore royal blue.

They all looked nervous and stared at Jikata. She sat up straight in her own regal pose. The Singer ran an eye down them, then addressed Jikata. "These Friends have voices closest to the Exotiques you will be Singing with."

Her heart clutched. She'd figured that there was one special spell she'd be required to lead, and that the other women would be with her—why else would she be Summoned?

The Singer waved to the youngest boy. "Scales, please."

He complied.

When he was done, the Singer said, "I have heard Exotique

Lady Knight Swordmarshall Alyeka myself and his voice is close. She is a very small woman and has a high range. The Volaran Exotique, Calli, too, I have heard." She pointed to a woman who opened her mouth and Sang—an alto. The Singer nodded when the woman was done. "The Volaran Exotique has yellow hair and blue eyes. She is the strangest-looking one of you all."

Jikata's own eyes narrowed. She'd been the brunt of enough prejudice not to like it here, in reverse.

"I recently heard Bri, the Exotique Medica's voice enough to find someone whose composition is close." She nodded to the one in blue and the Friend sang. Excellent control, but more, an underlying lilt of optimism, of sheer joyfulness.

Jikata had had that once, when she'd started her career. She frowned as she tried to recall when she'd lost it.

"Good." The Singer folded her hands, looked at the line of people before her and shook her head. "The voices of the other two Exotiques I have not heard personally. The Exotiques themselves have been wary of coming to see me." Her smile was sharp. "They, of course, were not Summoned for me, nor did they have any traditional duty to me as Alyeka did."

So Alexa had done a Marshall's Song Quest with the Singer. Damn, Jikata needed to read faster. Her mind flashed back to that first time in the Caverns of Prophecy. Despite how much she tried to recall she only had two vague memories: meeting five women, and getting a Grammy. The Song of the man holding her was vivid.

Then the Singer referred to him. "I have relied on Luthan Vauxveau to judge the quality of the voices."

His image came, handsome and dressed all in white leather. Jikata had heard various stories about Luthan when she'd discreetly asked. Not a Friend himself, but a Chevalier who rode the volarans, the flying horses. She was itching to see one of those up close, to ride one, but had not been out of the compound, even to go to the corrals and landing field.

The Singer wasn't taking any chances that she'd fly away, and Jikata was practicing patience along with all her other training. She *knew* that what she did here in the Abbey was vital, and the perks were lovely.

But the Singer was gesturing to the largest woman and saying, "This Friend approximates the voice of Marian, the Exotique Circlet, the Weather Sorceress who rides lightning, the one with red hair." That woman Sang, there was a natural huskiness to her voice.

Rode lightning? The words penetrated and Jikata stared at the Singer. Surely she'd heard wrong.

But the Singer said, "Raine, the last Exotique, the Seamistress and Ship raiser's voice is so." The Singer pointed to the last person, the older boy, who let loose with a strong, pure soprano. It held pulses of Power that had Jikata asking for a longer song. He rolled into a sea shanty and Jikata finally realized that there was a rhythm to the Power, the sound of the sea...or the tide...or the surf, whatever. She'd grown up in Colorado and lived in the hills outside L.A. She didn't know much about oceans and tides, but it was fascinating to understand that the environment of a person could be found in the tone of their voice, by the Power of it.

"The Exotique Raine's natural element is water, of course, and it is heard in her voice as it is in this boy's," the Singer said. "Bri, the Exotique Healer with the short brown hair, is also water, like a bubbling fountain."

So Jikata was being given visual clues as well as magical and audio. For a moment she experienced the first vision again, five women standing in a line, and she *saw* their faces and not the people here in this room whose singing only resembled theirs.

"Marian is fire, Alyeka is earth, Calli is air," the Singer said.

"All the ancient elements," Jikata murmured, "and I'm fire."

"We will start working with knots tomorrow." The Singer slid her a sly glance, all the others moved restlessly and Jikata understood that knots—*knots?*—were important. Nothing in Alexa's Lorebook had said anything about knots.

With a wave the Singer dismissed the older boy and he left. She said, "It is not known whether Raine will remain on Amee. Most doubt it, due to her past circumstances."

That whole sentence snagged Jikata's attention. Maybe she should look at Raine's… Jikata didn't have a Lorebook from Raine, didn't know that name. She had five Lorebooks, had seen five women….

"Attention, Jikata!" the Singer snapped.

Irritation flared, Jikata suppressed it.

"So you will practice with these four more often."

Of course the Singer gave Jikata no time to ask about several interesting bits of information since one of the Singer's attendants handed out music.

"A weaving spell," the Singer said. "To weave the energies between you, merge your Powers, make you all stronger as a team than individually." She leaned back in her chair.

Jikata stood and Sang with the others, watching the smug old woman, willing to bet her entire fortune that the Singer had never woven together a team of equals. As she Sang, she knew this was practice for her, because whatever the general voices of the others, the Power of the Exotiques would be far different.

She wondered if the Singer was trying to truly build a team or set them all up for failure, and the oppressive feeling came back, the vision of a wounded Amee. *What was all this about?* And the understanding that Jikata was being given just enough information, or time to absorb that information, so she wouldn't be voiceless with terror.

She had to consciously steady her voice, and wanted to memorize this Song. Because with that feeling of impending doom, was the thought that failure would not be an option.

21

Creusse Crest

Faucon's castle was empty of the Exotiques and their men's Songs, though traces of them lingered, and Raine took comfort from that.

She mastered the art of raising the small ships both by herself, with Corbeau, and with anyone else who wanted to experiment with her, which was a surprising number of people from the Castle and some from nearby towns. The locals were checking her out as a resident Exotique…and as Faucon's lover. Probably as Faucon's future wife, but she tried not to think of that.

Though she recalled their loving more often than she was comfortable with.

She modified the ship's design as she sailed her models with and without Power. Again and again she worked on the masts and the sails, thinking how they should be angled to take advantage of the Lladranan wind, the best placement to endure the stress of the currents. She consulted with Corbeau about fireproofing the sails and ropes and ship itself from dreeths, and had some spectacularly explosive failures.

Each day she sailed. The fishing boats had become used to her, no longer had a person watching her for odd spurts and starts. Most often she took out a small one-person craft so that she worked the sails herself. The time on the sea was her reward, where she could stretch her senses and rest her Power…or let her Power roll like the swells and use it or not.

She sailed close to some of the Circlets' islands, saw the Towers each raised—raised like she was raising her ship, she realized—and thumbed through Marian's book. Raising a Tower was the last test to become a true Circlet of the Fifth Degree, and a Sorcerer or Sorceress did it individually.

At least Raine would have a community to build her ship.

There were two large islands, several small ones. Since she didn't know any of those Circlets, she didn't stop.

In the evening she studied maps of the invasion course… just in case. And to know the landscape that the ship would be sailing through, especially the twisty, narrow strait between two continents. A passage she'd been told had opened during an earthquake after the invasion of the monstrous horrors had begun and before the ancient guardians had devised the fence and raised the fence posts.

There was that word again. Raise. Alexa had discovered how to raise new fence posts. Marian had raised her Tower to become a Circlet. Now Raine would raise a ship.

Exotique tasks.

But Raine preferred the word *raise,* to *destroy,* which also seemed to be associated with Exotiques. Alexa had destroyed plenty of monsters; Marian had destroyed the old Master of the horrors; Calli had destroyed the person who intended to become the new Master; Bri and Elizabeth had destroyed plague and sickness sent by the Dark.

The greatest task of all would be untying the "City Destroyer" Weapon Knot. Destroying the Dark's island and the Dark itself.

Then there was the task of team building. Each Exotique had united a portion of Lladranan society with the rest. Raine was supposed to integrate the seafolk and Seamasters with the rest of Lladrana to complete the common goal of destroying the Dark. She'd held back speaking with them. This place seemed too close to the Seamaster's Market and the awful village where she'd been a potgirl at a lowest-class tavern.

Raine hesitated to go into the towns by herself and Corbeau didn't know the locals here since he lived in the north. Faucon knew his people, but he wasn't here. She figured the real team building would be at Creusse Landing where the ship would be built, the sailors hired as crew.

Every couple of days, she checked on her family in the mirrors. Her brothers seemed to be taking her disappearance and "co-opting for a secret mission" well. Huh. They really thought she was a weenie.

She didn't see Judge Philbert again. Her father appeared more worn, but seemed more settled than she sensed he'd been before. Resigned, occasionally hopeful.

Raine wanted to be hopeful, too. She wasn't.

Singer's Abbey

The next morning brought knots.

Jikata had been led to a new set of rooms in a small round building. The outside ring was nothing but an airy lattice of brickwork that housed a mixture of bubbling fountains, tall trees, windmills with chimes, crackling fires—all the four ancient elements to draw Power from. The inside was one room with a domed ceiling and she couldn't resist sending her voice around. Wonderful. She'd heard an album of flute and voice recorded in the Taj Mahal and this room matched those incredible acoustics…and echoes.

The Singer sat in a throne a little off-center of the pentacle in the middle. The center was Jikata's mark, and she went there with confidence. There were two Friends attending the Singer, probably to move the several standing trays around for her. Atop each tray was a series of knots, from a simple one to an ornamental one made of many strands of thread, each a different color. One small lacquered tray of mother-of-pearl held an intricate knot that seemed to pulse red. It sent a shiver of premonition down Jikata's spine and her eyes widened as she saw the translucent image of Amee quaver into existence behind the Singer, nodding with a serious expression.

The Singer caught her breath, twisted in her chair, but the vision vanished. Then the old woman Sang a short chorus of praise. The Friends looked startled but joined in.

That Amee had appeared emphasized these lessons were vital. They weren't very close to the Caverns of Prophecy, but Jikata's Power in that subject was growing stronger, too.

To the left of the Singer was a low tray with three knots; she brought it in front of her and smoothed out a pretty piece of sky-blue embroidery floss. Eyes narrowed, she said, "This is the most important part of your training because the main task you have before you will be to untie a knot."

Jikata felt colder.

"A very special knot," the Singer said with heavy significance. "But it would be well and wise to learn the tying of knots, the setting of Power in them for certain purposes."

Gesturing to the three knots, the Singer said, "These knots release Power in a pretty pattern that will transfer to your body if you care to decorate yourself, or you may simply absorb the Power for use in your next task."

Fascinating.

"Choose one." The old woman tapped the first—the simple knot—and Jikata knew this was a test itself. Would her pride lead her to try one of the more complex ones? Or would she take the simple knot and direction from the Singer?

Jikata reached for the second knot. Before she could take it, the Singer picked it up and passed it to her.

As usual, Power sizzled through the woman's fingers, Jikata breathed through the brief pain, took the Power she could use, then went to the center of the star, directly under the top of the dome.

"Listen to the Song in your hand."

So Jikata flattened one hand and put the knot on it. The length ran across her palm, Power tingling, notes rising. She heard the Song in the thread, listened to it wind, repeat, as she traced the loops. Definitely a spell.

"Ayes," the Singer said. "Now Sing and undo it."

Jikata stared at the blue silk, then at the Singer.

"You hear the tune?"

"Ayes."

"You can see the ends of the knot."

Tiny tassels. "Ayes."

"You may trace the knot with your finger and Sing the

notes. For a simple knot the rhythm, pacing and volume will not matter."

The condescending tone riled her, as it was meant to. But Ishi had taught Jikata well. She didn't impulsively respond to the spur.

She'd warmed up her voice on the way to the rooms, and knew the acoustics, so she touched one end, heard that note, Sang it and continued along in a pattern of rising notes. Behind her finger the thread lifted, she came to a knot...a series of deeper notes and one very high one.... She Sang them and the strand loosened, the end slipped through, blue wisps puffed into existence then hung in the air, forming into a pattern. Jikata inhaled sharply and they were sucked in with her breath, slipped down her throat like vanilla ice cream, then made her dizzy with a rush of Power directly to her brain. Incredible.

"Proceed, Jikata," the Singer ordered and Jikata looked down to see the limp thread on her palm, looking more like embroidery floss than a spell.

By the time she was done she had a pattern of green swirls on her face that smelled of mint, scarlet spirals on her palms, and a dark blue eye on her forehead. All were gently settling into her skin until she hummed with Power. She thought they'd only last a couple of hours, but as long as they did, she had more energy...and was sensitized to an extreme degree that she could hear the soft breaths of the Singer.

"That is sufficient for this morning," the Singer said with her usual smug amusement. She gestured and a Friend folded the top of the tray holding knots in half to make a hinged case. "When you feel steadier, you can practice on those. They will release light and other small spells. If you practice in your own rooms no harm should come to you or anything else."

The Friend with the case took Jikata's arm, then hopped back as static electricity arced. Or maybe it wasn't static electricity, maybe Jikata herself was giving off sparks. She nodded to the Singer. "I'll practice." Then she left, with the Friend following.

Waves of music enveloped her, from the blades of grass, tiny flowers she hadn't noted much before, even sunshine. The soundtrack of her life increased. When she met other Friends on the path, their greetings sounded shouted.

Fabulous spell, but once was enough. Perhaps she should have started with the simpler knot, but that would have meant giving in to the Singer's subtle dominance. This way was better.

It took Jikata the rest of the day to finish untying the knots, but it was practice well spent.

Each morning thereafter she practiced on knots in the domed chamber. It should have been boring, but instead was engrossing. Jikata had never seen such knots, some ugly and functional of twine or rope—the untying of which would lead to muscular cleaning and landscaping spells.

Some knots were beautifully ornamental, loops and twists. These were the most challenging because with these, rhythm and volume and beat mattered. One wrong note and she'd have a knot burn on her hand, or could trigger a nasty green vapor that brought her to her knees and kept her nauseous for the rest of the day. Knots could Summon Chasonette, or Friends. Knots could make meals appear.

Jikata got the impression that they were an old magic, not much used, and had fallen out of favor. She believed it was because they were so touchy, the Singer had to be perfect.

To her own surprise, mostly she was. By the end of that week she could untie simple knots she'd never seen before, sense the pattern from the strands.

Sometimes, in the afternoons, they went to the Caverns of Prophecy and worked with the knots there...with odd results. Once Jikata saw horrible little *things* falling in a rain, once a Chevalier dying in a battle, eviscerated by a swipe of a black-furred monster's wicked claws.

Since the Singer insisted Jikata tell her every detail, each session was more exhausting. But when she learned she'd saved the Chevalier's life—he'd had an emblem on his shield—it was truly worth it. That one act made her whole time here on Lladrana, in the Singer's Abbey, worthwhile.

One evening the monthly prophecy for Lladrana was scheduled in the crystal chamber. This was one of the Singer's main duties and had been for time out of mind. It was one of these prophecies that had convinced the Marshalls to begin the Summoning process two years ago.

Beforehand, Jikata had been led to the outer room of the Singer's suite, but she could still feel the buzz of people's Songs from the room next door, *hear* a conversation.

"...not ready for at least a month," the Singer was saying. The door opened and Jikata saw a group of people who appeared dressed in their best clothes...and Luthan. Jikata's heart bumped a little when she saw the man in white leather. He was much more handsome, his Song more potent, than she'd recalled. She smiled at him, opened her mouth to greet him, and her arm was clamped by the Singer's boney fingers.

"You can see she is well," the Singer said. "Now we must go. Moonrise is soon, the time for the prophecy. Jikata *must* learn this Song." She pulled at Jikata and the sheer Power of the woman lifted her off her feet and moved her.

"Salutations, Jikata." Luthan bowed.

His greeting was echoed by others, then a florid man waved

at them as he rose from his bow. "And she will need to learn the Equinox Prophecy Song later this month," he said in a native accent Jikata hadn't heard before. He shifted his gaze to Jikata, with an approving yet calculating gaze. "A beautiful woman for our thousandth Singer. Unmarried…"

"Salutations," Jikata said in her smokiest voice.

Everyone stared at her and she donned her performance manner. She hadn't decided her course of action before the Singer and hefty Friends hustled her away with mutters about Krache men.

Down in the prophecy chamber the Singer became all sharp business and Jikata had learned to be wary of this mood.

A map spread before them, and though she'd seen one in Alexa's book, and in the beginning of Marian's, this map throbbed with color and action. Cascading notes became chords, transformed into melodies, then rushed through her like wildfire, flickering visions. Deep rolls of ocean waves; cheering as volarans and fliers dipped and whirled in aerial acrobatics; the glint of the sun on what looked like reflective sails of a ship; Luthan and a road through arching green branches— those were the flashing images. To her nose came a fragrance of summer and growing things, flowers, then the ocean.

The Singer wound down the spell serenely. The Power and connection with the music of the spheres had worked on her as well as Jikata. Jikata's ears rang and the Song settled in her blood and she knew she could Sing that spell in the future— any of the great spells, of Equinox or Solstice. It seemed like a gift that the Singer had given her, but Jikata didn't know why…until they were outside the door of the room and she was Singing it shut and locked.

Turning to her with fiercely bright eyes, the Singer said, "You are the only person who can open this door. When I die, there will be no other unless you train them." Then she turned and whisked away, leaving Jikata standing in shock that was a mixture of pleasure and terror.

Marshalls' Castle

As the second week ended without Faucon, Raine found herself wanting to be back at the Marshalls' Castle. It wasn't only because of Faucon, but because she'd bonded with the other women and heard their Songs in the back of her mind...and she thought they heard her Song. More than once in the past couple of weeks she'd felt their thoughts touch hers—usually during that time of serenity when she was sailing, and she believed they took some of that peace into their busy lives.

Great things were happening at the Marshalls' Castle and Blossom and Enerin wanted to return, though they hadn't actually said so. Blossom was fretting about the other volarans who were testing to go on the invasion. Status in the herd was changing daily and she wasn't there to assert her presence.

Enerin's parents were doing all sorts of feycoocu business, mostly at the Castle, sometimes showing up at the shore and whisking the little one away. Raine believed the magical beings were keeping their words not to manipulate the Exotiques, but she sensed they were trying to manipulate other events.

On the second to the last day of testing, Raine left Creusse Crest after breakfast for the Marshalls' Castle, Blossom handled the Distance Magic and Enerin matched their flight as a baby warhawk that made Raine ache inside.

Because of the trials, they couldn't descend to the Landing

Field, or even inside the Castle itself, so they landed just outside the front gate. The guards there bowed lower and had more respect in their eyes for her, as well as a wink. They knew she'd been attending to her task. Raine also reckoned she was carrying herself better, had lost the last little cringe of the lowly potgirl.

Before Raine and Enerin and Blossom had even exited the long passage through the main gate, Calli was running to welcome her. The Volaran Exotique enveloped Raine in a hug that smelled of the animals—rich, crumbling amber. A beautiful scent.

"Come on," Calli said, "you're just in time for the start of the trials today." She grinned and Raine noticed that the sun had lightened streaks of her hair. She was beautiful.

And Raine was blessed to have such good friends. She linked arms with her. "All the others are there, of course."

"Sure," Calli said. "It's the best entertainment there is, a mixture of circus and wild west show, and rodeo, and…and…"

"I get it," Raine laughed and kept up the fast pace.

"You have your own seat, of course, with the rest of us, in the Exotique stands." Calli flashed a grin. "They play to us. Well, to me and Alexa anyway."

Enerin squawked. *I want to see!* She zoomed away.

Calli laughed. "Her parents are there, perched on the rail of our box as hawks, preening."

As they entered the stable area, Blossom trotted away to be groomed. *Later,* the volaran said to Raine, *There is much gossip to hear.* Her rump wiggled and she lifted her wings and settled them in anticipation.

Then Raine and Calli were through the stables and onto the Landing Field, where bleachers had been erected around the edges. It was packed. Raine's nose twitched. She halted to sniff, but Calli dragged her on.

"Wait. Popcorn? Do I smell *popcorn*?" Raine asked.

"Bri discovered it growing outside Castleton. I don't know how she knew it was popcorn, but it's a new favorite. We have some for you."

Raine's mouth watered. "Oh." She was suddenly swamped with feeling for this place. It wasn't Earth, it wasn't home, but it, too, was beautiful.

Especially the people. Faucon came into sight, running.

22

"I don't know how I spent the nights without you," Faucon said and hauled her up. As he touched her, their connection throbbed with music she thought the whole Castle could hear. Then he put her down and kissed her soundly. *Raine.* His whisper was in her mind and she knew she'd missed the closeness of it, his touch.

Breathless, she said, "I don't know, either."

"Come *on!*" Bri was there sharing a smile with Calli. "Sex later, trials *now.* They're holding up the start for you."

"What?" Raine asked, dizzy from the hormones surging through her. She wanted a dim room with Faucon, not this bright carnival atmosphere of hundreds of people looking at her, them.

But Faucon had twined fingers and was tugging her along in Calli's and Bri's wake. He grinned, too. His smile made her heart flop around in her chest. "I matched the best score— Luthan and Mace and his Shield and I. All at the top."

Raine bumped her hip against him, teasing, just before they took the first step up the stands to a canopied box. "I expected no less."

His hand went from her fingers to around her waist, the touch more intimate and also to steady her if she missed a step. Courteous, protective. More churning inside her. She wanted this man. He had every quality she'd ever admired.

They entered the box where Alexa was nearly bouncing up and down on a trio of blue-green velvet pillows. "What *took* you so long, Raine?" Then she winked at Faucon. "Oh."

Before Raine could answer, trumpets sounded and the Marshall Loremaster announced, "The trials will now begin. Will those in group number twenty-two take their marks."

Raine sank into her seat on an emerald-colored velvet pillow and looked around. All the Exotiques and their men were there, the feycoocus were clustered at the corner of the box, claws curled around the rail. The stand was placed in one of the long sides of the irregular rectangle. To her left were the stables, to her right the maze, and before her was the width of the Landing Field. Beyond that the Castle wall and the cliff. No sound of surf here, but the laughter and hustle of energetic people who had rising expectations of a show. No scent of the beach… "Give me some popcorn!" she demanded.

Faucon passed her a warm pottery bowl and the siren sounded and six volarans rose gracefully into the air, two pair of Chevaliers and one set of young Marshalls. The sight caught her breath.

"Go!" shouted the Loremaster and they swooped around the field, racing.

Faucon slipped his arm around her and reached into her bowl and their hands brushed as they grabbed popcorn. He smiled down at her and life became a gilded bubble of perfection.

* * *

That night Raine was one of the few to take part in a "par-enties ceremony." It was a godparents bonding thing for Calli's children. The little girl and older boy already had godpar-ents—Marian and Jaquar—but those two were part of the invasion force. The new godparents were the chief Marshalls who'd stay behind, young Pascal and Marwey.

The ritual was solemn and touching, Luthan officiated as the "representative" of the Singer, though it was an open secret among them that he no longer considered himself so. The chil-dren cried and Raine found tears slipping down her own face. Pascal and Marwey would be good parents, but the invasion—the stealth mission—loomed like a shadow over them all.

After the ceremony Alexa and Bastien livened the Temple by providing tables of excellent food and sweets to buzz the kids.

Studying Alexa, considering her personal Song, Raine realized that the woman truly believed that the Dark would be destroyed and some would survive. Alexa knew the odds were long that she and her husband, Bastien, would live since they were the premier fighters of the land, but she was willing to put all her effort into the task. Her innate optimism matched her husband's and being with them eased Raine's own fears. Maybe she *was* a weenie.

So she talked and laughed and watched the feycoocus paddle as ducks in the sacred pool. Her spirits lifted and she paid attention to the little hum at the back of her mind. A trickle of melodic notes that had always been there when she was in the Temple. But now, after her time on the ocean and practicing her own unique Power, she could hear them better.

Frowning, she drifted around the huge room sectioned off by fancy wooden screens until she stood before the huge silver gong.

Of course.

She studied it again and listened hard. Over the last week she'd been working with the navigation stones—the compass point gems and the hematite Power spheres. Corbeau had taught her how to tune them, infusing them with Power.

She'd set them to frequencies that corresponded to magnetic north and south, the great plinths east and west of Lladrana. She'd become accustomed to hearing certain humming in the back of her mind, feeling it slide against her skin.

The gong had the same effect on her, had since she'd first heard it. It hummed with some sort of navigational Power. As the builder and captain of many ships, she recognized a navigational instrument when she saw one.

Light burst inside her head. Giddiness claimed her. She laughed and it rippled the chimes and vibrated the gong itself.

"Raine?" asked Faucon, standing by the buffet table.

She turned in wild joy. No one she'd prefer to celebrate with more. She ran and flung herself at him. He caught her weight and only stepped back. Good, solid man. Tough guy. Noble warrior Chevalier.

"I've got it," she shrieked and it echoed throughout the Temple, plucking notes from the chimes. Crystals in the beams flared bright, reflected glorious colors on the stained-glass windows. Raine remembered Archimedes in his bathwater. "Eureka!" She squeezed Faucon on the shoulders. Kissed him hard on his sculpted mouth. Man, what a zing that was!

He grinned. "What?" As if he felt her joy, he whirled her around.

The others crowded in a circle.

"What?" The word came from the Exotiques in unison.

Raine squeezed the top of Faucon's shoulders, then wriggled so he'd put her down. "I know. I know."

"Know what?" asked Bastien.

"Know what the Dark wants!"

That quieted the room. Raine would be concerned, too, after the joy of discovery—of fulfilling one of her tasks—diminished and she settled down.

Marian, the Circlet Sorceress, swept up in a long robe. "Congratulations." Her lips were curved. She, as a scholar, would understand the rush of a problem solved. "What does the Dark want so much that it has been invading Lladrana for centuries to retrieve it?"

Raine threw out a fist and caught the gong square in the center. It reverberated through the room, perhaps through the Castle and the town below, perhaps even through the land.

Luthan stepped forward, saying quietly, "Sometimes when the gong is rung the Dark sends horrors to invade."

She sucked in a short breath. "Oh, no!"

But Faucon slipped his arm around her. "If there's an invasion, we'll handle it, as usual."

"The Dark wants the gong?" asked Jaquar, Marian's husband, another Circlet-Sorcerer-Investigator-of-the-Great-Unknown. He studied it, brows down, ran fingertips close to the surface of the huge circular piece of silver. Or silvery-colored metal. "Odd," Jaquar said. "It doesn't feel like silver."

"It's not." Raine stood tall, proud. "What it is, is a navigational tool."

"The Dark has a transdimensional ship?" Jaquar scowled.

Raine shrugged. "Maybe, maybe not. This could be a compass."

Marian said, "So this might be a tool the Dark uses to traverse the Dimensional Corridor whenever it wants. To wherever it wants. A compass and a key, perhaps."

"It isn't only this planet, Amee, it wants to have as its own," Luthan added.

"It wants everywhere." Alexa bared her teeth.

"Everything," Marian said.

"Naturally." Bastien crossed his arms. "Big, predatory, greedy evil always wants total dominion." He flashed a charming smile. "It's up to us to make sure it's destroyed."

The alarm klaxon blasted: Northern invasion of horrors.

Bastien's smile widened. "That's our cue." He swung an arm around Alexa's waist and lifted her to him, loping from the Temple into the courtyard, where the sound of wings of dozens of volarans landing came.

"Shit," Raine said.

Faucon turned to her, laid a heart-pounding kiss on her mouth, brushed her temples with his lips. "I'm on rotation."

Raine stiffened her spine, released his hand. "Go." She sounded choked, but that was too bad.

He tilted up her face, his eyes intent. "Stay in my apartments." A corner of his mouth lifted in a smile. "I've had a new wardrobe brought in, rearranged the space so you can look out the window if you work at the drafting table."

He'd had a drafting table brought in, had noticed she liked it close to windows. Rising to her toes she kissed him. "Go."

Hesitating, he met her eyes. "A new bed, a while back."

She hadn't thought of that important fact. Elizabeth had shared his bed here in the Castle. "Thank you for telling me."

Taking her hand, he lifted it to his lips, then tugged her along as he ran outside, calling for his squires and his second team of Chevaliers.

Bastien and Alexa were already in battle gear, on volarans. The Swordmarshall met Raine's gaze, then Alexa raised her voice. "We'll meet again as soon as we get back." She tilted her head to listen to the repeating pattern of the alarm. "Sounds like we need to reinforce the line on the northwest coast." She turned in her saddle to Bastien beside her. "I told you that one fence post was weak, didn't I tell you—"

He leaned over and kissed her words gone, then said, "Ayes, you did." Nodding at the rest of them, he said, "I anticipate that we'll be back in two hours at the latest. We'll see the rest of you then." They rose, following other waves of Marshalls and Chevaliers flying northward, waving the newest Marshalls, their previous squire team, behind them protectively.

Numb, Raine nodded. She'd already been nudged aside as squires dressed Faucon for battle. His volaran trotted up, and then there was one last press of his lips on her own before he took to the sky with his team.

After all the warriors left and only dust stirred in the yard, Raine gave in and clenched her fists. "I did this. I… awakened it…called it…something," she said to the remaining Exotiques.

"No harm done." Jaquar patted her on the shoulder. His voice was considering, his eyes looked like ideas were zooming in his mind a thousand miles an hour. "The incursions have been getting smaller. We haven't had a casualty for weeks."

Marian said, "As if the Dark knows a final showdown is coming."

Thunk. Back to reality. Being here at the Marshalls' Castle would always do that. She shifted her shoulders. She felt a lessening of a burden. One of her tasks that kept her on Lladrana was fulfilled.

Then Faucon disappeared from sight.

Castleton

Raine just couldn't stay in the Temple or the Castle. With Enerin trotting beside her as a miniature greyhound, Raine walked with Calli and Marrec and their children to their suite at Horseshoe Hall. They invited her in, but she declined, too itchy under her skin to be with them.

Faucon hadn't flown to battle since they'd been lovers. She wouldn't have wanted him to stay—hell, yeah, she wanted him to stay—but she wouldn't want him to forsake his duty, couldn't ask him to do that. That unquestioning attendance to his responsibilities was something she deeply admired.

But she didn't like him gone to battle.

He will be fine, said Enerin.

Raine stopped in her tracks on the way to the stables, stared down at her companion. "Do you really *know* that or are you just being sympathetic?"

Enerin sat down and scratched her ear with her hind leg, tilted her head, gave a puppy grin. *I really know that.*

Letting out a pent-up breath, Raine said, "Thanks."

"You're welcome. Where are we going?"

Raine hesitated. "Back to the house in Castleton."

"Good."

"I have stuff there."

"Ayes," Enerin said.

Blossom was waiting and nuzzled Raine, greeted Enerin with a whuffle, and the two-mile flight to the house was quick.

I will stay at the end of the street instead of going to my stable, Blossom said. *Since we will be returning to the Castle.*

Everyone expected that Raine would be in on the discussion of the gong, and of course she would, but she sighed.

When she walked through the house to her bedroom everything seemed different. It wasn't the house, this beautiful place crafted for the City Exotique...Bri, before she found her own home in a local tower. Raine knew it was herself.

She looked at the house differently.

No longer was it a refuge from the awful months of living like the lowest of the low. Nor was it a prize, a symbol that she was someone special, an Exotique.

In the few weeks away, she'd changed.

This was no longer home. A beautiful house, but not her home. She sat on the bed and looked out the window to the pretty park, the lovely houses surrounding the greenery, the passersby cheerful and prosperous.

Looked around at the room with the pitifully few personal items she could call her own. Atop the handcrafted dresser was her cowboy hat—"the Exotique gang"—that could still make her smile. On the desk was a stack of books, all the others' Lorebooks, including a copy of Elizabeth's book. She'd read it and it hadn't revealed many of Elizabeth's feelings for Faucon. It was more a factual account than anything else, and focused on the plague and the Chevalier's sickness that she and Bri had to whip. But one thing was for sure, Elizabeth's actions had changed Raine's life, even though they'd never met in person.

If Elizabeth hadn't been in the picture, would Faucon have

loved Raine? Raine thought so. He had an innate attraction to Exotiques, and heaven knows, Raine was attracted to him. But Elizabeth had made Raine's and Faucon's coming together more difficult.

Sitting in the lovely house, Raine realized that was no bad thing. Because Faucon's heart was tougher now, wasn't it? He'd believed Raine when she'd said she would return home to Earth, as he hadn't believed Elizabeth.

Home to Earth. She thought of her little cottage and the boats she'd made and how she'd been dissatisfied with her family and her work. She'd had an offer from a French firm....

But she was no longer that Raine Lindley. She had grown far beyond that young woman, and she didn't know now if the cottage could remain her home.

She'd lived several places on Lladrana. A few inns, ever closer to the sea until she stayed at the Open Mouthed Fish on a pier where she'd gotten a job as a potgirl through the kindness of the gruff female owner. A night at Faucon's deck-house, then a room in the Marshalls' Castle, finally this beautiful house.

But not one of them was home.

The image of her rooms in Faucon's castle came—that was the closest place that had actually *felt* like home.

She went to her desk, opened Elizabeth's book, looked at the medical doctor and her new husband. Obviously Elizabeth loved that man, had had an affair with Faucon on the rebound from a previous breakup. Had gone back to Earth where her love was. Bri, Elizabeth's twin, had stayed with her love, Sevair, as had all the other women. They'd made lives here on Lladrana.

None of them were Raine.

She snapped the book shut. She didn't know what to do. Didn't know what life on Earth or here would hold.

Enerin trotted in with a small bag of toys, the strap in her mouth. *I am ready to leave.*

"How did you know we were leaving?"

You are the Seamistress. Your place is at the coast.

True enough—Earth or Lladrana, her home, when she found it, would be on the coast.

Enerin sniffed. *You are not packed yet.*

Raine narrowed her eyes. "That sounded like a cat sniff to me, a cat comment. You are a puppy, loyal and true, happy to be with me."

Plopping down on her butt, Enerin let the strap fall from her mouth and lolled her tongue, made big eyes. *I love you.*

"Oh." Tears burned behind Raine's eyes. She forced them back. "I love you, too." Raine hauled out a duffel, folded clothes into it from the wardrobe and dresser drawers. Squeezed in the books, a few knickknacks the Exotiques and their men had given her. She'd been given everything…or had worked for it. She didn't recall actually buying anything.

She put her hat on her head and felt weird, as if she really were part of the Exotique gang and would be staying, but where else would you carry a hat?

Blossom neighed outside and a few seconds later the Castle klaxon rang. Raine tensed, listening to the pattern she'd learned to distinguish. The horrors had been killed, a new fence post raised, no Lladranan casualties. Her knees felt weak and tension drained.

The Chevaliers and Faucon will be back soon, Enerin said. *You should move your things to Faucon's rooms so we can all talk about the gong.*

Raine wasn't sure she wanted to talk about the gong.

Enerin nosed under her pantleg and slurped on her ankle. *You did very well. You discovered what no Lladranan, no other Exotique had. You know what the Dark wants.*

She did. The Dark wanted death.

Still, Raine shouldered her duffel, and left the house, saying a silent farewell to it. Once again she'd changed and outgrown a place. Her time here was done.

There was a man sitting in the park. His manner and dress seemed rougher than what was usual in this part of town. When she passed him and nodded a greeting a look of pure revulsion twisted his features so he resembled the guy who'd stalked and attacked her.

Her step froze, then she moved on, though a chill slid along her spine. She just wasn't used to this reaction. The house on the square had been chosen for Bri, the Exotique Medica, because none of the locals had the revulsion reaction.

The incident added to the rest of her unease and she called Blossom, then hurried to the end of the street.

Her mind went back to her tasks. She may have accomplished one, but she had two more to go—integrating the Seamasters back into Lladranan life and raising a ship—before she went home.

Wherever that would be.

23

Singer's Abbey

Jikata was awakened from an after-dinner doze by a feeling of tugging strings inside her and a ringing in her ears that made her think she'd heard something in her sleep. She listened but no unusual sound came. There was sibilant whispering outside her door and a sense of activity in the Abbey compound.

With a little four-note hum, she swept the muzziness from her mind and rolled her shoulders as she rose from the chair she'd fallen asleep in. Marian's Lorebook was on the side table.

Stretching, Jikata walked to the outside door of her rooms where someone hovered, and opened it to her maid. The young woman's face cleared.

"What is it?" Jikata asked.

"The Abbey bell echoed the Marshalls' Castle alarm."

That took a few seconds to sink in and when it did, Jikata tensed. "The Marshalls and Chevaliers are flying to battle?"

"Ayes," her maid said and stepped forward to enter the rooms. "We've been told there have been small incursions of the horrors, but nothing triggered our alarm." She hurried to a cabinet in Jikata's sitting room, opened the top narrow map drawer, lifted out a built-in frame, pulled out the second drawer and snapped the whole in place. A piece of tapestry taut on the wood turned from blank linen to a Lladranan map, then became animated.

Jikata stared. Looked at the maid. "Is this a map like that one in the Marshalls' Castle?"

Her maid nodded. "But this is much smaller." She stood straight. "The Singer's Abbey has everything the Marshalls' Castle has—" she paused "—except the gong. But we have the Caverns of Prophecy. That's why the Abbey was built here. And because it's in the south, well away from the invading horrors."

Jikata nodded, drawing close to see the map. Little shields were moving from the Marshalls' Castle northwest to the coast.

The maid sucked in a breath. "I thought we'd replaced those fence posts. It's not good that we're fighting in the northwest." She frowned. "It must have been the very last one, don't you think? I heard the land was weak there, it might have crumbled into the sea." When Jikata stared at her she flushed, knotted her hands in her apron, glanced around. "I thought you should *watch*." She lifted her chin. "You are an Exotique, too. You should see what the others are doing." With a roughened finger the maid pointed to blue-green shields. "That's Alyeka and Bastien." The maid frowned. "I don't see Calli and Marrec, so they remain at the Castle with their children. Marian isn't going, either, though she does occasionally, probably not a big enough challenge for her. Bri is a medica and only went to battle once so she could train other medicas. Last I heard, Raine was on the coast."

Jikata grabbed onto the topic, the first time someone had mentioned the other Earth women. "What of Elizabeth?"

The maid's eyes widened and she put a hand over her mouth, as if realizing she'd been indiscreet.

Jikata gestured to the books. "I'm reading them all, so you can tell me of Elizabeth."

"She returned with the Snap," the maid said in a hushed voice.

"Alexa and Marian have written of the Snap." Jikata tapped the map, the largest island. "This is where Marian's tower is." She didn't know for sure, but knew it was Bossgond's island and that there was a spot on that island that attracted Marian, so it was a good guess. "More about Elizabeth, please."

"She was—is—Bri's twin and went back to Exotique Terre. I didn't know that she'd written a Lorebook." Suspicion was in the maid's gaze.

"The Singer gave me all the books," Jikata reminded her.

"Ayes." But the maid retreated to the door. "Watch the battle in the north. You should see that." She opened the door and snicked it shut behind her.

Jikata stared down at the little animated map. There were a lot of shields moving around the northwest edge of the country. Some pairs were long and pointy, and different colors with tiny bars on them, like wands. The blue-green shield with the green bar was Alexa's, the black-and-white one, Bastien's. Definitely Marshalls. The shorter, squatter shields would be Chevaliers then. There were a lot of orange-and-red ones milling around.

Then there was a flare of bright light that dimmed down to

a steady blue, sent a ray of blue light to the east, and Jikata's eyes widened. She'd just seen a fence post made! The blue line with blue dots must be the magical border that kept the horrors out. It ranged all the way across Lladrana with a tiny gap here or there, and a ragged opening in the east. If Alexa and the Marshalls had replaced the entire fence over the last couple of years, it was an impressive feat. And a lot of battles.

A sweet bonging of the bell tower came…and the sound almost made sense. On the map the shields were winging south. To the Marshalls' Castle, where the action was. Never as far south as the cloistered Abbey.

Marshalls' Castle

Raine and Enerin and Blossom flew back to the Castle. To Raine's surprise one of Faucon's squires met her at the Landing Field and cooed at Blossom, leading the volaran to the stables. The squire looked at Raine's cowboy hat, winked, then took her duffel. "You'll want to be going to the Temple."

Not really, but she did, anyway.

There were people in the Temple, Chevaliers and Marshalls who had not been on the fighting rotation, soldiers of the Castle, even the odd little guy who ran the Assayer's office. The doors of the place were not quite shut, letting in the night air to mix with incense someone had lit. Low talk filled the Temple. People had filed up to inspect the gong but none of them touched it. What had been a common object taken for granted had suddenly become dangerously lethal.

Marian and Jaquar were still near the gong, and Raine couldn't tell whether they'd remained the whole time. They *were* affably answering questions.

Robin D. Owens

Then Alexa's bootsteps rang on the stone, no mistaking that sound. Raine turned and the doors opened for her. She was followed by Bastien and Faucon.

Faucon's face was ruddy from the cool flight, but his grin was wide, his eyes a trifle wild. Raine ran to him and didn't stop when she scented monster gore. He grabbed her, whirled her around, and she figured that would be their new standard greeting. His body was warm under cold armor, his breath puffed against her ear. "The new fence post is *mine!* I was the one who killed the horror and planted the post!"

"A great honor," she said.

"Ayes." He kissed her. "My luck has been in lately. I now have four posts in the border."

He didn't look like he had a scratch on him. Some dirt and sweat and a bit of sea-scent, but no blood. Her last, lingering fear for him vanished. She kissed him back, dimly hearing Alexa's yell for attention.

Faucon slid her down his body and she felt his burgeoning arousal. With easy strength he set her on her feet beside him.

"Listen, all! We will discuss the gong. Those of you who want to stay are welcome, though I recommend only those who have made the invasion force remain. Bastien will be invoking a no-tell spell."

Bastien swept the space with a penetrating gaze, and most people were moving out the doors. "The spell will last until your death and will only be able to be removed by me or a Circlet."

No chance at all for gossip, then.

"From now on, a no-tell spell will always be a requisite at our conferences." He took Alexa's hand. "We Marshalls have been more open than ever before about our plans, but that ends now."

Alexa frowned but said nothing and Bastien continued, "The stakes are too high. All our lives, our land, our world."

The tenor of his voice, backed by his strange black-and-white magic, rippled through all of them in a spell. Then he smiled. "Feel free to speculate ten different ways when you talk and spread rumor."

Even more left, some nodding, some raising a hand in farewell. A few people settled on the colorful fat pillows gracing the built-in stone seats: the Captain of the Castle Guard, a couple of Townmasters, but as was happening most often, only the core group remained.

Everyone who was anyone was there, clumped around the gong. All the Exotiques and their men, Luthan, and Koz, Marian's brother, along with some nobles—Marshalls and Chevaliers—and Citymasters. And Bossgond, the greatest sorcerer of their age.

When the doors were closed, Bastien raised his voice in the no-tell spell, and they all joined in. The Power of that song-spell was such that no one in the room could communicate in any way about what occurred with anyone who was not there.

Alexa stalked around the nine-foot gong, mouth a thin line, jade baton out. "Could something so small hold such a Powerful thing as the Dark?" she asked, doubt in her voice.

"Look at you," Bastien, said. "You're small and Powerful."

"I don't eat planets," Alexa pointed out.

"Mass doesn't always equate with Power," Marian said.

Alexa's face scrunched. "A ship."

"An interdimensional ship that surfs the winds in the corridor," Marian said on a shaky, horrified breath. Raine had never seen her so pale. "Or a compass or a key. We still don't know, but it must be valuable to the Dark if it's tried to retrieve it from Lladrana for centuries."

"I think it made a mistake," Luthan said quietly.

They all turned to him. Bastien said, "Tell us."

Luthan said, "It plans to leave. One of the futures—a less likely one—is it leaving as it came, strong and looking for a tasty planet. With or without creatures living on it."

"The mistake?" Alexa asked.

"Amee is richer than most in Power, but she wasn't quite as weak as the Dark believed, has fought more. Her atmosphere is colder, less hospitable to it."

"We all know of Earth's global warming," Alexa said grimly.

"But Earth doesn't have a great deal of Power," Marian said.

"Not magic," Marrec, Calli's husband agreed. He was the only Lladranan man who'd been to Earth. "But it has some other *power*. There was a tang, a metallic taste in the air."

Koz, Marian's brother, also from Earth, stared at everyone, then said, "Nuclear power. Fusion. What could a being like this do with that sort of power?"

"What it has done for millennia, to Amee and other worlds. Leech on it, feed, until the world is dying or dead, move on."

A shudder went through the room.

"But why would it leave the gong?" Raine asked.

Luthan said, "I think it was strong from its last feed, the energy of killing a planet, the last of the life force. It arrived here, a miscalculation. Cold, it had to hurry. There might also have been attacks on it from whatever creatures Amee had summoned to defend her. It was not in a hot volcano, but in cool hills. It left the gong. Or—" Luthan's brows came down "—it thought it would destroy Amee quickly, come back for the gong when everything was dead."

Staring in fascinated disgust at the gong, Marian said, "Do you think the gong itself can open a dimensional portal?"

Koz answered his sister. "Perhaps, maybe that's why all the Summonings here to the Temple have been successful. But I think there's a natural portal at Singer's Abbey."

Now everyone looked at him.

Shrugging, Koz continued. "The Singer wouldn't let me in the Abbey but I could feel the energy." He rubbed the back of his neck as if hair had risen there. "I've learned a lot about interdimensional energy working with placing mirrors on Earth for Bri and Raine." He gave them a warm half smile.

Marian asked, "Bossgond?"

But the small man was already coming through the crowd, people moving aside from the sheer force of the Powerful aura surrounding him. He was skinny and ugly, but there was no mistaking his magic. He walked right up to the gong and *sniffed,* backed away without touching it. "Definitely not from Amee." He coughed. "Older than anything I've ever sensed."

"Well, if the Dark wants the gong, let's give the thing to it." Alexa's smile was fierce.

Everyone shuddered. "Are you crazy?" Marian asked.

"No. Listen to me." Alexa raised her baton and everyone stepped back. Raine bumped into Faucon and he put his hands on her shoulders, strong and comforting.

"If the gong is that mysterious and dangerous, we should take it with us to destroy it when we blow the island."

"The Dark will send everything it has after you, all the horrors, the Master, come itself…" Bossgond said.

Alexa said, "That will take time. If the horrors and the Master are busy fighting Marshalls and Chevaliers on the *outside* of the mountain, and we're down the old lava tube and inside…"

Raine hadn't heard any specific plans before, wanted not to know, maybe even to run. Faucon massaged her tense shoulders.

Alexa turned to Marian, whose mouth had dropped open. "You were in the Nest. How much do you think the Dark moves?"

Marian trembled, Jaquar pulled her against his body and wrapped his arms around her, his mouth grim. Then she answered. "I only sensed it. I interacted with the former Master. I don't know. Perhaps the Dark doesn't move at all."

"Can't be very fast." Alexa flipped her baton. Fire in her eyes, she looked at Luthan. "You've been having a lot of visions about the battle and the outcome, I know, and you don't tell me hardly anything, but tell us all this. What's the percentage of times that the Dark slithers away from that battle?"

Luthan hesitated, and the silence in the Temple was complete, only the faint tinkle of water from a small fountain breaking it.

"Luthan?" Alexa prompted.

"In all the times I've had the visions, the Dark has only escaped twice." His lips went grim an instant before he went on. "Most of the time it is destroyed, in slightly less of the visions it is damaged for eons."

"So we take the gong." Alexa nodded decisively. Despite her smile and the bursting of the top of her baton into flames, she put her free hand in her husband's and her words echoed hollowly around the room.

There was cheeping and flapping and the three birdlike feycoocus circled down to land on the frame surrounding the gong.

We can hide the gong from the Dark and will take charge of it during the final spell, Sinafinal said. *We will put it in a crevice. The Dark will go after it, not you.*

There was silence, then Marian said, "Fine."

The feycoocus whistled approval and flicked their wings.

Raine felt Alexa's optimism, that of everyone else in the room. But it was hope. At the core was the lingering knowledge that those who went into the battle could all perish.

Singer's Abbey

The next morning Jikata was in the practice room that was good for "creating" spells. She snorted. She thought the Singer just liked moving her around, keeping her off balance, though it was true that the colorful wallpaper in this room was studded with Power crystals as part of the pattern. She'd never seen the like either here or on Earth. The whole place gave her a buzz.

She was becoming accustomed to the buzz or hum or melody or her whole damn life-soundtrack of Power, tried to be blasé about it and thought her manner covered a lot of the daily surprises. Keeping the Singer and her Friends off guard.

She smiled.

One of the windows had an excellent view of the horse and volaran stables down the way, which she studied. She still hadn't been outside the Abbey walls, met any of the flying horses that Chasonette told her were telepathic, and yearned to. Jikata was getting restless, like some internal clock was counting down.

Despite the warm tones of great Power that imbued the chamber, she felt isolated. As isolated here as at home in the States. She just recognized it easier.

Today the knot spellbook was open to a successful harvest, one that prayed for good weather, no accidents with sharp implements. She shook her head. She knew precious little about harvest.

Yet as she scanned the spell, she recognized it was a good one. Simple. Strong. Essential.

Idly, she turned the pages, stopped when words caught at her. "To Summon Friends." Her heart picked up a beat…dared she? She had no idea when the Singer would appear, always a power play, or whether she'd be Singing with the others. The harvest spell could be Sung by as little as one "of the Singer apprentice level"—and that word still stung—or "a chorus of ten good voices." If organizing meetings here was anything like on Earth, it wasn't surprising that knot spell casting had faded away for simpler methods.

To Summon Friends. Again she studied the large window empty of anyone she knew, anyone familiar with who she was. Not Jikata the popular singer so much as Jikata the Earthling. Alexa had welcomed Marian warmly and Jikata thought Alexa would do the same for her. From what Jikata had read in Marian's book, curiosity was a driving force and might be counted upon to bring her.

The spell would "call to" three friends—which three of the five Exotiques? Alexa and Marian, since Jikata knew them better because she'd read of them? Who else? Wouldn't it be interesting to find out? The knot needed blue floss ranging from dark blue to sky blue, six stranded silk. She opened a small cabinet and pulled out a drawer. Her hand went to the mixed blue, the exact shades.

She glanced at the text—the amount of floss needed was a wrist length. She lifted a skein.

"If you attempt that, they may knock at my walls," the Singer said.

Jikata flinched inwardly, smoothed her face into a mask. She put the floss back into its proper place, pushed the drawer into the cabinet and turned to meet the Singer.

She stood on the threshold, hands folded at her waist, a

frown between her brows. Her eyes were calculating, head tilted as if she examined Jikata's Song—sensing restlessness? Jikata hoped not, *she* was in charge of her own life. "Ayes?" Jikata raised her brows.

The Singer glided forward. Jikata stood her ground. The Singer didn't even glance at the book before humming one note. Pages flipped back to the harvest lesson. She took her usual throne seat, this one was wooden and brightly gilded, the cushions a deep, rich brown.

"Should you Sing that spell and knot that knot, then release it, the other Exotiques will be knocking at my walls. You have much to learn, are not ready to leave."

The more the Singer said that, the more Jikata disagreed.

"You have not finished the Lorebooks?" the Singer asked.

"I'm reading Marian's," Jikata said.

The Singer's head turned sharply, then she hesitated.

Something was in Marian's Lorebook—Jikata would have to read faster.

Lifting and dropping one shoulder in an overly casual manner, the Singer said, "The Exotiques have agendas."

Who didn't?

For an instant there seemed to be the sound of multiple voices in the back of Jikata's mind, but they faded, along with the impulse to be with them.

The Singer's lips tightened, then she said, "Luthan has been deleterious in his reports." She turned to Jikata and repeated, "The Exotiques have their own agenda regarding you." The Singer smiled and it wasn't nice. "You will be ready for your task when *I* say you are ready."

She waved a hand and the door opened, the boys and women who approximated the Exotiques surged in, varying expressions of concern on their faces. For her? Or for the Singer? Perhaps these, too, were friends. She'd worked with them and valued them, treating them well. As the Singer hadn't.

Whether they were friends or not, they were only "a good chorus of voices." They could never be the quality and strength and the Power of the Exotiques.

Jikata was sure that the Singer wouldn't let her go until the Exotiques demanded her for "their agenda." Then Jikata would feel like a commodity, as she had a few times before in her life. She hadn't liked it.

No.

She could cast the knot spell to bring friends—strangers who could be friends—but, no. This was *her* life and she would take action.

She smiled a true welcome to the other singers, turned a false one on the Singer, who studied her, nodded complacently. Was this why the Singer's Thomas had returned to Earth? Had the Singer always been so sure of herself, misread people of Earth background? Hadn't worked to understand them? Sad.

The Singer Sang the first line of the knot spell and the cabinet opened and strands of living green and rich dirt brown and straw yellow floated out and settled on the book. Jikata hit her cue along with the others and she Sang.

And plotted.

24

Marshalls' Castle

Making love to Faucon all night long had been simply delicious. He'd had a little leftover wildness from the battle, from the triumph of stopping the horrors and raising a fence post, and Raine had loved every energetic moment of it. Every slide of body against body, every rough word and urgent demand.

Raine smiled and stretched against fine linen sheets. Delicious. She blinked at the light in the room. Another sunny day, and that was reason for smiling, too.

The door swung open and Faucon walked in with a tray that smelled of ham and eggs and warm toast from fresh bread that had Raine's mouth watering. "Hey, sexy," she said.

He looked a little startled, then put an extra swagger in his step. His chest and feet were bare, the lower half of his body encased in black leather pants.

"Breakfast for us both." He set the tray over her lap, settled beside her against thick pillows, grabbed a piece of toast and a fork and ate some scrambled eggs.

They ate companionably. This felt simply *right* to Raine. She was tired of thinking about the future, worrying about it, letting it shadow her. She'd deal with it when it came.

She sipped orange juice, let it lay on her tongue to savor the sweetness. Even here at the Castle, orange juice was rare, but Faucon was a merchant prince. Though he looked more like a scruffy rogue with his light beard, longish tousled hair and worn leathers.

He drank from his crystal goblet, sent her a sideways glance. "Last day of trials today."

A piece of ham got caught in her throat. She swallowed it down. "Then what?"

"Alexa and the rest are impatient to move north." He cleared his throat, seemed to study the brownness of his toast. "They 'won' the discussion with the Circlets and the invasion will leave from my northern estate, Creusse Landing."

He'd hadn't mentioned the ship.

"Especially now that I'm fine-tuning the ship's design."

"Especially that," he agreed. "It will be easier to gather people and supplies in one place." He frowned. "Though I think it will take folk here a little more time to get ready than they anticipate."

"A few days, then?"

"Ayes."

Raine considered that. Her time at Faucon's castle in the south was over. She should have been ready for that change. It never seemed as if she was. After a long breath in and out, she said, "I'd like to go to the manor first, look around without so many people."

Faucon shoved the tray to the bottom of the bed, took her hand, rolled close, stared into her eyes and kissed her lips. Tender. Supportive. "I thought you would."

"I'll leave after breakfast." She looked around the room. She hadn't unpacked. Just as well. "Do you have to stay?"

"It might be better," he said, lifted her fingers to his mouth and kissed them again. His gaze was steady on hers. "But I'm also tired of being away from you."

She smiled and that, too, felt real and right, then kissed him. "It won't be for very long. We'll be together soon."

The alarm sounded and they both tensed, but it only indicated that the trials would start shortly.

She pushed him onto his back, crawled on him and rubbed her body against his, savoring him, too. Then she kissed him deeply, taking his taste into her, and rolled away. "I'll shower, then I'm gone." She fluttered her lashes at him. "I think everyone is expecting you at the Landing Field."

He groaned and subsided on the bed and she laughed.

Raine didn't say goodbye. As she walked with Enerin puppy to the lower courtyard where Blossom was awaiting her to fly to the north, the crowd at the Landing Field roared with shouts and applause. No need to interrupt the activities with a brief appearance of one who wasn't a permanent Exotique.

She'd see them in a few days anyway. The corners of her mouth quirked up. She couldn't escape Exotique togetherness.

She stepped over the security threshold at the gate between the wards and smiled at the guards' snappy salutes. They met her eyes briefly, then at another eruption of noise their gazes went yearningly to above the Landing Field, where four volarans raced.

One of the guards said, "Friend of ours, just graduated

Chevalier class, trying out for the invasion team. She's good."
He heaved a sigh. "No soldiers on the force…otherwise…"

His companion nodded. "Otherwise…"

Raine felt her smile freeze. She'd just have to get over the
casual mention of the invasion and the battle and death it
would bring. It was like a ten-ton elephant following her
around, or Bri's roc flying over her head, not something she
could ignore. She hitched up her duffel and nodded to them
once more. "Good days ahead to you. I have a ship to build."

"All the luck to you, lady," one of the guards called, then
turned his attention to the air show again.

Blossom trotted to her, then stood as Raine fastened the
duffel behind the saddle. Raine hesitated. There was no need
to say goodbye physically anyway, when you could do it
mentally. *Hey, Alexa, I'm off to Faucon's northern manor.*

Immediately Alexa's attention focused on her. *Faucon told
us. Keep well. We'll be there soon. Virtual hugs.*

Raine laughed. *Virtual hugs back.* Which was better since
Alexa tended to hug too hard. *Love you, Calli and Marian.*
Those two were at the trials, too.

Love you, Raine, came in stereo from Calli and Marian.

Raine stretched her senses and found Bri between patients
in Castleton. *I'm leaving for the north, love you, Bri.* Just repeating the sentiment warmed Raine, made her smile real.

Love ya. See ya soon, Bri said, then through the common
channel added, *How's it going there at the trials, any surprises?*

Maybe, again in unison, from Calli and Alexa.

See you! Raine called.

See you! they all replied.

They didn't add anything about the ship. Because they
fully believed that whatever Raine was doing was right. She

understood that from their feelings toward her. They'd never doubted her.

As she and Blossom and Enerin took to the air and flew south and east to prevent any intersection with the Landing Field, she thought of how close she was to these women, sisters she'd never had, instead of brothers. She snorted at the thought of any of them linked up with her brothers. Never would have worked.

She'd bonded with the women and all of them would be on that invasion force. She loved them, a blessing and a curse.

Then she turned her face and Blossom to the west so she could taste the sea air.

Singer's Abbey

Jikata ate lunch alone with Chasonette on the balcony off her sitting room. After ensuring no one could overhear them, Jikata said, "So, what do you think of Singer's Abbey?"

Chasonette stopped parading along the thick rail. *It is pretty but boring. Not much to see or do. I have perched on all the spires and weather vanes and towers and looked at all the views.*

Jikata nodded. "I think I've had enough of the views myself, and it's time to move on."

The bird swivelled her head, fixed a gleaming yellow eye on Jikata. *We are leaving? The Singer won't like that.*

"It's not the Singer's life, it's mine."

It's everyone's.

"Do you want to expand on that comment?" Jikata asked.

Chasonette rippled her comb. *No.* She turned so her tail was toward Jikata. *When do we go?*

"Tomorrow evening. That will give us time to prepare. I'll

walk the perimeter this evening, check out the walls and find the best place to go over them." She considered her companion. "You can scout for me, go farther afield than the Abbey." The psychic shielding on the walls let in creatures and humans that meant no harm to the Singer, so they shouldn't be any deterrent to getting out, either. Jikata didn't think the Singer had a clue that Jikata might want to leave.

I will look for a good clearing. Chasonette groomed her upper wing feathers. *You can call a volaran and it will come and pick us up for the flight to the Marshalls' Castle.*

Jikata's breath came in sharp. She hadn't thought too much about going to the Castle. Where others would be the stars of the show. That didn't matter as much as *meeting* all these people and seeing their expectations of her in their eyes.

Since all the others had been brought for a specific task, it was only logical that she had been, too.

To help Amee, to destroy the leech that Alexa and Marian called the Dark in their books. Finally she would have time to read the books and discern what was ahead of her. She was sure there would be specifics.

"I'm not ready to go to the Castle. I want some time to myself. If a volaran will only take me to that Castle, I don't want one yet." Liar.

A while back she'd gone to the western gate, the simplest path that led to the volaran stables, corrals and landing field. The gate was two hefty pillars at the ends of high stone walls with an equally tall iron gate and an always staffed little sentry box. The gatekeeper had put on a pleasant smile but shifted into a militant stance that set him solidly in front of the gate when she'd spoken to him. His action told Jikata that before he became a Friend he was a warrior.

Jikata was fascinated with the flying horses, who wouldn't be? When she was high in one of the Singer's towers, she could sometimes see them outside the window, sometimes soaring alone, sometimes with a person winging away. The idea of flying on a volaran tempted her.

She'd once had a relationship with a third-generation California rancher, but she'd been on her way to the top and he'd wanted someone who'd fit her life to his. Wasn't meant to be and she thought they both regretted that. But she'd learned to ride and acquired some knowledge of horses. Enough that she'd made owning a horse property one of her wishes to fulfill once she made it to the top and could spend a decent amount of time with them.

So she had questioned the gatekeeper guard about volarans. He'd eased, but didn't move from the gate. He'd been a Chevalier, sworn to a noble lady who'd fallen—he'd gone mum. Then he'd switched back to volarans, talking about their intelligence, their mindspeech, mentioned that great changes had come when Exotique Calli had been Summoned, then frowned at himself and made busy work, waving Jikata away.

She told him that the Singer had discussed the Exotiques with her and the man's expression had relaxed, but she'd known she wouldn't get any more out of him and had left.

But the Singer's volarans might not let her fly with them, and others might take her to where she didn't want to go, yet. She had no idea how much they would obey her, consider her wants.

An incredulous Chasonette was staring at her. *Not want a volaran?* Her beak clicked. *How will we get to the Castle then?*

Jikata raised her brows. "Walk?" Though she'd never liked hiking and would have given a lot to have had her Mercedes here. Absurd idea. She hadn't even shipped it to the spa.

Robin D. Owens

For a moment she recalled "Club Lladrana" and had a vision of one of those party-colored golf carts with a fringe canopy in hot pink. She chuckled, then put aside fancy for reality. "I know there's a village to the north. I can hire horses or a carriage or perhaps a volaran. I have jewelry I can sell."

With a whir of feathers Chasonette was gone, bulleting toward the north, to the Castle? To whom? "Wait!"

I will return by tomorrow evening.

Jikata snorted. It wasn't a sound she often made, but it was satisfying. So she did it again.

So much for companionship. She allowed herself a scowl.

25

Creusse Landing

Even with Distance Magic, it took Blossom, Raine and Enerin a while to reach Faucon's northern estate. It was a beautiful summer's day, warm and sunny and with a breeze that brought the scents of the changing land beneath them as they flew above trees, flowers, growing crops. There was the richness of turned earth, a whiff of animals and manure: cattle, sheep, pigs.

They flew due west toward the ocean until the sea breeze and the taste of salt was in the air. Then followed the coast until they were flying over the large bay that curved into Lladrana.

Raine was familiar with the coastline from the maps, and from working with the ponds on the southern estate, and dismissed the Distance Magic bubble so she could see the shape of the land where she'd raise the ship and from which the force to destroy the Dark's Nest would sail. The estate was on the southern coast of the last part of Lladrana that jutted into the ocean, so they would actually have to sail around land before they set course to the Dark's Nest. *They*. Her stomach jittered as she realized she was thinking of captaining the boat herself.

It was just projecting herself into the mind of those—or he, or she—who would sail the ship, visualizing the coast. In any event, that first turn around the bulge of land would shake down the crew and the people on the boat. She shook her head. How would restless Alexa cope with hours onboard a ship?

But a ship was the way to go. It could carry stores and the people and volarans and they'd be fresh for the battle of their lives. Everyone seemed to think that the Dark would notice a massive flight of volarans arrowing to it over several weeks.

The ship wasn't going to be small, more like a galleon or a man of war than a graceful schooner, but Raine would guarantee that it would go faster than the volarans, using the Power stones and the wind Amee would fill the sails with.

Then Enerin cawed, lifted herself from the bag she'd been traveling in and launched herself off Blossom. Raine looked down to see a pretty U-shaped manor house of cream-colored stone, the long bottom of the U faced southeast to the ocean. The landing field was to the east along with several other outbuildings, and a lot of people.

When they circled down to a newly expanded landing field she noted busy activity in setting up more corrals and storage sheds.

Corbeau hurried up, lines in his face smoothing as he met her. He grasped her hands and she heard the beat of his blood that held a note of the sea, just as her blood and her Song—and Faucon's—did.

"Welcome to Creusse Landing. It's good to see you again, Seamistress Exotique."

"You're back already."

"I left shortly after you did, but came here." He glanced around, forehead wrinkling. "Much to be done if we're going to house an invasion force and stage the debarkation." Then he turned his attention back, leaned down and kissed her cheek. "I'll show you Faucon's and your suite, introduce you to my family and the staff." Another frown and he took her arm in a firm grip. "The Exotiques came last year and very few of our people had the repulsion reaction."

Raine tensed. She *knew* the man who'd stalked her was unusual in letting that emotion rule his actions, but this was another reason she was wary in meeting other people.

The Castle was free of those who had that reaction, or, like Luthan, they'd grown out of it or mastered it. In Castleton, she'd only met that one.

But Corbeau flashed her a smile and patted her hand on his arm. "I let everyone know the place would be teeming with Exotiques and encouraged those who wouldn't be comfortable with you to go." He shrugged a large shoulder. "Gave them a little settling money along with about twenty different rumors as to what would be goin' on here."

"Thank you."

So she met Corbeau's wife, who carried a baby on her hip and eyed her warily.... A lot of people were being brought onto their land, necessitating a lot of work, Raine got that, so Raine was especially polite to her. Raine winked at the baby, who reached for her hair and pouted when his hands snatched air.

That made the woman's lip twitch and she hitched him over her shoulder. "I'll show you to the Master's Suite."

Realization struck. It wasn't just that Raine was a stranger, it was that Raine was Faucon's lover. Despite Corbeau's words, she hadn't absorbed the fact that he—they? how many people?—considered her and Faucon a pair. Raine's heart leapt and she understood some other things. She liked being thought of as Faucon's lover, a woman he cared for. More, she had to squash a little slice of glee that *she* was Faucon's Exotique, not Elizabeth. Elizabeth had never been here.

So she walked through the house that was dappled with sunshine shafting in from large windows, and up polished wooden stairs passing a yelling bunch of children coming down. She paused and stared.

Corbeau's wife laughed. "No, they're not all mine, but the staff's, and another cousin of Faucon's lives here with her husband." Her gaze went serious. "Do you worry about that?"

Raine shrugged. "It's his home, or rather yours." She smiled. "Faucon prefers Creusse Crest."

The woman sighed. "Petty of me to be glad of that, but I am." She looked around her home. "I love this place and have been the mistress of it for many years."

"Your care for it shows," Raine said. "Like your love for the children showed."

"Thank you." She led Raine up another flight to the third floor and toward the middle of the hallway, then opened the door. No sunshine here, for all that the room had French doors and was bright with cream-colored paint. The suite faced east, inland, and would let in morning light. Sunrises would be magnificent from the long balcony beyond the windows.

"We keep this for Faucon. It has a sitting room and even a bath with a tub. No hot springs here." A little huff of breath.

"Still miss that since I came from the other estate." She shook her head. "Maybe that's why Faucon likes that place."

"He likes the castle," Raine said without thinking about it.

Corbeau's wife laughed. "Indeed he does, and those dramatic cliffs of his. The land slopes nicely to the ocean here. The beach is better, less rocky, but as a dock and port, not as good." She waved to the room. "Make yourself at home." Then the woman went outside the rooms and shouted. "Corbeau, you coming with that bag of the lady's?" Again the woman shook her head. The baby imitated her, cooing. "That man enjoys all this bustle." Her black-eyed gaze met Raine's. "But it's a hard thing we prepare for, and glad we are that we're staying behind."

The light in the pretty chamber seemed to dim. "I understand perfectly," Raine said.

Corbeau hurried in with Raine's duffel, put it gently on the bed that looked to be larger than a California king, but then the Lladranans were larger, too. Raine thought she saw a little color under Corbeau's cheeks, making them peachy. "Got caught up in a discussion about where to raise the Ship."

His wife tsked. "You all have been talking about that for days." She glanced at Raine. "Do you need a personal maid?"

"No, thank you," Raine said.

Corbeau slanted Raine an apologetic glance. "We're still considering the best place to raise the Ship. Were, before I left, and I used the crystal a few times, too. We think the little cove with the long beach—"

"Didn't you decide that was too narrow? Let the girl freshen up, rest a little. Then you can show her the spots. She's the Exotique Seamistress, she'll know what's what." With that unstated acceptance of Raine, the woman turned to leave, and

Corbeau followed. The baby twisted and looked at her with big, round eyes, before his mother gently shut the door.

Raine hopped up to sit on the firm bed, wriggled her butt. Faucon liked his beds softer, so did she. Yet he hadn't had it changed. Ayes, he preferred his southern estate.

The people who'd just left were good, solid folks, like the majority of Lladranans must be. Raine had fallen in with the most adventurous, the warrior and noble class, and she sensed that class knew exactly what kind of folk they were fighting for. People like the Corbeau Creusses.

However ordinary the Exotiques had been in their lives on Earth, they'd been Summoned to lead this adventure.

To accomplish great tasks. To build great magic.

To lead others to battle and death.

Marshalls' Castle

The trials had paused for lunch and Luthan was in the stables, grooming his volaran, Lightning, when a bright red Lladranan cockatoo came soaring in accompanied by two feycoocus in hawk form.

His heart gave a hard thump, then settled back to a slightly speedier beat. It had been unexpectedly difficult to wait until the new Exotique wanted to leave Singer's Abbey. He'd been to the Abbey several times but hadn't been allowed to speak with her, had seen her only once. Yet the small mental link between them remained, and the feycoocus had reported of her often.

When he'd seen her, he hadn't had the revulsion, and he hoped he'd mastered that shaming instinctive withdrawal, but he sensed her Song was yet muted.

The cockatoo lit on the door of the stall next to Lightning's and ruffled her feathers, then smoothed them. He could have sworn she was smiling. *The Exotique Singer wishes to see more of Lladrana. She will leave tomorrow evening when the Singer retires to her chamber for her private time.*

Luthan knew the schedule.

You should go and get her, and bring this one, too. Chasonette poked her head more into the stall and chirped at the beautiful buckskin with dark brown mane and tail there.

I can speak for myself, the volaran stallion whickered. *In the language of animals and even some bird, though that is not a pleasant-sounding language. I, too, was meant for Jikata, the Exotique Singer. Not only you, pink bird.*

Chasonette screeched and flapped her wings, turned and pooped in the stall.

Lightning snorted at the new smell, put his head over his stall. *Ayes, bird rude.*

Luthan didn't know if the volarans meant the language, Chasonette, or both. "That's enough."

I will carry the lady to the very nest of the Dark, the Exotique's volaran continued, raising his head. *Where will you be, fluffy bird?*

With another screech Chasonette took off. *I go now to smell the spice of the caves under the Abbey, those that no volaran in memory have been admitted in. I will see you later, riding on Jikata's shoulder.*

It is a trial, sharing feathers with birds. Lightning lipped the fastening of his door and Luthan moved so he could exit.

"I wouldn't say that within the roc's hearing," Luthan said.

His volaran stopped, sidled, no doubt thinking that rocs had considered volarans food. He blew air from his nose. *The roc will probably fly to the Dark's Nest, too.* Lightning stepped nervously from the stables.

"Probably." Luthan rolled his shoulders. He didn't want to think about the final aspect of the mission, who would destroy the Dark itself—the Exotiques—and who might live and die. He didn't want to court any more visions of the final battle.

He glanced up at the feycoocu hawks who'd perched on a rafter in the stables. Those magical beings always knew more than they said. He didn't know if *they* knew the outcome of the battle, didn't want to ask.

The Dark almost always dies. Tuckerinal lifted a wing.

That is the important thing, Sinafinal agreed. *All other destinies are continually in flux, as you would understand if you accepted your gift.*

Once the Exotique Singer is away from the Abbey, it will fall on you to help her with her prophetic gift, Tuckerinal said. He clicked his beak in encouragement. *The Exotiques are not the only ones with specific tasks in this matter. This is one of yours.* He glided down from the rafter and perched on a post outside the stable. Looking at Jikata's volaran, he said, *We will take care of the gong, then will be down in the Dark's Nest for the untying of the Weapon Knot, the City Destroyer Spell. I would never desert Marian.*

So will I be, said Sinafinal. *I will not desert Alyeka.* She raised her wings and joined her mate. *The future is in flux, some of us will live, and some of us will die.*

As long as the Dark is destroyed it is worth it, they said together.

Luthan felt cold. "We must destroy the Dark. I do not want to leave it for the future." Everything around him whispered that there would be no future if the Dark survived.

Singer's Abbey

That evening Jikata explored the compound with an eye to escape.

The wall was high, and imbued with Power to warn and keep people out, but had no defenses to keep people *in*. As she strolled she probed the walls' Power. Their strongest Power was against something Jikata could only think was "the Dark" mentioned in Alexa's and Marian's Lorebooks. The songspells for this were keyed to something bigger and meaner than wild beasts and bad humans, something…evil. A cloud went over the sun and the graying of the light caused her to shiver.

She continued her walk along the outside wall. Sometimes buildings abutted it and Jikata noted the ones with a window just above the wall—newer buildings. She also tested her own Power by trying to sense what lay beyond each section of wall. The compound was on a low hill and surrounded on all sides by a cleared area covered with short summer grasses and wild-flowers. Here there was a stand of trees deepening into forest, there the rise of hills, there a road….

If she discounted Amee's appearance and the looming Dark and only considered the place as if it had been "Club Lladrana," this had been the best vacation she'd had for years. She'd had her rest, her pampering, her spa time. She'd been treated like a star and been mentally stimulated.

And spiritually renewed. That she treasured even more. The constant music around her had fed her soul. Her subconscious had rested. When she returned to composing, her melodies would be strong and potent.

Her music would be valued here. Everything from simple tunes a person could dance to, to ballads cheerful or sad, to complex pieces, would go over big. As if her compositions had always been more for Lladranan tastes than American ones. She'd miss the technology to manipulate music as she wanted and the huge variation of instruments—strings, winds…

She stood still. Once more she'd been thinking of staying.

Inhaling deeply, she centered herself, *felt* the wisps of prophecy around her, saw the sparkles in the air, the distinctive crackling of a fire that meant "prophetic Power" to her. Below her was one of the Caverns of Prophecy, seething with wraiths like steam from a hot spring.

So she opened herself, let the flicker of prophecy flare and *saw.* Like most of her visions, it was ringed by a circle of dark, roiling thunderheads, but when she focused on the center, she saw the Abbey grounds. Zooming in, she saw herself, older, with lines on her face, standing at a window in the Singer's Tower. The sky was sunny between a break in great clouds, the morning cold from the ruddiness of her cheeks.

She was laughing and Jikata didn't think she'd ever seen that expression of serenity on her own face, didn't know if she'd ever experienced such fulfillment. She was more accustomed to dissatisfaction and ambition. Older-Jikata held a scroll and brush in her hands, one finger had ink stains. She was here and the Singer, wearing a heavy silk robe intricately embroidered with silk, her hair arranged in complex braids, dressed to do a formal Song Quest.

Almost, she heard a man speaking to her, knew without a doubt that a lover—husband—was in the shadows.

Then light dimmed, there *and* now, and her vision grayed and faded and vanished.

In the future she'd just seen, she was the Singer. The top of the heap, the star of the show. For life.

Never, ever worried about being the most popular singer, always working hard to maintain her career, her status, her fame. Not dissatisfied.

How fabulous. This could be hers, she knew it in her bones. Jikata knew the rewards.

The price was freeing Amee from the leech, fighting the awful Dark that had human servants and sent horrible monsters to Lladrana.

But she still didn't know the details of that price.

After she was snug in her bed that night, Jikata contemplated her future—not the vision she'd seen earlier in the day that she'd tucked away in the corner of her mind. That particular skill she'd developed after her parents had died and she'd gone to live with Ishi. The technique had served her well during her climb as a pop singer.

She considered her immediate future. She hadn't learned nearly everything the Singer could teach her, but she'd mastered the basics, had the tool chest to teach herself voice work and songspells and prophecy. The restrictions of the Abbey and the Singer were chafing. She was used to thinking for herself, plotting her own course and career.

This had been a wonderful break, but she had no real work here. Her unconscious was still playing with compositions not quite ready to manifest. A change of scenery would be good. She'd made the right decision.

All she knew of outside was what she'd read and the bits she'd gleaned in the time she'd spent here.

As her mind sank into the grayness of sleep, she thought she heard the whir of wings and smelled Chasonette's sweet fragrance. Ayes, Jikata's decision might be good, but she wasn't sure she could trust her bird guide.

And the dream came. Even as the Dark coalesced around her, Jikata's sleeping mind knew she should have expected this.

26

She heard the low laugh that seemed to rumble and hiss at the same time like hot, surging lava. The Dark stifled her. Every breath she took seared her throat, her lungs.

Yes, little Singer. The Dark snapped its jaws. *I will absorb your Power. Eat you.* She felt horrible pain as it bit into her and crunched its teeth on her bones.

She screamed.

And woke with Chasonette rubbing her face with her feathers. Jikata couldn't breathe! She shot up straight, panting, ran a hand through her mass of hair that had tangled around her.

Found herself trembling. Again. As usual.

Chasonette fluttered around the bed. *What? What? What?*

"Will you please perch somewhere?" Jikata reached for the tissue she kept under her pillow, patted her face free of cold sweat, let out a long and shaky sigh. "Just a bad dream."

Chasonette's comb stood straight up. She turned her head so a beady bird eye gleamed at Jikata. *Dream or vision?* she asked.

"Dream." Jikata lifted her hair from the back of her neck, touched her nape. No dampness there, her body hadn't reacted with all the terror that she'd felt in the nightmare. Perhaps she was getting used to night fears, learning to endure them. She plumped her pillows. "Threats," she said. "From the Dark. It's waiting for me, somewhere."

In its Nest.

"Ayes."

Do you want to stay here? Chasonette asked.

Jikata's heart gave one hard thump, echoed through her blood to her temples. Yes, she did want to stay here in the Abbey. Which was why she couldn't. She would not let anyone, any*thing*, manipulate her. "We leave tomorrow…." She listened to the sounds around her, knew it was deep night, early morning. "Today." She punched her pillow. "So it's waiting for me. For us. We'll see how tasty it really finds us."

Waiting for us? Chasonette launched from her perch again. *Will eat us!*

But weariness was weighing Jikata's mind down again as the herbal scent rose from her pillow. In that instant, she knew her pillows, perhaps even her room, had been bespelled somehow to cause sleep. The reason she hadn't read very much of the Lorebooks in bed.

If she were staying, she'd confront the Singer and her Friends on this issue, and win. Right now her anger couldn't even get started, and tonight she'd be gone. No use bitching about it. Live and learn. "We leave today," she mumbled and let the fragrance waft her into sleep.

Creusse Landing

The next morning, after a late and lively breakfast with Corbeau and his family, Raine decided to survey the area. The brief tour she'd gotten from Corbeau had been interrupted every other step by people wanting to meet her or needing his input on preparations.

She'd been shown three places where Corbeau and tagalongs had figured a ship could be raised and none of them had settled well with her, though the others had stood around a nice meadow not too far from the shore and decided that was best. She'd just stared at them. Apparently they all figured there would be huge Power in the ritual to move the ship to the Sea. Power from the Exotiques, and Raine, and the Chevaliers, and Raine, and the Marshalls, and Raine, and the Circlets, and Raine... Her insides jittered as she heard the big plans. She wondered if she could pull it off. Designing, yes; supervising, sure; building with her own hands, that she could do. Designing and building with only her brain and Power? Holding a ritual circle together? That she wasn't so sure of.

So she walked off her nerves while Enerin played as a miniature greyhound puppy alongside her.

She let her feet take her to the wide spot on the beach that had given her a tingle the evening before. It was just long enough to accommodate her ship...at low tide and with sandbars rising out of the shallow water. At dinner Raine had asked about building a ship in the water and was told that it couldn't be done. She figured it could.

Again she mulled over the map of Lladrana. This *was* the best place for the ship to depart from. She shivered in the cool morning breeze and at the touch of fate that the estate had been in Faucon's family for ages, just for this time...?

The beach was large and sandy, the promontory rising gently to higher ground, not the cliffs and bay at his southern estate, but Raine liked that panorama better. An image of the land she'd been offered formed in her mind and she felt a warmth at the notion of her own castle by the sea, the ship-yards...she recalled how the men had waved at her. She should send word for the best to come...or have her design sent to them to vet....

Ayes, I can do that! This very morning, Enerin said. She'd been puppy prancing and Raine realized she'd been thinking aloud, probably muttering.

She glanced down but saw no dog...a funny, pinkish sand-piper hopped up and down in the edge of the tide before her.

I can take a model, too. So they would see how it should be built! A sharp whistle of excitement came after that.

Raine eyed her. "I don't think you're big enough to carry a model." She'd been making them much larger than Enerin. She heard hawk cries, saw two shapes in the sky—Enerin's parents, the mature feycoocus. One veered off toward the manor, the other came straight toward them. There were no trees, so the hawk lit on the railing of the boardwalk to the manor a few feet away.

Salutations, Seamistress Exotique, Sinafinal said.

Raine inclined her head.

Sinafinal turned her beak to scratch above her wing.

We can fly, fly, fly! Enerin said. *Take a model to the shipbuilders of Seven Mile Peninsula, have one or two or three come back here!*

Ayes, we can, Sinafinal said, then turned an unblinking stare on Raine. *It is good you are progressing with the Ship.*

"Thank you."

At that moment, a three-foot square of thick paper swirled down to lie at Raine's feet.

It was Raine's turn to stare. She looked at the design she'd modified the night before, working instead of thinking of Faucon at the Castle where the last of the trials would have ended and the huge celebratory party would be going on.

Plink. Plink. Tuckerinal spit out four Power stones in the forecastle of the ship, gems appeared, then he joined his mate on the railing.

"You want me to make the model here?" Raine asked.

Sinafinal cocked her head. *The* real *Ship will be raised here, ayes?*

She had a point.

Tuckerinal chuckled.

Enerin flew up next to him, a small hawk, now. *We will fly, fly, fly!*

His gaze, much warmer than a hawk's should be, was indulgent on his child. *We will, as soon as Raine builds the model.* He glanced to the sky. *We will be there by noon.* The sun was well up, and the way was very long, but the magical beings moved much faster than anything else in Lladrana.

Raine picked up the paper. As she straightened she drew in a deep breath, loving the sound of the surf and the scent of the sea—brine and fish and seaweed and the depths. Then she turned in place and *listened,* curled her bare toes in the sand to connect with the ground and the planet. Where was the exact spot she'd thought would be perfect? She'd noticed the buzz, but had also been dreaming of Faucon.

All the feycoocus watched her, Sinafinal consideringly,

Tuckerinal with complete assurance that she'd do what she needed to, Enerin expectantly.

Another breath and the breeze caressed her face, lifted her hair. She walked the yard and a half to the ocean into the shallow water. It was cold, but not so much that would numb her feet. Again she closed her eyes and now she felt the ebb and flow of the tide, sensed the confines of the Brisay Sea, the land nearly circling it, the lap of wave against the rock of islands jutting from the water. And Power.

Natural power of wind and tide and the tug of the moon, of currents and the slow spin of the planet.

The power of the pure life energy of beings who lived in the sea, small schools of fish, gently waving coral, crusty creatures deep in rifts.

Power that was magic.

She thought the seas and oceans of Amee were a greater source of it than any place on land where humans had smudged it or used and reused it, or, in countries other than Lladrana, had ignored and denied it.

Her body swayed with the rhythm of ocean Power and she took that in to feel the flow of it in her own blood.

She turned slightly south and walked until her feet throbbed and Power washed through her from land and sea. When she looked toward the ocean, she saw this was the shallowest part of the inlet, with several sandbars just under the water. Perfect for building a boat. Human Power would hold the planks in place.

As she stood in this place, she thought that nothing was beyond Lladranans and the Power of Amee.

Not even destroying the Dark and surviving.

Shutting her eyes again, Raine felt the paper with her hands, her mind, visualized the two-dimensional plans she'd worked on for weeks, the other models she'd raised. She set the paper on the sand and Sang. The ship on paper bent and bowed and became a ship, tiny details of walls and rooms and decks separated and folded into place. The excess of the paper was whisked away in the breeze and all three feycoocus launched themselves from a nearby dune to play in the wind and catch bits, making a game of it, piling scraps where the wind didn't reach.

Done.

Raine glanced down at the model and received a little shock. The model was colorful, painted somehow, as perfect floating in the shallow water as it had been in her mind. The hull was a dark blue and painted near the prow were curling waves of turquoise. The masts were dark brown like wood and the sails also turquoise. She stared. She hadn't ever seen a Tall Ship with turquoise sails, but it worked.

It is beau-ti-ful! screeched Enerin in a sea bird's call. She lifted her wings and rose on the wind, a small bird. No, a small magical creature in the form of a bird, surely a bird would have more weight than Enerin.

It is a good ship built in a good place, a blessed place, Sinafinal approved.

Raine shrugged away the thought and touched her mouth. She was grinning, like she hadn't for a long time…certainly before she'd arrived on Lladrana, even longer, before her arguments with her father and brothers.

Maybe since the last time she'd built a boat by herself.

Before she could say anything, the three feycoocus had swooped down and snatched the model, carrying it among them. All of them looked more gull than hawk. In an instant they were nearly out of sight, only one last cry from Sinafinal.

Go to the village now. They await you.

Raine stared after the birds. Go to the village. A coastal village where fisherfolk lived.

She'd fulfilled one of her tasks for Lladrana and Amee, she'd figured out why the Dark invaded, what it wanted. She was well on the way to fulfilling the next task, raising a ship for an invasion force to sail to the Dark's Nest.

But she hadn't done anything to complete her last task, that of integrating the fisherfolk, the Seamasters, with the rest of Lladranan society, so it was less a culture of segments and more of a whole that respected its parts.

She'd thought she'd been ready to do this, but she'd been fooling herself.

Go alone to the village with people like those with whom she'd spent the first terrible months of her life in Lladrana. Perhaps face doubt and suspicion and people who had a revulsion to her kind—Earth women, Exotiques.

Breathing in a lungful of good sea air, she set her shoulders. The birds wanted her to overcome her fears. If worse came to worse she could fight and scream. She'd saved herself before. She could do this.

She repeated that as she took step after deliberate step to the docks a couple of miles down the beach. There were three docks with the middle one being a main pier.

That brought back memories. She'd been Summoned in December and lived most of the winter in a tavern on a pier. Swallowing hard, she kept her breath even. These docks and the clean streets with tidy houses radiating out from them were not the creaking and cracking pier she'd loathed, the huddle of miserable houses in a hamlet she still didn't know the name of.

She looked at the prosperous town, noted an inn sign moving in the wind. The tavern was called the Orange Shield and looked nothing like the Open Mouthed Fish. Not much like the Chevalier place, either, the Nom de Nom in Castleton.

From the title of the inn, it was owned by Faucon, and she wondered if the whole town was. It was certainly well cared for. The people who stared at her smiled. She marched up a short dune and found some women gathered in the sun, mending fishing nets.

A tall, strong-shouldered young woman jumped to her feet as soon as Raine appeared, setting aside her portion of the net less carefully than it deserved. She smiled widely, showing line crinkles beginning at the edge of her eyes. Her temples showed a few strands of silver Power. Raine noted her clothing and decided she was from a prosperous fishing family. Eight and a half months ago Raine would have wept to have such good sturdy clothes with a tight weave. The young woman moved with enthusiasm toward Raine.

The feycoocus had been right, these women had been waiting for her.

"I'm Ella and I've been asked to speak to ya, Seamistress Exotique." She offered her hand.

Raine met her palm to palm and shook. A little sigh came from the folks—Raine noticed a withered old man or two—and Ella nodded toward the tavern. "Come on into the Shield and we'll talk, I'll treat you to a honeyed rum."

Running the sentence through her mind a couple of times to make sure she'd heard it right, Raine said, "Thanks, but it's a little early for rum. I'll take some ale, though." Coffee or tea would be out of the question in a small town like this. She swept the group with a glance, saw listeners at the end of the street. "And we all know that though I've designed a boat and sailed some with Faucon Creusse and by myself, I am no mistress of the Lladranan seas, certainly not like you people are." She sucked in another deep breath and added, "The Seamasters haven't accepted me."

"Pigheaded men," Ella said, then turned on her heel and led the way at a brisk pace toward the tavern halfway up the street. "We'll talk a that."

The Orange Shield was dim even with large front windows that were clean, as was the whole place. Well, the Open Mouthed Fish had been as clean as Raine and the owner and other tavern girl could make it with inferior soap.

A couple of minutes after they walked in, a man rose from a bar seat in the shadows and shuddered with revulsion. He didn't meet Raine's eyes, but looked beyond her to one of the windows and walked stiff-legged out the door, never acknowledging her. Raine sighed. Would there be more of those who had an instinctive dislike of Exotiques among these northern fisherfolk? More than the southern or the towns and cities she'd been in? About one in ten that felt that.

Raine and Ella received their ales from the rotund barman, who sat down with them with a mug himself.

After her first sip, Ella leaned over the table of the booth toward Raine and got down to business. "The Seamasters…." She shook her head. "They'd grown haughty." She tapped her finger on the table. "And all of them men. *That* started happenin' a coupla generations ago. Mind you, life on the water isn't easy for a woman and not many of us feel the callin', but my foremothers never shoulda let us be squeezed outta the higher spots of the Seamasters' council." She snorted. "Not that I think it's much of a council, either."

"Ella…" prompted the barman.

Ella shrugged her big shoulders. "That's past, but there was a good shakeup, after we heard what they'd done midwinter, Summoned you poorly and on the cheap." She sniffed. "Then screwed up, didn't even know you came. There've been resignations. The only ones who weren't pressured to leave were the four who went to the Castle to help with your tuning. Now we got new blood, younger blood in, and some women." She nodded decidedly, thumped her chest. "I was just accepted a few days ago, when we all knew you were comin' here and the rumors were true, that the Ship to destroy the Dark would be raised and launched from here." She sent a glance from under lowered brows to Raine. "Right?"

"Ayes. It will be built in the shallows."

Ella nodded. "What sorta crew you need?"

"Fifty good sailors, some good navigators among them. We'll need practice, too, since the rigging I have in mind isn't something I've seen here." Raine waved a hand and was startled when someone put a thin charcoal drawing stick in it. She blinked in surprise and found the tavern crowded, everyone watching her, listening quietly to her words. A sheet of rough paper was slid before her and she made a rough sketch.

One man whistled, stepped closer. He was middle-aged with a streak of Power on his left temple. "I'm Jean. This is like some'a the ships I seen outta the seatowns of the Pinch."

The Pinch was where the Brisay Sea flowed westward into one of the world's major oceans.

The man sent her a crooked smile. "Hear you called the shipbuilders of Seven Mile Peninsula. They're the best."

"Word travels fast."

"Feycoocus spreading it," he said nonchalantly, grinning as everyone stared at him. He tapped his ears, his Power streak. "Heard it in the wind."

"Maybe you should be one of the fifty, then," Raine said.

His face hardened subtly. "We'll be a'puttin' that to the test of skill, just like the Marshalls and the Chevaliers."

"Ayes," Ella agreed. "But the Seamasters, the *new* council, must mend the rift with Raine, here, first." She leaned back so her back was straight. "You haven't heard from any of us 'cause the men are ashamed. They Summoned you and didn't provide for you, didn't care and protect you, and now mosta' us think you'll return with the Snap, after the Ship is built."

All gazes fastened on Raine. Her smile twisted. "True."

"'Cause you weren't welcomed here." Ella's eyes fired, she ground out the words. Raine sensed someone slipping out of the tavern…a former Seamaster?

"Who's going to Captain the Ship, then, to the Dark's Nest?" the barkeeper said.

Raine stared at him, at them all. "Surely you can't think that I'd be a better sailor than any of you all?"

"Don't you hear the music of the sea to tell you the right course? The music of the wind to tell you how to angle any sail?" Jean asked.

She had.

She did.

They all stared at her. Raine couldn't answer. Couldn't. Her throat had simply closed.

27

Raine tipped her mug to wet her dry mouth and found it empty.

Ella got her off the hook—she glared at the barkeep, who got out and made his way through the crowd to the barrel tap and pulled another ale for Raine, returned and set it carefully before her. Raine drank, and it was good. She nodded her thanks.

Ella said, "We gotta fix this here problem. The Seamistress Exotique has graciously taken the first step to meet us an' include us in all the goings-on with the Ship at the Manor." Another serious glance. "You're gonna let us participate in the ship-raising, aren't you?"

"Of course." Now that Raine had met them, recognized them as much like the people she'd known at home, she wouldn't have dreamed of excluding them.

Nodding, Ella said, "Ya see? She came to us, she'll speak on our behalf to all the other Exotiques, she'll help us decide who to crew the Ship. That's the kinda woman she is. Good. So now it's up to us to take the next step to make her comfortable." She frowned again, gulped at her ale, put it down with a rattle of pottery on wood.

People started talking loudly, offering suggestions. After thinking a moment Ella let out a piercing whistle and said, "I'm the local Seamistress here, and I gotta idea."

She waited until folks subsided, every eye on her. "Ayes." Ella nodded decisively. "We'll have a gathering, of fisherfolk and Seamasters old and new. All the former Seamasters…everyone who Summoned you wrongly…will Sing you an Apology Chorus."

Raine's mouth dropped open. Satisfaction surged inside her, then her mind caught up. She knew a whole lot more about pride than when she'd left Earth. A whole lot more about a lot of things, but right now she was concerned with pride.

She cleared her throat. "I don't think…"

"An Apology Song is necessary." Ella's jaw turned stubborn. "The Power and feelings of the Song will make things better."

Magic could help release her lingering anger and bitterness? That would be a relief. She didn't like feeling the emotions. As Bri would say, they were too negative, but Raine couldn't just think them away.

Confronting those who'd yanked her life around, uncaring of the consequences, without her consent. Wasn't that something victims did? She'd tried not to act like a victim, thought she'd gotten her act together. Everyone waited for her answer and Ella turned as if to order everything done. So Raine had to speak. "Then the Apology Song will be sung in private." She lifted her chin. "It's between me and those who Summoned me." She looked at Ella. "When can we do it?"

Ella chewed at her lower lip. "Five days'd get everyone here for a ritual in the town hall meeting space."

"Five days!" someone said. "Won't give 'em any time to practice the chorus as a group."

Raine couldn't help saying, "Probably as much practice as they did for my Summoning."

There was a moment of quiet and Ella clamped her lips together, then succumbed and let out laughter, and others joined in. Ella leaned over and thumped Raine on the shoulder. "You're a good one, ta be able ta joke about somethin' like that, Exotique Seamistress."

Raine was surprised, herself—there'd been more humor than bitterness in the remark. "Call me Raine." She raised her voice and looked around. "You all can call me Raine."

"A private forgiveness ceremony." Jean shook his head, tucked his thumbs in his belt. "I'da liked to of seen it, but all in all, I don't envy you. Not a damn good voice among those old Seamasters. Not a one."

More laughter.

Ella shot an index finger at someone Raine couldn't see. "Tell the old Seamasters to haul their asses here in five days. No excuses accepted." She hesitated. "Inform the other current Seamasters of my—Raine's—decision so they can come, too."

"Wise," Jean said, smiling. Raine liked him. He had a roguish glint in his eye that made her think he'd get along well with the Chevaliers and Marshalls.

"The sailor crew trials—" Raine started.

"Will take place on the Ship once it's raised," Jean said.

"Of course," Raine said. This was all moving fast.

Leaning over the table, Ella fixed her gaze on Raine. "Tell us about the Ship."

Rubbing her temples, Raine said, "I'm refining the design of the ship, but I can make a current model of the ship today, pass it around so the sailors know what they're getting into."

Jean grinned. "They're 'getting into' a Ship like the world has never seen, to crew and sail it, be its mind and blood. Signing on for an adventure of a lifetime." He swept his hand. "An action that will go down in legend." His eyes went distant, reminding Raine suddenly of Luthan. "Names will be remembered, every one. For as long as the seas flow against Lladrana's shores there will be Songs and stories naming each hero."

Raine shivered, she still didn't want to go, still didn't see it as adventure, only a course straight to death. She turned to Ella, saw the young woman's gaze set on an image only she could see, eyes gleaming. Raine's stomach twisted.

"Why you, Ella?" she asked brusquely.

"Wha—?" Ella jolted from her bedazzlement.

"Why are you bringing this together, not Faucon or Corbeau?"

Ella blinked. "Because it must be the fisherfolk who call our own to crew the Ship. Faucon is a noble and Corbeau is his man, more of a merchant. If Faucon ordered we'd come listen, but not think of the adventure as ours." She put a fist over her heart, thumped. "Would not think of ourselves as heroes of the adventure."

"Of course you are! The most important, to sail the ship," Raine said.

Beaming, Ella looked around as if gathering gazes, returned her stare to Raine. When she spoke it was a quiet voice into throbbing silence. "That is why you are *our* Exotique, the Seamistress Exotique, because you put *us* first in your mind. Your loyalty is to us."

Raine just stared at Ella, at the others around her. She knew these people. Oh, perhaps not the Lladranans individually, but she knew people who worked with the sea, who fished, and sailed and built boats and ships…. She could look into these Asian-like faces and read familiar expressions, sense familiar emotions. She sat up straight and scanned the people herself. Old folks, women and men who were married to those out on the boats, people who knew and treasured the life of a coastal village. Her kind of people.

"Ayes," she said. "You will be the real heroes, and you will not go unsung." She'd make sure of that, ensure that Marian and Jaquar and every Circlet who ever wrote about this had a list of the crew and those who sailed *The Echo. The Echo.* She'd chosen a name for the ship, and despite any arguments, she'd stick with it. The ship was hers to name. A very good start.

Ella was nodding. "Five days then, for Seamasters to gather and others come for the trials." Ella stood and shouted, "Then we will raise the Ship!"

"Then we will raise the Ship!" Everyone shouted until Raine's ears rung.

Singer's Abbey

At breakfast Chasonette picked at her food, throwing kernels she didn't care for onto the floor, making more of a mess than usual. *You are ready? We will go?*

Though they were irritated with each other—the bird had been close-beaked about where she'd been and what she'd done—and now seemed afraid, Jikata answered her. Flighty or not, Jikata needed the bird. "I'll tell the staff I'm skipping dinner this evening, want some meditation time. That way they'll go about their own concerns and we can leave right after the afternoon practice in the Caverns of Prophecy. I'll wait until I sense the Singer is taking her evening nap."

Chasonette rose from her perch and flew through the French doors out onto the balcony, then to the curving stone top of the rail, walked back and forth. *It will eat us.*

Drinking her morning tea, Jikata joined her, looked out onto the compound. Pleasant, manicured, constricting. If it had been hers... But it wasn't. If her visions and Amee's promises came true, she could live here, but now she had to leave.

She ran her fingers down the bird's soft feathers. "So it said." Stroking Chasonette, Jikata continued, "Don't worry. I'm sure we can find a safe place for you."

The bird said nothing more, but looked aside. So Jikata went inside and took her pack from the chest, checked all the things she'd brought from Earth: the water bottle, some instant energy bars, her various pouches. She added two large muffins from breakfast and left space for a wineskin filled with additional water. She lifted it, and it was heavy. Would be heavier still with the five Lorebooks inside.

Morning lessons passed quickly as Jikata strove to make more knots for the Singer and the Friends to use—knots that stored Power, knots good for general spells, knots to start fires... She'd memorized that one, knew quite a few of the songspells to tie and untie them by heart. At the first village, she'd pick up thread or yarn. She'd seen sheep, there must be yarn.

The Singer reprimanded her for not concentrating and Jikata said nothing, but left soon afterward for lunch in her own rooms, away from the old woman.

Jikata spoke casually to her maid, said she wanted to skip dinner. She'd done that several times before—they fed her too well here. Her maid patted her on her shoulder and said she shouldn't forgo meals, but gave no other protest to the plan.

Jikata could be a demanding woman, a difficult woman to those who made her life a misery, but all in all she'd been well-treated here and had been courteous herself. If this truly had been "Club Lladrana," she would have left the staff a good tip. As it was, she sorted through her jewelry case and chose a couple of nice pieces that she would leave for her maid and the staff. She didn't know what the future would bring, but she'd never felt she'd go poor and hungry here. She could Sing for her supper.

The afternoon in the Caverns was trying because the Singer was in several difficult moods, and Jikata wondered if the old woman sensed Jikata was leaving. For an instant anxiety flared, then she beat it back. If the Singer *knew* Jikata was leaving, she'd assign guards, and she hadn't. A blind spot of the Singer's? Or had she never asked herself such a question?

Was Amee or the Song itself keeping the knowledge from her?

Jikata finally decided that whatever prophecies the Singer had "heard" in the Caverns about Jikata, her future was not set. That certainly matched her own visions.

Both disgruntled, they left the Cavern. During the session, half-formed vision wraiths had dissipated when Jikata attempted to focus on them, on the questions the Singer had assigned her to ask. Jikata hadn't *heard* any illuminating Songs at all. The Singer's experience seemed to have been the same and she acted like a woman thwarted. She wasn't accustomed to that.

Jikata had Sung the door open, and now Sang it shut. The Singer gave her a sharp glance. "You were off on the beat."

She hadn't been, but said, "I've been slightly off all day." Jikata shrugged. "There are days like that."

The Singer sniffed. "There should *not* be days like that. You should strive for perfection each and every moment." She narrowed her eyes.

"Ayes, Singer," Jikata said mildly, keeping her mind blank, her own Song tamped down, revealing nothing.

The Singer stared, then turned abruptly. "You are the only person besides me who can open this door."

Jikata swallowed. That admonition, too, wasn't unusual, but it was odd that the woman said it after this particular session.

"Ayes, Singer."

"You have worn me out. You are dismissed for the day."

A bend of the head, of the torso. "Ayes, Singer."

They walked to the elevator in silence and when they reached the main level, Friends clustered around the Singer as usual to see to any need of hers. She left without a backward glance.

Releasing a long, quiet sigh, Jikata went back to her rooms. Chasonette was already there, walking back and forth on her perch, her food untouched. *I have never lived in the wild.* She flicked her comb up and down nervously.

"We'll be fine," Jikata soothed. "We can make the northern village easily by nightfall, but I want to go west toward that village, though it's longer." On Earth, she'd spent time on outdoor activities, on riding, and now that she was about to leave the constraints of this place felt intolerable.

It's a long way to the ocean. North would be better. Chasonette clicked her beak.

"When they look for us, they'll go north first." She'd been packing the Lorebooks and wineskin, Chasonette's food in a handy bag she'd had. Jikata zipped the pack shut and grunted as she put it on her shoulder. Then slid it back onto the chest, tied a knot that lightened loads on a strap. It wasn't a pretty knot, but made a world of difference.

She and Chasonette undoubtedly would be seen, and having her bag appear light was a great deal better than if it looked as if she were carrying gold plates in it.

Carefully she placed her jewelry pieces on the bedside table as tips, left with a couple of the marks she knew: For you, thank you. She gave one last glance around, and slipped from the room with the bird on her shoulder. When she extended all of her senses, she found that the staff was gathered in their own portion of the building. Midafternoon was melding into late afternoon and evening, and most people were inside.

Jikata didn't say goodbye. When she thought of it, there was no one she wanted to say goodbye to. Not unusual.

It had been years since anyone truly cared whether she was around or not…at least for herself. Jikata wouldn't dwell on that. Her life had been what she'd made of it.

She'd wanted to say goodbye to Ishi, had intended to, but perhaps Ishi had been right in that as she'd been so "right" in other things. They had nothing much to say to each other.

What would have Jikata said? "I loved you once? I'd like to love you now? I'd like you to be proud of me now?"

That wouldn't have gone anywhere.

Ishi had turned away from Jikata, and she didn't even know if the woman had ever loved her. Jikata only knew she'd disgraced the family by becoming a popular singer and not practicing the right ways.

Probably all to the good they had no last meeting. Ishi might have asked Jikata to give up her career. Jikata would have lied and they both would have known.

This particular pity party was depressing. She put a spring in her step and tuned in the lovely music around her. If she hadn't spent years with Ishi, Jikata probably wouldn't have tolerated the Singer for as long as she had. Especially not at this point in her Earth career, where she could choose her own projects.

That was the good that had come from the hard.

She nodded to the few people who were on the grounds, then making sure they were unobserved, went into a storage building and climbed the stairs to the second floor.

It was absurdly easy to slip out the window of a room that was no more than two feet above the west wall, throw her pack to the ground about fifteen feet below, slither on her belly 'til she hung from her hands and drop to the ground. She wasn't even out of breath, though her heart beat quicker.

She picked up her pack, checked to see how her various pretty pouches had fared. All beautiful. The variety of them made her smile—the recycled silk saris, the embroidered Irish linen, the fancy velveteen, the cheerful and casual clear plastic for her makeup. She looked at her energy bars. They seemed fine. Smiling, she shrugged it on. Food for the first little while, Chasonette would be a magical guide to the village, and then…new vistas.

She walked for about a half mile down the hill, a short ways into the trees and through a meadow dappled with long shadows, the grass underfoot giving off a sweet scent. She'd had a good pair of new cross-trainers in her pack, and her feet felt fine. She could walk as far as necessary.

They probably had actual cobblers here, and she liked the idea of shoes handmade for her feet, but didn't know how long that would take. Now she was away from the Abbey, time pressed more upon her, as if there were a deadline to a show coming up and she should be putting in twelve-hour days of practice.

Was it the Abbey that was under a spell, or her? Best she was away from it. Without the sleep Songs in her rooms, she should be able to read the Lorebooks faster. They'd tell her what needed to be done.

Now she was closer to the forest, the trees gave off trickles of mysterious tunes, wild trees with shadows beneath and between them. Old trees with long lives and rings of melodies emanating as if describing those lives. Different than the cultivated, beautiful, pampered trees in Singer's Abbey.

As Jikata had been cultivated and pampered to be useful.

When Luthan stepped out of the shadow of large trees—and how had he managed to hide wearing that pristine white?—she knew a sense of inevitability. A handsome white knight, followed by *two* volarans, one of which might be for her. It only needed this to be a European fairy tale.

Or a standard story of a quest against great odds.

28

Chasonette whistled a ripple of bright notes of welcome and Jikata's jaw flexed. This was why her companion had disappeared. Scanning the man up and down, Jikata couldn't complain.

They met at the edge of the forest. He bowed, but kept his dark brown gaze on hers, tilted his head as if listening hard to her personal Song. Then he relaxed. "Salutations, Exotique Singer."

She could understand him. She bowed. "Salutations, Luthan Vauxveau."

He turned to the large white volaran. "This is my companion, Silver Lightning Spearing into the Dark Mountain. I call him Lightning."

Intelligence was in those eyes. More than a horse, less, she thought, than human. Or very different than human. She didn't know how different they were temperamentally from Earth horses, but they still had eyes on the side of their heads—

prey animal eyes. She dipped a bow. "Salutations, Lightning." The lilt of his name came naturally, matching his personal Song.

The other stallion pranced forward. He was a beautiful buckskin color with dark mane and tail, wings a golden brown edged in darker brown. Stunning.

"This volaran was sent by the alpha mare for you, Exotique Singer. He is, simply, Hope."

Fabulous. Jikata held out her hand and fell in love. They didn't have hair but tiny feathers on their hide. Their wings were made of varying sizes and lengths of feathers. They looked horselike but were not. Their wings were angled across their shoulders, making a perfect place to ride, with legs before or behind the wings. Maybe even two people could ride, though the volarans were smaller than Earth horses.

"Now we've been introduced, I'd like to know your plans," Luthan said with an intensity that let her know she'd better *have* plans, otherwise they'd be following his.

She smiled. "I was going to the next town to hire a horse or a carriage or a volaran."

His brows went up. "You have zhiv?"

"I have jewelry."

Nodding, he said, "That would do. Where do you think this transportation—had you been able to find a stables or get one from the local noble—would take you?"

She widened her eyes. "Why, through Lladrana." She glanced around. "From what I see, it's lovely."

"It's the most beautiful place on Amee, here in the south the land is very pretty. The north is mountainous. All but one of our Exotiques…you know of the Exotiques?"

"Ayes."

"All but one is from a place with mountains, and you?"

"Originally. And you?"

He appeared surprised, then his smile flashed and it warmed his expression, hinted that his eyes could be lively. "I have a manor close to here, a few miles, should you care to visit?"

"Perhaps. So you're a southerner?" She didn't know what that meant here.

His face closed again. "The main family estate I inherited is north of the Marshalls' Castle." Again testing her knowledge?

"Which is in central Lladrana. I've seen a map." Her own lips curved. "Plenty of interesting maps."

Lightning pawed the ground, removing a divot of rich black earth. *Too much talk…bird…castle.* He said something more but Jikata didn't catch it. The volaran spoke more in images, feelings, than in words, and the words weren't pronounced by the volaran mind the same way they were by the human tongue.

Jikata frowned. "Sorry?"

"Lightning is impatient. He wants to fly, though we came from the Castle this morning, using Distance Magic."

She straightened, tapped her bag again. "I recently received some Lorebooks. I've read Alexa's and part of Marian's, so I've heard of Distance Magic and of flying on volarans." She gave him a smile. "She flew with you…and Lightning."

Ayes! Lightning's affirmative came in Jikata's mind, along with a small, silver-haired woman.

Luthan nodded. "Calli has ingrained the idea that we 'partner' with the volarans."

"Ah."

"Lightning and Hope would like to know if you plan on going to the Marshalls' Castle."

There was that word again, "plan." Though she'd left the Singer's Abbey, a lot of other people would have plans for her.

"What if I said I wanted to see the city of Krache?"

Lightning's ears pricked forward, and he whinnied in excitement. A city of square buildings and steep spires flashed in her mind.

Luthan's brow lined. "I wouldn't recommend Krache for an Exotique new to Lladrana, but we would accompany you." She heard a rapid beat as if calculations marched in his mind.

"However," Jikata continued smoothly, "I had planned to make a slow journey to the Marshall's Castle. Now that I don't have to worry too much about being followed and taken back to the Singer's Abbey." Her gaze surveyed his wide shoulders, the muscularity of his body. He was a Chevalier, a fighter, no one—no group—of Friends from the Abbey would prevail against him.

He bowed. "I am at your service. I will protect you with my life."

He'd said it simply, but it rang like a vow, and the air and Songs around them stilled for a moment. Red sparks of vision coalesced in front of her, she heard the distant shrill of Chasonette's cry, the stamping of the two volarans, but that didn't stop the prophecy.

They—she and Luthan and the volarans—were circling down toward a smoking volcano. What she could see of Luthan's face within the helmet was grim and determined... and she saw herself, dressed in strange Chevalier leathers, too. Helmeted, too. Determined, too.

Her mouth was open and she was Singing and she knew it was a great Song, and that the moment they plunged was the climax of her life.

Then the vision haze vanished and she saw Luthan, standing

straight, feet braced, hand entwined in Lightning's mane, face nearly as grim as in the vision. He blinked.

She said, "You can see prophetic visions, too."

His chest rose with a deep breath and he nodded. Rustily, he said, "I will…help…you with your gift of prophecy."

She tilted her head. "You sound uncertain of that."

He met her eyes squarely. "It is my gift, too, though not as great as yours. Not something I ever wanted, and that I usually suppressed."

Jikata nodded. "I know about that. On Earth—Exotique Terre—I mostly suppressed it." Her face stilled. "The Singer didn't allow that."

"Of course not. The Singer has definite ideas about what should and should not be done." He scanned the area. The Abbey was out of view, but Jikata believed he was extending his senses to see if anyone was checking on her…or him, the Singer's representative.

"They haven't missed you yet. Good." He gestured to her stallion—a very male "Hope"; and Jikata would have to get used to that name—and said, "Perhaps we should progress."

She went to Hope. "Salutations, Hope. May I admire your beauty?" She rubbed his forehead, then ran a hand down his neck, along his back to his rump and dock, walked around him. He stood perfectly still but shifted his stance to one of pride.

I beautiful. Very status large.

Luthan's volaran, Lightning, snorted. *Because you fly with her, the Exotique Singer, not because you have proven yourself in battle.* Lightning formed each word/image/feeling better, as if he'd already learned Jikata's speech limitations.

Hope grumbled but said nothing.

"We'd better get going," Jikata said lightly, and swung into the saddle. It was comfortable and she'd already noticed that the volarans had no bits, but only thin halters.

The sound of Hope's Song increased and flickered through her, then his mind was *there,* next to hers. An easy mind.

"Ride first," Luthan said.

"So you can see my form?" she asked, leaning over and patting Hope's neck, staring down at his beautiful wings. She wished she had boots.

Luthan raised his brows. "Exactly. I want to see your form."

She chuckled, and said *Run!* to Hope and he took off to angle down a long meadow. The wind whipped through her hair and she couldn't suppress a cry of glee. So wonderful! And it had been so long. Why hadn't she made time for horses in her life?

But a horse would never be as lovely as Hope. He turned, and with lifted wings, ran back to Luthan and Lightning, who had not moved, though Luthan had mounted his volaran.

"So you can ride," Luthan said. His seat was such that he looked as if he'd spent much of his life on horse—volaranback. Not even her rancher lover had looked as well in the saddle.

Mmmm. She caught the hum of pleasurable attraction in her throat before it rose to her lips. Though when his mouth quirked she supposed that he'd heard something in her Song that betrayed her interest.

We well-matched. Hope pranced in place and tossed his head.

"Indeed," Luthan said. "Interesting. Four of the seven Exotiques Summoned were horsewomen before they were Summoned."

"I know from her Lorebook that Alexa didn't ride," Jikata said. "Who else?"

"Raine and Elizabeth."

"Ah. The one who returned home. I have her Lorebook."

Luthan slanted her a glance. "Of course. Who do you think obtained those volumes for you?"

"Oh. Of course." She inclined her torso. *"Merci."*

"You're welcome."

"Shall we ride?" He smiled. "Slowly. North toward my manor?"

Jikata studied him. "You're the Singer's representative. Won't you take me back?"

No, he said mentally.

She heard his voice in her mind, easily, clearly, as if they were on the same wavelength.

I am not the Singer's representative, though I have not formally turned in my resignation.

Ttho? she questioned. But she knew he didn't lie. There was more than a "ring of truth" in his mental voice, it was as if he were incapable of lying telepathically. She listened closely, finally decided that it was the background lilt of his mental voice, as pristine as his clothing.

Ttho. I did not want to tell the Singer I was done with her until you were out of the Abbey in case you needed me, he said simply.

She'd heard him called an honorable man and knew it was true. Knew everything he'd said was true. He would protect her with his life, had determined to do that long before he said the words to her. Had done so from the moment they'd met when she'd been Summoned.

Merci, Chevalier Luthan Vauxveau.

He smiled again and her heart twinged. She'd met plenty of good-looking men here, but all had been Friends and usually devoted to the Singer. Not one of them had had appreciation of her as a female in the back of their eyes.

She stretched a little—physically, mentally and emotionally—when she saw his look, then let her lips curve. She was free of the Singer's constraints. "Won't the first place they look be your home? And won't the Singer call on you to find me?" She shifted in her saddle, a cue to Hope to proceed, and he lightly stepped through the meadow northward.

Luthan shrugged. "Perhaps." He and Lightning turned to join them. "But since you want to see the countryside, we will need provisions and shelter."

"Shelter?"

"A tent. I have one with three rooms."

Jikata's mind went from the image of green canvas to a parti-colored medieval tent. She realized she was right when she received a mental picture from Lightning and Luthan of a campground with many tents in all colors dotting it. Then one of rusty red and dull gold, rectangular…with two outer rooms and one in the back. It appeared totally charming.

"A tent sounds wonderful."

"Also, I've a training field where you can learn to partner with Hope. We'll have you flying before we leave at dawn."

Jikata winced. She'd had to rise early plenty of times to travel or to prepare for performances, but she didn't care for that. "Very well."

A smile hovered around his mouth. "I'm sure we can evade those Friends who will be sent to search for you."

An offhand apology for rousting her out of bed if she'd ever heard one.

They rode in companionable silence, through copses and woods, and once when they reached another long meadow, she sent a mental message of running to Hope and he did, but then he lifted his wings and they glided. Airborne! Maybe only a couple of feet off the ground, but flying.

She laughed, let it ripple from her like a banner of notes, a melody…Jikata's first flight.

In a show-off move, Lightning sailed by them, a full ten feet off the ground, legs tucked close to his belly. Luthan was grinning, something Jikata sensed was not common, and the sight fired more flickers of awareness of him as a man inside her, as lovely and joyful as the flight itself.

Then Hope was galloping across the field and in the distance Jikata heard the bells of the Abbey ring the hour.

Her mind whirled with a slight dizziness, the headiness of escaping—once again in her life—an old woman who commanded her, though Ishi had never been as autocratic as the Singer.

No, Jikata would not go back to the Abbey willingly. She didn't know what her fate was now, but she would fight to hold on to it.

Marshalls' Castle

Faucon had said his goodbyes to his friends during the long celebration the night before. It was more of a "see you later," since the next day those on the invasion force would be preparing to leave for his place and the start of the true adventure.

Which meant he had to be there first. He trusted Corbeau absolutely, and knew preparations there were going apace, but Faucon wasn't sure how Corbeau would mix with the Chevaliers and Marshalls.

Not to mention the fact that Faucon yearned for Raine, was ever conscious of the short time he'd have with her before she returned to her home.

His foolish heart. But he was a man of his time, risking all—love, life, soul—to live the fullest and kill the Dark.

So he and his volaran, and his Chevalier team that had been on alert the day before and was still sober, flew to the North. The second team would remain assigned to the Castle.

Two pairs of his Chevaliers had made the expedition force. Only three pairs had tested. Most of his people had signed on with him for the reward at the end of their service—a bit of land of their own. He'd have to revise his will before he left.

As he arrived at his northern home, he saw the bustle of the inhabitants and townsfolk preparing for an invasion of their own.

Below, on the newly extended landing field that would hold fifty volarans, Raine was waiting for him.

His heart lurched as he saw her unbound brown hair lifting in the wind, her long-limbed body held like a sailor's, the creamy skin of her face lifted to him.

His sex stirred and all thought of doing anything except taking her to bed for the rest of the day went from his head.

They landed and he dismounted, running toward her…he was always running toward her…catching her and feeling her body against his and tasting her mouth and hearing her Song—*their* Song—that ripped through them like an undertow.

This woman was his, and he was hers.

For the moment.

Living in the moment was all he had.

29

Creusse Landing

Raine spent the day in sumptuous sensuality…making love with Faucon with a hungry urgency. It had shocked her, the feeling they had for each other, but it hadn't stopped her from exploring the man, making him tremble, making him sur-render to the passion between them. As she'd been explored and had trembled and had surrendered.

A moment out of time with no expectations beyond plea-suring themselves.

Reality had come in the need to satisfy other hungers, namely their stomachs, and a discreet knock on the door told them it was time for dinner.

After dinner there was a slight commotion. The shipbuild-ers had arrived by volaranback, looking a little stunned. Three men and a woman, and the way they carried themselves sent a twinge of loneliness through Raine, reminding her of her family. People who worked with their hands, who sailed, who were completely confident of their abilities…though the woman was old enough to be the mother Raine lost early, the obvious matriarch of the family, just as Raine's father was a patriarch.

She wondered how much difference that really made.

The woman was stiff—and not just from the volaran ride—until she saw Raine. Then she smiled and bowed low. "Salutations, Exotique Seamistress."

Raine inclined her torso, recalled her name and said, "Salutations, Madam Deauville."

Striding to her, the older woman held out both hands. Faucon and his family were observing closely. Raine accepted the woman's grip, but Madam took Raine's hands and turned them over, studied them, nodded as she saw calluses in the same place as her own. "I knew you would do," Madam said. "Even if the Seamasters did a poor job of Summoning, our beloved Amee would ensure we seafolk would have an Exotique to be proud of. My boys could tell you were a good one when you flew over us."

Raine couldn't see how, but all four of the shipbuilders had wide streaks in their hair. The men, all quite a bit older than Raine, bowed. Madam had started childbearing young.

Faucon moved smoothly forward. "Welcome to Creusse Landing. I hope you will be comfortable here. Corbeau is the master of this place. We have a suite for you on the main floor facing the sea."

Madam's curtsy was deep, her sons' bows quite low and none met Faucon's eyes. Raine was picking up nuances of the culture.

"You are all very gracious," Madam said, bowing more to

Corbeau and his wife. Then she turned back to Raine, and Raine thought she saw relief in her eyes at dealing with a strange Exotique who knew ships more than with high Lladranan nobility. Someone she could identify with, and that touched Raine.

"The word has gone out and is spreading that there will be a great gathering, that testing of sailing skills will occur to man the Ship to the Dark's Nest." Her tone shimmered with excitement. "Sailors will come from all the land, Captains will come to be your second in command, Exotique Seamistress." She glanced at Faucon. "There may be a great fair...."

Corbeau said, "We are preparing."

"Good, good." Madam rubbed her hands, then her face took on an additional inner glow, her Song lilted. "We are honored to be the ones to help you raise the Ship. The design is brilliant."

"Only to be expected from an Exotique," one son said.

"Thank you," Raine said, "and thank you for coming to help."

"This is what we were born to do," another son said.

The next morning, they finished with the last of the design, all in charity with each other.

Then the shipbuilders, Raine, Faucon and Corbeau began crafting the ship-raising Ritual. It wasn't going to be easy, and Raine was going to be the one holding all the Power and directing all the others.

She must not fail.

Luthan's Home

Jikata received an impression of shabby comfort from Luthan's place, something that surprised her since she thought of him as an elegant man.

But the house, the first she'd seen on Lladrana, was nothing compared with flying. She learned the basics easily, mostly because she could mentally hear/see instructions from all three of them...and Luthan was the best of her teachers.

In fact, he'd been the most patient of all her teachers, equaling her childhood Japanese voice instructor, who'd trained her in several languages.

The next morning they were mounted and with an older, sedate volaran carrying packs, on the road and walking through the thick forest before dawn. Jikata marveled at the sunrise in a forest, the lessening of dark into shades of green, then sunlit oblongs slanting in, beautifully illuminating the forest floor.

She sensed that Luthan felt the mystery, too, then he glanced over to her and began Singing a lovely tune of praise for the sunrise and the Song. He Sang it through once, then emphasized the chorus. When he started on the second verse Jikata twined her voice around his, only adding the notes since she didn't know the lyrics, and joined in on the simple chorus. Chasonette Sang with them.

That set the tenor of the day, walking and talking and singing. She was learning today, too, simple folk tunes and a complex Song or two...and listening to the soundtrack around her change as the landscape did. She soaked in the underlying tones of meadows and forests and villages.

Much more satisfying than in the Singer's Abbey. This, too, could be considered Club Lladrana, the local tour.

Chasonette took off on little flights of her own, coming back with bits of gossip...the closest village was having a market day, the Singer's Abbey's bells had rung as usual, so they were keeping her disappearance secret.

Midmorning Jikata had a mental discussion with the Singer.

You come back, the Singer commanded.

No, Jikata replied in English.

I will have you brought back. But there was more anger being flouted than desire for Jikata in the Singer's tone.

Jikata couldn't resist a cliché. *You and what army?* They both knew it was Jikata and Luthan who could call an army.

The Singer had hissed, snapped their communication. Luthan had stiffened beside Jikata and she could almost hear the Singer scolding him. His face had darkened, he'd made a cutting gesture and urged Lightning forward.

For a few minutes they'd galloped, then flown, slowing when the old pack volaran complained. Luthan had met Jikata's eyes. "I am no longer the Singer's representative."

She laughed. "Good. I'm no longer the Singer's apprentice." But she sensed he was purposeful, set on the same course as the other Exotiques.

Now that she was away from the stultifying and shielded walls of the Abbey, she could hear, even *feel,* the links between her and the other women. Because they were all from Earth. More, all were from the States, and most held a common lilt— the signature of Colorado in their tunes.

Oddly enough, she was most curious about Raine, and could feel that woman's Song ebb and flow like the tide. Probably because there wasn't a book by Raine in Jikata's saddlebag.

As they'd transferred her possessions to saddlebags, Luthan had seen the books. His mobile mouth had curved, then flattened as he'd held them in his hands. He hadn't opened the covers, and she was sure he didn't read English, yet she thought he partially recognized the alphabet.

Jikata didn't bring the subject up of the other Exotiques,

why they were Summoned, the monsters, or the Dark. She selfishly wanted the rest of the day to be as pastoral as the countryside. He seemed to understand that, and quiet sensuality
spun between them.

When they stopped for the night, she helped build a fire,
tended the food as he erected the small, fancy pavilion. The
volarans flew off to forage and Chasonette settled down on a
branch and went to sleep.

They ate chicken breasts he'd brought in a cold-spelled
food bag and potato cakes that had heated in the same pan.

Jikata knew from what she'd read of Alexa's and Marian's
books that there hadn't been any potatoes in Lladrana, so one
of the other Exotiques must have brought them, but when? And
how?

She'd had a lot of things in her pack, but usual items a
woman would carry, and jewelry—costume and good—for
the tour. She had energy bars and a small stash of chocolate.
But potatoes? She'd certainly never carried them in her backpack.

After dinner she cracked open Marian's Lorebook, but had
no better luck reading this night than others, her eyes blurring.

Luthan took the book from her hands before she dropped
it and half carried her to one of the tent's "rooms" that was her
own. After he left, she skimmed off her clothes, put on a nightgown and snuggled into the surprisingly soft mattress.

They weren't traveling light, and it seemed odd that all this
stuff had been in the packs on the third volaran. She sighed.
Like most of her entire experiences here, it could be summed
up in one word. Magic.

She dreamed of Ishi. Jikata walked with the old woman
through the overhanging trees along the road she and Luthan

had taken. This time there was the added benefit of the sound of a rushing stream. Pretty and soothing.

He's a handsome man, Ishi said, glancing over at Jikata. *But do you think you should go with him?* She gestured in a smooth and graceful movement and Jikata followed her hand to see they were walking back to the Abbey. *It is safe back there, dear one. You should return and learn a little more, stay safe. Here outside the walls is much danger.*

Something rustled in the bushes and Jikata walked with a wary step, scanned the lush greenery along the sides of the road for threat. They rounded a curve and the Abbey buildings were just ahead, shining white as sunlight poured down on them.

Jikata stopped. *I don't think…*

Ishi and the dream vanished. Jikata awoke with a suddenness that had her heart jolting.

Luthan was crouched near her, she could barely make out the gleam of his eyes. She sucked in a shocked breath.

He held out a white cloth draped softly from his fingers. "You cried out. Nightmare?"

She sat up, looked at him. How much should she tell him? How much would he understand?

Slowly, he touched her cheek with his forefinger. "You weep."

She felt dampness between his finger and her face. When she started to speak, tears coated her throat. No, she didn't trust him enough yet to tell him of the nightmares, those of the Dark. But of these other dreams…. "I lost my great-grandmother just before I was Summoned." She took his handkerchief and dabbed at her face, blew her nose.

"I'm sorry for your loss," he said in a steady, deep voice.

"Ayes. She was old." Jikata managed a smile. "And she was difficult. But I loved her."

His Song surged and she understood she'd touched a chord in him that resonated the same. She tilted her head—he'd experienced this, too, exactly. So exactly that she knew *he* understood that she hadn't been completely truthful about her own feelings. So she cleared her throat of thickness and amended, "She and I disagreed on many things, and I loved her once, and I always wanted her to love me back and be proud of me."

His face tightened, as did the muscles of his body, and again his Song swept her. Then he relaxed, rocked back to his butt and folded his legs until he sat cross-legged in front of her. With a ghost of a smile, understanding lit his eyes.

"You, too?" she asked.

He nodded. "My father." He glanced through the canvas doorway to the other room and she thought he could see outside from that angle and looked into the night. "I never made my peace with him." He rolled his shoulders. "Not that we would have made peace. He was a very autocratic man." He hesitated, then went on, nodded at the saddlebag with Lorebooks. "You might have read that Bastien managed to connect with him, Reynardus, before his death."

The man had died in battle, Jikata recalled. Her throat went tight again. "Ayes."

Luthan's expression settled into brooding. "I have not resolved those feelings."

He made it sound like a fault. She crossed her legs under the cover, leaned over and touched his hand, a little sizzle of sexual tension stilled them both, but she'd meant to offer comfort. "Neither have I, which is why I still dream of her, I suppose."

Robin D. Owens

One side of his mouth lifted. "I'm spared that. But I... think...unresolved emotions could be fatal in the battle with the Dark. So I must find a way to accept what I feel...felt about him." His face went grim.

He'd brought up the topic they'd avoided. Precisely what Jikata didn't want to talk about in the middle of the night so it could give her nightmares. If Luthan had been female... Eyeing him, she reached into her pack and dug out half of the chocolate bar she had and offered it to him.

His eyes gleamed. "Chocolate." He broke the half into quarters, gave her back half.

He knew the word, then. Jikata hesitated, ate hers. "Do you have it here? I hadn't heard."

Luthan shook his head, a negative action common to both their cultures. After he swallowed a small bite, he said, "Ttho, but Marian brought some."

Jikata stared at him. "But I thought Marian arrived nude." The woman had felt humiliated enough to note it in her Lorebook.

Slanting Jikata a look, he finished his chocolate and said, "She brought it from Exotique Terre the second time." He rose, nodded to her. "*Merci,* lady. May you have sweeter dreams." Then he bowed and walked to his room. Jikata shut her mouth, which had fallen open, an unattractive trait that Ishi had deplored, and which didn't happen to her very often.

The *second* time Marian came from Earth. She looked at the thick, heavy book. The biggest book. The tent was dark except for some moonlight from a flap near the top.

Jikata could Sing a soft light into existence. Or practice meditation techniques and sink back into sleep, another puzzle in her head to be discussed...later.

On the Road

Jikata awoke early the next morning, refreshed and energetic. She was out of the Singer's Abbey and on an adventure, a slice of time before she faced whatever gruesome thing came next. Singing a terrible knot undone, perhaps. She glanced at Marian's book, but didn't want to spend her morning private time reading it.

So she dressed and trod silently past a still sleeping Luthan, thinking that no one did much around Luthan Vauxveau that he wasn't aware of. Then she stood at the threshold of their— his—pavilion and looked at him.

He was gorgeous. Not just his handsome face, and tough muscular body, but his personal Song. She'd been aware of it since they'd met up in the forest. More, she'd realized that his Song had lingered in the back of her mind, an unacknowledged melody since the night she'd been Summoned. An interesting fact that curved her lips. No, she hadn't forgotten him.

There was an undeniable attraction between them, as if he, too, had recalled her Song over the weeks. She liked his courteous manner, the way he acted with the volarans and Chasonette, his flashes of humor. She'd fallen in with honorable companions.

She liked the sexy tickle of warmth spreading through her, the awareness she had of herself as a woman, and was reminded that she hadn't had anything more than quick, satisfying bouts of sex for months.

Yes, ayes, traveling with Luthan Vauxveau might be a very nice adventure indeed.

The volarans began to Sing in her mind, calling to her. So she turned her back on the sleeping man and the sweet contemplation of the pleasures they might share and went into the summer green misty morning. Stretching, she hummed a tune that was forming in her mind, part air rushing through soft volaran feathers, part wingbeats, part simple notes of quiet moments of contentment.

She greeted the three volarans, rubbing their noses, clucking to them, listening to their Songs, and thought again of her old goal of her own little retreat in the California hills, with a horse or two.

But these were *volarans*. They looked horselike, but were so much more. Wings would define a species, wouldn't they? She leaned in to Hope and smelled his lovely crumbling amber scent. She could feel his vitality in the solid muscle of his strong neck, heard the pulse of his blood and his *ki*.

Good sunshine to you morning, Hope sent to her. It wasn't his mental tune that was fractured but her hearing. The volaran language was called Equine and to her embarrassment, she didn't master it quickly but spoke to them in fractured images. Perhaps it was because she listened to the entire Song of them, the Power and blood and the way their feathers shifted together on their skin instead of just their mental projections. She was hoping it would soon all mesh together in her head.

She chuckled and rubbed him, but felt a little stiff, so she walked to a bright patch of sun warming the earth, refining her composition. There she stood, centered herself and listened to the land. Up ahead a sparkling waterfall burbled cheerfully, the course and the drop ages old but the water ever new. The rocks around it Sang of minute, not unpleasant change, of polishing.

Grass whispered under her feet and beyond that the planet throbbed satisfaction with her, Jikata.

She heard cloth against cloth and looked over to see Luthan frowning at her, hair rumpled. He studied her closely, head tilted, then relaxed.

He'd dislike that she'd seen him less than perfect, so she cut her stare short and flowed into the first pattern of the tai chi forms she'd once practiced on Earth. She wanted something to warm the body and settle her mind, especially after touching a planet's awareness.

In her childhood she'd done the stretches and patterns with her parents every morning before breakfast, school and work. A shared familial moment that she'd grumbled about at the time, but now cherished memories of. When they'd died... Well, tai chi wasn't Japanese and Ishi had disapproved. When she'd been on her own she'd done them again. After a while life had gotten "too busy" and they'd dropped by the wayside. Now she was determined to make them a priority in her life. Every morning, and a couple of breaks during the day, would be good.

"One moment," Luthan said and withdrew back into the tent, not quite stumbling, but with less than his previous grace.

As she waited for him, Jikata did a few simple patterns, a little routine for health. Before she was done, he was back, dressed in white, as usual, but this looked like raw silk. He bowed to her and it was a different bow than before, a bow of one practitioner to another. She returned it, saw lingering surprise in his eyes. Then he moved to her left.

"I have not done these since I was a child," he said. So he, too, had neglected a skill until it had withered. Not completely perfect after all.

They moved into the commencing pattern, flowed on, and

when they reached "grasp the bird's tail" Chasonette appeared and had them both smiling. She Sang her own morning Song.

He said, "One of my nursemaids knew this discipline. I always felt better after it. I should have thought of it before." He glanced at her as they stepped into a lunge, smiled, and she felt her heart wobble.

Once again she focused, felt the air around them as it heated incrementally into a summer day. She was very aware of him, their arms extending, their hands flowing at the same time, knowing he was very aware of her, as if the air between them was charged and they were an inch apart instead of a yard. She was almost able to feel the press of her skin against his. Or his against hers. She trembled a little. "Listen," she said aloud to remind herself.

He raised his brows, dipped his chin in a nod, then his expression smoothed and she sensed his Power as he heard the Songs around him. His slow, genuine smile bloomed, the line of his shoulders lost a slight stiffness. "This place has no propensity for prophecy," he said with an exhalation that would have been a sigh if it had been deeper.

That was something she'd been aware of unconsciously. He was pleased. She was a little disappointed, and as her body went through the motions, wondered at her feeling. Did she like being an oracle, then? She recalled the sly smiles of the Singer, knowing secrets, more than any other person. Usually the first to learn of any future, and being able to decide whether she should share or not.

Jikata hoped she wasn't like that. She inhaled and let the thought flow from her, negative energy. Let the sense of self and...destiny...come. As she moved, she understood the Power of prophecy was like these exercises, which pleased her body; like her Singing, which pleased her soul. A talent that she enjoyed using. Wasn't that what life was all about?

She murmured it out loud. "Power is a blessing, using it a joy."

The silence between them turned harsh, the motion of his fingertips jerky where they should be smooth. She heard his breath. "It scares me."

Slowly she turned her head and met his stark gaze.

"Especially now," he said.

Club Lladrana was about to come crashing down again. Jikata glanced around at the pretty campsite, the volarans who'd wandered close to watch them after their morning feed. Chasonette, who stared with bright, beady eyes.

A beautiful setting for scary words, and that would help. "Let's finish and you can tell me."

He glanced away as if he'd been rude and they finished the pattern in silence together. She bowed and he did the same, then she slid a leg behind her to sit and he followed, sitting across from her, meeting her eyes.

"Tell me."

He did, of the Dark and the weapon knot and the coming invasion and battle in the Dark's Nest.

And her previous ideas of herself and her place in this world shattered.

30

To Jikata the next few days on the road and in the air were all the more precious for the looming task ahead of her. Hours to be treasured. The shadow of the Dark made the serene and pastoral days all the brighter. She cherished the moments of living and worked on her morning Song, let other bits of tunes crowd her mind, available to become compositions.

The days wavered from dream to acute reality at differing times. Southern Lladrana was full of beautiful scenery and ravishing music. Occasionally they went into towns, Luthan disguised in regular leathers, and once they stayed at the castle of an old, discreet noblewoman.

Those were the dreamlike times, when she let music engulf her.

The real times were when she sensed serious pulses through her links with the other Earth women, the progress of the great scheme she didn't examine. She didn't read the Lorebooks. Then there was the feel of Amee, the planet, angry, sorrowing, anticipatory. Songs more overwhelming than that of the landscapes they traveled through.

Nights were more difficult. Three times running, Jikata had suffered taunting nightmares from the Dark and Luthan had awakened her, then he began sleeping in the same room as she and Chasonette.

Ishi had made no reappearance.

As an escort and knight, Luthan was wonderful. He knew when she wanted to talk, or hear stories of the countryside or Sing.

Or fly. He continued to teach her volaran partnering.

Luthan had relaxed, she got the idea that he hadn't had a vacation in years and she was pleased she could offer him this.

The tingle of awareness between them was ever present, had gone from a sensation like the warmth of the sun sinking into her skin to a fire living within her, stirring her, ready to flash into flames. Shared glances, more touching than necessary. Heavy-lidded eyes full of sensuality. She saw that in him, knew she gave off the same sexual signals. Knew that they'd share sex and more, soon, and her spirit sang.

Creusse Landing

People streamed into Creusse Landing bringing with them the carnival atmosphere Raine had experienced at the Marshalls' Castle. That completely baffled her. Sure, getting together looked fun, *was* fun, with merchants setting up a regular fair. Enerin visited everyone, was often out.

But didn't the Chevaliers and the Marshalls realize that the reason for this fair was to raise and outfit a ship, then to sail away to invade an evil Nest and kill the Dark that had been there for centuries, if not millennia?

She rarely forgot that fact.

Such a weenie.

The Marshalls and the Chevaliers brought their own pavilions and made a beautiful little city. Most of them had the tents from the year before when they'd camped in the north, and those who didn't had friends who had loaned them some. Koz's large white tent with the trident banner he'd copied from Maserati was set up, though he was bunking with the rest of the Exotiques and highest-level Marshalls in the manor house.

The one VIP Raine hadn't seen was Luthan.

She'd shaken Faucon off to visit the sailors' camp that fringed the southern edge of the gathering. The high-level Seamasters were either in the manor or scattered throughout the campground, enjoying hobnobbing with the nobles and Marshalls.

Ella introduced her to laconic sailors who'd arrived to try out for the force. Most of them were big, tough men with scars aplenty from a life on the oceans and wide enough streaks of Power in their hair. Raine had asked around and few of them had wives and children and she was glad, though the amount of them who showed up made her think that a lot of communities might be missing a son or sister or friend by the end of this business.

Some of the men stared at her with flat gazes, shuddered, then picked up their stuff and left. They didn't want to be around Exotiques and no one else wanted to be around them.

But Raine got a feel for the sailors' tidy camp—tidier than

the Marshalls, who were nobles and usually had servants to pick up after them; cleaner than the Chevaliers, who practiced living in the moment—and liked the quality of the people who were there. Even a few minutes talking with them had her re-designing the ship plans in her head, to make it more like the ships they were accustomed to, more comfortable for the crew.

Then Faucon found her, snugged an arm around her waist and was introduced around himself, along with the ship-builder Deauvilles who'd followed him. They spent a while together discussing matters and when they were done, Faucon pulled her out into the evening and back into the noisy, crazy fair.

There was tasty food and drink, interesting wares. Faucon bought her a wide belt that was made up of snapping pouches in a deep green. They watched jugglers and tumblers and dancers and listened to minstrels.

They even danced a reel or two themselves, until Raine couldn't bear to step on his feet one more time.

After the stars came out, Faucon drew her down to the shore. Here some Chevaliers and staff of the manor patrolled to make sure no one camped on or trashed the beach.

The wash of the surf drowned out all other sounds except the music between them and depths of the sea. As they walked and spoke of little but the day and their friends, she relaxed.

Then he turned her and drew her into his arms and she felt the strength of him and sighed. He lifted her chin with a tip of his finger and their gazes met and she knew her expression was as yearning as his.

"Let me take you to a special place," he said and kissed her.

She ran her fingers through the silver hair denoting Power at his left temple. "Every place with you is special."

He inhaled, took her hand in a hard grip. "You strip my control from me," he said roughly, then pulled her along as he ran on the firm beach.

"Faucon!"

"I want to make love to you in the cove, and by the Song we'll do that."

Raine didn't really see the cove. There was a special music to it, the way the tide splashed and echoed around the steep rocks of the narrow inlet. That's all she noticed beyond the man and his hands and his tongue and the music they made together.

Each time they made love it was more wonderful than the last, as if their Songs were changing to match each other and Raine *so* didn't want to think of that. Better to acknowledge that the sex was the best she'd ever had...and Faucon the most tender lover.

So she lay with her head on his arm and they looked at the stars blazing in the sky...a naturally lighter night sky than Earth's. The sand beneath her, which sifted into her clothes, would have her moving soon enough, but it wasn't the first time she'd made love on the beach—hadn't been Faucon's first, either.

As she watched, a meteor flamed out, looking as if it had fallen into the sea and lit the surf with bright luminescence.

"How are you going to handle tomorrow?" he asked as he nuzzled her neck.

"What about tomorrow?"

"The Seamasters' Apology Ritual."

"Oh. That."

He rolled to his side. "You'd forgotten."

She said, "Ayes."

Kissing her nose, he said, "Because you've already forgiven them. You're such a generous person."

"I'm glad you think so, and I don't dwell on how I came here anymore. So much has happened since then, in the last few days. Crammed full of events." She stroked his cheek. "You." Winking at him, she said, "All the wonderfulness of you."

He choked and they rolled around in the sand, then had to get up and run in the surf to wash off. Play.

She'd had no joyous moments, no play when she'd arrived. And doom was coming up for sure. She didn't quite know how she felt about the Apology Chorus. She didn't doubt there were hard feelings still tucked inside her. When you grew up with four brothers and a father, you kept your emotions to yourself.

But the stars and moon were bright and a sexy man wanted to play in the waves with her, and this moment was the best life could offer.

It was midmorning the next day when Raine left the manor for the village hall and the Apology Chorus. Faucon and Ella walked with her. Faucon kept the conversation light, commenting on the changes between the manor and the town that had occurred since his last visit, nodding to Chevalier acquaintances.

Ella glowed with righteous glee. She, too, met gazes. Nods and smiles of sharp agreement were given her. So she walked proudly as if escorting a rightful queen ready to take up her crown. The people gathered together were sympathetic to Raine and condemnatory of their former leaders.

Though Faucon kept his manner casual, Raine noted his

eyes were keen for any discourtesy, any hint that someone in their path would be those who innately hated an Exotique. His Song was a compressed line of intense emotion.

This was an apology to Raine, and her opportunity for forgiveness.

She didn't think that either Ella or Faucon was ready to forgive.

Once she reached the townhall, she was taken to the meeting room to sit in a fancily carved chair with driftwood whorls, the seat of the Townmaster.

Twelve Seamasters trooped in, including the four who'd kept their jobs after the fiasco. Most expressions were stoic or shamefaced, but a couple of them had burning anger and contempt in their gazes. So she put on a mask of serenity herself.

They shuffled around in a semicircle, two rows, shorter men in front.

Ella introduced them and Raine nodded, then gestured for the girl to leave.

Sitting straight, Raine said, "I thank you for this courtesy. As you all must know, one of the tasks of an Exotique is to build connections between the group that Summoned her and the rest of the segments of Lladranan society." She sounded like Marian and allowed herself an inward smile. "I believe this will be helpful for doing that."

"We're grateful you're lettin' us Sing this apology in private," one of the men she recognized from her tuning at the Marshalls' Castle said.

Raine looked right at another guy whose jaw was clenched. "Before you start, I'd like you to imagine how it might feel to be yanked into a new world in the dead of winter, not knowing what happened to you."

He didn't blink. No empathy or compassion there.

"I didn't even know that traveling between dimensions was possible."

Most of the men shuffled.

Well, she hadn't changed any minds. But seafolk were usually a stoic and stubborn lot. Those who could empathize had already come to terms with their actions. Those who were still bitter that their secrecy had been unveiled, their incompetency revealed and the disgust of them that followed…they wouldn't Sing with true hearts.

"That's all I had to say." She cleared her throat. "I'll leave you to align your personal Songs to that of universal Song." How pompous, but dammit, *she'd* been wronged by these men. "And blessings on you."

"Never cared to be cross-wise to the Song," one muttered.

The leader hummed a note, and the chorus began.

Raine liked the tune, the rhythms of rolling water, of a team of sailors working. And they *were* working at this Song. The two grouches wanted to hasten the beat and their grudging and flat voices stood out. A couple of the men had the usual good voices of a people who were an aural society.

She didn't quite catch the words, but it sounded a little like a prayer, a prayer sung to her. The music surrounded her, echoed around her in the acoustic hall, enveloped her, and reached into her.

It drew deep emotions to the surface, and she found that the men's voices had become quieter and her own personal Song loud in her ears. Her ears only? She didn't think so.

The terror of the storm rising on the choppy, cold winter sea.

Falling into the mirror, whirling in the dark, winds whipping at her, chilling her.

Landing on a soggy ground on a gray day, lying, panting, completely uncomprehending of what had happened. Her tears, her shouts, her despair.

That seemed to fill the room and she blinked rapidly to keep tears from falling.

The strangeness of a place not hers, where she couldn't understand the language. Stumbling from town to town, from job to job, sick and fainting anytime she moved more than a few miles inland. Finally the job as a "slow" potgirl in a poor tavern on a pier, the Open Mouthed Fish.

Again and again the men Sang their apology until that, too, sank in. Most were truly ashamed at what they'd done, and now and again a voice broke as if they, too, felt her emotions, her memories. They acknowledged their fault in Summoning her with a half-assed ritual, only half-believing themselves, breaking the circle and leaving, not looking for her since she hadn't appeared in their shoddy circle.

They Sang until all the lingering anger and hurt was drawn from her, begging for forgiveness at treating a fellow human being so. Those were the words, and the emotions that came from most hearts. All but two who Sang because they were forced to.

They Sang until Raine sagged against the back of the chair, then lifted a hand to dismiss them. "Thank you. I accept your apology." She was worn out.

Then they bowed, as a group, and Ella opened the door.

Ten of the twelve stopped near Raine's chair, met her eyes, nodded and made personal apologies, bowed or touched her hand.

"I'm sorry." The words echoed in her mind from the timbre of many voices.

Then they were gone and Ella was at the open door.

"Go away," Raine croaked. She was going to fall apart, she knew it, and she didn't want Ella to see that. "Please." Her voice was rough as if she'd Sung all the choruses, too.

Face sober, Ella nodded and closed the door quietly.

It opened the next instant as Faucon stepped in. He came to her and swept her off the chair, sat himself and held her as she let out awful choking sounds.

Then she wept.

Raine had recovered her spirits and was walking hand-in-hand back to the manor with Faucon when an awful shrieking pulse split the air.

31

Faucon tensed beside her, silence fell over the fairground crowd. Then shouts came as Chevaliers called for their volarans and took off into the sky.

Faucon steadied her and himself, grimaced.

A hefty merchant plucked at his sleeve. "What is it, Hauteur?"

In the quiet, people turned to Faucon, awaiting his answer. His face hardened. "It's a relay alarm from the Marshalls' Castle, notifying us there's an invasion." Tilting his head, he listened as the siren blasted again. "In the far northeast."

People looked stunned, then glanced around at others. Raine realized that she'd become accustomed to a siren, Chevaliers and Marshalls flying to battle. War.

It seemed these folk had never had the circumstances of battle so emphasized before. Reality check.

Everyone watched as teams took to the sky, one of them

wearing the red and orange of the man who owned the land they were camped on.

The quiet stretched and Faucon tugged Raine through the crowd. "There's an animated map in the manor library."

Muttering arose, the phrase passed through the fair… animated map. Suddenly, it seemed, the people wanted to know more.

Faucon's stride had lengthened until Raine had to hurry to keep up with him, an unusual discourtesy. His Song had picked up an irritated note and he was muttering to himself. "What did they think we were doing all these years? This is the north, by the Song, they should have been more aware."

Raine couldn't answer him, found her throat closing once more as she wished that *she* hadn't learned what the siren meant. She didn't want to go to the library and watch as Chevaliers and Marshalls fought and maybe died. But she didn't feel like she had any choice.

And the pressure on her to raise a ship soon had just increased.

Every single person here would want that now.

The next couple of days Raine and the Deauvilles discussed and refined the ship's blueprints. She'd never worked so hard or long or modified a plan more. But she'd never built such a massive ship, had to design it for people who'd see it as revolutionary. And the design and ship had never been so critical.

They'd set the time for the ship-raising for the next full moon, before the week's end, and Raine and Faucon checked on the materials for it every day.

By the time they'd finished the very last changes to her design, Raine believed the ship would be exactly what the

Exotiques needed for an invasion battleship. It looked like a galleon, with a lot of space for stores, areas for hammocks for the crew and the Marshalls and Chevaliers, six tiny cabins for the Exotiques and their men. There was a quarterdeck for the volarans, and additional space on the deck for them and observers. It wouldn't be the fastest or most wind-efficient ship, but it would serve its purpose.

She and the shipbuilders pushed back from the study table and the oldest male Deauville reported the last of the materials had arrived. Raine was impressed when he said all would be laid out on the beach and sandbars—he glanced at her here—just before the raising. Only his family, Raine, Faucon, Corbeau and the three feycoocus would be aligning the materials. Circlets would provide Power for them to use in moving the huge timbers for masts, the great planks for the rudder and hull, lesser ones for the decks, the sailcloth and the miles of rope.

Raine thanked the man, thanked them all again, then said, "There's one thing I don't understand. You didn't mention the great Power stones, the hematite. Where will we get those?"

They stared at her, then looked away. Madam Lucienne Deauville smiled, then ducked her head. "Why we will raise them from the deep. Many of the great stones are found that way. Amee provides."

Raine's turn to stare. "You're serious?"

They all nodded. "Ayes," Madam said.

Raine rolled her shoulders. "When do we do that?"

The family shared a glance. "We make the rudder and the hull below the stones, set the Ship plan out, then raise the spheres." Lucienne shrugged. "Not a difficult matter."

"Ttho?"

"Ttho," Madam Lucienne said firmly. "Amee provides."

Raine just shook her head.

The night before the raising went well. Raine found laying out the materials for the ship taken out of her hands as the Deauvilles hustled around her. She "supervised." The sea stayed calm, barely lapping over the beach and the sandbars where Raine had felt the ship should be built, and the family seemed to accept that she'd chosen well. Madam Lucienne made a humming noise Raine took for approval. The eldest son held the design plans and watched the pattern form with an eagle eye, sharply correcting any missed detail.

Finally it was ready. Except for the stones.

The ship-raising pentacle had been incised in the proper spot on the beach by the great Circlet Bossgond himself, and the way he hovered near it, Raine figured he'd be spending the night to make sure that design wasn't smudged.

Madam Lucienne ignored that drawing, gestured for her sons to follow her example and roll up their rough pants, then slogged out to the area slightly under water where a section of the hull had already been assembled...by Power. It had snapped together easily with just a little Song and imagery and Power from Raine.

Lucienne waved at Raine to come, so she turned up her pants and went on out. The water was cold but not frigid.

All this preparation had strung her nerves tight.

Madam patted her with a heavy hand on Raine's shoulder. "All's well."

"If you say so."

"I do." A decisive nod. "All is well." Lucienne rubbed her hands. "Now we call the stones from the deep."

She scanned the beach, gestured to Faucon and Corbeau to join her and her sons and Raine. The feycoocus were already floating on the water, eyes sharp, waiting for the ritual to begin. Lucienne pointed at Alexa and Marian, who'd been watching with curiosity. "You come out here and help!" she shouted.

Alexa grinned and took off her boots and socks, folded up her jeans. Marian huffed and sang a little couplet that was snatched away by the wind and her magical gown shortened. By itself. She walked a couple of steps and her shoes and socks fell away and she was barefoot.

"Nice trick," Madam's eldest son muttered.

He was standing next to Raine. For this Song, she was between him and Faucon and they alternated male, female, even when Jaquar, Marian's husband, joined them.

Lucienne hummed the starting chord rustily, and her sons drowned her out.

Then she Sang, of the sea, the tide, the wind. Boats Powered by stones...

Raine let the cadence of the ocean take her, closed her eyes and swayed and Sang. Sang of the tide going out, of settling down, down, down into the sea, where secrets lay, treasures hidden by Lady Amee to keep them safe. All the riches of the planet were in these depths.

Rising once again to the water's surface, feeling the foam of wind and wave, breathing the sea air.

"And done!" Madam shouted.

Her son and Faucon squeezed Raine's hands, dropped them and Raine opened her eyes and staggered back at the sight of four huge shining round hematite stones.

"Ha!" said Lucienne, trudging back to the shore and her linen socks, sturdy shoes.

"Looks good," Faucon said with satisfaction, kissing Raine's temple. He carefully placed the directional jewels on each stone, then walked with Raine back to the beach.

"Huh? I missed it!"

"It was a sight to see." Still grinning, Alexa zoomed her hand up. "Four big pieces of rock shooting out of the ocean, plopping down on your ship. Incredible." She glanced at everyone. "And easy. Hardly took any effort."

"Amee provides," Lucienne said smugly.

"Amazing," Marian said. Raine could tell she was already framing her report in her mind.

"A good bit of sea magic," one of the shipbuilders said.

"A good omen that the raising will be a success," said another. Raine hoped so.

As was their habit, the Exotiques and their men had after-dinner drinks in the library. It had spread throughout the gathering that the group was available for any casual problem-solving that wouldn't go on the record, and in a much better mood as a bunch than if one approached them individually.

They'd already dealt with a young, stuttering teenaged Scholar—the level below Circlet—who'd been accepted in Marian's academy. He'd come from a sea family and had been sailing and working on his own maps of the northern waters and passageways for years as a hobby. Did they want to see them?

They wanted copies. As soon as possible. He left with a sweaty and proudly shining face.

Then came a young female Marshall pair, Sword and Shield, fingers entwined. They'd passed the trials, and were on the invasion force. They'd had second thoughts—Raine sensed it was the Sword—and wondered if they could be released?

Alexa heaved a dramatic sigh of relief, hand on her chest, then jumped up and hugged them both. It seemed she had wanted the Shield to stay and work with the understudies posing as the Exotiques at the Castle.

The Shield had a special gift for luring horrors, which was needed to make the magical barrier strong. Alexa and Bastien sent the women off with their blessings. Alexa went immediately to her waiting list and used her crystal ball to call the Castle and the head of the Marshalls there to tell the next pair of Marshalls to report to Creusse's Landing at once.

She shared a troubled glance with her husband as she was told their former squires, the newest Marshalls, were whooping loudly enough to be heard throughout the Castle.

Raine hadn't questioned anything regarding the trials before, but now she was weighing the seafolk who'd crew the ship. Hesitantly, she said, "The new replacements will be as good as those who just left?"

"Better," Bastien said, snagging his wife as she paced back and bringing her in to sit on his lap. "The Sword wasn't ready, but we can't dismiss on slight feelings if the scores were high, and theirs were, individually and as a pair."

Alexa grimaced. "Our scoring system was public—as I thought it should be after all the secrecy of the Marshalls in the past—but it didn't really allow for hinky feelings."

"On the other hand, that was the Pair I had the most concerns about," Bastien said philosophically, kissed his wife briefly, then looked at Raine. "The entire list of those who qualified were ties, sometimes three or four had the same score. We could replace the entire complement of Marshalls and

Chevaliers on the Ship three times with those who scored at the top."

Something within Raine eased. She wanted the best to go. To protect her friends. To have a better chance to destroy the Dark.

The doorharp strummed, and Corbeau's wife came in after an *"Entre"* from Faucon. Her eyes were wide and her expression was of suppressed excitement. She shut the door behind her and said, "There is a contingent of Friends here who wish to see you. I believe they came from the Singer's Abbey itself."

Everyone focused on her and she straightened to her tall height. "They didn't tell me what they wanted, but there's been snatches of whispered rumor that the Singer has lost the new Exotique."

"I heard that," Jaquar said.

Bastien sat up, holding Alexa tight. "Luthan. My brother hasn't been around lately."

"Luthan." His name came from Raine's lips at the same time as everyone else's. This phenomena didn't surprise her anymore.

Grinning, Bastien said, "He's got her."

Faucon said, "Show them in." He smiled, too, and Raine felt the fizz of interest and satisfaction in his Song.

The woman smiled back at him. "I don't think they are expecting all of you." She made a wide gesture.

"Even better," said Marian.

"And we don't really know a thing," Alexa said with satisfaction.

"But it would be good for them to stay and participate in the ship-raising tomorrow," Raine said, considering. "Friends from the Singer's Abbey itself." She nodded decisively. "Show them in."

The woman curtsied to her. "Yes, Lady."

All the Friends said was that they were told to come by this date. They did ask if the Exotique Singer had arrived.

Sinafinal and Tuckerinal and Enerin, who'd been dozing on various laps as cats and kitten, perked up and began cat-chattering. Then they stalked over to the Friends and sniffed their hems.

Marian said the feycoocus informed her that the Exotique Singer was a volaran ride away and enjoying herself. The fey-coocus went to see her every day. With a piercing look Marian asked how the Singer and her Friends had come to lose Jikata.

The Friends shuffled, and muttered inaudible answers.

Alexa invited them to spend the night and take part in the ship-raising ritual the next day.

That perked them up and they left.

Luthan is taking care of the Exotique Singer, Sinafinal said with authority. *She will join us when it is right.*

And that was that. As usual, no more could be gotten from the feycoocus as cats.

On the Road

Jikata's Song drew Luthan. Not just her personal Song that had woven around him from the moment they'd met, and that he'd breathed in every moment they were together. This was actual Singing of a tune he'd never heard before, a tune she'd begun making one morning and had refined note by note, over a few days. She wasn't only a Singer, but a composer, and her talent awed him.

Her voice and the Power behind it snared him. As he walked toward where she sat in front of the pavilion as the stars came out, he finally admitted to himself that he'd had prophetic flashes of the Song and look of her all his life. Dreams that had awakened him sweaty and yearning for something he knew wasn't found on Lladrana.

Now she was here, and there had been no instinctive revulsion for her. Surely a blessing.

All he had to do was offer her his hand. Problem was he didn't want to do that, he wanted to yank her to him, feel her soft body against his, under his, wrap himself in her long hair and bury himself in her and race to the top of the mountain of ecstasy.

But she Sang a Song of dawn becoming a soft summer morning and volarans playing in the pearl-pink lightening sky.

He looked at her with jaw clenched, quivering in every muscle, wanting her. It had been a long time since he'd had a woman, couldn't remember the last, any other woman, when his eyes were on Jikata. And he'd never had a woman like her. Would never have a woman like her, a Songsmith, a Singer, an Exotique.

A woman born to Sing the Dark to its Doom.

He could see that in her, the courage and strength and Power it would take to do that—Sing a weapon knot loose, bond with other women and meld their Songs together to rid a world of an evil being.

She looked toward him where he stood in the deep shadows, watching. He didn't think she could see him, but she'd heard his Song, just as he heard hers. That intricate Song that was as utterly beguiling as the scent of her skin, the ripple of her laughter.

So he stepped from the shadows into the firelight and she glanced up at him with a smile...then stilled.

If she'd shown fear he wouldn't have touched her, but her

gaze warmed and her smile curved and deepened into that of a woman looking at a man she wanted to touch her.

He was lost.

With the measured step he'd learned after his wild days—days that were flickering in his mind about how to take and love a woman rough—he came to her. Grasped her arms and lifted her from her feet until her face was even with his.

She deserved tender and gentlemanly.

He feared he'd give her rough and wild.

While he fought for control, she pressed her lips against his and sent her breath into him and he shuddered with need. Her tongue swept his lips and he opened his mouth and her taste was that of rich sweet cream.

He swung her into his arms, and trusting his feet to be sure while his mind was spinning, he took her into the tent. He didn't stop at the spareness of his space but went into the luxury he'd brought for her—the thick rug, the plump pillows, the small feather mattress all bespelled to inviting softness.

There he laid her down.

That was the last bit of gentleness between them.

They fought off each other's clothes, panting, moaning. He might have sworn at a stubborn buckle, then it was open. Her hands clutched his shoulders, kneading deep into muscle, and his explored the texture of smooth woman and silky hair.

They came together as if they'd always fitted to each other, mated, and the ride was wild, her Song spiraling them high, matched with his, until they flamed together and he was consumed.

He lay atop her, not wanting to move, knowing he was heavy on the smaller woman, but he could barely put two thoughts together, let alone command his muscles.

She purred, nipped at his biceps, and bliss shot through him and he shuddered again.

"Much better," she said in a husky voice carrying the Exotique accent, "than sleeping alone, with you near."

He'd only be able to grunt, so he said nothing.

Then with a satisfied hum she rolled them over until he was pressed into the mattress and she was atop him and having her breasts and soft body settle into him so wonderfully it was near pain.

"We won't sleep apart again, will we, Luthan?"

He had to find his voice. His arms tightened around her. "We might never sleep again."

She chuckled and it tugged every nerve in his body.

"I've wanted this since we've met." She propped her arms on his chest, her voice came above him.

He realized his eyes were closed and he needed to see her. Fabulous woman, beautiful sparkling eyes, cheeks with a hint of rose, lush mouth. His mind went blank again, but he managed to say, "Me, too."

She wriggled atop him and all sensation centered back to his sex, which rose. "No," he said, putting his hands on the globes of her bottom, loving the roundness, the texture. "No sleep tonight."

But they did. They slept and dreamed. Together.

He walked in a smooth tunnel of rock, holding her hand. Beneath them was the rumble of molten earth and the stench of evil. Outside he could hear fighting, Marshalls and Chevaliers and volarans battling monsters. Screams of pain and dying. Shrieks of mindless fury.

Jikata blinked and looked around her. "What is this place?"

32

He looked down at the woman and was blinded by her physical beauty, then heard nothing but her wondrous Song. "You know where we are, and you really should read the Lorebooks," he said mildly.

She tilted her head. "I think they would be too fearful all at once."

He considered, nodded. "Maybe."

"I would rather you tell me bits as I ask."

"Done," he said, then shook his head. The woman was Powerful enough to receive prophecies anywhere on Lladrana and draw him into them with her.

They came to an opening that was one of several around a huge cavern within the mountain.

She frowned. "What *is* this?"

"The volcano of the Dark's Nest." Outside the mountain, the

human voices became lost in monsters' roars. A liquid chuckle rose from the depths. Jikata shivered. Luthan moved until he was at her back, his arms wrapped around her.

"I know that sound," she said. "The evil leech on Amee."

"Ayes." He hadn't thought of it that way, but it was apt.

"Is this the future or the now?" she asked.

He turned his head away so his senses weren't lost in her, focused, saw the wavering atmosphere. "Future," he said, though he should have known. No humans were on the mountain tonight...this morning?

Voices lifted in excitement, triumph and glee came barreling toward them. He recognized Alexa's. Before he could draw breath, they flashed past him...the Exotiques, grouped together, flying on the gong. On their way to the last confrontation.

"I must join them." Jikata strove to break his grip, jump into the cavern, into the dark depths.

An ominous silence came from outside the mountain. He should be there, lending his arm to the fight.

He dropped his arms, let her loose. "Ayes, go."

She jumped with a battle cry.

"I'll follow," he said, and did....

Luthan woke up gasping for air, drew clean cool breaths that soothed his lungs from the hot rancid air in the dream.

The night breeze fluttered the outer flap of the pavilion that had come undone. Outside came the rustles of volarans, and the physical/mental sound of Equine conversation, with the feycoocus, softly calling him.

Jikata was wrapped in his arms, skin to skin. Her personal Song gentle waves, dreamless.

Not in the Dark's Nest. Not.

Had not lost Jikata.

His cold sweat dried.

That was in the future.

Jikata awoke to Chasonette tugging on her hair. It was still dark. Luthan wasn't near and she felt a pang of disappointment. "What?"

Luthan says time to get up.

Jikata would have stared at the bird, but couldn't see her in the dark. Could hear her, and smell the lavender scent of her wings.

She shoved herself sleepily to her elbows, then to her feet. If Luthan were waking her so early then it was important, but all the minds around her held excitement so nothing bad had happened.

Luthan was outside packing and a glance at his space told her it was bare. Humming a little spell light she went to the corner of the tent where a waterskin hung from a peg. There was also a collapsible canvas basin and a sponge for a quick clean-up. The sponge was already damp and held the faintest hint of Luthan. Memories of their passion heated her.

It had been a while since she'd had sex. There'd always been a sex buddy around. Now that she thought about it, she'd most often enjoyed herself with her sound engineer. He'd been clean, good in bed, and had no expectations of her.

He'd have gone wild here on Lladrana, she almost pitied him back on Earth.

This night with Luthan had been more than sex. How much more she wasn't sure, but what she had learned in the days she'd spent with him was that they had many things in common, something she wouldn't have guessed. Her feelings for him were unusually strong. They'd see where it went.

When she reached for her jeans and a shirt, Chasonette whistled a sharp negative. *Flying leathers today.*

After she was dressed, she tossed her head, Sang a little tune to arrange her hair just the way she wanted, and was pleased she could do that with Power instead of brush and comb or hours under the stylist's hands.

The moment she stepped from the tent, it opened up at the top and collapsed around their things—her things. Both volarans were saddled.

Luthan simmered with anticipation, exhilaration, and she had to smile. She went over, twined her arms around his neck, pressed her body against his and kissed him soundly, then raised her head and said, "Good morning."

His eyes gleamed brighter now than before. He brushed a kiss on her lips. "Wonderful morning."

When she stepped away, she felt his reluctance and that pleased her. "What's going on?" She helped pack her room and roll up the tent in bundles that seemed too small.

"There's an event that is taking place you won't want to miss—*none* of us want to miss." He raised a hand as she opened her mouth, his own was curved. "You'll enjoy the surprise more." He turned to her bags and with a flick of his fingers had them settling on the volarans. The ties whipped themselves into excellent, practical knots.

"We'll be flying far, using Distance Magic." He checked the bags and the volaran tack again, opened a new pouch that hung on her volaran. Chasonette flew to the top of the stiffened leather, then lowered herself into it until only her curious head with gleaming eyes showed.

I do not have the Distance Magic of the volarans.

Jikata caught the excitement from the others. "Are we going to meet the other Exotiques at the Marshalls' Castle?" She wasn't sure she was prepared, and Luthan had agreed that it would be her decision, but she trusted him. If there was something she should see—hear—then it was right.

He ran a hand down Lightning's neck. "Ayes and ttho."

No answer at all.

"There's a...ritual...I think you'd like to see."

"Will I be expected to take part?"

"Not unless you want to."

Ah, he thought she'd want to. Too many questions and she felt his impatience to *go,* not linger and dodge more queries.

"Fine." She looked around camp. It showed little signs of having been occupied. Good. Crossing over to Luthan, she kissed him again, let him help her mount, settled her seat on Hope and stroked a finger on Chasonette's head.

The bird looked at her. *We will watch history.* She flicked her comb.

Luthan kicked the dead embers of the fire apart. He walked to her, set a hand on her knee and looked up. "Do you recall our lessons in Distance Magic?"

They hadn't ever gone far, a mile or two. "Ayes."

"Good." He squeezed her knee, then surprised her by kissing it. "Beautiful Jikata." Another smile. "There is no part of you that isn't lovely."

She chuckled. "You should know."

He swung into his saddle, sent her a glance under lowered lashes. "And I'll know more, again and again." Then he stared at the open sky, the space around them. "You're a quick study,

Distance Magic will come easily to you. We'll be some time in the saddle."

Her eyes had become accustomed to the night so she could stare at him, handsome in his white leathers. Not his usual travel leathers, they appeared to be a newer set. Ayes, this was important. He looked much like the formidable man of her first impression.

"I'm ready." She stroked Hope's neck. A real road trip. "We can stop for a very few minutes now and then for a break."

He grimaced, then called, "Feycoocu."

A hawk spiraled down from the air, perched on a nearby branch. Chasonette chirped a greeting. Jikata thought it was the female one, Sinafinal.

Salutations, Jikata and Luthan and Chasonette and Hope and Lightning and Socks.

Luthan mindspoke, *How are the preparations going?*

Sinafinal lifted her wings. *Everyone is still gathering and the schedule is lagging. If you leave now you may arrive just before the ritual begins.*

Luthan frowned. *I believe it would be best to arrive after the circle has formed and the event has started, less distraction for the others that way.*

Less questions, Sinafinal agreed. *Shrewd thinking.*

Thank you.

Do you want to tell me what's going on? Jikata asked.

With a ripple of amused notes, Sinafinal shook her head. *You will see. And hear.* She launched herself from the branch, rose quickly into the sky out of sight.

Luthan picked up his reins and Jikata followed.

"Let's *fly!*" he said and Lightning took off. Jikata followed and understood something else, the slow pace she'd set for them had chafed at Luthan, yet he'd said nothing.

And real flying on a volaran was wonderful.

Addictive.

Creusse Landing

Raine was dozing as the sun brightened the windows, warming the room. It was full morning when a quick strum of doorharp strings sounded and the outer door of the suite opened.

Marian entered the bedroom, unheeding of Raine's yelp as she pulled the covers up. Faucon just grinned.

Then the Circlet Sorceress unfolded what she'd brought and held it up, and Raine forgot about everything else.

It was a gown of shimmering emerald and sapphire, like it had been lifted from the ocean itself. Around the hem of the dress and the sleeves were embroidered golden stylized waves. And in the satinlike fabric itself shone other silver symbols that Raine couldn't quite see.

But she could feel them.

This was a gown of the utmost magic.

Marian smiled. "You like it, then."

"It is the most beautiful thing I've ever seen."

Nodding, Marian said, "All the Exotiques bespelled it, as did the feycoocus and even the roc. A Circlet wove the fabric and made the dress." Marian chuckled. "One of the water persuasion." She held it out, admired it. "I couldn't make a dress like this for you in a million years."

Raine jumped out of bed, uncaring of her nudity, of Faucon's indulgent and admiring gaze. "Oh, thank you." Tears prickled behind her eyes.

"A magic gown for a magic day," Marian said lightly. "I see that you had a good night and a good sleep, too."

"Yeah." Raine was stroking the dress, but saw Faucon's eyes roll at her understatement. So she sent a grin to him. "Excellent sex and excellent sleep." He subsided back onto his pillows with a satisfied grin.

"An excellent breakfast awaits you both," Marian said.

"Should I dress in this?" Raine loved the dress but it wouldn't be better with egg.

"Absolutely," Marian said.

"Ayes," Faucon said.

Marian aimed a stern gaze at Faucon. "After he's gone. I know all about men and magical gowns."

She would.

Raine said, "I'll go shower then." Reluctantly placing her dress on the end of the bed, she left.

She was reviewing the ritual, the Song and the steps for raising the ship in her head when Faucon joined her in the shower.

They made love, but Raine felt a slight tension in him that hadn't been there before, and a little withdrawal. This was the day she would finish her task for Lladrana and Amee.

After that the Snap could come at any time.

So she made lusty and tender love with him.

In Flight

Jikata and Luthan flew over green land, rolling hills, and angled over the ocean and Circlets' islands that belonged to the Sorcerers and Sorceresses. Since they didn't land, she guessed they weren't visiting any of the chief magic workers and wasn't sure how that made her feel. She was used to having more Power than those around her.

Or thinking she had more Power. She sensed Luthan had a great deal of his own that he hadn't revealed, and the other Exotiques, of course, would have as much as she, wouldn't they?

But they wouldn't have *her* skills.

As she wouldn't have theirs, and that felt right.

Creusse Landing

It was a half hour before noon and the tide was ebbing, would be at the low mark at midday when the ship should be raised. Though it couldn't be seen, the moon was full.

Raine went to the middle of the pentacle drawn in the sand, faced west toward the sea where the materials had been laid out for the ship on the beach and in the shallow water and on the sandbars.

Everyone took their place, bonded pairs alternating with each other on the beach. It was a large circle and inner joy welled through Raine as she looked at them. All the Marshalls and Chevaliers, of course. Townmasters like Sevair Masif, Bri's husband, and others who'd been curious enough to respond to the invitation. Circlets and Scholars of the Tower community matched the numbers of the warriors, led by the greatest of them all, Marian's mentor Bossgond. All the Seamasters and many seafolk, Raine's own community. Even an acceptable number of Friends, those who lived in local villages, some from a small nearby abbey, and those who'd arrived from the Singer the night before.

Most wore colorful, formal robes, though none as gorgeous as her own, and the people themselves were beautiful.

All the segments of Lladranan society had come to support

her and this task of hers. For the first time in ages they would all be working in concert.

More than pride washed through her as she took her place in the center of the circle, Power rose.

Only a few had no mark of Power at their temples. This could also be the most Powerful circle ever and that made Raine's breath catch. *What was she doing?*

She set her shoulders. She was building—raising—a ship. Something she'd been born to do, something she'd been doing, with a twist, since she'd been old enough to be taken to the shipyard and sand the boats her family built. She could do this.

Bastien Sang the blessing, and with his wild black-and-white magic, he invoked a no-tell spell on everyone, sent it rippling around the circle. Raine saw some disconcertment and an angry look or two, but the spell was effective. No one could talk about this except to others who had participated.

She was the center of a vortex of Power like she'd never known before and would never feel again. This was *her* moment. The fulfillment of her being, her fate.

Power sizzled around her, time to harness it and raise the ship. So she winked at Faucon, opened her mouth and Sang the first note of the ritual. Everyone joined in. Then she continued with the simple verse, gathering the Power, steadying it, melding it for her use. Harmonious voices rose around her.

When Power peaked, filled her, swirled around her in a sparkling, golden cloud, enough to raise the ship, she started the first chorus with the ebb and flow rhythm of the sea. She Sang it slowly, visualizing the outline of the hull, began building from the bottom up.

Time passed and planks curved and snapped together with woody groans, bound by pressure and Power into a watertight whole. She rearranged the great Power stones a trifle, lifting them as if they were marbles, though her dress now gave off the sweet scent of herbs brought by her sweat. She built the hold, storage and cabins, and now the ship was high, throwing shadows from the sun reaching its zenith. Decks came next and she had to use Power to propel her breath, keep her voice even, but Power came as those around her marveled at the ship, Sang louder, wove the melodies for her.

Finally, near noon, Jikata and Luthan flew across a bay to a peninsula and dropped the Distance Magic spell. Immediately, Jikata *heard* a Powerful, fabulous Song as if Sung by several choruses in perfect harmony.

She could only wonder what kind of great spell they were doing, could hardly wait to see, to listen close up. Soon the volarans reached the shore with a large manor house set back from the ocean and a wide beach.

Gathered on the sand was a huge circle of people, all linked and Singing. All wearing bright clothing indicating different groups. There were those with leathers like Luthan's—though not white. Others wore rich robes, some long, or for those actually standing in water, they were belted up above legs, like people Jikata had seen in the towns, urbanites, then, and nobles.

Headbands glinted from several with marks of great Power—Circlets, the Sorcerers and Sorceresses.

Chasonette had been right, this was some historic event, pulling in all portions of Lladranan society. Who else?

Ah, Marshalls. Marshalls came in pairs, and as the volarans began to land, Jikata saw couples in colors—ruby red, sapphire, emerald…each had a sword on one hip and a tube on the other, for their batons. Armor was under the matched tunics.

There were people dressed roughly and wearing some sort of scaly ponchos.

Luthan landed near a couple who wore Friends' robes. So even the Singer was represented here, though Jikata only vaguely recognized them.

Narrowing her eyes, she saw they all surrounded what looked like a bunch of planks set in a regular pattern of a...boat?

Then, as Jikata watched in amazement, the boat came together as if a giant were building it, snapping it together like it was some sort of great model.

She turned her attention to the woman Singing the lead, the focus of them all, a Caucasian brunette Singing her heart out, totally concentrating on the boat. *She* was the one pulling the planks together, Jikata realized with wonder. It was her vision and her skill and her Power that was actually building the Ship, others were supporting her, funneling her Power, but she was the creator.

Raine heard each lilting Exotique voice arrowing to her with Power they'd had on Earth but was magnified a thousand-fold on Lladrana. They joined with her in the giddy delight of *building*, seeing a design of her own form before her eyes. No double-hulled aluminum racing yacht this, but a warship.

The masts rose majestically. Sails, lines, blocks and tackles, threaded themselves, arrayed themselves.

An idea had occurred to her, an extra defense for the ship. Something she hadn't spoken to anyone. Too many things about this invasion were too well-known, too few things were secret.

She was a twenty-first century shipbuilder and twenty-first century woman, so as all the others gasped in awe at a ship like the planet had never known, she used that awe, the surprise, the out-rushing of feeling and Power, every last mote of water and air and earth and fire and spirit to coat the ship, protect it, with a layer that could be activated at the right moment.

Raine Sang on.

33

"Wait here," Luthan said to Jikata and the volarans. Jikata knew none of them would obey. They were all too curious.

Luthan went to stand behind a man slightly shorter than he with striped black-and-white hair. Carefully, Luthan placed his hands on the man's shoulders and Jikata knew at once they were brothers and that Luthan's presence hadn't surprised the man, nor had his becoming a part of the ritual. That was Bastien, then, the husband of Alexa. The woman next to him, the small one with white hair and an attitude, was Alexa herself, not looking much like the holograms Jikata had seen.

Luthan Sang.

Jikata was caught in the moment, in the Song, then realized that the main Singer was flagging. Her voice was clear and true and still had incredible Power in it for the task, but she tired.

The rhythm was of a sea shanty and the main purpose or

element was creation—physical building. Not surprising since the deck of a ship was settling on lower structures inside the boat. Ship.

Jikata shouldn't disrupt this great spell, but she could help. Matching the note, she added her voice.

Luthan's head jerked up and he looked at her, but no one else seemed to notice. She was just part of the chorus, a melding of voice and Power. It had been a long time since she'd been satisfied with that, but she was now. She felt unusually shy. All these people gathered together for one purpose, trusting each other to practice Power together and Sing and make a great thing.

Togetherness and trust.

She hadn't had much of that in her life except the recent days with Chasonette and Luthan and the volarans. If she wanted to do a "poor little me" she could cast a glance back at her life and think that there hadn't been a feeling of real togetherness since she'd lost her parents. Ishi had been an emotionally isolated person. As was the Singer.

Her gaze went to the five Caucasian women, one at each cardinal direction and one in the center of the circle. The Exotiques. All the Power of the others flowed through them. Every single person there—even the Friends—trusted these women implicitly. The personal Songs woven into the pattern also resonated with affection, admiration for them. Personal knowledge of each other was of a depth that Jikata hadn't even had with her own touring crew.

She wanted that, hadn't earned it yet.

But melding her voice and her strength and her range and her Power into the Song was a good start.

She blinked, thinking that the bluish atmosphere surrounding the Ship held a new sheen.

And suddenly she heard more than the soundtrack, the setting around her, the voices. She *heard* the mental contact of the women.

That's enough for today, the voluptuous redhead with a gleaming gold band around her forehead said. Marian, the Circlet. *We would do better to save the masts and rigging and sails for tomorrow.*

The woman in the middle, arms raised, gave a slow shake of her head. *No! Today, now. I feel...* She flung her arms wide and Jikata *heard* her Song take on strength and Power. With surprise, Jikata realized that the woman had connected with Amee and the planet was pouring Power into her. A minuscule amount for Amee, a thread too thin to see, but huge to the woman. Her Song gathered strength, her expression became beatific. A ripple went around the circle of Singers and more Power pumped from them. Jikata strengthened her voice, slowly moved to stand behind Luthan. No one was looking at her. All were focused on the woman at the center who glowed like a goddess.

Her fingers moved gracefully, tiny swoops, and more planks for a top quarterdeck flew into place, snicked together. Jikata saw several layers—coats—of energy slide over the construction, into each fiber of the wood. Huge masts rose, settled with efficient thunks into the boat, rigging threaded like embroidery, sails slowly unfurled.

Jikata yearned to be a part of this, to contribute more. Gently, gently, finger by finger, she set one hand against Luthan. He trembled. The man in front of him arced, but the Power surge was regulated, swept around the circle, by strong minds.

Teamwork.

Many of these, including Luthan's brother, were intricately entwined in a team that had worked, fought together. Life and death. They knew their Songs, their limits, their strengths. Jikata nearly gasped in amazed pleasure at the link, but kept her voice steady, and curved the fingers of her left hand around Luthan's waist, helping modulate the Power herself.

Song was all.

Raine should have been tired and hoarse—she had been. But then she'd been sucked downward deep into the dark heart of the ocean. Darkness! She struggled against it, then discovered it wasn't the darkness of evil, but the blackness of the absence of light. No more evil than the brightest sunburst.

The dark of the true deeps, the bottom of the ocean where water glided over the lowest crust of the planet. She accepted this darkness, this water, this Song. And connected with Amee. She knew it couldn't be anything else, such a surge of Power that washed exhaustion from her, made her stronger.

The other Exotiques had spoken of their connection with Mother Earth, and then their connection with Amee, but Raine had never been certain of that. Now she knew. Mother Earth had a saltiness to her water, a faint metallic harshness from all the years man had used machines. A taste Raine'd grown up with and knew. Now an underlying sweetness, from the planet's nature, she thought, flowed through her.

She smiled, feeling *Powerful,* in every way. And she noticed a couple of new voices added to the mix running through her. Luthan's, just recognizing his individuality now. Another, the…strongest, most flexible. She welcomed them but concentrated on her work. The Deauvilles and other sailors had wanted some carving on the rails, the inside panels of the ship, around the deck and below, so she let them direct her. She worked fast, this energy connection with Amee could burn her out if she let it. So she added pretty carved flourishes.

Her hair went damp as she lifted the figurehead—a statue of a woman whose image had just come to mind.

It was a gigantic ship. It had to be to accommodate the volarans, though they had informed her that since the ship would travel at volaran Distance Magic speed at night, they would rotate off it so they might be free of constraints that hampered wingless humans.

Greater than anyone on Lladrana had ever seen.

Then, as her breath faltered and the sun hit the middle of the sky and beamed bright and shining on the sea, she Sang the last of the ritual, her voice alone, and added the name to the side of her ship, in fancy Lladranan and in English.

The Echo.

All she knew, all she had, she sent into the ship and she let the dimness of exhaustion, sparkling with the fading bits of Power, claim her.

Somehow Jikata was drawn to the center, along with the other four who'd been part of the circle. Their knees gave out at the same time as Raine uncurled her fists and let the Power sustaining them all go. The women tumbled into a heap, Jikata felt soft body parts under her arms, she thought her head was pillowed on Raine's thigh. With her last puff of breath, she said, "This isn't the vision I had of us meeting."

Then, with careful steps, Luthan was towering over them, breathing deeply but raggedly. "Not my vision, either. We met on a road. Alexa accused me of betraying the other Exotiques for not bringing you immediately to them." His voice changed from flat to almost wondering. "I gave that vision a ninety percent chance of happening."

A chuckle came near Jikata's right elbow. She didn't have the strength to look down, but when Luthan's brother strode up, then hauled up the small woman by her waist, Jikata saw silver hair and an upside-down face. Alexa. The Swordmarshall was flipped into her husband's arms and she leaned against him, but grinned at Luthan. "Just goes to show that not all your visions come true. Not even those in the ninety percentile."

Luthan gave her a slightly wobbly bow. "You reassure me."

"It reassures us all," his brother said and kissed his wife.

"Welcome back, Luthan," said another man and Jikata couldn't guess who he was. "This must be the famous Jikata."

She was so limp, she could only snort inwardly.

"Time to clean up this heap," said another man. "Where's my Bri? I can't see Raine, either. Raine, I congratulate you on an excellent piece of work. Everyone is still here admiring it."

Which meant everyone was still here seeing the famous Jikata, the Exotique Singer, in a heap. She was amused at herself for thinking of her image. Just in these few moments she received the impression that the other Exotiques had formidable reputations but not sophisticated ones. Though if this is how they all usually ended up after a great performance—ritual—that was understandable.

There were a couple of gleeful chuckles, a child's piercing shriek that had Jikata flinching. A small foot hit her in the shoulder blade as a little girl scrambled over the pile of them with great cheerfulness and disregard.

"Calli?" said a man in a voice that held the timbre of a good singer. "Sit up, the children are concerned."

Jikata recalled Luthan had told her that Calli, the Volaran Exotique, had adopted children. The little girl thought all this was a fine game, but an older boy radiated desperation.

"Sitting," a woman said in a slurred voice that held a bit of western twang.

Jikata decided she should right herself and her image and rolled to hold out an imperious hand to Luthan. He took it and smoothly pulled her to her feet, kept a hand under her elbow. She was the focus of many gazes, so she stood straighter.

Alexa's green eyes scanned Jikata up and down and she smiled impishly. Still leaning against her husband—more for love than for support, Jikata thought—Alexa held out a hand. "I like your work."

That was said at the same time another hand was offered and another voice said, "I admire your work greatly." The tall, voluptuous redhead, Marian the Circlet Sorceress.

"Thank you," Jikata said in a composed tone that was at odds with her sudden inward nerves. In an impulsive gesture, she took both their hands and a *snap* sizzled through her—them.

Bastien grunted and stepped back, Marian caught Alexa's hand and closed the circuit of energy that whirled through them.

"Let me in there," said a light voice. "And, Marian, I'll remind you that you didn't have any songs by Jikata on your PDA, but I did on my music player. I'm Bri Drystan Masif and you're just as gorgeous in person as you are on stage and in videos." Jikata's hand was detached from Marian's and taken by another, a vivacious brunette with hazel eyes. The circle was connected again, though the energy was dampened.

Marian said, "Bri and Raine have an affinity for the water elements. I'm fire, like you."

"Just as well I come between you, then," Bri said, grinning and squeezing Jikata's hand.

Jikata should have been withdrawing into her public persona, but she wasn't. The sheer connection she had with these women, the bond she seemed to share, was a wonderful feeling she didn't want to give up. It was as if she were meeting sisters she hadn't known before. And, again, that feeling should have dismayed her, would have on Earth, but here on Lladrana it felt right and natural. She returned the squeeze of fingers to Bri, passed it on to Alexa. "Thank you," she said for Bri's compliment.

Then Jikata turned her head and her attention to the performer of the day. "Raine?"

A startlingly handsome man was helping her to her feet, kept a possessive arm around her.

"Fabulous dress," Jikata said, even the Singer had nothing like this one. Especially since Jikata sensed it had been made with affection and love. It must have been a long time since anyone felt affection and love for the Singer. Admiration, devotion, respect...many of the cooler emotions that Jikata had been the recipient of herself, but she wanted more, and here on Lladrana she could get it.

"Thanks," Raine said. She stood a moment where she was, her bare toes digging into the sand. Centering herself? Grounding? There was a distance to her gaze as if she still felt the effects of the ritual. Not surprising.

"And I'm Calli Torcher Gardpont." A blond woman inserted herself firmly between Jikata and Bri. Another new Song that immediately became precious, adding to all the things Jikata had sensed about the volarans, more nuances to Songs of herd and flight.

Marian, the Sorceress, shook her gold-banded head. "Two waters and two fires, with only one earth and air. I don't know how this will work, or why—"

"Raine was needed to build, raise, the Ship," Alexa pointed out. "And there's only one Jikata," Alexa said. "Only one strong four-octave voice."

"The weapon knot demands a four-octave voice," Jikata said, she hoped calmly. She had extrapolated that from the Singer's range and what Luthan had told her. She was sure she could Sing at a great ritual such as the one she'd just witnessed, but untying the weapon knot called "City Destroyer" in the heart of the Dark's Nest—a volcano?—was a whole different matter.

"Ayes." Marian sent her a penetrating glance. "Haven't you read the Lorebooks I sent?"

Jikata returned her stare with a cool one of her own. "I just came off a long tour, have spent weeks with the Singer learning Power, and," she added pointedly, "your Lorebook isn't exactly a tiny volume."

Alexa snorted.

Before Marian could answer, Raine stretched out her hands, curiosity in her eyes.

"Jikata, the new Exotique, the Singer," Raine said softly.

"Ayes." Jikata nodded, then shook Raine's hand in disbelief as she followed the woman's stare to the Ship. "Fabulous job."

Raine glowed.

Jikata took her hand and got another kick…definitely a water element, whirlpools of the deep sea at the bottom of the ocean where there never was any light.

But there *was.* There was fire in the depths if she listened. The heated opening of a vent to the core of the planet.

Raine gasped. "Darkness and light. Cold and heat."

Bri sent a surge of head-clearing energy, healing energy, around their closed circle and Jikata caught another mixture of darkness and light. The darkness of infinite space and the bright pinpoints of stars.

"We're together, finally," Marian said.

"We're where we are fated to be." The words came from Jikata without volition.

It was true. A future of darkness and light awaited them, this time evil and good. Would the Dark swallow them? Or the light bless them?

34

The rest of the day was spent watching teams of Circlets move *The Echo* from its precarious raising point out to the open sea of the bay through Power. Lucienne Deauville also allowed that the Ship needed to "settle into itself."

Alexa had called a conference, limited to the Exotiques and their men, a few minutes before the celebration. It was Jikata's first conference and she sat back and observed.

"How much do you think the Dark knows about the ship?" Raine asked.

Bastien shrugged. "We've spread rumors, the Circlets have set a befuddling spell on the manor and its grounds, kept most of the crucial information to ourselves. Even done some meetings with no-tell spells. Done the best we can to minimize our risk. What gets out, gets out. Anything else?"

Luthan hesitated, then nodded to Chasonette. "The bird has

brought murmurings of some folks banding together to defeat the Exotiques before they lead us to extinction. Several times." He shifted uneasily. With a grimace, he ran his fingers through his hair. "I sense that it's based on the same affliction I have, the repulsion reflex."

"Hate crimes." Alexa's eyes narrowed, her lips thinned. "Nothing I despise more than hate crimes."

In that instant Jikata knew the shadow prophecies that had trailed after Alexa had been true. She would have made an excellent federal judge in the States.

Expressions hardened. Bri's husband, Sevair Masif, the stonemason and Townmaster said, "I've made the rounds of the village, of the fair, every day. I haven't heard anything like that here."

Raine frowned. "There were some sailors who had that reaction to me when I first came, but I don't know that I've seen them again…don't know that I saw them well enough in the first place to recognize them. Also…"

"Also?" Alexa's tone was cross-examination sharp.

"Also there were a couple of Seamasters who Sang in the Apology Ritual, but didn't mean it."

Faucon said, "I'll check that out."

"Good," Bastien said.

Marian sighed. "We can only minimize the risk. But it's still…"

"A big, whomping risk," Alexa said.

Raine fidgeted again. Jikata realized that of all of them, she was the one that fear weighed down the most, the heroine of the day.

It was the strangest launch party Raine had ever attended and was interspersed with talk, talk, talk. None of the Exotiques, particularly Raine, could escape for more than the few minutes it took to go to the bathroom.

Exhilarating to have all this praise heaped on her, the launch party to end all launch parties—though the ship had just been raised, not actually launched.

Raine noticed Jikata got her fair share of attention, but people tended to be more wary around her—a new, unknown Exotique, one who had been trained by the Singer and might even replace the Singer. The vital woman Raine and the others had connected with had disappeared behind a public mask that Raine envied. She wasn't used to being a star.

When all the discussion and celebration was over and silence encompassed the manor, Raine left the house and walked down to the beach.

Song still rolled within her like a low undercurrent, something that might stay with her forever. The Song of the deep oceans of Amee, the streams and flows of the waters, the ever-lasting surf against shore.

Perfect.

And there, anchored out a ways, in just enough water to accommodate her draft, was her ship. *The Echo* sat in the moonlit night as lovely as any dream.

She thought it was more beautiful than any sailing ship built on Earth. Her design, but the sweep of its line had a Lladranan flair.

For now, there was no one on her. Tomorrow sailors would swarm over her, learn her planks and her paces, her sails and her speed. The next day they would start the tests for who'd crew her.

Tonight the ship was Raine's and only Raine's.

She stripped down to the long underwear Lladranans wore,

waded into the chill sea and let the shock of the cold take her first breath, then swam fast and hard to the lowered rope ladder.

It took more exertion than she expected to climb up the story and a half, but she was still cold and shivering when she went through the hatch and slipped onto the main deck. Through chattering teeth, she Sang a spell that dried and warmed her.

For long minutes she stood still and soaked up the sounds of the sea, the quiet creaking of the boat, decks newly formed and smelling fresh, the movement of the rope rigging, the whisper of the sail.

Her toes curled at the gentle rocking under her, the feel of the deck under her. One of the best feelings in the world, standing on your own ship, ready to sail away.

Others had helped, but without her, *The Echo* would not exist. *She'd* done this, designed and built this beautiful ship, the greatest achievement of her life.

Slowly she walked the length of the ship, staring at the wonderful detailed carving of the inside, scrolls and garlands she'd half recalled from ships on Earth and those the sailors and Deauvilles had wanted.

Peeking out from a wooden leaf an eye seemed to wink at her. She went closer.

A gargoyle! And not just any gargoyle. This one was a car-icature of Bastien, a sly smile on his face. The carving was fabulous, with a delicacy that she didn't think the Deauvilles had. Then she knew. Sevair Masif, the Townmaster and Bri's husband. He was a stonemason, but obviously could also work his craft in wood. Blinking to make out details in the shadows and silver of the moonlight, she looked for others, continuing aft past the cabin to the poop deck reserved for the volarans.

And she knew they were all here. Every Chevalier, every Marshall, every volaran, with blank spaces ready to be carved for the sailors.

The Echo was a visual testament to those who sailed her to destroy the Dark.

She gulped down tears, put her clasped hands over her heart and heard the bump, bump, bump. How could she let someone else captain this ship?

Drawing in a clearing breath, she took the ladder up to the volaran's deck, for them to lift off and land. The winged horses had made it clear that they would be rotating who would sail and who would fly. *The Echo* would make faster time except at night.

More decoration here, with Chevalier and Marshall figures.

She wondered if Sevair had carved her, the designer, and where her figure might be, what expression she might have.

"Raine." Another whisper of sound, almost lost in the breeze, a caress wafted to her.

But she knew the soft call, the personal Song of the man splashing quietly below in the water.

She hurried down the ladder to the main deck, to the access portal, and looked down to see Faucon swimming in the water. "Raine."

Water slicked his hair back from his face and once again her heart squeezed as she felt the attraction of him, her lover. More beautiful than the ship.

"May I come aboard?" he asked.

"Ayes."

With widened eyes, she saw him easily swing up the ladder. He was nude.

Not shivering, either, which meant he had some sort of swimming-warming spell that she didn't know about.

The quiet within her now changed to thrumming anticipation.

He was simply gorgeous, in shape and in movement.

When he reached the deck, he looked around with awe.

"There is nothing like your Ship on all of Amee," he said, striding forward to take her hands, then lifted them to his lips and kissed each finger. "You must be so proud of your triumph. *I'm* so proud of you."

When had anyone from her family said that to her? She'd had to see in the mirrors how much they valued her skill.

All her insides wrenched.

And wind that was not of Amee whistled around her, slapped the sails. The air shimmered again, not a natural phenomena, then a hole opened, showing a corridor.

The Dimensional Corridor, the dimensional winds.

The Snap!

Faucon's eyes went bleak, his face expressionless after a flash of agony. He let go of her hands, stepped back, said nothing. Just stared as the winds of the Dimensional Corridor whipped around her.

Her heart broke at the sight of him. As if he'd known all along this Snap was inevitable and that she'd leave, though she hadn't mentioned going since they'd become lovers.

She knew he'd shouted for Elizabeth to stay. He said nothing to Raine, but kept his gaze locked on her, surely that meant something?

He'd never said he'd loved her.

Slowly the winds turned her and the Corridor solidified more around her. She caught a blur of movement from a balcony of the manor house, knew it was Jikata. Did *she* see the Dimensional Corridor? Even as the thought went through Raine's head she *saw* in a different manner.

Home.

The house she'd shared with her father and brothers, had grown up in. Herself there, celebrating Thanksgiving, laughing, surrounded by love. It was noisy and active, as it had always been. Children surrounding her, a couple of them hers. The vision shifted and she saw two buildings, facing each other. One was the old shipyard where they all worked, the newer one was smaller, sleeker, as were the ships docked near it. The sign read Raine Lindley Racing Yachts. A glimpse inside the door showed photos of grinning men and women holding trophies. One of the guys was blond and handsome with a charming smile and bright blue eyes and her heart squeezed, knowing that he'd be her husband, her love on Earth.

She had what she had wanted there, she knew. A prestigious reputation for building the fastest, the most modern ships, a good life with a husband and children to come. A wonderful, fulfilling, easy life.

She looked back at the man who loved her now. His shoulders were stiff, his biceps bunched, his hands fisted.

His gaze burned with intensity and she knew that no man would ever love her the way this man did, no man would ever love her more. She wouldn't love that guy on Earth as deeply as she could love Faucon.

If they lived.

She'd already suffered for Lladrana, for Amee, already paid for whatever they'd given her with tears and blood and sweat and fear. The ship below her…she couldn't feel the ship, the lovely rocking on the Lladranan seas so different from Earth.

Glancing down, she saw the gleaming deck, but she wasn't truly in Lladrana anymore, she was hovering here until she chose.

She could ask Faucon if he loved her. She opened her mouth. That wasn't fair, to make him prove his love and return.

Her decision. The man, this man who would not draw back from the last battle against the Dark. He could die soon, so could she if she stayed. She *knew* that as well as she knew she'd be the preeminent yacht designer on Earth if she left Lladrana.

What was love in this moment worth?

She hovered. *Heard* the strong Song of him, of her own, of the oceans of Lladrana, of Amee.

More than simply love, the richness of this life, the intensity of this life was such that she didn't want to forsake it. With focused vision, she now saw the carving of herself set in the prow. No caricature at all, but a sculpture of her, eyes distant but haunted, a model of the ship in her hands. Surely if she returned to Earth, some small droplet of her blood would yearn for Lladrana the rest of her life. Her long, lovely life.

She returned her gaze to Faucon. His eyes were wet. Still he said nothing. Offered nothing, but his Song was ragged with an agony that tore at her.

"I'm staying!" she yelled, and her world went dark an instant, the vision of her loving family disappeared, the familiar scent of home and ocean that she hadn't even known she was smelling, vanished. A last beat of charging rock and roll she hadn't known was running through her head stopped.

She dropped and clunked on the deck.

Faucon's eyes went wide. He shuddered and gasped, then he grabbed her. Held her tight. "I love you."

"I love you," she said.

They lowered to the deck under the throb of their emotions, her clothes stripped away. His body was slick under her hands...sea spray and sweat. Then his mouth covered hers and all his urgent movements swept her away, too. Her clothes disappeared. She needed the scent of him, the feel of him on her, in her. Needed his hard hands stroking her breasts and between her legs. Needed the throbbing words of love, his breath in her mouth that they'd share.

Needed life.

She loved him, but was terrified of the future.

She didn't want to die.

Worse, she didn't want to see him die. She clutched him as their loving turned fierce. "I love you."

Jikata found rough, cold brick against her back and realized she'd retreated from the rail of the balcony to the wall of the house. She breathed shallowly and wiped a hand across her eyes.

So that was the Snap. She had no doubt what she'd seen. Everyone had been discussing Raine's Snap out of the woman's hearing, speculating whether she would return home to Earth or stay here in Lladrana. Jikata hadn't heard it all, but something had gone wrong with Raine's Summoning. The odds had been seventy percent that she'd leave.

Alexa and Bastien and Bri had all wagered she'd stay. They'd been right.

Jikata *shouldn't* have been able to see it, not Raine on the Ship at this distance. But she had. Closely, brightly, too, as if it had been day instead of a moonlit night. Tendrils of damp iridescent mist, reflecting all colors, had gathered around Raine. Different than the mist before Jikata's eyes that signaled a coming vision. But something that Jikata half recognized, something that had her shivering in the summer night. Dimensional Corridor misty winds.

Jikata had seen what Raine had—a family dinner, a successful business, a loving husband and children, a long and fruitful life. Jikata still didn't know why Raine hadn't returned. Because Raine, like Jikata, had seen the blank emptiness ahead of her here on Lladrana. Hadn't she?

Yet she'd stayed anyway.

A quiet almost-sound, a sigh, alerted Jikata to the presence of someone in the darkened room behind her. She jolted, but stopped herself from whirling, knowing it was Luthan.

And how much had *he* seen?

With a firm step she walked back into the room, saw his shadowy form silhouetted black.

"Raine's Snap has come and she has stayed," Luthan said.

"Yes," Jikata said, deliberately using English.

His chest emptied of another sigh and he shook his head. "Amazing what people will do with just a little hope…and love."

The air thickened around them and Jikata was aware of an ache she had to hold him, be held by him.

"My Snap won't come until after the battle with the Dark," she said matter-of-factly, but the truth of it began to nibble at her self-control. She'd have to fight and survive before she could leave.

"All of the Exotiques fought and faced death before their Snaps came." He answered her thought, not her words, strode across the room and took her in his arms.

She looked up at him. "Not Raine—"

"Not recently, but she was abused, and the English word is 'stalked' before we found her."

"Found her?"

"You'll hear the whole story sometime." He bent and brushed her lips, she opened her mouth for him.

He tasted anxious, matching his Song. He hadn't liked whatever he'd seen during Raine's Snap.

Then came a shout, running footsteps, banging doors, a wordless yell.

The moment broke and Jikata breathed easier, there was reality to deal with.

Luthan snorted, his teeth showed white in a grin. "Alexa rarely bothers to be quiet and discreet." He gave her a last tight hug, then indicated the balcony and they went out on it, holding hands. Just in time to see Alexa sprinting across the sand, yelling. "The Snap, the Snap came for Raine!"

Bastien sauntered behind her, bare-chested and with the drawstring of his casual pants untied.

Alexa dove into the water and thrashed to the Ship.

Faucon withdrew from Raine, rolled them over and cleaned them up with a quick songspell. He was panting. Even after the explosive release of sex, his nerves seemed wire-tight. His face was wet and though he'd like to think it was sweat and sea spray, he knew there were tears, too.

His woman had stayed.

Had stayed *for him*.

He hadn't pleaded with her as he had Elizabeth, hadn't even believed in his heart of hearts that she would ever stay after what she'd already experienced. Hadn't told her he loved her.

Yet she'd stayed.

A frisson of fear drained away the heat of loving. She'd stayed. That meant she might Sing the terrible spell to destroy the Dark. How could he keep her safe?

He hadn't thought he'd keep himself safe. Hadn't thought he'd have much to live for except to destroy the Dark with his last breath.

Everything had changed.

She had changed their futures, and he didn't know how much of a future they had.

Thumps and curses came as Alexa climbed up the rope ladder. Her shouts had warned him that there would be no resting and gazing at the stars with Raine, any tender words after loving.

He wasn't overly modest, but wished for pants.

Alexa plunged through the access hole and halfway across the width of the deck.

"Raine!"

Raine sat up beside him. He put a hand on her thigh to keep contact, though the way their Songs had fused together in incandescent heat, he didn't think they'd be totally separate ever again. More fear would come, more dread. He shut it away.

"Geez, Alexa, why don't you wake the entire country." Raine sounded aggrieved, pushed her fingers through her hair as if to straighten tangles. That didn't work.

"Raine!" A happy cry, now. "You *stayed.*"

"Yeah, and I'm rethinking that decision right now. Umph!"

Alexa knocked her over.

The women flopped around together a little, hugging and separating, and Faucon was glad that his spell had included a perfume that dispersed the scent of sex. Not that he would have minded, but Raine would have.

"That's a nice sight," Bastien said, coming so quietly onto the Ship that he startled Faucon.

"Ayes," Faucon said.

The women were upright and hugging and crying, talking in fractured English. Faucon wiped his arm across his face.

Bastien crouched down beside Faucon. "Might not want to do a bloodbond with her."

"No!" It was nearly too loud, and he hadn't thought it completely through, but Bastien was right. Such bloodbound couples would die together. Much as it would have hurt for Raine to return to Earth, at least then she would have lived.

Bastien said wistfully, "You want to keep her safe."

"Ayes. And you want to do the same with Alyeka."

"No way to do that." A sad half smile. "Can't keep her out of this fight. We'll survive or go down together taking the Dark with us, Song willing."

"Maybe—"

But Alexa had jumped to her feet and grabbed Bastien's hands, pulling him to his feet so she could throw herself into his arms. "Raine has stayed after the Snap!" She tugged him to dance around with her. "You know how much zhiv we've made?"

Raine slanted Faucon a wary look that he read. He lifted his hands. "I didn't bet."

Then Sinafinal and Tuckerinal and Enerin were there, three peacocks. Enerin was obviously following her mother's example of disregarding sex for beauty. Sinafinal spread her fan, walked toward Raine, ducked her head and spoke.

35

Thank you for staying, Exotique Seamistress. The Ship needs such a fine Captain, Sinafinal said.

Raine appeared a little startled. "I've already had a good idea for the Captain—"

Jean will step aside, as he should. You have increased our chances greatly against the Dark.

"Thank you," Raine said.

She loves us! Enerin trilled.

Faucon rose, stepped over to Raine and picked her up, then whistled for his volaran. "We won't talk of battles tonight." Not anymore. "We have something wonderful to celebrate, another Exotique has decided Lladrana is her home!"

Cheers came from Bastien and Alexa, some volarans who'd landed near them, and shouts from the shore and house.

Raine smiled, and it seemed that some of the shadows that

had dimmed the brightness of her eyes had vanished. She put her arms around his neck and triumph surged through him. Nothing he'd done in all of his life, no joy he'd felt before, equaled what flowed through him now.

He set her bareback on his volaran, and swung up behind her and they rose to more cheers.

People dotted the beach, and all the lights in the house were on.

The flight was short, but reminded him all the same of the first night he'd met her. A dazzling light burst in his head and heart as he finally allowed himself to love her without believing she would leave him.

She was supple and wonderful in his arms, and though danger and death loomed, before they reached that last instant, he would cherish her in every moment.

They stopped at the stables where Faucon could snatch some old trousers for himself and a long tunic for her. His volaran pranced out to discuss the events with the rest of the herd. The status of his winged steed had just increased because Faucon was the mate of a *permanent* Exotique. Blossom, Raine's volaran, was also trotting around, head high.

He gathered Raine up, feeling more and more like she was a prize, and took her to his bed. There he loved her again, gently, tenderly, and she fell asleep in his arms.

His selfish wish had come true and now he was torn, rejoicing and regretting. She was here, she loved him enough to stay with him despite all that had happened to her. That was the greatest gift he'd ever had in his life. She loved him enough to Captain the Ship through the dangerous waters to the Dark's Nest.

He hoped she loved him enough to stay behind, safe on the Ship, when he went into battle. But he thought she had a different definition of their love—love mixed with responsibility and duty. Other, sisterly love—that would have her going to battle with him. Going further to unite with the other Exotiques and Sing the City Destroyer spell.

The spell that would destroy the Dark and might destroy them all.

He regretted that she stayed, knew the fear gnawing at him now was part of the price he'd paid for this great love.

Still he wrapped his arms around her, brought her close to smell her scent, rub his face in her silky brown hair, listen to their Songs as they wove melodically together. He was blessed and would always be blessed if she was in his life.

Quashing his fear into a tiny wad, he put it in a locked chest deep inside him where it would not cause panic and shame him. Better he keep this to himself as all the other men were doing. Though the pairbonded ones knew they would die with their women: Bastien and Alexa, Jaquar and Marian, Marrec and Calli, Sevair and Bri.

Others in the force: Mace and Clua, the newest male Marshall pair…*all* the Marshalls and most of the Chevaliers. When one fell, both would die, the bond and fate ensured that.

He would not pairbond with Raine. He wanted her to live if he died…though he did not think he would live long if she perished and he survived.

A small mutter of protest came from her and she sounded as if she was rising from the sleep she needed. He'd let that fear out already, so he punched it back again, snapped chains around that inner chest. Held her close and murmured words—a mixture of Lladranan and English. He chuckled deep in his throat as he thought that now he'd linked with two Exotiques, and Raine was not from that same place as the others, he might very well know the language better than any of the other Exotiques' men.

For a moment he thought of Elizabeth, let the experience sift through him, part of his life, part of how he'd treated—and would treat—this new woman he cherished more.

Elizabeth had been a sweet rippling stream in his life, but never quite his as he'd wanted, and he accepted that was a good thing.

For he and Raine fit so much better together. Raine was an ocean swell of love that surprised him, inundated him, took him under. Kept him forever.

He let Elizabeth go, the last splinter of hurt vanished.

He could love Raine so much more because he'd had time with Elizabeth, and Elizabeth had been—was—a good and true woman. But she'd never been meant for him. He'd tried to force fate and had stumbled and fallen.

As he let sleep creep up on him, and listened to Raine and breathed her, he only hoped his true destiny had a better ending.

Pounding came at their door, rousing Raine. No gorgeous gamalon scale of strings attached to the lovely harp on Faucon's door, but small-fisted banging.

"Come *on*, Raine!" Alexa yelled in accented English. A shiver went down Raine's spine as she realized that she'd decided to stay. She, too, would begin to speak English with a Lladranan accent, God willing.

Song willing.

Struggling from the grip of man and covers—and wasn't that

wonderful, a man who'd held onto her all night long, when they weren't making love—Raine stumbled from bed. She grabbed a coverlet and wrapped it around her and went into the sitting room to crack open the door. "We're not up yet. Go away."

Alexa scowled, shifted from foot to foot. "Why aren't you up?"

"So, like, you sprang right into action after your task was done and your Snap, right? Well, I want to bathe and eat."

"But we want to go to the Ship! Nobody will until you do, Madam Lucienne Deauville says. I want to see my quarters. I thought we could hold another battle planning conference there. Get our sea legs."

Raine stared at Alexa. "No one is going to get their sea legs on a ship floating in a calm bay."

Alexa lifted wide eyes, smiled a winsome smile. "It's a start."

"Go. Away. I'll be down in about an hour."

"Make that two," Faucon said in a morning-rough voice from behind her. "It's still very early, hardly dawn."

Alexa huffed a breath.

"Don't make me call Bastien," Raine threatened.

Eyes narrowing, Alexa said, "You think that man can control me?"

"Ayes," Raine replied and heard the word from Faucon at the same time.

Bastien's bulk showed behind his wife. "Come on, Alexa, a gift for you arrived from the Castle."

"What? A present? For *me*?"

"And you might want to bother, I mean *talk* to Jikata," Raine said. "You probably didn't get your fill yesterday."

"True, very true," Alexa said. "Later. A gift. From whom?" She began to badger Bastien.

Faucon chuckled and Raine turned to him, feeling a little embarrassed. She'd thrown a different life away for this man and he knew it. As grand gestures went that was pretty damn big.

"I am so lucky," he said.

She relaxed, then lifted her brows at him. "And are you going to learn to control and manipulate me like Bastien does Alexa?"

Grinning, Faucon said, "We'll manipulate each other. And Alyeka—Alexa—likes it. But if everyone is waiting for you—which is only right—perhaps we should rise a little earlier."

"You just want to know what Alexa's present is."

He tilted his head. "I already know, her new mount is ready, the young volaran that will come on the trip. Arrow for the Dark."

"Oh." So many volaran names indicating their destiny.

At that moment sunlight slid through the windows. Raine smiled. "Another pretty day."

"With a pretty sight to come, your Ship."

He *was* proud of her, and she was proud of her achievement. And now that she was staying, she would call it "the Ship" like everyone else. There was only one. "My Ship!" She tasted the word, then hurried over to the windows.

"We're facing east, inland," Faucon said. "The sea's to the west," he teased.

She rolled her eyes, muttered, "I knew that, but I'm used to an ocean on the east." Heading for the shower, she said, "I *do* want to take a good tour." She flashed her lover, her man, a smile. "See if all the details are right."

She led several admiring tours until the Ship felt familiar under her feet. Groups of volarans streamed to alight on the quarterdeck, sniff around it, march along the regular deck, then return to their Landing Field and stables.

The Chevaliers and Marshalls grinned, even when they saw the hammocks strung with little room between them where they'd sleep. At noon Alexa dismissed the last lingering Chevaliers, welcomed Corbeau and his family, who brought lunch. Along with them came all the Exotiques and their men, including Koz, Marian's brother. They adjourned to the main cabin belowdecks that Raine called a lounge and Alexa a war room.

Raine and her charts of the course were up first, pointing the way with her forefinger, talking about tides and shoals and wind patterns. All the information was in her mind, easy to recall, and she knew fatalistically that her father had been right. She would have to Captain this Ship of her own.

Then they rolled up the other maps and brought out the one of the island. It was mostly volcano, no good harbors, no cove that would accommodate the draft of the Ship.

"So the plan is that we go in at dawn. They shouldn't be able to see the Ship, Raine and Marian and Jikata will be cloaking it." Alexa hesitated a little on Jikata's name. They didn't know her very well yet, only that she was key.

They all looked at Jikata, she merely nodded. "If there's such a songspell, I can do it." Then she looked around pointedly. "As for the City Destroyer weapon knot, Marian showed me the spell yesterday evening and I can handle that, too, the lead and the ritual and the Power. *But* we *must* practice as a group. I understand that you have been practicing together, which is all to the good, and the Singer brought in people whose voices approximated yours, so I have had some practice that way. *But we must practice together.* Is that clear?"

"Clear," Marian said.

Jikata looked at Alexa. She gave a little cough. "Clear."

The rest of them spoke together. "Clear."

Nodding decisively, Jikata said, "Good."

After one more cough, Alexa said, "Now the actual battle plans." She shifted a map with geographical gradations away to reveal a map of the island easier to read. "I anticipate that the minute we drop the cloaking spell, or invade, the Master will order out the horrors. Hordes of horrors."

Raine felt sick but nodded.

"The sailors who wish to fight will land with the first wave of Chevaliers. The goal of those fighting outside the volcano will be to distract the monsters and the Master from us Exotiques who are going in."

"In a volcano?" asked Jikata. She moved closer to the map.

Alexa said, "It's mostly inactive."

"Huge mountain," Jikata murmured.

"You're so right," Alexa said. "Here's a ledge where all of our volarans can land. We'll take the gong which will also distract the Dark, and maybe the Master, because the Dark wants it, and wants it intact. It's dangerous and should be destroyed. The feycoocus will hide it." Alexa gestured and Marian rolled out another map that showed a cutaway of the mountain.

"We've been working on this map for weeks and we owe the intelligence to Sevair, Bri's husband, who attached a spy-eye to the Master. Since he doesn't bathe, we're still receiving information. Circlets monitor the eye twenty-four seven and we may even get information during the battle."

"Priceless," Bastien said. He was leaning against the door, arms crossed.

"So, we land here, and send our volarans back to the Ship."

No one wanted to doom the volarans, and the knot's magical shield could accommodate a limited mass.

"Then we take the gong—" Alexa trailed her finger down and across the mountain "—to an inactive lava tube here. The Master rarely uses these tubes, so he won't think of them as access points first."

"Take the gong," murmured Jikata. "I don't hike."

"*Ride* the gong," Alexa said. "There's probably snow, and if not, we have, uh—" she waved "—anti-grav."

Raine's mouth dropped open. Her mind boggled, trying to imagine what Alexa was saying, then she decided she didn't want to.

"It will work!" Alexa assured.

"Yeah," Bri said, grinned at Alexa, who beamed back.

Raine and Jikata looked at Calli. She shrugged with an amused smile. They turned to Marian, who sighed. "Crazy as it sounds, it *will* work."

"Anyway," Alexa said briskly, "we ride the gong down the mountain to the tube. Then we go down the tube to this cavern."

It was a huge space in the middle of the mountain.

Jikata frowned, tapped a well-kept nail on figures. "Are these the dimensions?"

"Ayes," Alexa said. "Plenty of room to do a ritual."

But Jikata was shaking her head, pointing down to another tube angling deeper into the mountain, threading her finger down it to a smaller dome-shaped cavern. "And these are the dimensions for this chamber?"

"Ayes," Marian said.

"Do we have any information on this room?"

Marian shivered. "Not much. I think I was stashed there for a while. The old Master called it the larder."

"Is there food in there?" Jikata asked.

"One moment," Jaquar said as he leafed through papers. There was quiet until he looked up. "No, the old Master kept prey for the monsters there, but nothing's there at last report."

"The acoustics will be better in this chamber," Jikata said.

"But—" Alexa started.

Jikata raised her head and there was something in her manner that had them all stilling. "There is a chamber of these exact dimensions in the Caverns of Prophecy, where I spent a great deal of time. If I were to speculate," she said slowly, "I would say that Amee has ensured the chambers were identical."

Alexa's eyebrows rose. She rubbed her hands. "Guess we get a little more of the gong thrill ride."

"Oh, joy," Marian said.

"Then the feycoocus take the gong to where it can be destroyed. Jikata takes the stage and we're her girl backup group. There's a time during the ritual for a warning. That's when we mentally notify the guys outside to break off fighting and retreat to the Ship, which has been hiding in a cove. Then we Destroy the Dark."

Raine was sure it wouldn't happen like that.

"We're going, too," Bastien and Luthan said in unison.

Alexa whirled to look at her husband. "Ttho."

36

Jikata stared at Luthan, the shell of her hard-held control nearly crumbling, as she tried to grasp the plan. She'd studied the Weapon Knot City Destroyer ritual, and had coolly determined that was possible. But this mountain-gong idea was absurd.

Luthan met her eyes and she saw his determination. That quality was matched by everyone else. She'd never met such a group of determined people. A people at war.

Bastien strode forward, set his large hands on Alexa's small shoulders, a fierce smile on his face. "You think I want you to die inside the mountain away from me when I die outside? Or vice versa? We're bonded with the coeur-de-chain, we die at the same moment, so let us die together."

Bri linked hands with her husband, Sevair, looked at him. "The gong will only hold us."

The craftsman was the right one to ask. A smile hovered on his lips. One of satisfaction. "I've made a sled."

The women switched their gazes to him. Jikata's heartbeat spiked as she looked at Luthan. He wouldn't be outside, fighting the monsters and evading them the way he'd done all his life. He'd be inside with them.

"A sled," Bri repeated.

"Ayes. Wooden, waxed runners." His smile curved deeper. "Marrec lived in the north, he knew of sleds."

Koz cleared his throat, and Sevair glanced at him. "Koz lived in Colorado like you. He will steer it."

"Koz's body has no muscle memory of sleds. Even as a boy, he didn't sled much," Marian, his sister, snapped.

Tapping his temple, Koz said, "My mind recalls, we've all studied the physics of it, and I've been practicing. We'll be a seven-man bobsled team."

Marian gathered the glances of the women. "All those who have sledded before the last couple of weeks raise their hands."

Jikata joined the rest of the women shooting their hands up, a brief memory of laughing and tumbling off a toboggan with her mother and father during a winter holiday coming back to her.

Koz lifted his hand, Marrec's stalled halfway up. Not much skill among the men.

Koz leaned back in his chair. "Good thing you're all experienced. A saucer is harder to steer than a sled."

Marian snarled. Jaquar took her hand and lifted it to his lips, they locked gazes. "We, too, are bound together, will die at the same moment. If I must breathe my last, I want to be looking at you when I do."

Jikata met Raine's eyes. They shared a look. Neither of them wanted their men to perish if they did, and Jikata was certain the men felt the same way.

Real discussion stopped at that point and the maps were put away and food brought out. Jikata didn't eat much and Raine picked at her food.

As Jikata ate, she sensed tension winding Luthan tighter and tighter. Or perhaps he was reacting to her. All the awful visions that she'd put out of her mind, or those she'd only recalled fragments of, swarmed into her head—the battle, people and volarans dying outside.

The women and their men dying inside, or in a terrible explosion.

That feeling that she'd live to be the Singer surrounded with these women as her friends seemed a vague wisp of past hope, impossible.

Luthan rose from the table first and excused himself and her, held out his hand.

A tiny muscle flicked at his temple. He, too, must be remembering all his visions. The different fates of these vibrant people. She couldn't leave the room quickly enough.

Hope and Lightning were on the quarterdeck, and Jikata and Luthan mounted in silence, flew to a stretch of empty beach a mile from the manor, then the volarans returned to their herd.

Luthan turned his back on the Ship in the distance and walked south, leaving hard dents of footprints in the sand. "Sometimes I don't think I can bear it," he said in a nearly conversational voice. His mouth twisted. "Everyone knows I have flashes of the future. I've kept a cool manner so people won't ask. I've spoken about the battle results once, to Bastien."

She'd caught up with him, matched his stride with long lopes. Reaching out, she caught his hand and he came to a halt.

Pivoting, he faced her, took her hands. A pulsing conflagration of Song whipped through her, through them, like wildfire.

Not a physical need, but emotional and spiritual. He needed her, hated his visions, had been punished for them as a child, felt apart from everyone because of his "gift." The only one who'd accepted him unconditionally was his brother Bastien— a man with striped hair called a black-and-white, with wild Power that usually caused madness. Luthan had bitterly decided his whole family had been mad.

All this flared through her and she dropped his hands to take him in her arms, comforting him as he'd done her the night before. "Sshhh," she crooned, holding him, not knowing when the last time it was that she had offered simple comfort, that anyone had asked it from her.

He drew in a steady breath and calmed, but she sensed emotions were still dammed within him and wondered if she could break that dam, whether she should.

"The Exotique Singer," he said in a low voice. "So serene, are you so confident of your place in the world?"

"On Earth, certainly," she said. For now, the next few years. Then she'd have to continually fight to stay on top. "You, too, are serene and confident of your place."

"I know who I am. My wealth, title, nobility," he bit out. "As a man, I'm loved by my brother—" he hesitated "—his wife, and the other Exotiques have affection for me."

"Great affection, love. I felt that. Great respect."

He shrugged. "It almost makes up for the fact that my father never cared and my mother prefers to live with her sister instead of her sons."

"Her sons are warriors."

Now he snorted. "And she prefers to pretend there is no Dark threatening Lladrana. Because being the best, most famous warrior was my father's driving obsession."

Jikata received a montage of moments with his mother, enough to say, "Her sons weren't normal, weren't allowed to be by their father, and she didn't understand that. But she loves you as much as she can," she said with solid certainty.

"You think?" His gaze searched hers.

"I know," she said.

"Perhaps when this is all over, I'll go visit her again, take Bastien." His eyes widened and he looked away.

"What?"

He tried to step away from her hold. She hung on. He subsided.

"I never got used to my gift. Never wanted to when it mostly showed events I didn't want to know of in advance." He smoothed her hair. "You should return to the Abbey."

The words echoed in her head and sparked the memory that Ishi had said the same thing to her last night in a dream, a continuing refrain of her great-grandmother's. "What have you seen concerning me?"

He stared over her head. "You don't want to know."

Didn't she? Or did she? She'd lived with *her* gift all of her life, though had allowed it to be dulled by hectic years.

She swallowed. "Tell me."

Taking two steps away from her he stared at her with eyes that had gone the color of bitter chocolate, his jaw flexed. "I give you a survival rate of approximately sixty-five percent."

Jikata caught her breath, surprised. "So low?" she rasped.

The twitch of his mouth was bleak. "Much better than most of the other Exotiques."

Her pulse pounded in her temples. She shouldn't ask. Back off now. A strangled, "Most?" fell from her lips and as if the word was a trigger, the air shimmered in front of her and the sunny beach vanished:

Instead she saw a horrible scene in black and grays and too much blood-red. She stood at the foot of a broken, black mountain. The Dark's Nest volcano. Hardly more than a crater. The day was gray with clouds and smoke and ash. Red with ember and blood.

Before she could shift her glance aside, she saw fragments of an entwined Alexa and Bastien.

Jikata gasped. Shuddered.

Luthan's hands clamped hard on hers, she felt every callous. The flashing energy of like minds chained them together. She turned away from the carnage of broken bodies, volaran as well as humans. The mass was too many for her to count. Sickening.

Other mounds showed pieces of horrors. There were more of them, but that was no comfort.

Her gaze fell on a woman in a green sorceress dress. Since her hair had leached from vibrant red to mostly silver, it took several seconds for Jikata to recognize Marian. Her left hand was mangled. Blood was a ribbon from her forehead to the sterile ground. Then her eyelids fluttered and opened.

A sob snagged Jikata's attention and again she turned, weightless, to see Calli wrapped in a stern Marrec's arms. His hair, too, was silver. Their volarans were crumpled and dead at their feet, in a pile with other singed horse flesh surrounding the couple.

What do you see? Luthan's voice prodded in the here and now, pulling at her. Gratefully she let herself be swept back. Blinking damp lashes, Jikata drew in a shaky breath, focused on Luthan's serious face. She'd never been so glad to see anyone in all her life. She grabbed his biceps to steady herself.

Her insides were trembling.

Shit, her whole body was trembling.

"We'll get you back to the manor."

"Ttho." She wouldn't let what she'd seen shake her so. Better get used to it, more visions would come. She would have to handle them. Better start now.

"What did you see?" Luthan squeezed her fingers, eyes resigned. "I don't want to let go of you." His words hung in the silence and she heard more, she heard his Song spiraling to intertwine with her own.

She'd think about that later. "Let's walk." She wanted the warm sun, the pretty beach.

Nodding, Luthan let go of her hands and she felt colder.

She took a wobbly first step, straightened her spine. She could and would handle these visions.

A breeze whipped around them, bringing the scent of brine, the taste of salt, sand sifted into her shoes. That was fine. It told her she was alive.

Safe here on the beach, walking to the manor. For the moment.

Luthan watched her, brooding. She sensed he was calculating what to say. She kept placing one foot in front of the other, calling on tai chi, thinking of her balance, inner and outer.

"What did you see, and who?" His tone was abrupt.

She hadn't seen what had happened to Bri, or Raine, their men or Koz. She hadn't seen Luthan's fate. If she probed the feeling of the vision she might know. She breathed in the air instead, concentrated on putting a glide in her step.

"Shall I tell you of my visions?" he asked evenly. "They happen too frequently, one every couple of weeks, and are ever changing, have plagued me for months." She stopped, turned so the sun warmed her back, so she could see the beautiful green land above the dunes.

Luthan's lips curled. "The only constant in them is…" He lowered his voice so even the wind couldn't catch it. "Calli and Marrec live. One hundred percent of the time. That is a given and true."

Jikata jerked a nod. "Yes, they were alive, thank God."

"Thank the Song," Luthan agreed. "Thirty percent of the time I see my brother alive—"

Which meant Alexa was alive since they were bondmates. Jikata blinked hard, tears stinging the back of her eyes. She'd grown so close to these women already…as if she'd always known them, their Songs, in the back of her mind, always expected them to show up in her life.

She held up her hand. "That's enough."

Luthan stared at her and for a moment there was a disconnect, and he appeared strange and alien. She shook her head to jar memories of their loving back into it, and everything settled into place.

"What did *you* see?" he asked.

"You *do* want to know."

He inclined his head.

"Why?"

His jaw clenched, he looked away. "I like to be prepared."

"If the visions haven't prepared you by now—"

"Your Power is stronger than mine, your visions may be truer."

"I hope not. Remember the ninety percent error of meeting with the Exotiques."

"I bless that fact. Was the mountain whole?" he asked.

"Almost a crater."

He looked surprised. "Good." His shoulders settled a little lower, giving up tension. "Who—"

"I didn't see all the Exotiques. Calli and Marrec lived, I think maybe Marian." The words bulleted from her, and she forgot gliding and began to stride. Luthan kept pace, silently.

"Was there a ship?" he asked.

"I didn't see the ocean." But it lay before her now, beautiful and endless and fathomless. A green matching Raine's eyes. The Ship was majestic, riding on it, appearing invincible.

"Did you see yourself? Or me?"

"No." Glad of it. "Leave it be. That's enough."

He lifted an eyebrow. "You think you'll be able to order this vision?"

She stopped and angled toward him. "Of course not. But I think that they are best taken in small doses." She gave him a hard look. "The others are not despairing, are hopeful." She managed a smile. "My volaran is named Hope, and Amee has spoken with me. The future may be wonderful. I *will not* despair."

Lifting her chin, she said, "I will follow my destiny, fulfill my task, and do what I must, which is lead the others in the City Destroyer ritual. I will *not* let them down."

The chances of all living were low, she knew that now, but some would survive. Even Calli wouldn't live if Jikata didn't Sing her part.

Luthan sighed. "I've been keeping a running percentage for everyone."

She looked at him. "Sixty-five percent?"

"Ayes. I can't…haven't been able to see myself."

"I'll let you know." The rotting smell of dying seaweed rose around them, turning the air bitter.

"Please do," he said politely.

Her stride turned into a march. Sixty-five percent. The

words drummed in her head, in a throbbing beat that matched her heart. She hadn't been working hard enough. That must change.

She must also work the others hard.

Because they *would* win, and more would live. She was determined.

In her mind, tendrils of a song unfurled like a banner, like the sails of the Ship ahead. A battle Song. It would need marching steps, and volaran wing beats, and a roc's cry….

She flung back her head and let her emotions pour out in Song. Turned to her lover for support and to give support.

The Song battered Luthan's ears, screeched, whipping away all the music of his life.

Alien.

It was alien and mutant.

The woman turned to him, screeching those hideous notes, smiling a hideous smile. She held out hands to him that speared him with noise.

She was mutant and alien.

He flinched and stepped away, shuddered.

37

Vaguely he knew what was happening. The innate repulsion reflex. Something he hadn't experienced with Jikata. It was as if her Song, *her* innate music, and speaking of their shared gifts, had finally yanked away the veil that had always been between them.

She was not Lladranan. Not of Amee. Too different.

The sound of her was driving him mad. She wasn't screeching anymore, but her personal Song was nothing but clashing chords grating on his ears and nerves. He slapped his hands over his ears, gritted his teeth, let the sting of painful tears coat his vision.

Her face changed into a grotesque frown and she stepped toward him, still holding out fingers pummeling him with noise drowning out the universe.

He could not touch her. Could. Not.

Her mind showed unnatural images of huge metallic shapes that hurt his head. Tall buildings that should not be. Sticks of trees surrounded by black tarry substances. Cities with no green.

There was the frenzied roar of thousands of voices, the woman standing in a harsh pulsing red ray of light with shoulders, arms and legs bare, wearing a tiny black dress.

He hurt. Why did she punish him this way? She was coming closer, closer, and he couldn't bear it. Not Lladranan. Not Amian. Alien. Alien sound, images, visions.

One blow would knock her back, keep her away from him, silence the unholy noise.

Ttho! The word pounded into his brain like a spike, giving surcease for a split second, enough time for him to remember that he must endure. Must not act. This was *his* problem, not hers. Nothing of his reaction had to do with her.

He only needed to wait these horrible minutes out. Then all would return to normal.

There was nothing normal about his life. Never had been.

"Luthan?" Her voice cackled his name, he couldn't bear the sound of it on her lips. He fisted his hands, stepped back instead of stepping forward to kill the alien who tormented him so, shrieking in his brain, rasping his nerves.

"Go," he managed to say as gutturally as she. "Run. Fast."

"What?" A scream now, scraping him raw.

"*Go!*" Even as he said it, something wrenched inside him, as if tearing. He cried out, thought he heard a shriller echo of his scream.

Then volarans were there with sweet scent and beauty beyond compare and Songs to soothe him and block out her cacophony. Lightning, beloved Lightning, pushed between them, shielded Luthan from her. He wrapped his arms around Lightning's neck, buried his face in his mane.

His ears popped, his eyes leaked tears, and suddenly there was the sound of surf. Lladranan sounds enveloped him, Songs wrapped around him.

The world steadied. Luthan breathed in volaran and Song and air and sunlight and a lovely day on the beach.

And the wonderful scent of his lover.

He lifted his head to look at her, but she had a hand pressed over her heart, was panting and backing away from him. Her face a mask he'd seen her wear too often, eyes dark with pain.

He found his voice again, rough, but his. "Jikata." He lilted it with the pleasure of a man on seeing his woman.

It wasn't enough, he saw that, heard it in their Songs, which were out of tune, the bond between them torn.

She shook her head, mounted Hope and they flew away.

Probably best. He was still coated with the cold sweat of the experience, his revulsion of her. His muscles still shook from the constraint he'd bound them with. It was over.

The veil between them was gone forever, and even now he could hear her faint Song, thought it mixed with his in his blood and bone. Her fragrance lingered in the air, reminding him of her taste of sweet, heavy cream. He leaned heavily on Lightning, wiping his forehead against the volaran's soft feathered hide.

The revulsion reflex was finally over. Luthan only hoped his relationship with Jikata wasn't, too.

He'd looked at her with disgust. Had rejected her. Jikata had seen he was in distress, suffering and tried to help. His hands had fisted, face contorted as if he were keeping himself from striking her.

She'd never had a man hit her and the thought of it—that it would be a lover she'd let so close, had stupidly believed she'd bonded with emotionally—shocked her.

Then had come a ripping pain inside her, from her heart, her mind…her soul? As if they'd bonded deeply and the bond had torn. That hurt her, too, scared her. So she decided to take a step back—to get over her hurt and see where they were when everything settled.

She concentrated on her task. That afternoon she informed the other Exotiques of their practice schedule of three hours a day. Alexa and Bri protested but she quashed that with the simple statement that this was now their most important priority and held up her hand. End of discussion.

The others had tilted their heads as if listening to her Song, then agreed. They'd even had a first session and had done well enough.

She began noting down her new battle Song, ready to refine it. Chasonette warbled it with her.

That night Jikata finished Marian's book and began Calli's, the smallest, read until her vision dimmed, then set it aside. Luthan and she had shared a room last night, but she'd requested a change of rooms. Instead, his squire showed up and transferred his things to somewhere else.

She was sure gossip had spread since she returned from the beach alone and upset, but no one said a word to her about it. A blessing.

Oddly, she felt soothing strokes from the other Exotiques along their connections as if their Songs aligned with hers to comfort. As Luthan's Song had once been in tune with hers, and was now missing, as if he, too, had stepped back.

She dreamt that night, of the Dark gurgling, chuckling,

whistling in its Nest, all horrible noises, nothing melodic about them, and it turned its black leech head and its nasty mouth formed the words, *I will eat you*. It began sliming its way to her as she was rooted in place, petrified.

The mountain had exploded, all her friends had died, and still the Dark surged forward to cover her and absorb her.

For the next couple of days, Jikata avoided Luthan. That wasn't hard, since he was avoiding her, too. She'd figured out there had always been a thin curtain between them—something she hadn't even sensed—and it had been swept aside.

She knew what had happened. He was one of those who had an innate repulsive reaction to Exotiques. She'd read about it, but since he'd never acted differently, it hadn't truly sunk in. But she didn't know why it had happened *then*. Delicate questioning of the other Earth women had revealed that Luthan had shuddered at everyone else when they'd first met. Was it the commonality of their gift that had masked her nature? Or the fact that she had Japanese blood and looks?

She didn't know.

But she had work to do, and she worked herself and the others ruthlessly. Since a later vision had shown Alexa living, Jikata believed she was on the right course.

Her nights were filled with bad dreams that she examined, then dismissed.

The other women hadn't said anything about Luthan's absence, and Jikata's and Luthan's mutual avoidance had had one excellent benefit—she'd completely connected with them.

Like Bri said, it was as if Jikata was the last piece of the puzzle that clicked them all together. They all fit. She appreciated all of them. She could hear their various Songs, how the

Songs wove together in a fabulous, ever changing, ever wondrous harmonious whole. She enjoyed being with them, and the more of them together, the happier she became at the loveliness of their combined Song.

But there was an emptiness in her where Luthan had been. She missed him, but wasn't quite sure what their relationship should be.

Today the women had lingered in the manor's third-floor common room after breakfast. They, and their men, were all housed on that floor. Corbeau's wife had made it politely clear that eating up here was a courtesy for the rest of the household. Staying out of their way. As a group the Exotiques weren't very demanding, but Jikata sensed they were exhausting or incomprehensible to many.

"Since Raine is going with us on the invasion, she should have dreeth leather clothing," Marian said.

Raine paled, gulped, set her shoulders and nodded.

Some bit of knowledge tugged on Jikata's brain.

Then they all looked at her. She straightened against the back of the loveseat she shared with Bri, not understanding their frowns.

"It's the strongest, most protective substance a person can wear into battle." Marian's gaze was piercing.

Calli coughed slightly, Alexa glanced away, rubbed her temples.

"And?" asked Jikata.

Marian sat in a chair angled close. She flicked her fingers and a big book appeared on her lap, its pages riffled until it settled open, facing Jikata, with a hideous picture of a winged dinosaur-like creature, nasty teeth bared, spurs on the legs, spines. Terrible. Jikata recalled the dreeth quite well. Her ominous feeling increased. "So?" She made her voice casual.

Alexa looked back to her with an intensity Jikata hadn't experienced before from the woman, as if she examined Jikata for warrior-woman qualities. Jikata kept her gaze steady. Alexa nodded, their glances locked. "The only way a person can wear dreeth leather is if they help kill a dreeth."

The words slithered through Jikata's mind. She'd known that, forgotten. Like Luthan's repulsion factor. She couldn't speak. Alexa looked away, a false smile on her face.

Marian tapped the book's page and the dreeth turned into holographic, awful reality, rotated in three dimensions, hissing, long neck snaking, beak snapping, raising its wings. It was as big as the Circlet Tower it attacked.

Damn.

"Raine and Jikata should probably have fire-breathing dreeth skin. We *are* going to—into—a volcano, even if it's inactive." Marian glanced sideways at Jikata. "The fire-breathing ones are a little smaller," she added in a reasonable tone. She turned the page and the new 3D dreeth, half the size of the tower, spit flame.

"We can wait for an incursion of horrors, a *small* force, but one that contains a dreeth, take you there."

Jikata nodded, but her palms went damp.

The bonding with the other women had been easy, one task done. Integrating what Friends were here and establishing good communication lines with them and the Singer hadn't been difficult once the Singer deigned to mind-speak with Jikata again, another task finished.

Now the rough projects loomed.

Alexa's mouth tightened, she said, "We'll make sure that you'll be surrounded by Powerful Marshalls. Minimize risk."

"We'll all go," said Calli.

"No, you won't!" Jikata found herself saying in unison with the others.

"I will guard her." Luthan's voice came from the threshold. Chasonette rode on his shoulder, had obviously told him an important meeting was in progress.

His voice was calm, his face impassive, but his Song reached toward her, unrolling like a glittering, sparkling ribbon that tempted. "No horror will get by me. I'm a warrior, I fight for what I want and that's Jikata...." He paused. "Her well-being."

Jikata glanced at him, away, wasn't sure what he wanted, or what she wanted. Chasonette soared from his shoulder to the back of the couch by Jikata's neck. The bird took a strand of her hair and gave it a gentle tug in affection, then fluffed her feathers and squawked. *I do not think I will go hunt dreeths.*

Calli smiled. "Probably a good thing."

Chasonette stepped off the couch onto Jikata's shoulder. *But I love my Jikata.*

"We love her, too," Bri said, "and we'll protect her from any dreeth."

More than affection welled in Jikata for all the women.

Luthan prowled forward.

Raine lifted her chin, swept a gaze at everyone. "We should do it ASAP." Her voice quavered.

Luthan moved his stare from Jikata to Raine, frowning slightly. And in that instant Jikata *knew* he'd had visions regarding Raine. What they were, she didn't know. She still hadn't seen Raine at the end of the battle and didn't know if that was because Raine was on the Ship or had died.

"You're recovered from the ship-raising?" Calli asked.

"Oh, yeah," Raine said, flushing a little. Another glance around the room. "Faucon and I are a Pair."

"You certainly are." Calli smiled. "And I'd bet that he and both his teams will be working with you to kill a dreeth."

"Surrounded by orange and red." Alexa snickered. "Okay." She fingered her baton. "We'll take both you and Jikata out the next time the alarm rings that a dreeth is with the invading monsters."

Marian rose. "I'll tell Jaquar to reprogram the alarm to notify us whether a fire-breathing dreeth is among the horrors."

"Reprogram?" Jikata used the same English word Marian had.

Marian flashed a smile. "It's faster than saying, 'remove the old alarm notification spell and study it, change it to recognize new parameters.'"

"True," Alexa said. "But how…"

"The alarm is tied into the magical fence and fence posts, and they gather and relay the information by spell to the Castle, that's forwarded here to the siren we installed," Marian said. "Do you need to know more? As Raine said, the sooner this is done, the better. I have a feeling the Master may be up to something nasty once the fence is fully active again."

Jikata hadn't thought of that. She glanced at Luthan, he shrugged. Then he was sitting, forcing himself into a too small place, making Jikata move over until she was thigh-to-thigh with Bri on her left and squeezed against Luthan on her right.

The spark between them flared, their Songs meshed, the bond that had ripped wove back together with remarkable speed. As if all they needed was to be in each other's presence. As if it were fated.

Alexa's fingers tapped a beat on her baton sheath at her hip.

"Might be a good time for me to change place with my under-study. Get the monsters and the Master accustomed to *her* being in battle instead of me."

She flashed a smile at Raine and Jikata. "Bastien and I will still be there, but disguised."

"All our disguise spells are prepared," Marian said. She made a moue. "Alexa, you don't get red hair. That's not a disguise. I can give you black with a deep auburn tint. But we'll all pass for Lladranans." Marian Sang a quick pattern of notes that Jikata barely followed, and Alexa's hair and skin color changed.

"Jaquar says you're consulting," Bastien said from the doorway. He smelled of the volaran amber resin scent. He stared at his wife. "Alexa?" His eyes widened. "Interesting look. Come with me. Our squires, I mean our new Marshalls, have some questions. Whatever you're planning, I agree."

Luthan watched them leave, his expression a mixture of admiration and love...and sadness. Which made Jikata's own heart twist.

She drew in a breath. "Right. Now I should practice how to kill a dreeth."

38

"Flying to battle and teaming, first," Calli said. She looked at Marian. "I think we should all go disguised from now on."

"Good idea," Marian said. She swept her wand down herself and her skin and hair color became very like what Jikata saw in the mirror, though Marian's eastern European features were emphasized.

"You've been practicing," Bri said. "Me next." She grinned. "I want to shock my Sevair. He'll disapprove."

Marian inhaled deeply, shut her eyes as if visualizing images she'd formed in her head...then they came strongly to Jikata, the "Exotique Gang" as Lladranans. Tapping her foot to a beat, thinking of the notes comprising the spell, Marian Sang.

Jikata picked up on the third word, harmonized and refined Marian's Song. She certainly didn't need any more Power behind it. All the Exotiques had an incredible amount of that.

Eyes popping open, Marian stopped the spell and stared at Jikata…as did everyone else. Jikata had led practices on knots, but hadn't just joined in on someone else's spell. She got the idea that her flexibility surprised them.

"She *is* a trained Singer," Luthan said.

"Boy, do we need you!" Bri said.

Jikata put some steel in her smile. "So Calli and Alexa will be teaching me flying and teamwork and fighting." Her turn to flash a glance around the room. "Marian will refine the City Destroyer spell. But *I* will lead that spell and Sing the main part. Therefore those other activities will be done after our three-hour practices."

They nodded.

"We *had* been rehearsing together, three and four of us," Bri said, "Marian's been doing her best to lead."

Jikata glanced at Luthan. "Lucky for you, the Singer brought in her own understudies, voices that resemble yours. I *have* practiced leading them. For hours." She studied the women. "Though I always knew the amount of Power would be off. You all have a fantastic amount of Power, and we're all from the States, not a mixture of Lladranans and me. So our Song has been very different."

"Three hours a day." Calli sighed. "Well we need all the practice we can get."

"Ayes," Jikata said.

"Well." Marian huffed out a breath, caught Jikata's eye then she and Jikata picked up the songspell again. Bri, Calli and Raine changed before Jikata's eyes. This spell was like an illusion spell. Narrowing her eyes, Jikata could see the true aspect of the women. Marian had even muffled and distorted their Songs.

"Very good on every level," Jikata said. "But I must be able to hear you all well during practice."

Marian gave her smug smile, twiddled a couple of her fingers and the sound-illusion portion of the spell vanished and the bright Powerful melodies of the Exotiques returned full force.

"Excellent." Jikata smiled.

Bri was examining her hands, turning them over to check out the skin tone. "Beautiful." She looked at Luthan. "The Lladranans are a beautiful people." Then she glanced at Marian. "How draining is this illusion spell? And how long does it last?" Bri's forehead furrowed. "I could probably change the actual pigmentation of our skin." After a few seconds she nodded. "Ayes, it could be done."

"And changed back when everything is all over?" Raine asked.

"If you want."

Raine's half smile was brief. "I'm committed to the battle and living here and Faucon. But I still cherish who and what I was—am. I'd prefer to be me."

"There have been instances of Exotiques who have yearned to be Lladranan so much that over time their skin and hair and eyes have changed," Marian said and they stared at her. "I think illusion should work just fine." With a snap of her fingers, the illusion disappeared. "This whole expedition is an open secret."

Marian said, "We've been spreading rumors about what's going on, and I don't know why anyone would betray us to the Dark—"

"Power," Luthan said, grim. "It's happened before."

"I don't understand that," Calli said.

"Me neither," said Bri, "since it warps a person into a monster." She shot a glance at Jikata.

"I've seen pictures of the Masters of the horrors in your Lorebooks," she said. "Ugly. Disgusting. Repulsive." That was the wrong word to say.

Luthan took her hand, lifted it to his heart that thudded more rapidly than it should. "My deepest regrets." *I have given you some time to be angry, to heal, but time is at a premium. I want what we had.* His song sounded richer than ever.

I don't think that's possible, but we can go on from here, slowly. If you want.

I want, but not *slowly. We will make something new,* he said implacably, then turned to listen, as Jikata was, to Marian.

"In any event," Marian continued with her point, you could count on her to do that, "we'll keep our disguises a secret."

"I agree," Bri said, again turning over her hands, which had reverted to Caucasian coloring, with the slight added aura of the green of a Powerful medica.

Marian walked up to Jikata, smiled. "I don't think we've formally welcomed you to the club."

For a moment Jikata had a wild thought about Club Lladrana.

"The Exotique Gang," Raine said huskily.

"The Exotique Invasion Force," Marian said. She hugged Jikata tightly. "Welcome, Exotique Singer." Marian's smile lit her eyes. "I'm sure Alexa has a cowboy hat and boots for you."

Luthan, close enough for his breath to stir Jikata's hair and make her remember loving that began to stir her emotions, said, "I gave Jikata's sizes to Alexa."

"Good," Marian said. "I'll go speak to Jaquar then and we'll reprogram the alarm for a fire-breathing dreeth. One should be enough for leathers for both Raine and Jikata." With a last nod, she left.

Calli went over to Raine, who stood shifting from foot to foot, and took her hands, kissed her on both cheeks. "I'm proud of you, Raine."

Raine's jaw flexed. "Thank you," she said.

"We'll do this together, Raine," Jikata said. "Everything."

"Ayes," Raine said shortly. She rocked forward onto the balls of her feet, glanced at Jikata. "So we'll have to be in on the dreeth kill."

Luthan looked at Raine, then Jikata. "It's best if one of you, probably Jikata, makes the killing blow."

Jikata flinched.

Killing.

Jikata had never thought about deliberately killing anything bigger than a mosquito in her life.

"It will be trying to kill you," Calli said.

Jikata could make an exception.

"This is war," Calli said.

The reality of war was suddenly inescapable.

Raine muttered something under her breath that Jikata thought she was the only one to hear: "We who are about to die salute you."

The siren screeched that afternoon while Raine was giving Seamasters a tour of the Ship. Everyone froze in silence. Raine tried to figure out the pattern and whether it told of a fire-breathing dreeth in the invasion. She hadn't paid enough attention to the alarm to know exact details. Her mind scrambled as she considered logistics of getting off the Ship and to Faucon's room where regular battle leathers, chain mail, shield and helmet were awaiting her on a wooden stand next to Faucon's.

Then Faucon was there, slipping his arm around Raine's waist, an easy smile on his face aimed at the Seamasters who were scanning the sky.

"The alarm will be answered by those remaining in the Marshalls' Castle," he said. "Our folk here are off standard rotation, and will only fly one more mission for practice."

Raine's stomach clenched. Killing a fire-breathing dreeth, some practice.

He led the Seamasters to some rope lines that weren't quite familiar to sailors of Lladrana and they were diverted from the thought of invading monsters that they'd never faced, to something they dealt with most days. Raine explained the sail setup, and they hummed in approval. A couple actually took notes.

Whether the invasion was a success or not, she was yanking Lladranan sailing closer to nineteenth-century Earth.

That night at dinner a morsel fell off her fork as the siren erupted again. Silence filled the room, then an older Marshall told a funny story and chatter and eating resumed. After dinner Jikata Sang a medley of Earth folk tunes and Raine was impressed at the woman's polish and showmanship.

"We couldn't have a better Singer," Faucon murmured.

"Ttho," Raine answered. But she felt a little ruffled by Jikata's continued coolness to Luthan, the first Lladranan man Raine had trusted.

By the time Jikata was done, the siren had played the "all clear, invasion rebuffed, no casualties" pattern and there was a collective sigh.

That night Raine unfolded her mirrors on Faucon's desk in their suite and checked on her family. All her brothers were gathered watching baseball at her Dad's, yelling and shouting and cursing. Drinking beer and ribbing each other. The sheer normality of it had her crying until Faucon swept her to bed.

Deep in the night, Raine was jolted awake by the third shriek of the siren. She popped from bed, heart racing, and grabbed a robe. Evading Faucon's grasp, she ran from their suite up the stairs and into the common room, where everyone had gathered.

Since Faucon followed her and Alexa was pacing, Raine reckoned that no fire-breathing dreeth was in this bunch of monsters, either.

Hanks of Alexa's hair stood on end. "The Master and the Dark are up to something, so many alarms together, all at once."

Jaquar, the Sorcerer Circlet, said, "I told you last month that we had reports that the Master had set up a breeding ground for horrors in the northeast."

Tugging at her hair, Alexa said, "But that was last month. How could there be monsters grown and coming for battle already?"

"Magic," Bastien said, picked her up and took her to sit on his lap. "Dark magic."

"They're up to something," Alexa repeated.

"Maybe because *we're* up to something," Calli said.

"Perhaps," said Marian.

Jikata, perfectly groomed and in a heavy silk robe, glided into the room. She glanced to the corner, where the manor's animated map had been placed, but didn't go over to it. Luthan followed her but didn't come from the direction of Jikata's room, so they were still apart. Pity.

"The klaxon and the waiting is getting on my nerves," Jikata said in a melodious voice, appearing perfectly serene. Raine envied her that composure. Everyone knew *she* was scared. Weenie.

Folding gracefully onto the couch, Jikata said, "Since I don't know what to listen for, I can't tell whether I should be preparing for battle or not." Her voice was still smooth, nearly careless. How did she do it? "Could one of you demonstrate the pattern I should listen for?"

They stared at her. Such a reasonable request and something they should have thought of earlier. Then Bastien leaned around Alexa to the wooden coffee table and rapped out a series. Thump-thump, pause, thump-thump-thump, pause, thump-thump. "That's the fire-breathing dreeth alert."

"Thank you," Jikata said.

Alexa hopped up and strode to a nearby kitchenette. "Who wants some jasmine tea while we wait for the battle outcome? The tea leaves are straight from Krache."

"I'd like some," Jikata said. She aimed a smile at Jaquar. "I've read Marian's Lorebook. You lived in Krache, tell me of it."

Everyone seemed to be settling in for a vigil. Raine couldn't take it. Her blood seemed to pulse in that rhythm Bastien had sounded with his knuckles. Thump-thump, pause, thump-thump-thump, pause, thump-thump. Her breathing kept beat.

She stood. "The sailors' trials start at dawn. See you later." She marched away, her steps following the series she'd recall for the rest of her days.

Faucon rose, too. "I'll distract her."

Bastien grunted. "Good job if you can get it," he muttered one of the Exotique phrases that was entering the Lladranan language. "I have to sit here and drink jasmine tea."

* * *

Jikata had another dream of Ishi urging her to return to the Abbey, woke again with tears on her face. Why couldn't she let the woman go? She'd thought she'd made peace with the fact they'd wanted very different things in life.

From the Lorebooks, Jikata knew she could speak with Marian or Calli. Both those Exotiques had difficult parents, too. But Jikata had had a mixture, loving parents and distant Ishi. She shouldn't forget that. More and more memories were coming of her parents now that her career didn't blind her—good memories and she welcomed them.

She thought of Luthan, wanted him, for more than sex, for the companionship they'd shared, the friendship they'd built. She was moving beyond hurt and that was good. He was giving her the time she needed, and she wondered if, despite his words, he needed it, too.

But this very minute she wanted another cup of jasmine tea.

She was filling the pot with hot water when Raine appeared at the top of the stairs. "I missed out earlier and the scent of it stayed in my head. Can I have some?"

"Sure." Jikata poured two cups, put them on a tray and carried them to the low table in front of the loveseat where Raine sat. Jikata took hers and sat next to Raine, who reached down and cradled her cup in her hands.

"Ready for the battle?" Raine asked.

"No. I will never be ready."

Raine seemed to ease at that. "Neither will I." She looked to the darkened doorway to the bedrooms. "Sleeping alone?"

"Ayes."

"So, when are you going to forgive Luthan for something he has no control over, say, like skin color?"

Talking about this only made Jikata weary and sad, but she didn't want to go back to her bedroom and didn't think Raine would drop the subject. "I'm working through it at my own rhythm. I would have expected you, of all people, to understand."

Raine blinked. "Why? Luthan's always been honest and honorable and good to me. *He* never stalked me. *He* never hurt me. *He* never tried to kill me. Did he do that to you?"

"No, he only made love to me. *Before* he showed how repulsive I was to him, thought of hitting me, tore our bond. That hurt, and takes some time to heal, too."

Tilting her head, Raine said, "Okay, tough blow. But a tough blow to him, too. He's had to fight this innate disgust from the moment Alexa arrived, experienced it with the aftereffects and consequences." She frowned. "You know, I—we—have always accepted that what Luthan and the people like him do is unnatural and wrong."

"Perhaps because the first one Alexa met tried to kill her, and one like that attempted your murder, too," Jikata said.

"True. But *why*? What really happens to them?" Raine touched her heart. "What do they feel that makes them act that way? The guy who stalked me was a lowlife bully, but Alexa was attacked by a Marshall, and they're well-respected. There's no one more honorable than Luthan. Maybe we should have asked that question before. If we know what it's like, then maybe we can change or prevent it."

"I'm the last Exotique," Jikata said, though her thoughts and speculations were following Raine's.

"For now, and from Earth. Who's to say there won't be more from somewhere else? Those who might affect more than a small minority with the revulsion?" Raine paused. "It seems that a woman so in touch with Songs like you could understand how they're affected and tell us about it. Marian, as a knowledge keeper, and Bri, as a healer, could take it from there."

Jikata sighed. No, she hadn't wanted to talk about this, but it was one more good thing to think about. She finished her tea and rose. "Good point, and good night."

"Sweet dreams," Raine said.

"I hope so," Jikata replied.

"Raine?" Faucon called in a sleepy voice from the bottom of the staircase.

"Coming," Raine said, and took the dishes to the sink.

Jikata went back to her lonely bedroom, ignoring her envy.

Raine, Faucon, Corbeau and Madam Lucienne Deauville were aboard for the first sailing trial—when a full crew took *The Echo* out. Their mental link was the only thing that prevented disaster. But many of the Seamasters and the sailors learned quickly—especially Jean and Ella, so a core group was chosen including them and Madam Deauville for the rest of the trials.

So Raine was stuck sitting in another grandstand while people fumbled at sailing her Ship.

Thump-thump, pause, thump-thump-thump, pause, thump-thump.

It took a moment for Raine to realize that the siren was echoing the pattern that had shadowed her dreams, circled in her brain when awake, stayed in the back of her mind as the first, then second, then third hour of the sailors' trials passed.

But on her left, Jikata was rising from her seat, face impassive. Alexa had already leapt from the Exotique spectator box, followed by Bastien, both running toward the stables. Calli's volaran waited for her, caparisoned for battle, hovering beside the stands.

Blood drained from Raine's head and her knees felt weak when Faucon took her hand and drew her up.

Jikata passed them and her telepathic whisper came in Raine's mind. *Showtime. I'm petrified.* The Singer didn't look petrified. Raine figured she did. Then Faucon was moving fast and she was running, mind completely blank.

They sped to the manor house and up the stairs to Faucon's suite. Three squires, one male and two female, were already there, and the moment Raine stopped, one of the women started undressing her. As the light silk blouse was drawn over her head she realized she should have already been wearing leathers, like Faucon, but his were dreeth leathers. He hadn't said a word to her about that when they'd dressed this morning.

"The teams?" asked Faucon, drawing on his gauntlets.

"They are standing by, prepared to fly with you and the Sea-mistress Exotique. She will be protected at all times. We have our orders to bring down one of the fire-breathing dreeths so that the new Exotiques can deal the killing blows."

"Dreeths? Plural?" Raine squeaked, then sucked in her breath as the buckles around her waist were pulled tight.

"Three," one of the women said, handing Raine her helmet, turning to tighten a fellow squire's tunic.

"Three." Raine panted, tried to envision three fire-breathing flying dinosaurs raking the sky with their talons, spewing flame. She thought her eyes would roll back in her head. So stiffened her knees. "Let's go," she said, making her voice normal.

Faucon glanced at her, gave her a sweet smile. *You will be wonderful.*

Yeah. Sure.

They stepped out of the suite and Koz was waiting. He held a tiny box and earbuds. "Here."

Raine's eyes widened. "What?"

Tucking it into a small pocket in her tunic over her chain mail, Koz grinned. "My backup music player."

"What?"

"Okay, it's my second backup. I brought three, and I charge them with Bri's solar-powered pack."

"We need to go." Faucon was impatient.

"Battle music for Raine," Koz said.

Jikata and Luthan, together but not touching, stopped on the staircase, came over.

"Better not be 'Ride of the Valkyries,'" Raine muttered.

"Nah, that's strictly Marian's cup of tea," Koz said. "I heard you like heavy metal." He jerked his chin. "That has it. Industrial, power metal."

Raine put a hand over the pocket. "Those aren't the same."

"Yeah, yeah," Koz said. He fit the earbuds in her ears. Raine heard rippling strings. She snorted, reached for the plastic buds. Koz brushed her hands away. "Traveling music first, calculated to last 'til you get to the battlefield. Starts soothing, then goes to energetic. Works good with Distance Magic. Subliminals." Koz was talking faster as Faucon frowned. "Once you get to the battle, the heavy rock'll kick in." He grinned. "Help you kick ass."

"Thanks." She left the new age sound humming in her ears, thought if she listened closely she might sense the subliminals…confidence? All to the good.

Koz raised his voice. "Faucon, spread the word that all dialogue with Raine should be telepathic."

Ayes, Faucon said. *Battle is too noisy for anything else.*

Raine's insides jumbled, then she stiffened her spine.

Looking at Jikata, Koz said, "You want my backup player?"

She laughed, shook her head. Her long hair had been bound up in a braid circling the back of her head. It looked like it might give her extra protection under her helmet. Her leathers, like Raine's, were pristine. Not one singe, claw scrape, or any sort of monster or human blood. Luthan's white leathers were perfect, too, though that was expected. Dreeth, of course.

Anyone who was anyone wore dreeth to battle. Which is why this whole thing was going down.

"Ttho," Jikata was answering Koz. "A multitude of Songs surround me always. And if I want music…" She opened her mouth and her voice soared in a purity of notes that reverberated through the hall and through the earbuds and had Raine staring. Jikata smiled at Raine. "Not the 'Ride of the Valkyries,' but classical. Hildegard Von Bingen."

It sounded like something nuns would sing. Well, the woman had just come from an 'abbey.' The complete opposite of metal. Raine nodded. "Beautiful."

Jikata smiled. "Thank you. I'm working on a battle Song." Her forehead creased. "I should have had it for today."

"These things can sneak up on you," Koz said.

"I hope not," Faucon said. "Let's go. Later, Koz."

Koz was only allowed one more battle by the healer, Bri. This wasn't it.

Raine forced out the Chevalier blessing to Jikata and Luthan, wondered when they were going to kiss and make up. "Good hunting."

Another smile from Jikata, this time almost impish. "And to you. See you at the dying dreeth."

"Gotcha," Raine murmured, and gave in to Faucon's tug. They ran down the stairs, all of them, and out the side door where their volarans waited. Then on the flying horses and off they went.

To battle.

39

Battlefield, Northeast Lladrana

Whether it was the harp music with subliminal messages or the fact that she was surrounded by fifteen seasoned Chevaliers wearing orange and red, Raine was as prepared as she could be by the time they banished the Distance Magic bubble and flew into battle. She clutched her sword in her clammy grip, gritted her teeth to keep from whimpering.

Another bubble snapped around her—defensive force field, provided by a Shield, a Chevalier specializing in defensive magic. Raine was still looking around for Alexa and the Marshall team when Faucon's voice came to her, to all his people. *Let's take the small brown one with the yellow spines.* He arrowed to it, and there was nothing Raine could do but follow.

Heavy metal thumped into her ears, pounded into her blood,

bolstering her determination. She *would* do this. She was a fighter.

She found herself screaming with others, a burst of flame came close and Blossom squealed, dodged. Raine looked up and up and up.

There it was. A dreeth.

A little one, only about the size of a bungalow.

The magical 3D pictures didn't do it justice.

They missed the pure evil in its beady eyes, the glee as it snapped its wicked curved beak with sharp teeth, swiped with the claws at the end of its wings, aimed its spiny legs to kill.

She hated it at sight. It was an abomination, a monster with only one purpose—to kill.

Not if she killed it first.

Yelling, with the music thundering in her ears, she raised her sword, checked on Blossom as she'd been taught, gathered the volaran's thoughts to her own, infused them with confidence and resolve.

Aim for the wings, cripple it. She recalled tips. Go for the belly to rip and kill.

Blossom outflew others, taking chances they shouldn't have to kill.

A small warhawk accompanied them, whistling its battle cry.

The distended belly. Ayes.

Dodge the beak, the legs, the spines.

Drop! Down under the flame!

The belly, the belly, the belly.

Blossom was shouting wordless challenge in Raine's mind.

Faster! After the warhawk!

Raine was there, stuck her sword in the belly, ripped. The sword stuck and she lost it.

Next to her was a battle scream and a huge beak plunged into the dreeth's underside. Bri's roc.

Horrible glistening organs pushed through skin, the smell was gaggingly gross. Blossom and she and Enerin zoomed away, rose above the flailing dreeth. Saw it spinning out of control.

Faucon was next to her, sent her a battle grin, eyes wild. Then he and his volaran dove, slipped under a wing.

Blood up, Raine followed.

She and Blossom caught on the wing, sending all three of them tumbling. The world tossed around Raine, Blossom pulled out of a steep curve. The dreeth screeched again, a death cry, plummeted to the ground.

Raine had to kill the dreeth. Had to! Her task. She leapt from Blossom, lit on her feet. The dreeth thrashed around, but she was nimble, dodging jerky claws, snapping teeth. Nasty, nasty stink. She ran toward her sword, still sticking out of its stomach.

Even as its eyes glazed and it thumped around, with its snakelike neck aiming the head at Enerin the warhawk, Raine set both hands around her sword and jerked *down*. Next time she'd get a bigger sword.

One. Last. Horrible. Gurgling. Cry.

The dreeth was dead and Raine was screaming triumph when Faucon swooped down and plucked her up and away from a render's claws.

With strength and agility, Faucon set her before him, hunched them both low over his volaran's neck. Flew to the sidelines of battle, stopped and turned his volaran to face the carnage.

The monsters on the ground had no chance against the scything Marshalls, the best Chevaliers.

Raine shuddered in Faucon's arms, panting, crying. Hating the beat in her ears, she flung off her helmet and pulled out the earbuds.

The battlefield noise overwhelmed her and she wept more.

Faucon waved a bright clean orange handkerchief and she took it, wiped her runny nose, blew, used a corner for her eyes.

"I did it," she moaned as she panted.

"Ayes." His strong arm around her middle tightened. "You could make a Chevalier." He paused. "Not a good Chevalier, you have battle impulsiveness."

She didn't know what that was, didn't care to. "I'm a ship-builder. I'll stick to that."

"Ayes." His breath was a long sigh as if he'd thought she'd want to do this again. Not in this or any other lifetime.

Except for that last battle. The Dark's Nest.

She scanned the fight. "Where's Jikata? Does she have her dreeth yet?"

"Ttho." Faucon pointed with his gauntleted hand. Up to the sky.

The noise was incredible. Cacophony. Jikata shut it out with the Power of her own Song, of Hope's, of Luthan's. He was there, his arm swinging to kill monsters before they reached her.

He was so close that their Songs were mingling, and she knew he was determined to protect her and prepared to die doing so. All her feelings for him came rushing back, overcoming her heartache. Now was *not* the time. Put it away.

Now was showtime.

Hovering in the air, Jikata stared at the buff-colored dreeth, then found a quiet place within herself and *listened* for its sound signature. As it pulsed in slimy, staccato, minor key sharps, she clenched her jaw and learned to anticipate its movement. That squeal, there, it would dive. It did.

She'd been holding back, watching, learning, legs clamped around Hope's barrel. Calli and her husband Marrec, Shield and Sword, were with her, as was Luthan. He'd vowed to protect her with his life and was honoring that.

She heard a triumphant roar and glanced to her left, where Raine was ripping the guts out of her brown dreeth like a warrior woman. Then Faucon grabbed her, took her off the field, as was the plan...that Raine had obviously forgotten during the excitement of battle.

Chevaliers wearing orange and red streamed toward Jikata.

Luthan smiled. *You'll be wonderful,* he repeated the words Faucon had said to a nervous Raine, packed them with the same sincere and confident punch.

Jikata blinked, inclined her head. Took a deep breath, focused on "her" dreeth. It would be...right *there*...in a minute. Short-term prophecy. A good skill in battle. Did Luthan...

Now!

She whipped out her sword, Sang the spell Marian—the other fire Exotique—had taught her to make it flame, made sure she and Hope were of one mind, and flew.

Just think of something you'd like to kill, Calli said.

Jikata had just the person in mind. The sleazy promoter who'd wanted sex for favors. She'd barely escaped and it had taken two years to work around him. Soon she would have had enough power to ruin *his* career.

The dreeth's eyes had Bobby's meanness. Big skanky flying dinosaur, little weaselly promoter. No problem.

"Fire!" she shouted and flame shot from her sword. Hit its left wing claw.

Howling, the beast flapped away, fanning the flames that ate at its wing. Jikata grinned in satisfaction. Too bad it wasn't Bobby's dick.

Then she was surrounded by Faucon's Chevaliers. The outer Chevaliers dealt with the ground horrors—the renders and slayers and soulsuckers.

Luthan flew just ahead of her. Yes, he was anticipating the next move of the dreeth and would be there when it—

He took an axe and cleaved its head. It went down. Still on fire.

Jikata dimly recalled what she was supposed to do. Follow Luthan down to the ground. She did.

Leave Hope with a Chevalier Shield. Done.

Walk to where the dazed dreeth lay.

She ran, puffing, heart beating too fast, Song not steady, agitated. Who the hell cared?

Six big men held the writhing neck. Luthan had already started the cut.

Eeeeeew. No, no, no. Jikata skidded to a stop.

Luthan held out a hand, eyes blazing. *You* must *do this. To be protected.*

She was shaking her head.

Thinking too much, Calli said from beside her. Set a hand on Jikata's lower back, urging her forward. *Think of that skank Bobby.*

Bobby!

She'd needed protection from him, hadn't had anything but her wits to save her. And she wasn't the first he'd preyed on, or the last. He'd destroyed dreams, shattered lives. He should *pay*.

Jikata stared into the dreeth's eye. It hated. Hated her for no reason. Opened its beak.

Defensive bubbles layered around her, protecting her from the short, searing flame. The Shields, who'd kept her safe, including Calli, stumbled into others' arms.

Jikata was endangering them!

She jumped the last few steps to Luthan, took the axe from him and went to work.

It was foul. Green blood spurted, brown sinews parted as she hacked.

Around her the battle ended and still she labored.

Luthan and Bastien stepped forward to cut the bone, and Jikata averted her head.

Then back to work and she was singing "Sixteen Tons," pounding, didn't know whether to be sick or laugh. Finally there was one last ropy blood vessel and she severed it and watched blood spurt and droplets fly and pump and pump and pulse and…die. She sank to her knees, axe dropping from her limp grasp.

This had been awful.

Luthan was at her back, lifting her by her elbows. He turned her, looked into her face, his expression stern, except his eyes, which held compassion. For her? Or for the hideous creature she had ended that had been bred to hate and kill?

This situation was no good for anyone. Anything.

The sooner they destroyed the Dark, the better. It warped everything it touched—monsters, Master of its horrors, humans, Amee, *all*.

A world out of balance. Amee was a place where evil had more sway than good.

Luthan held her and she liked his grasp. She shut her eyes

and strove to listen to the land, where seeds lay, waiting for the evil to be gone so they could grow.

That was good. She opened her eyes as she heard someone approaching.

"The lines have been drawn on the dreeth, Jikata, you must make the cuts on the pieces you need. Then the others who helped kill it will get their share, good dreeth leather for all. We only lost part of one wing," Bastien said cheerfully. He handed her a big knife that weighed in her hand.

Jikata stepped from Luthan's arms and looked at the beast. There were dashed lines scored in the body. She straightened her shoulders and followed Calli as that woman told her where to cut.

This part seemed easier, as if some of the Power that vitalized the dreeth had been extinguished along with its life.

"So, um, Exotique Singer," one of the Chevaliers addressed her, a female Shield dressed in Faucon's colors.

"Ayes?"

The Chevalier ducked her head. "Ah, um, do you want the teeth? Or could I..."

Jikata gasped at the idea, forced down her gorge. Swallowed hard. Glanced at the wicked beak and the sharp teeth angled out from it. "No, I don't want them."

"She's claiming the leg spines, though," Marrec said, murmured in Jikata's ear, "Equally valuable and I'll sell them for you, get you a good price."

"*Merci,*" she said politely. Obviously quite a few here on this battlefield had struggled for money—zhiv—as she had, no matter what their circumstances were now.

Jikata set her knife in the next piece of hide, gritted her teeth and cut. It took her around so she was facing toward where

Raine was doing the same thing across the battlefield. Their eyes met.

I am never *doing this again,* Raine sent, and Jikata realized it was a communication between the two of them. They'd bonded enough for that, then. Probably in the last couple of hours.

Neither am I, Jikata replied. *Once was too much.*

Ditto. Raine grimaced and resumed carving.

Jikata did the same, trying to avoid the sight of other monsters being butchered…soulsuckers for their tentacles, slayers for their poisonous spines, renders for their claws and teeth. It made her angry to see their marks on her friends. A nearby Chevalier was being treated for slayer poison, Bastien had the imprint of a soulsucker tentacle cup on his face. The white scar on Alexa's face stood out palely. So Jikata slashed at her dreeth.

When she moved around once again, she saw the third dreeth of the action. It was much less mangled, more neatly killed than the ones Jikata and Raine had ended. Professionals had done that, and were making the most of every inch of skin, every tooth and claw and spine.

Jikata was never so glad in her life to be an amateur.

Then Luthan's hand folded over her own. "It's done."

She let him take the knife.

Luthan led her to Hope, who watched from the sidelines with rolling eyes and flaring nostrils. He didn't like the smell, or the wild Songs of the humans, or the sight of raw monster meat.

Neither did she. Without protest, she let Luthan lift her to her saddle. Her mind was a whirl of images, actions of the last few hours. Most of them bad enough that she'd like to forget them forever, but she knew would haunt her nightmares.

Luthan placed his hand on her knee and the warmth of it, the pulse of his Song was so sweet everything inside her clenched.

"I have apologized, and before the Exotiques, do you want another one here, more publicly?"

40

"Ttho." But she met his eyes and scrutinized them. "You want to build anew, be lovers again."

"Ayes," he said.

She let out a breath. So much fate involved in this adventure of hers. He wouldn't remain a friend, couldn't the way their Songs twined around each other. She touched a small slice on his cheek, didn't know what had caused it, and he didn't, either—it didn't pain him because of the adrenaline still surging in his blood.

She needed to say the words aloud, knew he needed to hear them that way. "I forgive you, Luthan. You can't control your revulsion and didn't mean to hurt me. And I apologize if I hurt you. I…care…for you."

His hand pressed against hers. He said huskily, "Apology accepted. There's some wonderful hot springs caverns on the way back. We can—"

"Sounds great!" Bastien clapped his brother on his shoulder. "Meet you there." Then he sent over the "Exotique link"—*We are going to Azure Caverns to soak!*

The feycoocus gave piercing whistles and took off.

Luthan sighed. "*Merci*, brother."

Bastien winked and strode away.

Bathing Caverns, North Lladrana

Luthan was demanding. Jikata used the sex to pour out all the battle stress, used him, let him use her.

Then came the tender loving. The Song of the two of them, as lovers, mended and grew until Jikata knew it would last a lifetime. And in the afterglow, she asked about the repulsion reflex and he spoke of it.

Noise that would drive a person mad.

She could believe it and she let some tears come, for him, for her, for every damn thing. More battle stress.

She left Luthan sleeping, unusual for him after sex, but the last few days and the battle had been rough on him. He'd *seen* visions of this particular battle, too, that she hadn't experienced. Because he was more in tune with the monster invasions that had always been a part of his life?

She wanted to speak with Raine. The woman's Song had gone from triumphant back to plaintive. The note of fear that had vanished for a while had returned.

They had gone to the same battlefield and killed a dreeth, a bonding experience if there ever was one.

Jikata strolled to the large, steaming pool in the cavern where Raine was soaking alone. Faucon was up attending to the volarans, Calli and Marrec had left, and the others were still in their private hot tubs.

Raine waved, and Jikata took a seat on a rocky ledge next to her. The water came just above Raine's breasts like a straight-cut décolletage gown. Jikata was shorter by a few inches and the sensual slide of the water lapped against her shoulders.

When Raine looked at her with sad and vulnerable and anxious eyes, Jikata felt ages older than the woman.

Raine's voice was low and husky. "Why aren't you freaking out about this? The battle. You know you're going to have to Sing in the Dark's Nest, be the anchor for the rest of us. That's your task, a life-or-death thing, no choice about it. No choice and no Snap until you're done."

Jikata said, "You said, 'until' so you think that it can be done, that I'll survive."

Shifting her gaze to stare across the large pool, Raine said, "You are *Jikata* and your confidence is…remarkable." She sighed out a breath. "Ayes, if anyone survives it will be you." Her forehead furrowed. "I…hear an extra depth to your Song. A better connection to Amee herself, maybe."

That surprised Jikata. "Maybe so. I've seen her several times. Much like the figurehead you made for *The Echo*."

"I think I got that image from Luthan and you. It didn't come until you joined the circle, near the end." She sent Jikata a sideways glance, opened her mouth, closed it, blinked. "You see visions. The future. I won't ask. I'm afraid to."

"Good, because our futures are still undetermined. May be in flux until the very last moment when we succeed or we fail."

"How can you stand it!"

"The uncertainty? The thought of death? I have moments." She shook her head. "I just spent some time crying."

"Me, too, but you're still more sure than I am."

Jikata considered it. "Perhaps it was my upbringing. Perhaps because my parents died when I was a teen and I formed my philosophy of death at that time. Perhaps because I recently lost the last of my family."

Raine inhaled sharply. "I'm sorry."

"Don't be. We weren't as close as I'd thought, hoped."

They sat in silence for a moment before Jikata said softly, "What are you really afraid of, Raine?"

Mouth twisting, Raine didn't look at her and said, "Big scary Dark. Monsters. Death. A painful death. I've never lost anyone I loved that I can recall. I guess I haven't developed a philosophy for it. Failing to stop the Dark, hurting my family. I want to live." Her chin set. "I want to live and build boats and love Faucon."

"Children?"

"Ayes." Raine's eyes flashed. "I know it's rare for Exotiques to have children, but yeah. After what we've done—will do—we deserve children. Amee owes us that."

Jikata found herself chuckling. "Amee owes?"

Raine leaned back, lifted her feet from the pool and wiggled her toes. "If I'd made that Ship in Connecticut, I'd've charged a pretty damn penny." She sank back. "As it was, except for the Power spheres, which we raised from the deep sea, everyone kicked in zhiv for the materials. Amee didn't pay for it."

"No? What about gracing us with our Power, with the Power to build it?"

"Not enough," Raine said decisively, lips firming. "After all we've gone through, we haven't been paid enough." She looked at Jikata. "We all have nightmares. Every one of us. Each of us have given, will give, our lives to free Amee from the Dark.

We should get a good return on that. That sounds mercenary, but none of us asked for the Summoning, or this life."

"True love," Jikata murmured.

Raine's eyes went back to being hurt. "Ayes, that makes up for a lot. But we live with knowledge that our loves may die. That we may die. That factors into the cost. Physical, emotional, mental, Power, all are affected and are what *we* are paying to do this thing for Amee."

"Like last night, you have a point."

"And you listen." Raine brooded. "Maybe I'm just mercenary. Maybe it's that I don't have a philosophy of death or dying and fear the uncertainty of the battle and the future."

"Once you were in the battle for your dreeth skins, you lost that uncertainty," Jikata said.

"Yes. I'm hoping that will happen again when the time comes." She nibbled her bottom lip. "Alexa has a fierce spirit, and determination and knows what she's—we're—doing is right. So she thinks of that, will think of that. She's linked to Bastien and the Marshalls, a team, who all believe like her, and are connected to the rest of us. Excellent support. Marian is sure that her Power and that of the Circlets, their combined intellect and flexibility is better than the Dark's. So she has that…intellectual confidence, arrogance. Calli…is Calli. She's loved by all the volarans of Lladrana, connected to all of them. She thinks of better lives for her children, for the rest of Lladrana, and knows she will do her best and that's all she can do. Bri is naturally optimistic, and thinks death is just another adventure. She has that link to all the common folk of Lladrana, her healingstream, faith, I guess, in people and us and the Song as the All."

Jikata was stunned at Raine's reading of their friends, then

Raine turned her eyes on Jikata. "And you have that bond with Amee herself, and the Song, and your belief in your destiny?"

"Yes." Jikata shook her head at Raine's insight. "Ayes, and the payoff that I can become the most Powerful person in Lladrana. True love. Composing. Endless fame." Then she turned her head and stared into Raine's eyes. "What do you have, Raine?" She lowered her voice so it could mesmerize.

That didn't work on Raine. "True love. I love Faucon, more than I thought I'd love any man. My connection is to the sea, the ocean." She laid her hand flat on the pool. "Even here, I can feel the tug of the tide, how there's an underground river that feeds this and water runs wild to the ocean."

"The Seamasters?" Jikata asked.

Raine shook her head. "Despite the Apology Ritual, and… uh…bonding with individuals, we still aren't comfortable with each other. It takes a while to be accepted into the whole community." She frowned. "I guess I think that what I have now is more than what I'll have after the battle. What I have now is wonderful, I can only lose." Again she stared off into the distance. "My man, my friends, my family, my life. I don't want to lose any of that."

Before Jikata could think of a reply, they heard whoops and splashing as others jumped into the far end of the large pool and swam toward them.

Creusse Landing

The sailing trials continued until the best crew was chosen. The stores were packed and a launch date set. The summer days took on a hint of autumn coolness and the hours passed until it was the last brilliant summer day before the invasion fleet left.

Luthan kept tallies on the life-and-death percentages of his friends. With the hard work they and Jikata were putting in, the odds against them were lowering.

Almost to acceptable levels.

Since the dreeth battle, he'd actually had a few visions where they all survived.

He'd shared some visions with Jikata that they never spoke of to others. He was grateful that her standard survival rate was now seventy-three percent and his was the same.

But he'd felt the desperation of Calli's son grow. The boy had been adopted only a year before and still felt unsure of his place in the world. He was old enough and clever enough to do something foolish—like stowing away on the Ship. Luthan didn't doubt that the boy would be found, but it would cause more emotional ructions and could possibly delay the invasion.

So he took the boy aside and revealed to the child that Calli and Marrec would live—and made him vow not to tell anyone in case that changed the future.

When the boy had flung himself into Luthan's arms and wept, balance within Luthan had finally occurred. Or rather Luthan finally came to terms with his gift. He'd comforted a child, comforted himself and his woman with his foreknowledge. The events he'd guided—like getting Bastien back to Alexa in the first place—had helped to minimize death and destruction. He'd helped his brother, his friends, himself. Whatever came, he had done his best, would use his gift as much as possible to do his best.

And Sing and pray. And love.

Then the sun dipped behind the horizon and it was night.

* * *

Faucon rose early on the day they were to sail, stood looking at a sleeping Raine, his heart so tight in his body he could barely breathe. The day at the caverns, he'd finished grooming the volarans and had walked down and heard the conversation between his lady and Jikata.

Raine was so much more fragile than he, than the others, thinking she had more to lose than to gain in this battle. The one the invasion weighed on the most. *Not* the weakest link of them all, he'd never believe that, but the most troubled.

So he left her with a kiss and walked to a place he rarely visited—the chapel to the Song. Here at Creusse Landing, it was tucked away in the corner of the short southeast wing. It was a small room, decorated richly, above the altar was a large stained-glass window of sky-blue that showed multicolored butterflies rising in a helix through the air—living musical notes, representing the Song itself.

He'd actually thought he'd be the solitary reverent, but the room was crowded. He went to the small front pew and knelt, looking at the altar with a large lyre upright upon it. Next to him was Corbeau's wife, and Faucon sensed she was praying for the warriors and again his heart squeezed. The thoughts and prayers and Power of those remaining could be a great force for those who were going. He nodded to her and clasped his hands loosely on the rail before him, bowed his head.

He considered his life a celebration of the Song, the living of it a prayer, the moments he treasured also daily prayers, so he rarely felt the need to formally go to chapel. But he was here for Raine, to pray for solace for her, for the lessening of the weight on her, however that may come about.

He bowed his head and listened to the Songs of others, particularly those strong in faith whose Songs rose effortlessly to connect with the great Song that was the source of All. As he breathed with others, he let himself be suffused with music, sent his mind, his emotions, questing to link with his own personal Song that was part of the music of the spheres, contained in the great Song of All.

His prayer was simple, that Raine not lose anything in the battle with the Dark, that she survive and prosper and love and find all she needed and deserved. He visualized that for her. Himself as loving husband, homes, land of her own, a shipyard of her own. Being valued by the Seamasters. He set the images within his mind to solidify and bolster himself and Raine when he linked with her. Prayed for them to become reality.

The sun lit the window and brilliant color exploded through the room.

A woman's voice lifted in a glorious Song to the morning. Jikata.

Everyone turned to stare at her and they learned the Song she'd crafted and Sang with her.

A blessing.

The door opened quietly and Raine was there. Faucon heard her intake of breath. Linked with her, he *felt* the Song wash over her, suffuse her with hope.

That was what she needed most. Simple hope.

He stood, and still Singing, he went to her, put an arm around her and brought her to the pew and they sat, looking at the window.

Filled with hope.

The Echo, *Brisay Sea*

With Raine standing by Faucon at the helm, they sailed into the open Brisay Sea. She paid attention to her crew and her two lieutenants—Lucienne Deauville and the man she'd first met in town, Jean, who'd sailed a good part of the world. Everything went more than smoothly, her sailors were optimistic, buying in to the whole "great adventure" thing. Ella was enthusiastic enough for ten people.

The remaining Exotiques hung over the rail of the great Ship waving at people on shore—well, Jikata propped a hip against the starboard side and raised a languid hand.

There was a good turnout of folks: merchants from the fair, townsfolk, dignitaries from other cities invited by Bri and Sevair. The Seamasters were there, even the two who'd begrudged their apologies. They were smiling smugly and Raine didn't like it, but was glad she'd be out of their sight.

On *The Echo,* many of the landsmen and women were unpacking and exploring. Flights of volarans were circling, landing, playing.

The Echo was using a small portion of the Power spheres, was under full sail, and handling well.

She visualized the course. To hug the coastline would add many miles to their trip, and the course was set to go beyond all land. They'd angle to a point where they'd sail through the middle of a smaller sea, and directly to the relatively narrow strait between continents. That cleft had opened eight centuries ago when the Marshall Guardians had developed the fence posts. Lorebooks told the story of Amee causing an earthquake to ensure her warriors access to the Dark's Nest.

When asked the name of the strait, Jean had grimaced, avoided Raine's eye and swayed with the Ship, finally saying gruffly that it was called the Strait to Doom, because it led to the Dark's Nest.

The voyage itself would take four weeks, one week longer than the volaranback expedition the year before. But this was an invasion force, with fighters and weapons and stores.

She'd anticipated being less anxious on the Ship, where she was in control and command. That had happened to some extent, but the reason for the Ship always lurked at the back of her mind. She grimaced, nothing to do but endure. Survive.

41

Jikata didn't like the Ship. Nothing about it. Not the overly rococo flourishes, the masses of volarans standing on the quarterdeck, and especially not the large closet of her cabin that she shared with Luthan. At the start, she'd contemplated selfishly keeping the cabin and the bed to herself, but even a closet with Luthan was better than sleeping without him.

And the Ship was surrounded by water, a very strange sea that would open into a very strange ocean that would narrow to something called the Strait to Doom that sounded the strangest of them all.

She'd paid her dues on a couple of cruise ships at the beginning of her career. All right, two voyages, but the water hadn't been this...active, almost alive. The moment she'd stepped aboard, she'd experienced an ominous feeling that she couldn't shake, a depression of her spirits.

A loss of her composing ability.

It was now the end of the first week, and the nightmares were back with a vengeance, always ending in visions of mass slaughter of herself and her friends. Difficult to throw off even during sun-bright days.

The others loved the Ship. Bri, the most well-traveled, was on the deck all the time, talking to the sailors, learning a little of their craft. Alexa had been sick for the first three days and nights, adding her moaning to Jikata's dreams, but now she'd bounced back and hung over the rail, looking at the water, the land that had changed from peninsula to islands to the open sea, all with towering mountains in the distance to the east.

Marian, the other "fire" person, seemed to have no problem at all, either. Of course all the women were born and raised in Colorado, stayed there mostly, so an ocean voyage was a novelty.

Calli spent some time in the air with different volarans, and Jikata envied her, though it was obvious that keeping up with the Ship put a strain on them, so those flights were short. Easier on the beasts at night.

Furthermore, some of the sailors kept giving her sly glances, and Chasonette picked at her and whined.

The only time Jikata's mind felt clear and focused was when they were Singing, whether warm-up exercises, or the actual unknotting ritual. That was going well. All knew the chorus and the opening verse. Each was making progress on their individual verse, which spoke of segments of the Lladranan culture that were finally coming together: "I of the Volarans, lovely in flight"; "I of the Tower with Knowledge Bright"; "I of the Townsfolk, valuing right"; "I of the Marshalls, ready to fight..."; "I of the Seamasters and ocean's might"; "I of the

Singer, music and sight…" As usual, tailor-made to the Exotiques. Or the Exotiques had been specifically chosen for their culture and thus the Song. Which they had been.

Bri was the one who was having the hardest trouble with memorizing her verse, and Jikata was considering changing the beat for her. To Jikata's surprise, Raine had somehow incorporated a rock-and-roll beat that also echoed the sea. She was Singing well, but remained afraid.

Marian had tried to foist the weapon knot on Jikata and she'd refused it. The thing looked like an artery, pulsing red with a drumbeat that was disturbing.

Time and again, Jikata would sit down to compose and someone would interrupt, or her inkwell would be sliding around and the notes just wouldn't come. It was a never-ending irritant.

As day waned into night, depression and anticipation of nightmares settled on her like a polluted, foggy gloom. She usually picked at dinner, then retired to bed. Sex with Luthan stayed the nightmares, but didn't stop them, and he didn't seem to be sharing them, so she supposed her Power was that much stronger than his.

Visions didn't come during the day anymore, were as scarce as her composing ability.

Occasionally Ishi walked through her dreams like a balm, and Jikata welcomed her. Amee had failed to show after the first night, but she'd been dismissive of Jikata's mild complaint about the Ship and the water, had seemed to beam with pride at the Ship and her Exotiques.

It all set her teeth on edge. She should have stayed at the Abbey.

Disaster struck in the middle of the second week. Not to *The Echo*, but to Lladrana itself. The Marshalls' Castle sent an urgent message and Alexa announced with a serious face but vibrating with anger. "I have news."

Everyone gathered, everyone quieted.

Alexa paced, hand on her baton, jutting it forward in its sheath. A bad sign. "As you all know, we've been replacing the ancient fence posts as they've fallen, raising new ones so the northern boundary is a solid magical shield to repel the horrors." She stopped, sucked in a deep breath, addressed the crowd. "Early this morning *all* the old fence posts, those we didn't raise in the last two years, fell." Her jaw flexed. "There are holes in the fence. Five gaps, to be precise. And horrors are steadily coming through."

"*This* is what the Dark has been planning," Marian said. "It caused the old posts to fail and fall."

"Ayes," Alexa said. "The new Master of the monsters likes notes, he had one delivered in one of the incursions, gloating."

"He doesn't know of this Ship, the invasion?" Jaquar asked sharply.

Alexa shook her head. "It seems not. However, *we* are the primary team."

"We must turn back!" someone shouted, and Raine couldn't pinpoint the person.

"Ttho!" Alexa's voice resounded over the deck. Her face hardened. "We are not returning to Lladrana. The others must cope without us."

There was muttering, some grumbling.

Alexa ignored it and went on. "A discreet call has gone out to those Chevaliers and Marshalls who have retired. Chevalier classes are being sped up. Pascal and Marwey and our understudies must handle this." Her skin stretched tight over her cheeks. "None of you will be allowed to return."

Shouts of dismay. Bastien stepped forward and put one hand on his wife's shoulder, the other on *his* baton. His gaze swept the crowd, but Raine didn't think he identified the dissenters.

"You all know what you signed on to do. It's more vital than ever that we kill the Dark." He gestured to the cluster of Circlets—Marian, Jaquar, Bossgond, others. "The Circlets speculate that once the Dark is destroyed, the new Master of the horrors, the monsters themselves, will stop invading. They may even collapse."

Lifting her chin, Alexa said, "This endeavor is the best permanent solution of the problem of the Dark." Another audible breath from her. "We must pray and Sing that Lladrana will weather this." She glanced at Jaquar. "None of the scenarios that I ever saw speculated about how long it would take for a steady stream of horrors to overrun Lladrana."

"The Circlets of the Tower community are already working on that. We will have the information for you later today."

"Good." Again Alexa scanned the crowd with her cool, military stare. "What we *are* going to do is invade the Dark's Nest and destroy it!"

A cheer went up. Alexa fastened her gaze on Raine. "And we're going to wring every bit of speed out of this Ship that we can, right?"

"Right," Raine said, calculating course, speed with and without sails, and how she could shave time off the voyage without risking all.

There was plenty to worry about on the voyage. They had updates from the Castle daily, and the remaining Marshalls were doing well, but some monsters were slipping into the country. There were mutterings on the Ship about this and no one could determine exactly who started them. Raine was pushing herself, the Circlets and the crew as hard as possible, and the Ship was speeding through the waters, at a rate that the volarans could not match, not even at night, so the ship was crowded with them all the time except for brief flights. The two herds—humans and volarans—were irritated with each other.

But Luthan worried about Jikata. He said nothing to the others—not that they were unaware of the changes in her. Of all people, Bossgond the Circlet had informed the Exotiques that she was not to be confronted, that she must come to the realization that she was being influenced by the Dark itself.

When Alexa demanded whether that would happen in time, Bossgond had turned to Luthan and flat out asked about his visions of the battle—and of Jikata.

Of course they'd all stared at him. The odds for them all had gone up, and he was grateful for that, for the shining few that showed all the Exotiques living. But the visions came more often, and more vividly. He hated that he couldn't discuss them with his lover as he'd had. So, in the face of Bossgond's challenge, Luthan narrowed his eyes and examined Jikata's actions in the visions. He was unsurprised to find that when the battle outcome was the Dark living and most of them dead, she'd been an uninspired Singer.

Luthan had stared at Alexa and said, "Twenty percent of the time, Jikata is affected by the Dark and we fall."

Alexa blinked. "Twenty per cent?"

"Ayes."

"Oh." She gave him a brilliant smile and walked away with a bounce in her step, and that caused a little clutch of his heart. He'd come to love this woman his brother had wed, and he didn't want to lose her. His heart would be torn irrevocably if he lost his brother, too. As for Jikata…he already knew that if she perished he would, too. They weren't bound together in a ritual blood exchange ceremony, but they were close enough that he thought his mind and will would shatter if she died.

"Jikata…" Ishi's face was lined with concern. "Who are these people? How do you know them? Why do you trust them?" Ishi's standard questions for any friend Jikata had spoken about, wanted to associate with.

Jikata had nearly forgotten those questions, now memory came rushing back, along with annoyance and teenaged anger. She'd been in with a *good* crowd when in school. It was only when she had the first flush of success that she'd traveled with bad companions for a time, then she'd gotten smart.

In the dream, she and her great-grandmother were standing on a rocky point of land, covered with a sheen of ice. Ishi gestured and Jikata looked across the slate-gray ocean to a mountain rising out of the sea. One mountain, an inactive volcano, though Jikata sensed molten fire beneath it.

She sensed something else—the Dark. Close enough, terrible enough, to chill her insides and make her shiver.

"These people will get you killed."

Another graceful wave of Ishi's pretty hand and the base of the volcano was littered with the fragments of a great battle… humans, volarans, monsters all dead and heaped together.

She saw Luthan, body shattered in a way that hurt her soul, saw herself, flung far from him, hair singed, face still. Saw all her friends in a hideous pile, each death wound more obscene than the last so that she couldn't look closely, not that she could tell one from the other except for the size and hair color.

Which shouldn't happen because they were disguised, all with black hair and golden skin, like Lladranans.

The breath went from her lungs. Her chest constricted as realization blazed through her.

This being was not Ishi, had probably never been Ishi. She felt sick from more than the carnage she saw, the horror of the dream. She had been so gullible! Played so very well. Because she'd wanted the dream woman to be Ishi.

But Ishi would never, ever call her "Jikata." It had been that last change of name that had Ishi sending her a note of disinheritance. The old woman had seen it as a betrayal of everything Jikata was, when Jikata had felt it was giving herself a true name.

She widened and rounded her eyes at the fake Ishi. "Ishi?"

"Yes, Jikata?"

It wouldn't have been "yes." They didn't speak English in Ishi's home.

"Why do you scold Jikata?" She made her voice plaintive.

There was a flash of real anger in those eyes—red-tinged eyes?—that Jikata had always ignored before.

"Because you do not listen, Jikata child. You should not be here. You should not join with these people."

Ishi would have called her Fujiko. So she replied in Japanese, "Why don't you call me by the name my parents gave me?"

Ishi's face went blank, as if the thing that lived behind it had had no clue that there was more than one language of Exotique Terre, spoken in the States. Jikata could have switched to Spanish, or French, made her accent Canadian or British, and the result would have been the same. No effing clue.

She smiled a terrible smile. "Just *what* are you?"

Ishi's laugh started tinkling, then mutated to an awful rasping, gargling gurgle. Then the mask, the total illusion, was dropped and Jikata retreated a couple of steps in surprise before she settled into her balance and stood her ground.

The thing had once been a man. It was not the hideous thing shown in graphic 3D in Marian's Lorebook, nor the before-and-after pics that Sevair had imaged of his former assistant in Bri's Lorebook. Swallowing, Jikata could see that he'd warped from that man. No nasty tentacles around his mouth, but a knot of them growing out of each temple of his head that had a row of yellow spines front to back. Eyes a pupilless red.

She swallowed again, put a hand on her hip, examined him up and down. He was furious and his mind worked fast and loud, broadcasting information. Smiling, she sneered, "Go back to your hole, you disgusting creature." Then Sang the banishing chorus that was part of the weapon knot.

He snarled, raised deformed, clawlike hands to rake her, but vanished, leaving the smell of corruption.

Jikata woke, blood pounding in her head. She reached for Luthan but he wasn't there. He had taken to wandering the Ship in the night, soothing volarans.

When her breathing steadied and she could hear more than the rush of her pulse, she noticed rustlings in her mind from the other Exotiques, who were gathering in the cabin. She yearned for their companionship, but had the lowering thought that they might not want hers. She rose anyway, and left her cabin.

Alexa was already sitting at the table with a mug, hair sticking up. Calli was there with trembling hands folded on the table. Bri had her head propped in her hands, massaging her scalp. Raine was walking to a chair and drawing it out and

Marian was preparing drinks on the tiny counter space of the galley. "Bad one," Marian said.

"Yeah." Alexa hunched over her drink.

"What are you having?" Raine dropped heavily into the chair.

"Tea and mead," Alexa said.

"Mead," Marian said.

"Ale," Calli said.

"I'd like jasmine tea," Raine said.

"Water's here and hot," Marian said.

"I'll pour it." Jikata moved from blocking the doorway.

They all froze for a moment, their thoughts checked, too.

"I'll take some jasmine tea." Bri's voice was muffled.

"How can anyone drink tea and mead?" Marian asked Alexa, trying for a teasing tone and falling flat. Alexa shrugged.

"Really bad dream," Raine repeated.

Bri got up and went behind her and began to knead her shoulders, comforting them both.

It took little enough time to pour the tea over a strainer packed with jasmine tea in each of their individualized mugs with a cowboy hat and their name. Jikata gave the first to Raine, the second to Bri, and took the third, the weakest, herself.

She sat and so did Bri. They all drank in silence until Raine said, "We were all dead, and Faucon…" She shuddered and it went around the table.

"Bad one," Calli said and Jikata knew she was seeing the remains of her husband and herself and her beloved volarans.

After another long silence, Jikata said, "The new Master sent the dream. It and the Dark know we're coming."

Another mass shudder. Eyes showing fear then faces turning stoic.

"Shit," Alexa said.

Jikata lowered her voice. "He has dreeths for the volarans, doesn't think we can reach the hatchway in the bottom of the mountain." She'd caught that flash of knowledge from the Master's mind.

All attention focused on her.

Calli said, "The volarans will be fine."

They stared at her, and Jikata was sure everyone was listening hard to her Song and hearing her absolute confidence…and a secret she hadn't imparted.

Raine narrowed her eyes. "They can't know how fast we're coming." She looked at Jikata. "Did you get that? That he knows when we'll be there?"

Mulling over every nuance of her interaction with the Master, Jikata recalled that the weather seemed colder than she'd thought, more winter than autumn. The setting had always been determined by Ishi—by the Master Horror.

"Ttho," Jikata said. "You're right, I don't think it knows how fast we're coming."

Raine switched her gaze to Marian. "You think that because I built the Ship and the Master doesn't have any of my DNA or Jikata's we can get through the island shield."

Marian stirred from brooding at her mead. "Ayes."

"I have a secret, too." Raine looked at Calli, crossed her arms.

The mood at the table lightened a little.

"Good enough," Marian said, then stared at Jikata. "Can you describe the new Master as he is?"

"*Hai.*" Jikata showed her teeth in a smile. "He doesn't speak Japanese. He doesn't know my Japanese name. He didn't even *know* there was such a language."

"No other languages in Lladrana, *sí?*" Calli's smile was faint, but true.

"I'll want an image of him to pass around," Marian said with her old professorial authority.

Jikata grimaced. "No chance of missing him." She drank her tea, finally noticing the good flavor, and sighed. She'd loved it once, but not now. If she made it, *after they'd* destroyed the Dark, she doubted she'd ever drink it again. "Another advantage, he doesn't know our disguises."

"That's right," Calli said, and swallowed. "I had blond hair."

Alexa looked straight across the table into Jikata's eyes. "Tell me one thing, Singer and prophet. In your visions, do any of us live?"

"Ayes, sometimes all of us," Jikata replied immediately, recalling her previous visions, nothing the Dark had sent her. She still felt the heat of embarrassment at being duped, but set that aside, sending them all the truth in her heart. She looked around the table, hoping she lingered on each face equally. "And since we've been practicing, the more we practice, the better chance that we live, we *all* live." Though she hadn't had that in a vision lately, she was sure of it in her bones.

"Sign me up," Alexa said. With a little raise of her cup in a toast to them, Alexa gulped the last of her tea and mead and said with a wobbly smile, "Think I'll go make love with Bastien. It gets us through."

"We guessed," Marian said drily, finishing her straight mead. "But it works."

Men filtered into the room. A serious Bastien, who lifted Alexa gently into his arms, his face so tender with desperate love that Jikata had to look away.

Jaquar took Marian's hand and pulled her into waltz formation and they danced from the room, gazes locked.

Marrec held out his hand. "Calli, beloved?" She went to him, and he gripped her fingers, then sent her ahead of him down the short, narrow hall with a hand to the small of her back.

Sevair strode over to Bri, lifted her straight from her chair and put her over his shoulder, smiling as she giggled.

Faucon swung Raine into his hold, set his mouth on hers and walked out, obviously able to multitask.

Jikata sat at the table, examining every dream she'd had of Ishi, every nightmare. The Ishi dreams had been false, the Dark ones where it had threatened her all too true. But since embarking on the Ship, Jikata didn't think she'd had a true vision. So the awful dreams showing increasing death and destruction were sent by the Dark.

Her mind was all too clear. Reality bit and bit hard. She was petrified. She could die.

Did she have a philosophy of death? Of course. And it wasn't doing a damn bit of good now, in the middle of the night, with those visions of dead friends painting her mind. She hadn't anticipated dying for a long time, maybe in her nineties when she was old, like Ishi.

Now they were sailing to death and it was all too close.

42

She stepped back from herself, looking at herself as if she were seeing a vision, and she didn't like what she saw.

An infection had grown in her—from the Ishi dreams and the Dark nightmares. She'd been well on her way to becoming a woman like the Singer, or worse…and even more worse was that woman could have been easily manipulated by the Dark.

She'd nearly cost them all their lives.

Closing her eyes she sought music, the Song, and went to the very core of her to recall her own identity.

Ruthlessly she looked for the dark smudges of fear and arrogance and suspicion and hubris and eradicated them. She wiped them out with ideas of how she wanted to be, her own self-image she wanted to cultivate: understanding, supportive, confident. Not as easy to include those qualities in herself as it was to fall into selfishness.

She could and did nip most of the bits that the Dark had added to herself. The negative qualities that were innate, she'd just have to continue to work on, as always.

She was left with one stubborn bit of...something...from the Dark that she couldn't change herself. She wasn't as complete and as competent as she thought.

Sighing, she came back to herself, sitting at the table with a cup of cold jasmine tea. She saw a man in the shadowy doorway and jolted, realized soon enough that he wasn't *her* man. Luthan had not sought her out. Too much distance between them since the Dark had influenced her? She hoped not.

The man walked in—Bossgond, the best Circlet Sorcerer. He took a seat opposite her, giving her a sympathetic look. With a pass of his hand over her cup and one low note, he heated her tea. She curved her hands around the mug and returned his stare.

He wasn't the wizard of books and films, tall with long flowing white hair and beard, lines around wise eyes. He was shorter than most Lladranan men, skinny and boney. The knobs of shoulders and knees showed beneath his robe. His hair was golden. But when she withdrew her hands from her cup, he took them in his own—calloused, tough hands that matched the shrewdness, the sharp intelligence in his eyes.

She felt a connection to him—more than the common link they shared with Marian, his protégée. A great portion of the low vibrations of their Songs matched. Jikata caught her breath.

He squeezed her fingers, comforting. "Great talent makes great demands." He bowed his head. "I thank you for coming to aid us, Singer."

Then, without fanfare, without any noticeable stress at all, he drew the last bit of the evil from her, through their grip. Siphoned every smidgen of it out of her, and *cleansed* her inner self, leaving her feeling as if she sparkled.

He withdrew his hands, held them stiffly straight into the air. Blackness streamed from his fingertips to hang in a greasy cloud. With a short, sharp hum, the cloud ignited, flamed, was consumed.

The air should have smelled sulfurous, or acrid, but only the faint scent of jasmine tea lingered.

Bossgond rose, inclined his torso. "Be blessed, Singer."

He left, straight-backed, as silently as he came, and Jikata pondered his manner. Usually he was a grumpy, irascible old man. But she understood now that was a mask he wore to hide sensitive feelings. No one could have been gentler, kinder to her in this moment of crisis and doubt. She missed the potency of his Song.

She remained at the table, not wanting to return to the cramped cabin empty of Luthan. She thought back to when the Master had dropped his Ishi persona and she'd seen the true nature of the being—twisted and evil—and had been repulsed, as repulsed as Luthan had been with her that day on the beach.

Had he seen her monstrously warped and evil?

Ttho, never. Now, finally, Luthan had come to her. He stroked her hair, brushed it aside so he could trail his fingers down her face. Shaking his head, he said, "You were *different,* but never evil." He bent down to kiss her lips, softly, softly.

Tears welled in Jikata's eyes. "Thank you."

He sat next to her, took her hand. "You are better."

"Completely." She grimaced. "Back to my own self, which is not as delightful as I think."

"Very delightful." He kissed her fingers.

She asked what she wanted to know. "I haven't had any true visions on the Ship. Have you?"

His breath left him on a relieved sound. Nodding, he glanced around, narrowed his eyes, tilted his head as if listening. She followed suit, sensed everyone except the night crew, a few volarans and Bossgond were asleep. The Circlet was brooding quietly and she knew he wouldn't eavesdrop.

Luthan kept his voice low. "Lately I've been seeing us all survive."

Jikata let out a sighing breath. "I had a feeling, and one vision before we left."

"It's Faucon," Luthan said. "He is the key. I don't know how…but…"

Jikata nodded. "Ayes. I see a shining aura around him in the visions where we live."

Luthan stood, drew her up, held her and closed his eyes. "Let's go to bed, I have a need to sleep with you in my arms."

Jikata woke before dawn and waited until all the Exotiques were above deck, where she could talk to them en masse, before she got up. Luthan still slept, and she stroked his head, the silver at his temples wider, the lines in his face deeper.

She loved him and didn't want to die.

Most of all, she didn't want him to die.

She could meditate….no, that was putting the reckoning for her bad behavior off. Dressing carefully, she went up top.

So she went up to the deck and found the Exotiques had gathered to watch the dawn.

"I'm sorry I've been such a bitch," she said.

Alexa drummed her fingers on her baton sheath. "Visions?"

"Not so much."

"Nightmares every night," Calli said. "Chasonette told Blossom, who told me."

"Yes. Or dreams of my great-grandmother who just died, sent by the Master to turn me back." She looked at them all. "Can we mend the bonds between us that have frayed?"

Bri stepped forward and hugged her. "You only had to ask."

After a ritual that included Bri's laying on of hands to check her inside and out, some group mental activities—including untying a few spellknots with Song—and a volaran flight, Jikata felt as if she were truly grounded and whole.

"So, Jikata—" Alexa had calculation in her eyes "—can you finish that battle Song we want?"

It burst into her mind, fabulous notes, a strident melody. She scrabbled for pencil and paper, as if there'd be any on the deck of a Ship, but Calli handed her some and, muttering to herself, Jikata finished the Song with a flourish. That wasn't the only Song that came to mind, notes and chords and bars and bridges all the way to full orchestral pieces dazzled like fireworks, as if they'd been dampened and suppressed and now could cartwheel and be recognized. "I want to get some new compositions down. See you."

"Wait, the battle Song—" Alexa said.

Jikata shoved the paper at her and Alexa scowled down at it. "I can't read music."

With a sigh, Marian took it from her, scanned it and began to Sing, a strong alto. Chasonette joined in. *Welcome back, Singer,* she said mentally, thoughts loving.

Jikata smiled as she went down the hatch, all the women had good voices, but she'd trained them. She didn't think that

Marian would have read music or tried a new song in public before they'd met.

She was making a difference.

That's why the Dark feared her.

That afternoon, spellknot unbinding and Singing practice went extremely well. Another subject was added to the training: mind shields. Taught by several Circlets, including Bossgond.

By the time the Ship sailed into night, Jikata knew the Dark could not penetrate her dreams.

The Ship was sailing fast, and so was time…sailing by with nothing Raine could do to prevent it. She was pleased with the crew's response to the threat to Lladrana, and the new speed. They might match last year's expedition's time of three weeks. As if it were a race and not sailing to death.

But every second of speed she could squeeze from *The Echo* would lead to more surprise on behalf of the Master and the Dark.

Raine left Faucon sleeping in the tiny cabin and went up on the deck, too restless to stay stifled down below. She nodded to Jean, who Captained *The Echo* at night, but didn't disturb the quiet or insult him by asking how the shift went. They were making good time by the wind against her face.

She was on a Tall Ship—oh, not quite, they were mostly schooners, and this was definitely more like a galleon—but a big ship with masts, the deck vibrating under her feet and creak of rigging and swish of air filling the sails. Going starboard, she looked toward the east and the land.

The sea and the wind and the rolling of the waves beneath

the Ship itself soothed her until she felt sleepy. But like other times, she didn't want to go back to the cabin. Despite the porthole, the cabin was too confining. So she gestured to Jean that she'd be bedding down on a mattress kept for sailors who wanted to crash on deck instead of below in their hammocks and settled down.

She drifted, the scent of the sea and the pretty night, and the rocking of the Ship sending her into a doze she didn't want to give up for sleep.

They'd timed this night of sailing to reach the narrow passage between continents at dawn. Everyone seemed to think that she should be the one to Captain *The Echo* as they traversed it. That her special rapport with the oceans of Amee wouldn't lead them aground. Since no one else had sailed the curving strait, she'd agreed.

Once they were through that passage they'd be in the northern waters commanded by the Dark.

A shadow loomed over her, the hair on her nape rose. *Danger!*

A flash of a blade and she rolled, hearing the thud of the knife into the mattress. Adrenaline surged through her, she kicked out, yelled.

A heavy fetid-breathed man crashed down on her. She struggled, freed a hand to rake his cheek. He flinched, but made no sound, his hands went to the sides of her head.

To twist, snap her neck and kill her.

Waves of *wrongness,* of fury, of madness, rolled over her from him. She struggled for breath to scream. Set her nails in his bleeding cheek to claw again.

Then she was free. More than one set of hands clamped around him and flung him away from her.

"Mutant," he screamed. "Alien *thing!* You deserve to die. You *all* must—"

Solid sounds of flesh meeting flesh and quiet.

Bri was at Raine's side, crooning, expert medica hands checking her. Raine sucked in a hard breath as pain speared when Bri pressed a rib too hard. Finally, Raine could breathe again, short, choppy breaths, but air. She tried a smile, found that her cheek hurt and her lip was split. Wetness that wasn't sea spray dribbled down her chin. "Haven't we done this already?"

"Sshhh," Bri said, soothing. "Let me care for you."

Raine didn't dare close her eyes. She felt the heat of Bri's healing hands. Must have broken bones, then. Her cheek, maybe, her rib. Her arm hurt, too...so she concentrated on the little drama going on down the deck.

"How did he get on the Ship?" Faucon spit out. Anger radiated from him, being matched by Bastien and Sevair. Faucon glanced at Raine's attacker, then came to her, settled beside her so he could hold her in his arms.

Bri cast him a glance of approval, but a whimper escaped Raine as she was shifted.

"How did he get on the Ship?" Bastien repeated.

Jean stood straight, but his voice was as cool as the brine at the depths of the sea. "He passed the trials with flying colors, same as everyone else. I saw no sign of that hatred reaction at any time. He masked it well." Ire spiked Jean's personal Song.

"He'll be punished," Alexa said. "You," she said. Raine got the idea that she nudged the man with her toe. He was conscious then, not as hurt as Raine was. Anger spurted through her. Faucon kissed her forehead.

"You piece of shit, you'll be punished." Alexa's voice went silky. "Where there's one, there might be more. Covering for you as you hurt us, eh?" She chuckled and it wasn't pleasant. "We'll make you talk. By the time you're finished you'll sing us a pretty Song about this business."

"You can't," Raine's attacker said.

"Think not?" Marian said. "We have the Power of all the elements. Power such as you have never known. We have the feycoocus, also strange and disturbing to folk like you. We have," her voice lowered, "the roc."

Bri smiled as her hand circled Raine's wrist, sent heat there. Raine gritted her teeth against the pain.

There was a whisk of feathers and a short, melodious but threatening whistle. *I like men guts,* said the roc as it landed, forcing others to move aside as it took up much of the deck.

Raine distantly noted a splash as if someone went into the sea. Good riddance.

"Another's gone," Bastien said.

"The water is cold here," Jean commented. "He may not make it to shore, or once there, die of hypothermia."

"We can only hope." Alexa fingered her baton.

"The volarans won't help him. They won't attack, but they won't help," Calli said.

"Not even volarans accept what these mutineers have done," Alexa's voice rang out. "Their names will be noted for all time as betrayers, creatures of the Dark."

Raine's attacker thrashed. "Ttho! We are *more* loyal to Lladrana than you. More! We do not incite the Dark to kill us all!"

Alexa squatted next to him. "Tell us everything."

He hesitated.

The roc clicked her beak in what sounded like anticipatory smacking for food.

Words rushed from him.

The Echo, *Strait to Doom*

The attack on Raine had slowed their pace. They'd stopped at the mouth of the strait while she slept and healed, and they'd sent her attacker to shore with a few supplies.

Midmorning when she awoke there was a council of war. All the Exotiques and their men crowded into the main cabin. It was a well-run meeting, and Alexa had the names of the two men who'd left, and Luthan had checked each and every person for any innate revulsion. There was one female medica who had had it, but like Luthan, had overcome it. So she stayed.

The general consideration was that there were no more betrayers on the Ship and that they'd lost two good sailors who would have been with the invasion force. That was the outer conclusion. From the glances Raine got, everyone was worried about how it would affect her.

So, to lighten the mood—her own as well as others—Raine revealed her secret.

With a smile she raised her arms, and Sang.

The Echo disappeared.

Not really.

She was a twenty-first-century woman and had worked on many metal-hulled ships. She hadn't stopped learning once she came to Lladrana, had studied Koz's mirrors.

The Ship was nothing but reflective surfaces. The sails the same, thin mirrored fabric.

So the people in colorful Lladranan clothes were shown in

an eternity of images, but the Ship itself—masts, hull, even ropes—seemed to have vanished.

And as she Sang that spell, as all the others wondered at her skill, *The Echo* silently pushed through the Dark's shield.

Raine and Jikata and the Ship were not totally of Lladrana.

Then she simply concentrated on sailing. In itself, the Strait to Doom wasn't difficult to navigate. It was narrow and twisted and turned between great cliffs, and when sailors Sang, or Raine and the other women practiced, the reverberation was incredible. They went through it fast, the wind from the south-west filling the sails. Lladrana was left far behind as they sped toward the Dark's Nest.

The last full day before the invasion was a short one. Circlets gathered in a group listening to the Dark and the Master through the spy eye, making sure the Ship went unnoticed. A pall of silence fell on the Ship and people spoke in whispers and orders became telepathic instead of shouted out with cheer. The "fun" part of the adventure, the forging of new companionship and community, was done.

The "hard" part of the adventure, the fighting and dying, was about to begin.

Tomorrow.

Though Raine thought some fighters were looking forward to it, like Koz, to her surprise. They were checking their weapons for the umpteenth time, planning on going out in a blaze of glory. The Chevalier Representative to the Marshalls, Lady Hallard, and her Master of Volarans were like that.

Raine wanted to stay on the Ship and feel the swell of the ocean under her feet, Faucon's arms wrapped around her from behind and sail away beyond the horizon and forget war.

Trouble was, the outcome of this war, this battle, affected every living thing on Amee, and the planet herself. Not something that could ever be forgotten.

Night fell and Jikata sensed an outrush of relief from everyone.

"Of course the Dark or the Master or the horrors can still sense us and attack at night," Alexa said quietly.

"But they attack fifty percent less at night than during the day," Marian pointed out. "We've studied the horrors and their eyes aren't that good."

"Now we move the Ship to within striking distance," Raine said.

She'd Captained the Ship so efficiently that it amazed Jikata, not even the toughest sailor, or her brilliant second-in-command, hesitated when she gave an order.

Probably because Raine listened to the ocean all the time, her head slightly tilted. She heard tones and undertones and low notes that no one else did. Jikata and the others knew that. When they'd linked to practice Songs, they could sense what she heard clearly. She'd bring the might and force and Power of Amee's oceans, waters that *surrounded* the island to the City Destroyer spell. A huge benefit.

With little noise, everyone moved to their accustomed duties and the Ship was under full Power—both magic and wind. The sails caught the wind and bellied out, full. Sailors spared a glance at each other, a look Jikata now understood. The wind was being unusually accommodating on this trip. Having a planet on your side in a fight was a good thing.

Too bad it couldn't get rid of the Dark itself. But the huge, evil alien being had insinuated itself into the volcano, latched onto Amee's life force before she'd known it.

Marian eyed the sails of reflective fabric with a critical eye, nodded, held out one hand for her bondmate, Jaquar, and the other for her brother, Koz, the mirror magician. She turned and gazed at Jikata with an encouraging smile and Jikata felt her stomach dip with more than the smooth ocean roll.

On a breath, she set her expression in the one she used just before performances and stepped into the circle as everyone except the working sailors did. They were going to shroud the Ship in illusion and move it as close to the island as they could with the Power they had tonight, and bring energy to keep it cloaked all night.

She waited until everyone linked hands and looked to her, then set the first note high, only three voices followed her to that sound. Then she scaled down and people joined as they came within their range. When she'd gathered all the voices, held them on a sustained note in a mighty chorus, she met each person's eyes and began the spell chant.

It was different than Singing with the Friends, or a small group, or even her experience with all these people before. The Song cycled around, and each time a tiny bit of the energy stayed with her. She understood with a shock that these people were not only Powering the illusion spell, but they were also each giving her their magic—and their blessing, their confidence—for the terrible spell she would Sing tomorrow.

Emotion flowed through her as well, the predominant one was of determination, but there was affection, caring, love. Even a trace of passion from Luthan, who stood on her right.

She'd never felt so connected with friends, humanity, the universe itself.

A sphere of shadow, blacker than the night, rose as a bubble in the center of the circle, lifted to the tip of the highest mast, and draped itself over it like the folds of a huge cloth. Stars blinked out as it settled over the Ship, flowed over the sides and brushed the waves, ended a few inches into the water. Inside the "tent" sounds were hushed, the vague outlines of the island and the far shores were blurred into barely seen smudges against the night.

Jikata could only hope that the Ship had become one with the night, too.

43

The Echo, *offshore the Dark's Nest*

Jikata ended the spell and people folded onto the deck. Though she might feel energized, she knew the others had used much to move the Ship and cloak it. She let her own legs loosen and take her onto the planking.

Sailors brought sleeping bags up from below, for everyone, Jikata noticed. They'd all bunk here for the night, not separated by any distinctions of Power, or rank, or status or whether they were sailor or Exotique. A community.

No one wanted to forgo the fellowship before battle? That spoke of deep connections. Connections that Jikata dimly remembered from her parents. They hadn't been a demonstrative family, but Jikata had loved her mother and father, known she'd been loved in return.

She *listened* to the background music, the soundtrack, and could not tell sailor from townsman from Friend.

No matter how many survived, and Jikata *knew* some of each segment of Lladranan society would survive, they would take that sense of community back to their lives and spread that feeling of community to others. Whether the Dark was destroyed or not, Lladrana had come together, and she had had a part in that great undertaking. Something to be proud of, and a good thought to fall asleep on as she snuggled into Luthan's double bag and smelled the scent of the sea and her lover...and utter determination.

Alexa was the first one to stir in the chilly dawn. Since she'd been softly snoring every time Raine jolted out of sleep, Raine figured the Marshall had slept through the night. Must be nice.

Raine had a terrible feeling about this day, her insides were gnawed by fear and cowardice, and she wondered again if she would be able to stay the course, if she'd drop out at the last minute, her fear too huge to bear. No one would blame her for it, and the spell might be all right without her. They'd practiced with people gone, all the way to only three—and different trios—all with Jikata. Just in case.

Discreetly she stretched. She should have gotten more sleep, she *knew* it, but that was easier said than done and she was taut as a rigging cable under full sail. Nerves. They'd probably last all day and get her through...*whatever* she had to face.

Steadying her breathing, she didn't move, just scanned the heaps around her. There was a gray veil between her and the sky that she blinked to penetrate, then realized it was the cloaking spell. Closing her eyes, she listened to the currents of the ocean against the shore, the eddies of water across shoals. From her last glimpse of land the night before, they were very close to the island, no more than a few hundred yards, closer than any had anticipated. A good omen. Since she was waking on a creaking deck instead of in heaven or hell, they must have been overlooked by the Dark, the Master and all the horrors.

The feycoocus as birds were perched on the railing, staring at the island that they could see, muttering among themselves.

Sevair rose and started the tai chi exercises that Jikata had taught them. He and Luthan seemed to like them the most—Earth element people. Of course Alexa was too impatient for them, would rush the movements and preferred other exercise. Raine had seen her dance.

For herself, Raine sought the long, low, tones of the depths of the ocean and it soothed her.

She turned her head and looked at Faucon's aristocratic profile, the handsome lines of his face. He was the reason she'd never back out. He wouldn't. He'd go on and fight. It would be terrible if he fell and she didn't. She knew he felt the same about her, and would actually prefer her to live without him.

He opened his eyes and she jolted.

Touching her face with his warm hand, he said. "Anxieties are always worse just before the battle."

"I'm not going to stay on the Ship."

His eyes softened. "Of course you won't."

"You knew that."

His smile was the sweetest she'd ever seen. "Of course. You love the rest of the Exotiques. You'd never leave them to meet their fate alone." He paused. "As they, and I, and any of their men would never desert *any* of them."

She searched his face. Her fear now had a thin lid of resolve, keeping it from shooting into full-fledged panic. She could do that now. The months at the Open Mouthed Fish had taught her that. If she'd had to face this battle, this man, before, she didn't think she would have been able to control her fear. Not that she was grateful for the experience, or cherished it or anything. She still wished she'd learned whatever lessons she'd needed to in a gentler way. That was probably impossible, but so it was.

She rolled close to him, hung onto him, buried her face in his chest and smelled the man, the wonderful lover she had, through his shirt. He'd discard that, take a quick dip in the ocean before changing into new linens and dreeth skin leathers that would mask his scent from her. "If only I *knew*," she whispered. "I think I could face the known better than this awful unknown."

His arms clamped hard around her, brought her into his body and rubbed his chin on her hair, brought his mouth to her ear. "I asked Luthan." His words were barely breath. She wondered that he spoke aloud then realized she needed to hear it formed into words, would oddly question it less than if telepathically spoken. "Luthan said that the future was still too changeable to *know* which of us would live or die or survive broken."

Raine stifled a gasp. She hadn't thought of the last alternative. It was always live or die.

Faucon put his hand under her chin, tilted her head so her eyes met his flinty gaze. "I think I would rather die, too, than live broken, remember that."

Raine shuddered.

"What, you think one of us is going to take a sword and finish you off if you're flopping around like a fish?" Alexa said harshly and both Raine and Faucon flinched.

The small Marshall was standing, hands on hips, her gaze equally hard. "Think again, dude. We'd want you in our lives despite anything."

Smoothly rising to his feet, Faucon pulled Raine to hers, made a bow to Alexa, smiling, and it was almost carefree. "I am delighted to hear that, Alexa." He kept an arm around Raine's waist, looked at Bastien, who was irritably flinging away covers and grunting, hair in his eyes. "But that opinion is about a year and a half too late."

"Raine fits you better than I ever would anyway," Alexa said with a sniff, then walked over and yanked Bastien to his feet. The two Marshalls scowled at each other, then kissed so deeply Raine turned away.

"They know," she murmured. "At least they know that if one of them dies, the other will not survive alone. Faucon—"

"Ttho." He framed her face in his hands, kept his eyes matched with hers. "If I fall, I want you to *live*. As magnificently as you can." He cleared his throat. "I've left everything except Creusse Landing to you."

Raine opened her mouth. He put a hand over it. "Please, this is what I need to do."

She huffed out a little breath.

He scanned the stirring company, bent close and whispered in her ear, again with just the slightest sound. "I overheard Luthan and Jikata once. Calli will survive, and since he's bound to her, so will Marrec, with few injuries."

It wasn't her own good future, but somehow it eased Raine. Two would survive, the two with children. Her muscles relaxed infinitesimally. She leaned against Faucon, muttered into his chest, "Does she know?"

"Ttho, neither she nor Marrec. Jikata said they should not be told. They might become too reckless and change the way events should unfold. That would be disastrous."

"Huh." Raine frowned. What would she do if she knew she'd live? She looked into Faucon's brown eyes, at the other women. She'd try and save whomever she could. But she didn't accept that they would all perish. She *didn't*.

And they wouldn't. Calli and Marrec would survive.

Taking a deep breath, she let it go slowly, listened to Chasonette warble at the sun's rising.

Enerin came and settled on Raine's shoulder, Sang Jikata's morning Song. *It is a good day to live.* She rubbed her soft bird feathers against Raine's cheek and Raine felt the love. "Ayes, a good day to live."

With a smooth move, Sevair scooped up two hammers, one large and one small, and moved from meditation pattern into fighting pattern. His hammers whistled through the air, deadly as blades.

Then it was full light and people were coalescing into battle groups.

Raine strode to a muttering sailor who had to stay behind and man *The Echo*.

"Line up!" she barked to her crew in a tone she hadn't used before and that she hoped worked.

They fell into ranks she didn't quite understand—according to their duties on the Ship, their previous career, their birth status. No changing that at this late date.

"Those who tested for battle and are with the invasion force to the right." She gestured. More moved there than were supposed to.

Raine studied the sullen faces of those remaining, including

Jean and Madam Lucienne. "You were chosen for the skeleton crew." She turned her head, speared her gaze at several to the right who also had been chosen. They shuffled their feet but didn't move back to the lines.

Quiet crept over the Ship as everyone watched. Raine's neck heated. There were at least ten better leaders on this boat than she. But she was Captain and it was the seamen that she had to order.

She looked at the discontented expressions of the men and women who would sail the Ship to a deep harbor safe from an explosion and tidal wave.

Slowly she shook her head. "Don't you all know that you have the most necessary job of everyone here?"

The quiet became intense, not a cough, not a whispered aside, everyone riveted on her. Her throat tightened and she went on. "You will save the survivors."

She let that sink in. "We may be wounded, in need of rescue. Who will save us except those who stayed behind? How will we get home?" Home. Faucon's Castle. Lladrana was home now and how fiercely she loved it!

"Who will take the helpless from the shores or the sea? Who will heal us and tend us and return us to our lives if not you?"

People began to walk back to the ranks of the crew before Raine, those who now stood tall with sternly determined expressions.

"It will take enormous skill and Power to return fast to pick us up before we die, especially if we are in the cold sea." She glanced at the deck where the volarans stared at her. They understood better. She actually thought her own feelings were closer to theirs than any of the humans. "The volarans cannot help everyone." Many of them wouldn't survive or would be hurt, too. That caused an ache in her heart. "All our hope for our futures depend upon you." She cleared her throat, looked to the group to the right. "Who will stay to save us?"

With lowered gazes people moved from the group at her right back to the proud lines.

Jean lifted his head, the silver streaks of Power had widened. "We will Power the rescue Ship."

Raine inclined her head. *"Merci."*

Then her knees began to tremble and she went down to the cabin to change.

When she returned to the deck a few minutes later, Alexa coughed, wrapped her arms around Raine. "Good job." A shuddering breath came from her. "I only hope I can do as well with my St. Crispin's Day speech."

"What?"

"You know, 'rally to the cause,' 'go, team, go!'"

Raine hadn't thought of that, but she supposed that inside she'd anticipated such a speech, and from Alexa. The smaller woman stepped back, and though her face was calm, her eyes were a little wild. "I've made them before. I haven't worked so hard on a piece of writing since my law journal days. Marian's been helping. This speech has to be perfect."

"No," Raine said, and touched Alexa's breastbone. "It only needs to come from your heart, and you have plenty of heart."

Alexa blinked. "Thanks." She inhaled. "Well, you showed me how it's really done." With a nod she walked away.

Raine watched her in wonder. *She* had given advice to *Alexa.* And Alexa hadn't seemed to think that was unusual or strange.

Raine was one of them. She'd known that, known they had accepted her as one of them since the moment they'd learned of her existence. Had always treated her as an equal, a person with her own skill set. But *she,* herself, hadn't truly accepted that she was equal to them. She hadn't been Summoned by the Marshalls in a proper ceremony, hadn't been welcomed, hadn't immediately meshed with the portion of Lladranan society that she'd been sent to integrate into a whole, wasn't from Colorado like the rest of them. Something tight inside her hadn't accepted that she was equal, now that loosened and she knew. She *would* hold up her part in this undertaking, would provide her own unique Song when they did that dreadful spell.

Faucon was there before her, bowing deep, lifting her hand to his lips, eyes warm. "Well done, beloved."

She wanted to fling herself into his arms. Instead she smiled at him, feeling a little light-headed, and said, "Thanks."

And the morning progressed, quietly, efficiently.

Intensely.

Calli stepped to the middle of the deck and once again everyone quieted.

"I have a secret to reveal. Something that will reduce our casualties." She gestured to her volaran and the winged horse trotted forward.

Then, as they watched, it disappeared.

"This is a volaran's ultimate defense," Calli said. "They can, and will, carry us to the shores invisibly. They can even fight so, but it takes enormous Power. Use it well."

Calli turned to Alexa, whose expression was floored surprise. Calli smiled sweetly. "Your turn, Alexa." Calli settled herself, ready to listen.

Alexa cleared her throat. "Ayes. Well." Then she glanced at the tall black mountain in the distance and her face hardened. She lifted her chin, set her hand on her jade baton. Then she cut the top of the sheath away.

A shiver went up Raine's spine. No action could have been clearer that Alexa meant to fight, with all she had, all she was. To the end, using all the Power she could from the Jade Baton of Honor that she'd won.

Her speech was wonderful. She started out slow and low, so people had to strain to hear, then the cadence picked up and so did her volume until she was shouting and punching the air and everyone else was cheering.

Then Raine went up to Jean and handed him the small guidance gems...a formal turning over of the Captaincy. He glanced at the island and his jaw clenched, then he gazed down at her, most of his usual optimism gone in savvy awareness.

She said, "I need you here. Sail to where it's safe and...when it's all over...come back and pick up the survivors."

He nodded shortly, bowed in a sharp, military fashion. "I won't fail."

"Of course not." Standing on tiptoe, she kissed his cheek. "You are an excellent Captain, I'm glad you're with us."

He ducked his head. "Thank you." Then he mentally yelled, *Come about,* and the Ship turned to present her broadside to the island, better for the volarans to take off in waves.

The battle was beginning.

44

Alexa shifted nervously from foot to foot while Calli double-checked all the volarans' tack and mental states.

Then Alexa blew out a breath. "Since the volarans have that nifty little trick of invisibility, we should go with the first wave."

They all looked at her.

"We're pretty sure the dreeths will come from the top of the mountain."

"Ayes," Jaquar said. "All the reports indicate that."

"They don't know it's going to be today." Alexa showed her teeth. "No one would expect a force of this size to make it in under a month, let alone under the three weeks of the exploratory team. They weren't aware of us then, either." She gestured to the Ship, which a volaran had stated "did not look there," when it flew to the southern shore for that purpose.

Alexa shifted her shoulders. "If the Master and Dark fall,

the horrors will not be directed. Those in Lladrana can find them, clean them up. Hold the line, build a new border. The sooner we get in and do the spell, the less loss of life."

"So we go with the first wave." Bastien nodded.

Raine gestured to Madam Lucienne, who came over. "You've been watching Bastien as he counts down the waves of our army?"

"Ayes," the woman said.

"We're going first," Alexa said. She sent a glance around their little circle but no one protested.

Madam rubbed her hands, "Good idea." She nodded to Bastien. "I'll count down and release the teams as practiced."

Bastien took her hand and kissed her fingers. *"Merci."*

She nodded, went to her post, squared her shoulders.

Calli said, "Ready?"

They all replied, "Ready."

Raine grabbed Faucon and kissed him hard. "I love you." Then she set the earbuds in her ears and turned up the volume. Once they were committed, she'd be all right.

She hoped. The beat of the volume was the same as her portion of the Song and she muttered it in her head.

"Mount!" Bastien barked.

They did, and she felt better on Blossom, even stronger when Enerin sat on her shoulder, dug in her little war hawk claws.

Communication by mind, Exotique link only from now on, Bastien ordered.

They nodded.

Got the gong?

Calli and Marrec, Marian and Jaquar held up the soon-to-be invisible ropes.

Bastien looked at Alexa.

She nodded.

Here we go! she ordered and they all rose together, and when they were at the top of the mast everyone winked out around Raine.

She set her teeth and didn't look down as she trusted to Blossom that they all moved together. It felt as if she were a disembodied spirit floating toward the island. The speed of the volarans was significantly slower when they were invisible. She could feel the draining of Blossom's and her own Power. She wished she'd known about this sooner, so she could have prepared herself. This was good for the volarans, this was excellent, but the time it took to cover the distance aggravated her nerves.

They were nearing the shore when she heard Madam Lucienne's mental shout of *First wave, go!*

Wings whirred beneath the Exotiques as the other volarans flew toward the island with their burdens of sailors, Chevaliers, the Marshall team, two medicas, Bossgond and another Circlet. As they hit the beach, their invisibility disappeared and they engaged the horrors milling around the mountain.

They gave war cries and Sang Jikata's battle Song.

Noise from the battle rose and Raine looked down.

Ella was the first to die.

Ledge outside the Dark's Nest

Raine and Blossom bobbled the ledge landing, had to withdraw.

Steady, Raine—Alexa's voice was sharp.

Raine pressed her lips together, separated her grief from the rest of her mind, reassured Blossom. Definitely not the time for a volaran to panic. Blossom and she approached the ledge to land again, settled on all fours this time.

The women had all dismounted and were visible in their dark dreeth hide. The men were lined up—the seven-man bobsled team of Koz, Bastien, Luthan, Marrec, Faucon, Jaquar and Sevair—and their sled looked sturdy and efficient.

Raine ignored the tears running down her face, at least her eyes weren't continuing to well and blind her, and slid from Blossom. For one last moment of normality, she buried her face in Blossom's neck and drank in her scent and hugged her tight.

See you later, Blossom said.

One last squeeze, then Raine stepped away, lifted her chin, straightened her shoulders. *Fly safe to the Ship.*

I will.

Blossom lifted her wings, Raine could see the hazy outline of them and touched Blossom again, sending her a little more energy until they faded. *Go.*

With an almost silent whir of wings, the volarans were gone. Marian and Calli were holding the saucer on the ledge, a third of it was protruding over space. Raine gulped, went over and took her place in the lineup. Alexa and Bri would be at the front, Raine and Jikata in the middle, Marian and Calli in the back. At least that's how it was supposed to work. Raine prayed they wouldn't *go* spinning around. Going one direction—down a steep slope, and there *was* snow—was enough.

Ready? Alexa's eyes were compassionate and a little haunted. She, too, would lose friends today, had lost friends for the two years.

Anger spurted through Raine. Ella should have lived a long and full life. *I want this DONE.*

So do we all, said Calli, inclining her head.

Air spell initiated, Marian said, and the front of the saucer rose, steadied, as if it sat fully on the ledge.

Alexa and Bri climbed on, curled their hands in the thick woven edge that had been placed around the gong's rim.

Raine met Jikata's eyes and they settled in, legs stretched around Bri and Alexa. Raine felt the gong-saucer rock a little as Marian and Calli got on. Soon Marian's legs were snug around Raine's hips and the buzz of the Exotiques all in physical contact comforted her.

On, "go," Alexa said.

There was a little peck on Raine's cheek and she saw Enerin hovering near.

Sinafinal, Tuckerinal and I will be with you until it is time to take the gong, Enerin said.

Merci.

Alexa sucked in a breath, but shouted mentally, *Ready, set, go!*

Marian released the spell holding the front of the sled. They dropped and were off.

They zoomed down the mountain.

Rock on the left! Alexa yelled to Bri, who was steering.

I see it, I see it. Lean right, Bri shouted back

Raine leaned right.

Path is to the left, Marian reminded coolly.

Course, Raine corrected, recalled she was supposed to be projecting it to everyone's mind. Enerin gave her an overview, she picked out their position and set it on a green line.

Doing well! Alexa gave a shriek of wild laughter.

Raine opened her mouth and some snow flew into it and tears ran down her face, thrills from the ride and the others' excitement, sadness from Ella's death and the sound of distant battle. That was as close to laughter that she could get.

The men ranged themselves on the bobsled silently. Koz would drive, Jaquar would keep the course and help with air or weather magic, and the rest of them would give ballast and Power.

Faucon wanted to be with Raine. Whose idea was it to separate the men and the women?

Amee's.

Female planet. One of the men, Luthan, should have spoken to her.

Everyone on? Koz asked. He sat in the front of the sled that hung in midair, anticipation gleamed in his eyes. He was looking forward to this battle, having been forbidden Chevalier status by the medicas due to a head injury.

Bastien slid in behind him, slightly shorter than the other men, but he'd never driven a sled, and Faucon wasn't going to trust his life to Bastien's wild magic.

Luthan came next since they all figured it would be best if the brothers were together. Marrec took his seat, Faucon followed, and Sevair, the one with the most sheer muscle, stood ready to jump in after he shoved off.

Set? asked Sevair calmly, though there was an undercurrent in his Song that the men shared, they wanted to be close to their women.

Go when you're ready, Jaquar said. An image of the course came to Faucon's mind with the sled motionless and poised.

The sled surged forward and Faucon caught his breath as

they were airborne, then hit the ground and bounced twice then shot down the mountain. This was nothing like a volaran ride. He began to pray.

Outside, down the mountain of the Dark's Nest

Jikata Sang, her voice quavery. Better get over that, soon.

Since the wind whipped the sound of her words away, she didn't think she was alerting any of the dreeths that appeared in view.

Marian had inserted a cushion of air between the gong and the rock or snow and that made the ride smoother, faster than Jikata'd anticipated, more dangerous.

They were going too fast for the dreeths to catch them, weren't they?

So Jikata Sang out her fear, little limbering exercises before stepping onto a stage, some Song she knew from her childhood, but couldn't put a name to in her fear.

Hearts thumping fast and in unison, they leaned to the left or shifted to the right. Hit a bump and went flying, landed with a skiff of snow, gliding long and smooth.

Lava tube ahead, Marian said with tension in her voice. *Leave the saucer guidance to me. I'll be using Air Power.*

"Yeah!" Alexa yelled.

Jikata averted her face so as not to see the dreeths shrieking above them, circling, trying to get a bead on them. She brought up an image of all she loved, Luthan, these women who'd welcomed and helped her, Ishi, her parents...

Then they were slowing, circling a hole into the mountain.

Slowing! A dreeth cried and swooped.

A huge bird attacked it. Bri's roc companion.

The hole swallowed them. Jikata's heart jumped again, her stomach tightened.

Showtime.

They plunged into the Dark and the odor was foul. The mountain itself seemed to grumble at being a lair for the Dark, the Master, the horrors. Plummeting down an old tunnel made by lava, Jikata *felt* the Dark. Knew the others did, too. More, she heard its life force. Not a Song at all, something more like a huge, inimical hissing, low continuous thrumming of hatred for all life. Stirring…waking? It touched all of them in dreams more than awake because it was asleep and torpid? A terrible thought that they hadn't known this, hadn't experienced the full might of its waking power.

Luthan hung onto his brother, who was coping with this part of the action so much better than he.

Jaquar was skimming Power from all of them to push the sled along, gain on the ladies in the saucer ahead.

Women flying down a mountainside on a gong.

Inconceivable, except that it was happening.

Luthan's entire life had changed the moment one Exotique came and did inconceivable things.

Coming to the hole. Hang on tight, I'll have to raise and angle the sled, Jaquar said.

Luthan knew he'd hate that more.

Then it was happening with a terrible wrenching in his gut and they disappeared into darkness and the familiar sound of battle was lost and he was lost.

Until he heard the purity of Jikata's Song.

He opened his eyes and saw a sliver of red light ahead, the

large upper cavern. And the glint of the saucer-gong. Close, so close. They could protect the women.

Especially since he heard the sound of the Dark awakening.

They shot through the opening to the large chamber, saw Alexa pointing and shouting, "*There!* Across, across, across. Fly this thing, guys!" The saucer, the gong, stayed up even as Luthan felt their own sled lose momentum in the middle of the air, angle toward the bottom of the cavern.

Lift! Bastien commanded, but they were unused to flying on a sled instead of volarans. Luthan raised his voice in a flying spell, Sevair Sang a spell for lifting massive blocks.

The women glided through the room, spinning, laughing nervously, then went into the passage and vanished.

The sled began to tumble.

Stop! Jaquar commanded.

Luthan snapped his mouth shut. So did the other men. The sound of their clashing notes echoed and died.

I am a weather mage. Jaquar's mental tone was acid. *A Circlet of Air. You will leave this task to me.*

Everyone quieted. The sled righted itself, spun slowly as if in a slight wind. Settled onto a course toward the opening the women and the gong had disappeared into.

Then a dreeth shot into the cavern from another entrance, followed by masses of horrors from several other holes. Some monsters fell to their deaths, screaming. The cavern was filled with awful noise again.

Singing Chamber inside the Dark's Nest

Jikata gasped as the gong shot into the lower chamber, tilted and left them falling. With Song and swears, Marian slowed their descent. It was a short drop, no more than twelve feet, but at the rate they'd been going…

The feycoocus swooped down and took the gong away, darting back into the tube. The chamber *was* like the Cavern of Prophecy with crystals on all the walls and the domed ceiling, in the same colorful patterns.

Jikata lurched from her feet as the mountain began to roll and buck under them, *reached* for all that connected her to Amee. Couldn't find it here. Not like the Cavern she knew at all.

The volcano had been too shadowed in the Dark for too long.

All the others looked terrified. "We don't have a good connection to the planet," Marian said, her voice high and shaky, her face pale. "I hadn't thought of that. We can't—"

"Stop it! *No negativity!* We *will* do this," Alexa yelled, crawled over the ground to the lower left point of a pentagram etched in the stone. Alexa was the first Summoned, the warrior, she might have a better link to the planet.

Alexa found her place, sat, glared at them all and Jikata felt her huge determination. It buoyed her, steadied her.

"If we can't stand, we will sit. If we can't sit, we will lie down. We *will* do this," Alexa shouted.

A rock hit her in the head, clanging on her helmet. Alexa groaned, shook her head.

Jikata crawled to the middle of the pentacle and prepared to give the performance of her life.

45

Upper Cavern inside the Dark's Nest

The mountain rumbled, tossed the sled about, Jaquar steadied it.

Then the Master appeared, raised twisted arms, deformed hands and *grasped*. "We rule here, no fresh air here, no air that obeys anyone other than me. Fetid air, blow them down to die!"

He yanked his arms and the sled fell into the crowd of horrors.

More monsters died.

They jumped free, Luthan and Bastien and Faucon on one side, Sevair, Marrec, Jaquar and Koz on the other. Luthan and Faucon pulled swords, lifted their shields, fought. Bastien drew a sword and his Marshalls' baton and cut a swath as creatures flung themselves away from the bright, searing energy of it, fueled by his wild Power.

"Jaquar, look for the right opening, figure out a way to get us there," Sevair, the Townmaster, ordered. His grin was fierce. "Leave the Master to me."

There was a human cry and Luthan saw Koz pressing a hand against his throat where blood welled.

Jaquar shouted words and Koz was lifted to the hole in the middle of the wall, shoved down the chute to the lower cavern.

Luthan went after the sled.

The Master began to chant a spell to Summon all the horrors in the nest to here. Sevair hesitated, then broke away, fought through monsters toward the man who had betrayed him.

Singing Chamber inside the Dark's Nest

Following Alexa's example, they took their positions. Raine gritted her teeth and tried to pretend the shaking beneath her feet was a wooden deck, not stone.

It didn't work.

She took her mark at the tip of the western point of the star. Calli was opposite her, Marian was in the lower right point, Bri at the top, the north. Alexa was in the lower left point and Jikata was in the middle.

The earth tremors stopped and they all stood.

Raine began her breathing exercises, thumbed off the music player, removed the earbuds, flinched when she heard noise of fighting, of cries from monsters and men—their men— from the cavern above. She just wanted things to *happen*. All the nerves of her skin felt exposed, raw.

Marian had given Jikata the weapon knot and it lay at her feet, throbbing to a beat that seemed to match Raine's heart.

Jikata hummed middle C and everyone stilled.

"After the Blessing and opening chorus finish, the City

Destroyer spell is initiated, the knot starts to untie." They'd practiced with other knots so Raine was sure seeing thread wriggle wouldn't panic her. "After the first, basic knot is untied, the spell can't be stopped. The minute one of us moves from our mark the explosion will occur. We want that to be *after* our men are here and the final protective shield is Sung."

"Yeah, yeah," Alexa muttered, tilting her head as if listening more to what was going on in the upper cavern or outside the mountain.

"The sequence, Alexa," Jikata commanded.

Alexa said, "Blessing. First chorus. Calli Sings, Marian Sings, Bri Sings, I Sing, Raine Sings, you Sing. Each of us untying one of the main knots of the whole thing." She stared at the complex knot.

To Raine, it looked like it was growing and pulsing faster, redder. She shivered. Shouldn't she be hot? But she was cold, from the inside out.

Alexa continued, "The guys show up during the ritual. Before the last verse we do a mental broadcast for everyone to get the hell off the island and back to the Ship. Then the last verse with all of us to undo the thread, encase us in a shield bubble to protect us, then *boom*." She jerked her hands apart. "The mountain explodes, killing the Dark. We either remain safe here or go flying. Marian and Jaquar take care of us with their Power if we go flying." Alexa grimaced. "Too bad we couldn't practice that part."

"Too draining," Marian said.

"Yeah, yeah," Alexa repeated. "The Ship comes and picks us up." She pulled out her baton and waved it around, the flames on the end ignited. "Happily-ever-after ending."

"Exactly," Jikata said. She Sang scales, and they all followed, listening to the sound echo off the dome around them.

"Ah!" Alexa shuddered, put a hand over her heart, stood straight, looked at Calli, who was trembling, too. "Lost a pair of Marshalls and a pair of Chevaliers." She glanced at Raine. "One of Faucon's."

Raine should have known—she cast her mind to Faucon. Fighting, uninjured. She'd been too damn preoccupied with herself.

Alexa twitched a smile on her face. "Our men are winning." She looked at Jikata. "And we're going to win, too." Alexa's nostrils flared. "Time to kill this thing."

Marian said, "The Dark's aware of us and the gong. Moving in two directions sluggishly, calling for the Master of horrors."

Bri lifted her chin. "Sevair will take the Master out."

Raine didn't know if that was a good thing or a bad thing. Sounded to her like the "things go to shit" part of the invasion plan they'd anticipated had started.

"Focus, and breathe, and *now!*"

They began the Blessing and it was beautiful, six voices rising in a purity of sound, setting the crystals to vibrating around them. Calmness settled over Raine. It had begun. The beginning of the end.

Then Koz fell through the hole in the ceiling, wounded, limp. Ayes, the end.

On the last phrase of the Blessing, Jikata's voice broke, destroying the pattern. She shut her eyes, shuddering. She *must* control her voice, but the Dark inside the mountain hated them and she couldn't feel any link with Amee. Throat hoarse from the nasty air around her, she sent mentally, *We will start again.*

Ayes, Alexa said. Marian and the others echoed.

But they only got through the first verse again when the mountain bucked. Crystals fell, shards flew.

Marian shrieked and held up her left hand. They all stared. Her little finger had been severed. Bri scuttled over. She and Marian looked around. For the lost finger, Jikata realized, and knew if she didn't turn away she'd vomit.

Face white, Marian hissed a word and Jikata saw the flesh of her hand flash red with searing flame. Marian flinched as the wound was cauterized.

Jikata's eyes met Raine's. They shook their heads at the same time. Raine pressed a hand to her side. Jikata hated that. It reminded Jikata of Amee with the leech, the planet she couldn't reach, and without that connection they might all fail.

Dying was bad.

Failing was worse.

Evil cackled, an ominous smoke filled the small room. The Dark knew they were there, knew what they were trying to do. Sent a wave of triumph at them—*You cannot.* The words sliced at Jikata's mind like frozen razors. *Amee can't reach you in my domain.*

We must establish a link! Alexa said. With all her Power, Alexa *reached,* drew them all into the fight against the Dark, battled the roiling smoke back, then sent their minds plunging down, down, down, through the mountain, a spearhead, angled around the Dark in its innermost lair. Down into the earth beneath the mountain, first fiery lava, then frozen tundra. They *all* reached, they *all* Sang in their minds for Amee.

They all begged.

They felt a torpid tendril of support, a tiny wisp from Amee, and it refreshed Jikata, the others.

The Dark snapped it.

They wept.

Upper Cavern, inside the Dark's Nest

Luthan fought horrors, heading for the sled.

"I know you, Dapince," Sevair shouted the Master's—the once-man's—name. Names had Power. "You can't finish that spell to bring more horrors here correctly. You always screw up. You were a good assistant—" Sevair shrugged "—but not my best." Another shrug, casual for a man yelling at the top of his lungs. "Not creative. You only know what you're told, don't you?"

"That's a lie!" The Master didn't truly speak, more like gurgled, rasped. And even with those words, his spell dissolved.

His mouth worked, he looked at Sevair, terrified.

Froze.

Long enough that Sevair could throw his hammer to split the Master's head open and smear his brains against a wall.

The mountain shuddered, air clapped against Luthan's ears like thunder.

Some of the horrors dropped, unconscious or dead.

Too many remained.

Luthan carved his way through the horrors, swinging his sword relentlessly. Soulsucker, render, slayer. Behead, thrust, slice. Kill.

Act. Do not think.

Then he was within reach of the sled, droplets of body acid from a slayer burning on his cheek. Stings that meant he was alive. He grabbed the sled's rope, slick with blood of horrors. Turned back to see the other men fighting, shouting, killing.

Grimly hauling the sled back, he was close to the rest of them when the specter of his dead father rose. Dread filled Luthan as he saw the man. Ghost or projection from himself or splinter of the Dark?

It didn't matter. Anger flashed through Luthan. He'd needed his father, dammit! Needed him all his life, a *good* father, not a damned tyrant.

But he'd never needed him as much as he did now, when his woman's life, his brother's, his friends', his own and the fate of Amee all hung in the balance.

A render swiped at Luthan, hit, flinging him back away from the defense and protection of the others. No blood, only bruises—the dreeth skin had held.

"No, you will never be the man I am," his father gloated.

"Prove it," Luthan shouted. He flung up his shield against a flurry of slayer spines that thudded into it. His gaze burned into the cold form that was his father. "All your life you wanted fame, you wanted power, and you used the fight with the Dark to get it. *So fight the Dark!*" Luthan curled his lip, panted to increase the blood flow to his mind, his lungs, his limbs. "Those who fight this battle will be remembered forever. You died before you reached this pinnacle."

His father scowled, slowly turned as if looking around.

We are in the very heart of the Dark's Nest, Luthan said.

Bastien dispatched two soulsuckers.

Both your sons are here, fighting to destroy the Dark. Even your black-and-white wild Power son, Bastien. See how he fights and prevails. Ours are the names that will be recalled. Not yours. You will only be mentioned as our father, if at all.

Too long a speech, but Luthan fought through it, through the monsters to get back to the other men, drag the sled there.

Slowly the revenant looked around, then began to wield a ghostly sword, and horrors died.

Faucon watched Koz disappear, battled, worked toward the place where the others had gathered.

But some horrors had followed Koz, were going down to the women! The ladies, who were concentrating on Singing.

Palms slapped together. Grunting with effort, Faucon sent Power to Jaquar, found himself lifted, too. The sled appeared and they were tossed on it, grabbing onto each other.

And down and away.

Into the lower chamber where the women Sang scales. They hit the ground, picked their targets, fought. He ducked a render's razor claws, swung his sword and cut them off.

Singing Chamber inside the Dark's Nest

"We need a better link with Amee," Marian gasped, cradling her hand missing the finger under her breasts, sending worried looks to her brother, who was lying too still beside her.

"We don't have it." Alexa was grim.

"*We* do." Sevair's voice rang out, and Jikata glanced around, saw only their men standing, dead horrors scattered around.

"We do," Bastien echoed, yanking up Alexa, kissing her, keeping her solid against him, her feet not touching the ground.

Luthan came behind Jikata. "It was always meant to be this way. Lladranans and Exotiques together."

"Men and women?" Marian asked. Jaquar was kissing the place her little finger had been.

"Not necessarily," Jaquar said. "Had you pairbonded with women, this still would have been necessary. Exotiques cannot save a planet, not their own. Not without the commitment of natives. That is wrong."

"I believe you," Marian said on a shaky breath. She blinked and frowned. "I can't hear or feel the Dark."

"It, too, is alien," Sevair said. He held Bri and scowled. "You don't have much Power."

Bri lifted her chin. "Enough to finish this."

Alexa wiggled and Bastien put her down. She turned and set her feet inside his, another wide and steady stance, straightened her shoulders, hefted her baton, glanced back up at her mate. "You didn't save us!"

"We save each other," Luthan said, his breath on Jikata's temple and it was the sweetest thing she'd ever felt. She closed her eyes, cleared her throat.

"We can Sing with you," Luthan continued. "But we do not have the Power or the training to untie the weapon knot. You will save us all."

"We will save each other," Calli said, relaxing into her own silent, reliable mate, Marrec.

"I'll welcome the deep voices," Jikata said.

The mountain rumbled around them, the ground quavered under their feet, and outside she knew Chevaliers and Marshalls and volarans were dying. But now they *could* kill the Dark. Everything in her mind, soul and Song sensed that.

She opened her mouth and Sang the first note, at the lowest of her range.

Then they spiraled upward in the Blessing and she felt a bond with Amee again, given to her by Luthan, to the others by their men. The Blessing ended.

In the pause before the first chorus, more horrors fell through the hole. Luthan left her and the other men ran to face the monsters, fight them.

Jikata couldn't stop the spell, couldn't delay it. She glanced at the women, gathered their gazes, marked time with her hand and they started the first chorus on three.

The men joined in, Singing as they swung their blades and Sevair his hammers.

Pride surged through Jikata, matched by the other Exotiques.

The chorus ended and Calli launched into her solo, then Marian, Bri and Alexa. As the men killed horrors, they kept the Dark at bay.

Faucon whirled as a soulsucker tentacle lashed, probed for bare skin to drain his life. Slashed the tentacle, spun again and choked as he saw a slayer targeting Raine with his poisonous spines. Short distance, straight in the torso, able to penetrate the dreeth skin. He yelled her name, jumped toward her.

46

Raine forced her gaze away from the skirmishes between the men and the horrors, watched the last loop of Alexa's knot wave in the air, tug, and…pull…loose.

"I am from the Seamasters, know oceans' might!" Raine Sang, hitting the timing exactly! Relief and sweat trickled down her spine. These damn dreeth leathers were hot.

All the blue-green crystals in the room, the shades of gray, even black and white, all tints of the sea, glowed. Sound enveloped her, slipped along her skin, sank into her pores, reverberated in every cell. All the sounds of the sea, too. The surf, the lap against a boat, a ship, sloshing and splashing, the depths where sound was simply vibration. Her breathing evened, her voice steadied, her determination firmed. She waded, floated, swam. Sang.

Raine! Faucon's scream brought her from a trance. She turned. Agony lanced through her, took her to her knees.

You must Sing, Jikata yelled.

She must Sing. She rushed to expel a wavering note that she'd missed, bolstered the next. Concentrated on her solo, her Song of the sea, as she stared down at slayer spines in her body. One in her side, another in her hand.

Poison began to sink into her. Bracing, cutting one note a hair short, she ripped the spines out, hissed a breath, inhaled sharply, and let the next note tear from her throat, a low one, more groan than melody.

She *must* finish this solo.

Imperative.

So she thought only of the Song, the phrasing, the breath, the rhythm, all the little component parts that would make a mighty whole, like droplets of water in the ocean. Like raising a Ship. She could do this.

Jikata joined in to harmonize, even out Raine's tones. The Singer was doing well for a "fire" person, but hadn't she said she'd had a house in California? Bri, the other "water," joined, too, and her support—more sound of rushing rivers, trickling streams, rain—helped. Focus.

Sing. The. Notes.

Watch the knot, Marian said, and that was good advice, too.

Raine watched the thread slowly lift, push under another loosened loop. She was doing it, her knot! A knot she should know, a seaman's knot, but she couldn't quite figure it out. Her vision narrowed to the throbbing blood-red string.

Her hand burned clear to her elbow. She couldn't look at it or she might panic. Something gnawed at her side.

Bright flashes came at the edge of her vision, Alexa firing her baton at horrors.

Raine wanted to smile but her face felt a little numb.

That thought brought fear. She must *Sing*. Back to looking at the knot, back to listening to the echoes of the crystals. Pain returned and she ignored it, as she formed each note, strained to Sing them right. This part had a rock-and-roll beat.

Pain came because Bri was linked with her sending her healingstream through their bond, fighting for her.

One last sentence, a repeat of the first.

"Ahm frm th' Seamashters', kno oshuns' might!" She spit out the last word, saw the thread jerk and her knot fall apart.

Jikata's voice filled the room, strong and rich. Raine curled on her spot and let the pain take her, panted the continuing Song. She thought she heard Enerin's soft weeping in the back of her mind. Her vision blurred to turquoise...turquoise? Oh. The blue-green of being under tropical seas. Snorkeling? Scuba diving?

Not diving, dying.

Jikata was amazed that Raine had Sung her part, then Jikata sang hers and they all launched into the second-to-last chorus. Jikata used all her art, skill, technique, Power to bolster Raine's voice, surprised the woman continued the Song. Her hand was swollen to twice its size, red and with pus dribbling from the spine wound. Jikata was in awe that the woman could even hum. But she was doing her part, adding the lilt of the sea to the spell.

You are faltering. The words came to her mind. Not the Dark, but the Singer. Jikata had an image of her, dressed in a heavily silver embroidered sky-blue robe, sitting in the silver chair in the chamber identical to this one in the Caverns of Prophecy. *The songspell wavers.*

Not by much, and not Jikata's part, only Raine's. Jikata added more Power.

I will help. I will save you all.

Too late for that, Jikata was sure. She was also sure that they would do fine without the Singer. But Jikata let her Singing breath out in increments. They would do better with the Singer. And the old woman wasn't asking.

Rich Song added to the room, and Jikata sensed the others' surprise, then the Singer melded into Raine's part. The Singer didn't have Raine's heart, and was of an air element and not water, but she'd had a century of practice. She could match Raine's voice, blend Raine's Power with hers. Incredible.

The spell strengthened.

The accompaniment of ringing metal, human grunts and monster cries stopped.

Jikata blinked, saw all the men but Sevair run to their women, hold them, boosting their Power with battle adrenaline. Luthan's scent and touch behind her was the best thing of the day.

Faucon sat and propped Raine against him. Sweat running down their faces, the men prepared for the pause before the last chorus.

Sevair clashed his hammers together and they sounded remarkably like the gong. Must have been forged to do so. Another secret. The note was sweet, sweet, and Jikata knew it echoed through the mountain and outside.

"The others will withdraw now," Sevair said. He walked to Bri, lifted her into his arms, held her, spread his feet in a solid stance.

Alexa mind-shouted the command, *Return to the Ship!*

Jikata sensed there weren't many warriors left to heed the call, perhaps a quarter of the force. Now and again through the Song, Alexa or Calli had jolted, tears sprang from their eyes and rolled down their faces. Friends lost forever.

Or for just a short time if she and the others failed, and died.

The men stood behind their women, linking to them, providing Power surging with adrenaline and testosterone to boost the energy that carefully unworking the knot had drained.

With Luthan's arms around her, his chest touching her back, his breath in her ear, Jikata hummed one note, and they all, even Raine, started on the right beat.

All went well until the middle and Raine faded. The Singer carried on. Raine was supposed to be amplified for two lines, and Jikata could feel her muzzy mind focus on this one last task thinking of the rhythm of the ocean, could feel Faucon's Song intertwined with hers, helping.

I can Sing these last notes, the Singer said.

They were pure, beautiful. Until the Singer died.

Jikata felt the shock of it, of the old woman's passing, as she had weeks before, when Ishi had died.

Like then, she kept on, steadied herself and the Song as the others realized what had happened, as there seemed to be a void in the world. Until she became the Singer of Lladrana herself.

For a short amount of time.

Sweat poured down Jikata's body, and about three quarters of the way through the last chorus, she knew she might break her voice, strain her vocal cords beyond repair by the time the spell was ended. She got light-headed from the lack of good air, and the others sent her Power so she didn't falter, but her lungs worked like bellows. The other Colorado women were in slightly better shape from living at high altitude, but Raine was keeping her murmur steady at a high price.

They might escape with their lives, but they would be

forever changed. Jikata met Sevair's worried eyes, he glanced down at the top of Bri's head. She, too, was draining herself of her Power, pushing her gift to the limits.

Koz was dying. Raine was severely injured. They might not survive.

Grief poured through Jikata, added timbre to her voice, enriched it. But she couldn't afford clogging tears. She was a professional and this was the greatest Song in her life. A Song that would save a world, *worlds*, destroy great evil.

It didn't matter that her special voice would be gone.

The feycoocus shot down the tube, separated to their persons. Sinafinal sped over to Alexa as a miniature greyhound, added Power and yips to the Song, magic.

Tuckerinal raced as a huge hamster to Marian, glanced at her, then detoured to hop on Koz. His pumping chest eased.

Enerin ran as a kitten to Raine, settled on her lap, mewing.

Luthan's arms wrapped around Jikata and she focused more on the Song. The men were Singing low as the women continued to spiral high. As she watched, a throbbing blood-red strand of the knot lifted, slithered through a loop, laid limp.

Color seeped into her mind, images from Luthan. She was leaning against him now.

Look at the knot. Marian's mental voice was hushed.

Jikata did. It had swollen to the size of a snake, crossed over itself only a few times. It wasn't the red of blood as it had always been, it was covered with sparkles. Glittering tiny explosions popping like champagne corks. Getting bigger and bigger.

The knot grew and throbbed and sparkled, twelve small sparks growing into six larger ones.

A stifling, thick black ooze filled the lava tube entrance,

slithered down the wall of the cavern, defiling and killing the crystals, harming the spellsong. The Dark had reached them.

Jikata signaled everyone to speed the pace even faster, Sing louder, emphasized key words herself.

The air around her thickened, glazed. A bubble forming. The spells' defense.

Flames replaced the sparks on the thread, decreased from six to four to two...

The Dark whipped out a tendril, slashed the bubble, bounced off.

BOOM!

The mountain shattered around them, screams filled the air, horrors, monsters incinerated in an instant.

No! There was a shriek of disbelief and fury as the Dark died.

Stone disintegrated, and they were in the open air, falling.

Jaquar and Marian Sang, voices strong and competent, completely confident and the bubble encasing them all slowed and righted.

Bri huddled over Raine, sending healing energy through the injured woman, nasty pus and dark red stain drained from her wounds. Faucon was holding Raine and praying, his Song a counterpoint to Jaquar's and Marian's.

A dreeth dived at them.

The roc intercepted it.

They fought, beaks and claws, fell, ripped into the bubble.

It couldn't take the blow.

The bubble popped.

Jikata grabbed the pieces, held them together, Sang as she never had before.

Until her voice simply broke.

The force field disappeared and it was like a vision moment where she could see everything progress in slow motion.

Jaquar snagged Koz, Marian brought a wind to break their fall, pushed air at the others, slowed Bastien and Alexa's fall, but they hit hard, Bastien's shin bone poked through the skin. Alexa stroked him and yelled for Bri, then took her baton and his and had him arching, screaming, but the bone set. Alexa sobbed.

Volarans whirled about Calli and Marrec, brought them safely down to the fused glass that had been sandy beach beyond the smoking crater of the mountain. They were yards from Bastien and Alexa, and ran to them.

The roc, crippled and torn, grabbed Bri and Sevair, tried to glide, but they fell the last ten feet and there was a horrible snap and Bri's grief-stricken cry came as she flung herself on the dead bird.

Marian's air hit Jikata, Luthan, Raine, Faucon.

Jikata and Luthan came together, held on. The two older feycoocus were there, dug in their claws, slowed them until they were five feet from the ground then bulleted off toward where Enerin struggled to help Raine.

The planet jarred under Jikata's feet, she slipped, came down hard on her butt.

Screams of pain split the air, stopped short.

"Are you all right?" asked Luthan. He'd rolled in some sort of Chevalier maneuver and was favoring his left shoulder and leg, but looked okay. Alive. Completely and absolutely gorgeous.

"Ayes," she croaked, then remembered. Her voice was gone. Tears overran her eyes, she shook her head, let herself grieve for an instant, shook her head again impatiently. They were alive! They'd destroyed the Dark! She managed a quivery smile, touched her throat. "No voice, I won't be the Singer."

He held out his hand and she put hers in it, let him draw her to her feet.

Marian shrieked, and Faucon yelled, "No!" then, "Bri!"

Luthan met Jikata's gaze. "Raine," he said.

"Raine," she whispered sorrowfully. It had always been Raine who'd had the least chance of surviving.

"Koz didn't have the connection with Amee that the rest of you do, either," Luthan said. They ran toward the others.

Bri stumbled to an outcropping, set one hand on Raine, the other on Koz. They'd landed on the rocks.

"Bri—" said Sevair, her husband, but it was too late. Bri poured the healingstream into them, poured herself into them.

Jikata and Luthan drew near and he put a tight arm around her waist. It was hopeless.

But Bri continued until she toppled over, pale and still.

Alexa crawled over to her, stroked her hair. "Her healing skill is gone."

"Like my voice," Jikata said.

47

On the Glassy Island Beach

Raine's vision was dimming, black at the edges of her sight, colors bleeding out into gray. She was dying. She knew that and it wasn't as bad as she thought it would be. In fact, she thought that just...beyond...she could see a shining golden door a little like the portals of the Dimensional Corridor.

This dying wasn't so bad, the pain was a dull ache that she knew she could bear, and dying among friends who were more like sisters—and brothers—and in the arms of the man she loved after saving a world. Not bad at all.

Her gaze fixed on Faucon's face. She wanted that to be her last sight. She was sorry this would hurt him.

"No," he yelled. "Bri!"

But Bri's life force was nearly as thready as Raine's own. She couldn't heal, would be lucky to survive.

"No!" Faucon shouted again and it was deeper, more sonorous, almost a Song. "Jikata!"

Jikata opened her mouth but nothing came out, though Raine felt the touch of her Power. Jikata's special voice was gone, too.

"*No!*" Faucon's word was Song...prayer...*demand*. His brown eyes flashed and he rose with Raine, jostling her broken bones and piercing already ruptured organs. Terrible pain made the world bright again, tore a rattling gasp from her.

He shouted, "*No!* I am a true Lladranan, true Amian and I say *no*. This woman, brought here against her will, fulfilling all your demands deserves better!" A chant with Power.

She thought she heard a hum in counterpoint. Marian, exhausted, giving her all, tears streaking down her face as she and Jaquar held Koz, who was dying like Raine was, too broken to be mended.

"These native men and these Exotique women have *freed* you, Mother Amee. They *deserve* better from you, blessing and benediction!"

It all rhymed in Lladranan, and rolled over Raine like a wave, giving her the strength to smile up at Faucon.

Then it happened, the slightest wisp of a Touch, with blessing, with amusement. They all felt the Power of the world.

I pay my debts, Amee Sang.

Raine gasped again with strong, perfect lungs. Faucon collapsed with her onto the beach and they held each other tight.

Jikata wept in joy. She'd felt Amee Touch her...with Power that healed. She sang a low C and the next moment draped around her in a glittering shininess of Vision. Luthan's fingers tightened on her own and she knew they shared this prophecy.

She and Bri and Raine and Koz had been Healed, her voice, which had been gone, Bri's exhaustion of her healing gift, which had also been gone, Raine's and Koz's mortal injuries. In that Great Healing they gained more, all three of the women would have children with their men.

Time stopped.

"Look at them all." Luthan's whisper was hoarse, his grip tight. "Alexa…"

Jikata glanced at the Lady Knight Swordmarshall, did a double take. Alexa's hair had turned a flame-red. Jikata choked on a laugh as she saw the woman's future. Alexa had complained about being a Joan of Arc so Jikata didn't think she'd tell Alexa that she'd be George Washington and John Adams and Thomas Jefferson all rolled into one—a person who forged and held together a new nation. Oh, not like the democratic republics of home, but a culture that found its own way, melded together into one people through adversity.

Luthan, who was shaking his head beside her, jutted his chin toward Marian.

"Oh. Oh." Tears gathered in Jikata's throat. They'd all known that Marian was the most likely to have children, but when Amee had Touched the Circlet, she'd quickened a child that had been conceived by Marian and Jaquar the night before. Marian's left pinkie was still gone, but neither she nor Jaquar could hide the Power that made them faintly glow.

"Calli," Luthan continued the litany.

Calli had been the least hurt, beloved by her husband, her children, all the volarans of Amee, wrapped in a protective bubble of their love.

Since she hadn't been injured, her gift from Amee was less. She would never have children of her body, but have more children than all of the rest of them put together. She and Marrec would travel throughout the world, live the longest.

Bri laughed and poked Alexa in the ribs. "Your hair is red, like you wanted."

"What!" Alexa clamped both filthy hands in her hair.

Bri was back to normal, grinning impishly.

"Bri will be the greatest healer of all time, founder of many schools, revered," Luthan muttered. He met Jikata's eyes, his own sheened. "As you will be a legendary Singer, your voice returned with additional richness and Power by Amee herself."

"And we'll both have children." She leaned against him, felt his solidity, his love.

Koz struggled away from Marian. "Sis!" He propped himself on his elbows, looked down at his body showing health under the shreds of his leathers. He shook his head in disgust, glanced at Jikata and Luthan and his eyes widened. Jikata didn't know what he saw, whether their eyes had turned a different color as his had. Now his irises held a glimmer of silver like his own mirrors. "Wow," he said. He looked around. "We made it." He grimaced and shook his body. "Coulda done without all the pain." New lines were in his face.

Sevair grinned. "Ayes, we destroyed the Dark." Then his expression sobered as he looked around. "I can't get my bearings."

Jikata stood and moved slowly inland around the crumbling mass of the volcano. A gasp strangled in her throat as she looked down. There, about three feet underneath her feet, looking as if he'd been encased in a smoky glass coffin, was Bossgond.

He still held his long staff in his hand, his robe still showed his boney knees and shoulders, and his face had a look of startled surprise. His eyes were open. Jikata thought the black mark on his forehead must have been his death wound.

She must have made some noise because the others gathered. Marian stifled a sob and knelt down to touch the glassy surface of the ground over his face.

"But Amee takes those who fall into her ground," Raine said dazedly, leaning heavily on Faucon. She met Jikata's eyes. "Not the monsters, but Lladranans, the Lorebooks say so. Ella—is Ella here?"

Raine's gaze followed Alexa as she hurried, sliding a little on the glassy surface.

This was the battlefield.

Jaquar stroked Marian's hair, his jaw clenching. He said, "Bossgond went out fighting. He and all the others here bought us the time we needed to defeat the Master and the Dark."

Tears welled into Jikata's eyes at the sight of the man with whom she'd spent only a few comforting moments.

Alexa gave a cry and Jikata and the others followed. She'd only gotten a stride away before she saw a volaran and a female Chevalier in profile, as if they'd fallen on their sides—almost like they'd been caught in amber, her arm was raised, sword outthrust, her grin fierce. A yellow, poisonous spine was stuck in her neck. Jikata averted her eyes and stumbled on.

They all ranged what was left of the battlefield. Did they feel the need to witness as Jikata did? She walked over the smokily transparent surface, showing bodies beneath. Thankfully most of the death wounds were shadowed. Luthan held her elbow.

"A monument to all who fought the Dark, by Amee," he murmured.

Jikata caught her breath again as she trod over the Chevalier representative, Lady Hallard, and her Shield.

Then she stopped by Alexa, who wept over a pair of men

locked in each other's arms, between their volarans. All four seemed to exude love.

"Our old squires, the newest Marshalls." Alexa held onto Bastien. The men's batons weren't standing straight up in the ground like the pictures Jikata had seen in the Lorebooks, but were in their hands.

Like the rest of them, Alexa let tears trail down her face. She looked at the flat, glassy plane, glanced up at the jagged lip of the volcano crater. "How many are entombed here?"

Bastien shuddered. "It's not natural, to see them so."

"Ayes, it is." Jikata's voice was thick. "Like Jaquar said, a monument from the planet Amee herself." She began Singing the most beautiful, saddest Song she knew, Samuel Barber's "Agnus Dei."

The Exotiques wept around her.

Her Song broke again a few notes from the end, but music itself swelled through her, them, around them, echoing off the glass.

The feycoocus Sang, led by Tuckerinal, who knew the tune, and there were more than the three Jikata knew. More than a dozen perched on the rim of a furled glass wave.

Sing with us, said Sinafinal. *You are Lladrana's Singer now.*

Again a heavy weight settled on her shoulders, constricted her chest.

Truly, the passing of an era.

And thank the Song for such a terrible era's passing, Luthan said mentally. Like the other men, there were wet trails on his cheeks.

Koz limped heavily toward them. He'd taken the time to look at all the bodies between Bossgond's and the two new Marshalls'.

Jikata saw Koz shake his head hard, thought she saw tears fly away. His hands opened and fisted. He thumped his chest. "And I'm still here. All these, too late to save, dead before the explosion." He pivoted on his heel, pointed. "The Ship! Everyone else must have been rescued."

"A quarter," Calli said softly. "So many volarans dead."

The feycoocus' Song mixed with Chasonette's as she flew toward them. They looked to see the Ship sailing full power toward them with people cheering and volarans rising to the sky.

Jikata hiccupped with sobs.

Then it came, the call of Mother Earth, rolling over Jikata like an inexorable tide.

The Snap.

Jikata—Mother Earth, sending her own promises of the future. Jikata experienced the feeling of being on stage before thousands, all roaring in approval, joining with her to sing her latest platinum album. Oh, the rush of applause from such an audience! The scent of hot California earth came, directions from an impatient man who wanted her to say her lines just *so*. Her, a movie star. An Oscar and gold Grammys. A life of ease and wealth and luxury on a rich world. Her *home* planet grateful that she hadn't been invaded by any wisp of the Dark. Jikata would be creative and successful and loved.

Jikata, whispered Amee, echoing like it was from the chamber in the Caverns of Prophecy, all the way from the Abbey.

"Jikata." Luthan wrapped her in his arms. "Beloved," he said in a thick voice.

The winds came.

Not the tearing forces ripping through the Dimensional

Corridor just before it shifted like a kaleidoscope forever. But the real winds of Amee, with the hint of coldness this far north.

Earth pulled at her with its delicious melodies, its underlying soul-tune that was the pulse of her own blood.

"Jikata." Two voices Sang, Luthan's and another, one that put an English spin on her name. A voice she thought she'd recognized.

Mist surrounded her, them, then dissipated and Jikata saw they all stood together on one side of a stage.

"What *is* this place?" Calli asked in awe.

"Ghost Hill Theater," Jikata said and her voice wasn't mere words but a Song.

Alexa snorted. "Huh." She looked around, "Nice place."

"Ayes," Jikata said, lifted her arm and pointed. "Restored by him."

Trenton Philbert III stood, hand clasped with his wife, his lady, who Sang with a mediocre voice, but the pulsing colorful auras of light around her were awesome. They stood before a group of people dressed in evening clothes. Most were men who looked like Raine, but there was a threesome who clumped together in a manner that even Jikata, raised in Denver, recognized as ranchers.

"My father," Calli said faintly, "his wife and stepson." She looked down at herself, at Jikata, and Jikata was very aware that they appeared like they'd been in a fight to end all fights.

But they'd saved a world.

"I don't have anyone there," Alexa said in a strained voice.

Bastien picked her up and held her close, "Good," he said, then made soothing noises.

"Neither do we." Marian stood hand-in-hand with Koz, a

false smile frozen on her face. "Mother must have died." Jaquar stepped close and wrapped an arm around her waist.

Bri was sobbing openly, and Jikata finally focused on the elegant woman that had her face—her twin, Elizabeth, who was held by her husband, flanked by her mother and father.

Trenton put an arm out when a couple of powerfully built men surged toward Raine. "They have fought for an entire world—"

"Two," Juliet said crisply. "For Amee and for Earth, because if that Dark had triumphed it would have crossed the corridor to the nearest planet, which is our Earth."

"You can't go to her, but you can see she is fine, and can talk to her," Trenton ended.

"Fine!" Raine's father's shout hurt her ears. All her brothers and her two sisters-in-law were there, looking stunned.

Through her tears, Raine said, "Okay, so I was dying, it was rough. But I'm better now. Best, really." She wrapped her arms around Faucon. "This is my husband, Faucon. He's a nobleman here, so he'll keep me richly." She laughed and the sound rang with contentment throughout the theater.

Her father and brothers ceased their restless shifting. Her father crossed his arms over his chest. "He doesn't look Swedish."

She snorted a laugh. "Here in Lladrana we have no engines. So I'll start a golden age of sailing vessels. I love you all…" Her voice broke. "Be well, and those mirrors you put in your houses? We can see and talk to each other through them, if you want. Holidays maybe."

She sniffled. Faucon whipped out an orange-and-red hand-kerchief and she blew her nose, glared at her brothers. "I am *not* a weenie."

"Never said you were." Her father stuck his hands in his

pockets, rocked back on his heels, studied Faucon. "So the nobleman deal was true."

"Ayes. Yes." She grimaced a smile. "So was the stuff about designing a ship. You were right. *I* captained it."

Her father stilled. "That mirror. You *did* see us."

"Yes."

"I love you and am proud of you."

Bri and Sevair had moved close to her family, and she gestured to them to join Raine's shell-shocked men. "I'm Bri, and these are my parents and sister. You might want to talk to them about all this. We've been communicating for a couple of months or so with mirrors." She turned back to her delighted twin, her parents, her face showing she yearned to touch them. "Oh, Elizabeth," she sniffled.

"Oh, Bri!" Elizabeth twined all her fingers in her husband's, as if holding onto him would keep her from reaching out to Bri.

"So you whupped the Dark, eh?" asked their father.

Bri stood tall. "Ayes, yes, we did. I love you, Daddy and Mommy and twin."

"We love you, too," her mother said. "It's a blessing that we can see you one last time." She shook her salt-and-pepper head. "Though you're looking the worse for wear."

Bri grinned. "Life can only get better."

Jikata watched the emotional reunions of Bri and Raine. Was glad for them, but tired, wanted to go home. Back to Lladrana and wherever home was for Luthan.

He'd heard her thoughts, of course. "We'll visit the family estate, then go to the Abbey." He'd made peace with his father somehow, she saw *that* in his mind. She squeezed his arms around her waist. "Good."

Calli and Marrec walked tentatively over to the ranchfolk.

The father, his new wife and her son that Calli'd written about in her Lorebook.

The young man smiled at her.

"How's the ranch?" Calli asked.

Her father looked relieved at her question. Marrec's arm came around her and she leaned into it.

"Ranch is goin' well. We're followin' some new practices. Still a cattle ranch."

"I'm glad to hear it," Calli said.

They stood in silence that was all the more quiet for the babble of Bri's and Raine's loving families.

It would have been like that for Ishi and Jikata if Ishi had been alive, had come here.

But she wouldn't have. Jikata took Luthan's hand and went over to Alexa and Marian and Koz.

Alexa looked at her and Luthan, smirked as she touched her red hair. "You know, Jikata, both you and Luthan are totally silver-headed."

A shock rippled through Jikata as she looked at Luthan. It was true and she hadn't noticed.

He squeezed her hand. "More important things on our minds. You are beautiful."

Judge Philbert cleared his throat. "Time's up, folks." He took a heavy envelope from his breast pocket and slid it across the stage to Calli's feet. "Your investments, Calli, liquidated."

"Thanks." She bent down and picked it up.

"How do you come into this, Philbert?" Alexa demanded.

Trenton smiled at his wife. "I married into it."

Juliet Philbert's gaze was serene. "I was disabled in Lladrana, couldn't hear Songs well, saw auras instead. The old Singer gave me a chance to come to a place where my kind of Power worked better." She shivered. "A strange, frightening place, but the Singer put me in Trent's path and he found me." She glanced up at him and shook her head. "It took me a while to trust him, and for him to believe me, but we married and took on the Singer's work here. I am the equivalent of Earth's Singer, but I deal better with light."

She looked at Calli. "I was the one who tuned the crystal in the mountain for you to use it as a portal, and I helped destroy it. I worked with the Singer to provide mirrors in the Abbey and here at Ghost Hill." She sent her gaze across them all. "I love it here, and I love Trent. I let my Power here change my appearance to become Terran. Give them my Lorebooks, Trent."

The man went to a podium and pulled out two hefty leather-bound books, zoomed them across the stage and into their space. Jikata wondered how that might work and thought she should ask Bossgond…and grief caught at her again.

She looked down at the books—one was in Lladranan and one in English. The title was *The Lorebook of the Lladranan Aura Mistress Giselle Reneau Philbert*.

All the Lladranans stared down at the books, then Marian and Jaquar picked them up. After a moment, Alexa said, "Huh."

It seemed the right word.

Juliet continued, "Now is the time the Dimensional Corridor shifts, Sing the portal between our worlds shut with me, Jikata. You can cross over to this side or stay in Lladrana."

Jikata could have all she'd ever wanted if she stayed here on Earth, the validation, the fame and success. Everything that had meant so much to her. She'd unblocked her composing talent and could create soul-satisfying albums that would be wildly popular.

But she stepped back, into the group of ragged people who'd had the determination and honor to save a world. "I'll stay."

Juliet nodded and began the first note, low in the register, accompanied it with throbbing midnight blue light emanating from her hands. Jikata realized the spell would be a simple scale from the lowest note to the highest. She sang the next.

Raine shivered as the notes rippled from the throats of the two Singers, one of Earth and one of Lladrana, women who'd switched worlds. Strange colors pulsed around and from Juliet.

Swallowing hard herself, Raine cast a last glance at her father and brothers, her sisters-in-law, and stepped back to join her new family.

They lined up, holding hands. Raine's was gripped tightly by Bri's and Faucon's. The connection among them was roiling with emotions, spikes and dips of personal Songs. She and Bri stared at their families. Raine's gaze locked on her father. He raised a hand to her, smiled, said, "I love you." Then the air between them rippled and wavered and the sight of the stage and the people upon it faded.

There came a last flurry of sensation from Earth, each unique to the person, but shared—wind chimes; the scent of the water at her home dock; the sight of a skyline she'd never seen but flashed in multi-images and views and reverberated in the minds around her as "Denver."

Then, of course, the Songs of Mother Earth: castanets, rock and roll, Beethoven's Fifth, Irish jigs, gamelan chimes, bagpipes, chants in multiple languages, a swirl of sound that seemed to sweep around them, blessing them. Matched by the Songs of Amee: the rush of volaran feathers, the bells of the Singer's Abbey, the ring of a stonemason's hammer.

And with the last echo of the lost gong, the Dimensional Corridor shifted and the link between Earth and Lladrana was gone.

They had the final blessing a month later outside Castleton, after all the lingering horrors who'd invaded Lladrana were defeated. The invasion was already celebrated in Song and story, the three quarters of the force who'd lost their lives to be forever remembered.

Jikata and Luthan had carried the dry husk of the Singer's body from the Caverns of Prophecy. Sevair and Koz had fashioned a glass coffin for her and laid her inside. Marian and Jaquar had filled the coffin with Power to preserve the lady. All of them had transported the old woman's body to Glass Island, where the Circlets had melded her coffin to the land, showing forever that she'd helped save Lladrana and should be honored and remembered and revered.

They'd spent a little time on the island, once again saying goodbye to lost friends, easing their grief, then had returned to plan a great ritual.

People came from northern villages—some being resettled—and southern Krache city.

All gathered in a huge spiral, with Alexa and Bastien on one end, circling round with all the Exotiques. Marshalls and Chevaliers and Circlets and City-and-Townmasters and Seamasters and Singer's Friends of the whole country were interspersed throughout the spiral.

The population of Castleton was there, as were those who lived and worked on Exotiques', Marshalls' and Chevaliers' estates. Old folks and toddlers, children and teens. As long as they could link hands with each other, they were accepted in the spiral.

And they did link hands, with Luthan and Jikata in the very center. Then, finally, Alexa slipped her arm around Raine and Faucon's clasped hands and the circuit was closed.

They lifted their voices and Sang in a free Lladrana.

AUTHOR NOTE

The Summoning series came from stories I told myself before I went to sleep when I was a teen. I'm extremely proud that I had a chance to refine the ideas and write them. I enjoyed climbing the mountain and the wild ride down it. It's been an adventure.

When I first started the project, I thought of doing different female archetypes…Alexa the warrior, Marian the academic, Calli the nurturer, Bri and Elizabeth the healers, Raine the girl next door, Jikata the sophisticate. Some of these archetypes I used, some I bent.

As for settings, authors are using their hometowns these days, so I used Denver. Cheesman Park exists (and has a fascinating history of being a cemetery), so does LoDo (lower downtown), but the Ghost Hill Theater and its attached hotel was actually fashioned on a rehabbed Canadian theater that had plans available on the Internet. I chose Best Haven, Connecticut, because I knew Mystic is a shipyard, as well as the fact that my college roommate—who first encouraged me to write—came from Westport.

There's a lot in my head that couldn't make it into the books: some background of Lladrana when the Guardian Marshalls first set the fence posts; the extended lives of secondary characters Thealia and Partis, Koz; ideas about the feycoocus. I also have research materials for the books, everything from a small model of Windsor Castle upon which the Marshalls' Castle was loosely based, to a multitude of yacht designs, books on knots and wooden ships, and maps…so Lladrana will stay with me for a long time.

I *do* include some extras on my Web site, robindowens.com under the Worlds page, and all excerpts from my work are on my site under Reads.

I hope you enjoyed Lladrana and visit there more than once.

May the Song take you where you need to be.

Robin

CAST OF CHARACTERS

Echoes in the Dark

Raine Lindley, of Best Haven, Connecticut, is part of a ship-building family and was Summoned on the cheap by the Sea-masters, unknown to everyone else. She spent the first six months of her time on Lladrana sick and working at taverns, particularly the Open Mouthed Fish.

Faucon Creusse, a wealthy nobleman, leads one team of Chevaliers in battle, and fields another, innately drawn to Exotiques. He is a merchant prince with seaside estates.

Enerin, a baby magical being (feycoocu), shape-shifter.

Jikata, once of Denver, Colorado, now of Los Angeles, California, is a half-Japanese popular singer on the cusp of becoming a superstar.

Luthan Vauxveau, older brother to Bastien. Luthan is the representative to the Singer, the oracle of Lladrana and a nobleman and Chevalier. He has a touch of prophecy and wears white.

Chasonette, a Lladranan cockatoo.

The Exotiques, their men, their companions
(in order of Summoning)

Alexa Fitzwalter, *Guardian of Honor,* an attorney from Denver, Colorado. Alexa became a Swordmarshall in the elite noble warrior class, fighting the Dark.

Bastien Vauxveau is a black-and-white, a person with striped hair and wild magic, a Shieldmarshall, a rogue.

Sinafinal, a magical shape-shifting being (feycoocu), native to Lladrana.

Marian Harasta Dumont, *Sorceress of Faith*. A doctoral student from Boulder, Colorado, has become a Sorceress of the highest order, a Circlet, practicing weather magic and has founded a school with her mentor, Bossgond.

Jaquar Dumont, a Circlet of weather magic.

Koz/Andrew, Marian's brother from Earth, formerly suffering from multiple sclerosis, he brought wealth with him.

Tuckerinal, Marian's former hamster, now a magical shape-shifting feycoocu.

Calli Torcher Gardpont, *Protector of the Flight,* a horse whisperer who now teaches people to partner better with the volarans, winged steeds.

Marrec Torcher, a common man who became noble through his marriage with Calli.

Thunder, Calli's primary volaran.

Elizabeth Drystan Jones, *Keepers of the Flame:* Newly certified medical doctor, she was Summoned on the rebound of a broken engagement and had an affair with Faucon.

Brigid Drystan Masif, *Keepers of the Flame:* Massage therapist, Bri has "itchy feet" and has kicked around the world using her gift of healing hands.

Sevair Masif, a steady and reliable Citymaster, stonemason and architect.

Nuare, a roc who has attached herself to Bri.

Other important characters

Corbeau Creusse and his family, cousin to Faucon, a new Seamaster and the person who runs the northern estate, Creusse Landing.

Lucienne Deauville, matriarch of a Lladranan shipbuilding family.

Marwey and Pascal Raston, *Song of Marwey Online Read.* Marwey is former assistant to Alexa Fitzwalter and now a Shieldmarshall. Pascal is formerly an impoverished nobleman and Chevalier, and is now a Swordmarshall.

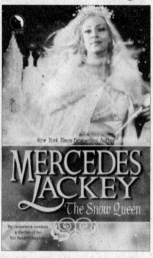

COURTLY MAGIC AND DEADLY INTRIGUE
COMBINE IN THE FOURTH ACTION-PACKED
INSTALLMENT OF THE CHRONICLES
OF ELANTRA BY

MICHELLE SAGARA

To ease growing racial tensions in Elantra, the emperor
has commissioned a play and summoned Private Kaylin
Neya to Court to help maintain order. But when her
trusted Sergeant, Marcus, is stripped of command, Kaylin
is left vulnerable, with two troubling cases involving
politics…and murder.

*Available October 2008
wherever trade
paperbacks are sold!*

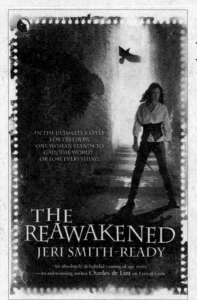

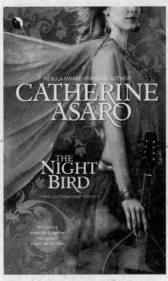